DOC SPEARS   **JASON ANSPACH**   **NICK COLE**

REBELLION

DARK OPERATOR   **BOOK 2**

GALAXY'S EDGE

Galaxy's Edge: REBELLION
Copyright © 2020
Galaxy's Edge, LLC
All rights reserved.

This is a work of fiction. Any similarity to real persons, living or dead, is coincidental and not intended by the author.

No part of this publication may be reproduced, stored in a retrieval system, or transmitted in any form or by any means electronic, mechanical, photocopying, recording, or otherwise without the prior written permission of the publisher and copyright owner.

All rights reserved. Version 1.0

Edited by Lauren Moore
Published by Galaxy's Edge Press

Cover Art: Tommaso Renieri
Cover Design: Ryan Bubion
Formatting: Kevin G. Summers

Website: www.GalaxysEdge.us
Facebook: facebook.com/atgalaxysedge
Newsletter (get a free short story): www.InTheLegion.com

JOIN THE LEGION

FOR UPDATES ABOUT NEW RELEASES, EXCLUSIVE PROMOTIONS, AND SALES, VISIT INTHELEGION.COM AND SIGN UP FOR OUR VIP MAILING LIST. GRAB A SPOT IN THE NEAREST COMBAT SLED AND GET OVER THERE TO RECEIVE YOUR FREE COPY OF "TIN MAN", A GALAXY'S EDGE SHORT STORY AVAILABLE ONLY TO MAILNG LIST SUBSCRIBERS.

INTHELEGION.COM

FREE SHORT STORY
TIN MAN

WHEN YOU SIGN UP FOR OUR VIP MAILING LIST

There's only one distraction from the stress of combat for a legionnaire—the next mission. For Sergeant Kel Turner and Kill Team Three, the wait is never long. Whether it's on a core world snatching a delusional genius who knows too much, or on the edge forging allies among a complex alien culture, Dark Ops are the foot soldiers of the House of Reason's galactic game for dominance.

Danger looms over Kel and his teammates like taxes over a Republic citizen. The promise is written in blood. Now they face a crisis that makes their worst firefight tame in comparison. Kel learns that sometimes there are no clear answers, manuals, or templates to follow. Isolated from Republic help, when the lives of thousands hang in the balance, a planet looks for a savior.

Fortunately, when there's a dark operator on hand, the odds favor the Legion.

01

Orbital freefall is stupid, Kel thought standing at the edge of the Talon's ramp. *So, what does that say about me? Stupid is as stupid does, I guess.*

Had anyone else been able to hear his thoughts, they might have thought them odd given the fact that he was one of the most experienced space divers in the Legion.

He had over a thousand sub-orbital freefalls to his credit, ranging from heights of a few kilometers up to forty klicks, where the atmosphere was thin enough to be unbreathable but dense enough to allow normal body flight. The most dangerous thing about atmospheric freefalls was taking the lift to the flight line. Child's play compared to falling onto a world from orbit. His logbook recorded sixty-five freefalls from space. Today would make sixty-six. If he survived.

Day one of freefall school they had a guest lecturer. The crippled leej had been one of the modern pioneers of orbital freefall. To have done what he'd done, the man must have been a wonder as a young leej. Now, though ancient and confined to a grav-lift, his voice was strong, his mind sharp. He spoke with the urgency of a man who knew this might be his last chance to help a young leej become an old leej. Maybe that was all that was driving the man—holding off death for the opportunity to share his wisdom with younger warriors one more time.

"Orbital freefall is a tool. Nothing more. Don't be impressed by it. Don't fall in love with it. During the Savage Wars we tried every method of infiltration you could imagine. One time, on the Sha'kal'an home world, we even swam in. Of course, there wasn't much choice there. Just remember what I'm telling you now—if mission success demands every member of the team and all the equipment arrive at the objective, let the Navy land you and walk there."

Kel hung on those words. The old man did the impossible, living to a ripe old age after doing what he'd done, time and again. There was a true badass still alive inside the husk of the floating corpse before them. A legend.

If that ancient leej knew what they were about to do now, what would he say? Would he scold Kel for ignoring his warnings?

"Look at him," Poul said. "He's in his happy place."

Kel ignored his friend. His attention was fixed on the wrist link projection as he looked off the ramp of the Talon flying aft-forward as it fell around the rotating planet below. They'd cross into the night terminator soon. The glow from the many dense urban centers blossoming on the rolling horizon made one thing obvious; if someone was expecting them, an invisible landing would be impossible. But conditions always favored those who knew how to best exploit them, light or dark, jungle or duracrete.

Almost time to stand the team and move them to the ramp, Kel thought as he half listened to the exchange behind him.

It was an old game. Knowing Kel's concentration was incorruptible, his teammates tried to get a rise out of him anyway.

"Man's working, Radd," Bigg said before Kel could form his retort. "Shut up and let him work." Their team sergeant wasn't gruff. Just reigning in what could sometimes be the euphoric banter that characterized their personal reactions to danger. It wasn't uncommon for laughter to break out among the team during a full-on blaster fight. Sometimes in the most absurd situations, that's all you could do. That, and KTF.

"So much negativity," Poul said, feigned hurt in his voice.

"Seriously though, Kel," Bigg said. "Don't kark this up."

Kel had been the one to bring the new vernacular to the team from his last mission. He'd let it slip only once. That was all it took. The word spread like a virus with no nano-immuno guardian to suppress it. Now it was, kark this, and kark it all, and kark the weather. Whatever it meant. Kel didn't know either. But it was catchy.

Poul, only temporarily restrained by Bigg, took this as a cue to resume his hypo-manic chatter. "Yeah, Kel. Not like we're keeping score or anything, but you're about due, Mister Perfect. No one has a flawless jumpmaster record, not even Bigg."

"Didn't I tell you to shut it?" Bigg growled. If he were sincerely disciplining Poul, it would be in a voice so quiet it made your skin break out in goose bumps.

Braley assaulted simultaneously. "Karking hell, Poul. You're wishing for Kel to make a mistake? With our lives depending on him? You're a genius, you know that? You can't lord over Kel if you're dead."

The only one to not join in the stress relieving chit-chat was the newest member of the team, Sims, who sat silently. It wouldn't be anxiety about the jump that prevented his joining in. Sims was an experienced space diver himself. No. Respect made him hold back. Sims came over from Kill Team Five. He'd only been with them a month since Tem, Kel's teammate and best friend, had been killed. The wound still ached. Sims knew it and stayed quiet, clearly not sure where he fit into the team dynamic. Wise men found their place cautiously among a group of warriors like Three.

"Good track," Kel said to the pilot as he dropped his arm and the holo projection disappeared.

"Roger, jumpmaster," the pilot responded. "Maintaining track. Descending through one-hundred fifty kilometers."

They would jump a hundred klicks above the surface to start the ten-minute ride like no other—shorter, if anyone's canopy failed to deploy. Most of them had seen the remnants of such a catastrophe. If the ground was soft, at least you dug your own grave on impact.

"Five minutes. Stand. Up."

Lorrian was a core world, nothing like the backwater edge planets they usually worked. Everywhere below glittered with civilization. The implication of this buzzed in the back of their brains, like a Styberian hornet inside your bucket.

Space junk.

Comets, asteroids, meteors, and other space-borne particles naturally orbited planets. But around worlds like Lorrian, clouds of artificial objects formed minefields. Ice shards from ship fuselages, parts broken off damaged craft, and centuries' worth of obsolete satellites and orbiting platforms collected in orbit before burning up in the planet's atmosphere. Space junk could kill you. The risk of collision was supposed to be astronomically remote, yet it happened.

Twice in Kel's ten years in the Legion, an operator lost his life during the early phase of an orbital freefall. One had occurred during an actual mission. The operator never made it to the surface. There were no remains to find, but the most likely cause of the operator's failure to appear below the mesosphere was labelled, "foreign debris collision."

The other incident had occurred over Area Doxy, the barren training ground of a planet that neighbored Victrix. That one had been captured on holo from the dropship. A small meteoroid intersected the path of the free-faller shortly after exit. The man simply disappeared as the object traveling at 70,000 kilometers per hour hit, the collision's kinetic energy so extreme that the event registered as a bright flash. Kel knew the hapless victim. It was beyond cliché to say the man never knew what hit him.

He and his teammates often marveled at the sand-blasted effect their armor displayed after they'd landed safely under a full nano-tubule canopy. Fine particles of space dust flying at tremendous speeds left scars on the Whipple layer over their armor. If any of those particles had been large enough and tough enough—say, a two-centimeter nickel meteoroid—they'd leave more than a faint scratch. There'd be nothing left of the operator to cremate.

Nothing you can do about it, so no reason to worry, he told himself. Not for the first time. *Just do your job. People are depending on you.*

It was the phrase his mind repeated to him most.

People are depending on you.

"Hope the House of Reason is right about this guy," Poul said as he shuffled toward the ramp. "We're going to a lot of trouble to nab some data thief. If it's my turn to intersect with a meteor on the way down, avenge me by punching some delegate's ticket, won't you?"

This time no one told him to be quiet. He spoke for them all.

Kel went through the jump commands. Sims pinchecked his container for him as he made the last confirmation of their plot against the landmark of the city below, the bright angular shape unmistakable. Plasma boiled in his veins as he gave the last command. The only command a jumper wanted to hear.

"Stand by. Go, go, go." He led, arching his body as he stepped off the ramp, and gravity took over.

Everyone's fate but his own was now out of his hands. It was up to them to arrive alive on the surface, but he would lead the way, minutely adjusting their track toward the target, working to the last to get them there in one piece.

In Kel's experience, perception of time was relative. There was no better example of this than when in freefall. For him, the minutes spent in freefall passed at a frozen pace, his hyper alertness slowing time in a way that allowed him to pay attention to a vast number of visual inputs—the ground, the other jumpers in his charge, the streams of data filling his HUD. Time crawled. Experiences became more vivid; information processed effortlessly. Whether perception or physics explained it, he didn't know. He knew only the one thing.

People are depending on me.

The drogue chute and freefall compatible armor overlays had done their job and kept them stable until the atmosphere condensed enough to allow them to steer by body position. The attitude jets and control surfaces attached to their limbs worked with the program in their buckets to keep them out of spins.

Atmospheric resistance grew, now dense enough to stabilize his fall. He arched harder while also relaxing. *That's the secret to staying stable*, an amalgam of voices repeated in his head as he hurtled to the ground at 200 kilometers an hour.

Kel didn't need the cursor to tell him he was on track. Hours of study burned the target into his mind. There was a dark space near the northern region of the city, and as he looked left, his body followed, now lining up on the longest axis of the dark oasis below. He checked his altimeter. Four kilometers. Now it would just be a pleasant ride down to 1500 meters until the welcome shock of gravity would return as carbon fiber parachutes deployed and assumed their angular shapes, causing them to slow like dry leaves drifting to the ground. He hoped. It was never a guarantee. Only hitting the surface one way or another was promised.

His faith renewed as his feet returned below him for the first time since leaving the Talon. Full canopies appeared behind him after his own inflated, and the smooth glide to the ground passed in seconds as he flared and came to a gentle landing. He stepped out of the carryall straps between his legs and grabbed his rifle before triggering the program to jettison and destroy his chute and its container. He retained the freefall overlays. Normally useless once on the ground, this time there would be a purpose for the extra layer. They hoped.

Everyone touched down smoothly. Silently.

Kel checked his map view and was already moving off the fairway and into the woodline when Braley interrupted his thoughts. "Nice job, Kel. Perfect calcs. Well done."

Kel kept his head up, scanning. The five operators were the only source of movement. Three hours before first light. The time when even a sentry would be fighting the curtain of sleep. From the time he'd stepped off the ramp a hundred kilometers above, only ten minutes had passed.

Sixty-six, Kel said to himself. *Sixty-six orbital freefalls.* He thought about the old leej and his last warning to them before they levitated him off the classroom dais.

"Eventually, gravity wins."

02

"Yeah, not too bad for a part-timer," Sims offered, the first thing he'd said since rigging in the back of the Talon an hour before.

Team Five was tasked as a primary orbital freefall team. As a result, they often found themselves home on Victrix, waiting on a mission that never materialized. Meanwhile Kel's team was always on the move. *Specialization is for insects*, Kel always held. Kill Team Three proved the adage true.

"Pfft, Kel has more jumpmaster time than you do, newbie," Poul retorted, though he didn't mind the dig from their new teammate. It was nice to hear Sims taking part in team talk.

"Nip it, ladies," Bigg grunted. "Time to go."

The UberGolf course they stood on sported manicured grass arranged in long curving lanes, concealing little of the unnatural glow from the buildings peeking above the surrounding trees. Having grown up on a world known as a destination for rich pleasure-seekers, Kel was familiar with the type of real estate they'd chosen as a drop zone. He'd never played the game himself; the tiny ball and the strange clubs never interested him. His father, a retired legionnaire, mocked the sport and those who played it as frivolous. Kel had vowed early to be the antithesis of whatever his father found childish.

Bigg was the last into the stand of trees. "Everyone good?"

Silence equaled agreement.

Braley pointed in the same direction as on everyone's HUD and ordered, "Sims, lead off."

Nervous relief at landing safely evaporated and with it, the team's banter. Even in the sanctity of their buckets, their mouths could rob their ears.

Sometimes locating the target site for the raid was a tense part of the mission. Locations were often inexact and based on sketchy intel. Not tonight. It was almost cheating to use the hyper-detailed terrain maps they'd used for planning.

And if you ain't cheating, you ain't trying. Words they all lived by.

They needed no deviation from the planned route through cover, sticking to low ground or the wooded intervals. Through open areas between the patches of orderly forest, the mimetic function of their armor—combined with their slow, purposeful movements—made their presence little more than a trick of the light. The object in your peripheral vision that disappeared when you turned to look. A figment of your imagination.

Sims took a knee short of the tree line and the open terrain beyond; Bigg and Braley did likewise. Kel and Poul turned to face backward. Sims spoke in a whisper, the unshakable habit of a hunter. "I've got no activity. Zero movement inside or out."

Braley grunted. "Looks like the holo. Hate to think what the upkeep is on this place."

Just past the tree line and shrubs lay the most ostentatious mansion Kel had ever seen. It was stunning. Spires rose and arches spanned. Transparent walls unbroken by frame or column fooled the eye into thinking that no barrier existed between shelter and nature. The spectral display in his bucket confirmed what they'd feared. Radiating like heat rising off duracrete, a shimmering drape lay around the entire estate. Disruptor barrier.

"Kel, Poul, swap," Braley said. "Take eyes on the target. Okay, Sims, do your thing."

Kel took a spot and knelt as Poul did the same, the exhibitionistic architecture now under their unblinking gaze. Sims took a few steps back deeper into cover and sat as Bigg and Braley knelt to watch him. One reason Sims stood out as a candidate to replace their fallen teammate was his mastery of data stream intrusion. A slicer. Or so had been claimed by his Team Five leader. Everyone knew it was one thing to have attended the courses. It was another thing entirely to be able to perform the magic on demand.

Tem was flawless under pressure, Kel remembered. *Flawless.*

He still wondered what his friend's last minutes had been like. Alone. Deserted by his troops. Overrun by zhee. He was found under a pile of donk bodies. Evidently, after killing more of them than a cyclax eats shepp, he buried himself under a hill of dead and called in the bombers. It just hadn't been enough to shield him from the blast. He'd probably already known what the end would be, but called in the strike anyway. Tem was like that. He never gave in. Never quit. Even so, not even a thousand dead zhee were worth losing Tem. Not by Kel's math.

Sims gesticulated in the dark as he manipulated virtual holos visible only to him. Kel checked his chrono. Two and a half hours remained until beginning morning nautical twilight, the witching hour when they would lose the cover of darkness. Kel kept up his scan. Only faint light issued from within the mansion. Under his visor, it was no different than daylight. The spectral enhancements allowed him to search for all manner of electromagnetic energy. Sensor beams and the radiation emitted from simple household appliances and cleaning bots roaming the floors framed the furniture. He saw the invisible. A human could not hide.

"I got good news and bad news, sir," Sims said to Braley, still not comfortable enough to address their team commander with familiarity. "I can spoof all the detectors and even turn off the alarms. Easy. For a rich guy, he cheaped out on the internal security. I might have advised him the same since he splurged on the disruptor field."

"Okay," Braley responded. "That must be the good news."

"Yes, sir. The bad news is I can't enter the disruptor field control net. It's in a hardened central node, not connected to any external link. There must be a remote way to silence the field, but I can't slice into it. It's more than just a simple signal. Looks like maybe it's a biosignature and it'll take too long to decode. Sorry, sir."

Kel knew it wasn't a deal breaker. They'd planned for this.

"Could be worse," Braley said. "Good job. Kill everything you can and let's get ready to hit it. Kel, Poul? Anything?"

"All quiet," Poul answered for them. "Nothing stirring. This is the time."

"I've killed all the internals, sir. What say I go first? Seems fair." Sims was taking responsibility for not being able to knock out the disruptor field, though the fault was not his.

"Bigg?" Braley inquired of the team sergeant.

"Okay by me. Don't worry, Sims," Bigg said encouragingly. "If it scrambles your brain, you won't remember it. Get ready to power up your Whipple fields and let's hit it. Ready? Move."

Kel had dealt with disruptor fields before. Without armor, crossing one was virtually impossible. It did more than cause a loss of consciousness. It scrambled your neurons into static. Sometimes permanently if the field was powerful enough. The barrier could be penetrated by attacking at a high rate of speed, but you'd reach the other side an unconscious, convulsing heap. Their armor was shielded against all kinds of radiation. Even so, passing through the security barrier was unpleasant and could damage systems. Kel bet this one was as high energy as could be made. The target was the type to make purchases excessive to his needs. It was a mark of the galaxy's wealthy.

They used their mimetic camo for cover until the last moment as they followed Sims, moving slowly through the manicured garden to the edge of the shimmering barrier in front of them. The camouflage effect faded as they diverted power to the Whipple layer, part of the freefall compatible overlays they still wore from the jump. They hadn't been able to test it, but between their armor's shielding and the extra layer to protect them from space debris, energizing the layer should minimize the disruptor field's effect.

"Here goes."

The team waited as the human dorma pig took the crucial step.

"We can always get another newbie from Team Ten," Poul said just as Sims stepped through.

Sims paused on the other side, still upright. Kel held his breath, wondering how he was going to retrieve Sims if he collapsed.

"Nice try, Radd," said Sims. "Looks like you're stuck with me."

"Go, go," Bigg hurried them all as he moved across the barrier, Kel the next to follow.

"Oww."

Poul's left hand contracted into a claw as he attempted to shake it back into life. The protective layer on his gauntlet must have been damaged during the jump, performing its vital function passing through the upper atmosphere only to leave it faulty for its final role.

"Serves you right, Radd," Sims clucked.

Poul shrugged. "Suppose it does at that. Just kidding about replacing you."

"Everyone good?" Braley inquired. "Poul?"

"Good to go," Poul said, flicking his wrist as if his hand were covered in biting insects. "Fit to fight."

Bigg was already moving to the covered entrance as the team fell in with him. Kel brought his K-17 up and turreted his body to look above through the transparent façade. Everything remained dark and still as they closed. Bigg flared his plasma torch and passed the glowing tip through one side of the door as Braley gave it a push from the other side.

They flowed like water through the threshold, an unstoppable force whose momentum couldn't be slowed, halted, or ignored. They were on the hunt.

Their priorities were securing the target and eliminating any threats. They had a good idea where the sentries and target would be at this time of night. Kel went with Braley and Bigg to the master suite; Poul and Sims split to find any guards. They bypassed rooms that held nothing but garish décor to arrive at the master suite. Kel reached for the decorative mechanical knob, an ancient device used as a design touch. He gently torqued the knob and was rewarded with rotation of the obsolete device. Unlocked. Bigg was in position for first look into the room. He pushed the muzzle of his K-17 forward, then back, telling Kel he was ready. Kel finished the motion turning the knob, resistance evaporating. He pushed. Bigg moved, Kel leaving only an electron's orbit between them as he glided to his side of the room.

The massive bed was untouched. Their illuminators filled the dark spaces like accessory suns. Wordlessly the three men moved through the adjacent rooms. Everything was as immaculate as a museum. Perfectly preserved and untouched.

"Dry hole," Braley sighed. "You got me, Poul? Dry hole here."

No response.

"Trouble?" Braley looked to Bigg.

Kel's ears strained for sounds of violence from elsewhere. He moved with Bigg to the door just as Poul's voice returned. "Sorry, boss. We were a little busy for a minute. All good. We've got a prisoner restrained after a little scuffle. Hey, did you say we came up with zilch?"

"Yeah," Braley answered. "Stay put. We're going to finish the house. Who's your detainee?"

"Security goon," Sims broke in. "We surprised him dozing at the monitor station. He didn't surrender right off and refused to follow commands. He was wearing a shield, so the shocker didn't faze him. I tried not to damage him, but I may not have succeeded. Sorry."

"Yeah," Poul picked up the rest. "Guy was fighting for his life. Not too badly, really."

"S'kay," Bigg dismissed. "We'll work it out." Bigg looked to their team leader. "We'll sort it out later, sir."

The man they were sent to retrieve was a criminal, but that didn't mean they could use deadly force against the target or any of his employees unless warranted. If they seriously harmed anyone on this operation and it later turned out it not to be justified, there could be trouble. Yet another reason Kel hated Dark Ops being used for non-military functions.

"Can you retrograde the guy if we need to?" Braley asked Kel.

He had drugs that could produce amnesia if administered soon after an incident, but if the subject had head trauma, it could be dangerous. "Won't know till I can examine him."

"Let's finish up. We're bleeding momentum," Bigg admonished. They made a detailed search to find only one other person in the residence, a housekeeper in her bedroom on the lower floor. She barely stirred as they entered the room, no time to even register surprise as Kel stunned her. He quickly placed the autoairway over her mouth and initiated the nanomeds. She'd stay asleep for the better part of a day, even if the device was removed prematurely. It would be unwise to do so though, as the airway protected her breathing while unconscious. Kel had a dozen of the devices. The target was the only person they would be taking with them. Anyone else they encountered would be staying in place, unconscious and unable to alert the local police—who could be on their target's payroll. They could depend on no one's help locally.

The detained man was enerchained to a chair and had a seal over his mouth. One of the guys had put a skin-pack over a gash on the man's forehead. His eyes were wide and alert with fear. Sims leaned over his datapad and sorted through holos above the monitor station while Poul kept watch.

"We missed him. There." Sims straightened and pointed at an image. "He left with two of his protective detail at 23:17." A thin man in purple stepped into the driver's compartment of the luxury speeder as two monstrous guards dressed in gray crammed themselves into the compact vehicle. Another view showed the vehicle disappear up the front drive.

"Great," Poul exhaled. "So, do we wait and ambush him when he returns, or do we go on a manhunt?"

Everyone remained silent.

Braley looked to Bigg. "Suggestions? I don't want to take us home empty-handed."

Bigg turned to the restrained man. "What we lack is information."

Surprisingly, the guard didn't need encouragement to talk. When Kel removed the gag, the man sputtered apologies. "Sorry. You guys startled me. Don't kill me, okay? I used to be one of the good guys. Republic Army. I know who you are."

"He was a basic, huh?" Poul said to Kel over L-comm. "Sounds about right. Sleeping on watch."

"What I mean to say is, I *don't* know who you guys are," the man said, backtracking. "You were never here. I get it, okay?"

Once he understood he wasn't going to be harmed, the initial trickle turned into a flood. "You know Xenon

Boothe is a paranoid mess, right? 'Course, living in a glass house probably ain't the best cure for that."

They hadn't removed the restraints. Braley sat across from the man while the rest stood, imposing their size on the disadvantaged guard. Sims was at work, looking for data stream clues to where their quarry lay.

"I've been with him three years and it's only gotten worse. He's never really trusted anyone. Insists on doing all his own driving, says there's less chance *they* can take him out that way. He's not afraid to get his hands dirty, either. Won't let anybody touch his speeder or his yacht. Does all the maintenance himself. Paranoid or not, what you've heard is true. Guy's a genius."

"How's it gotten worse?" Braley asked. "Paranoid about what?"

"That the Republic was after him, going on about how his days are numbered. It used to be the odd comment. Now it's all he talks about." The man jutted his jaw toward them. "Seems he wasn't wrong, huh?"

Kel was intrigued. Truth was, they didn't know why they were sent to retrieve Xenon Boothe from his home on Lorrian. They just knew the order was legal. The man was a celebrity in the business world, well known for his innovation and philanthropy. Kel was vaguely aware of how the man made his trillions; something to do with phantom tech. Their buckets utilized the tech, allowing flawless access to functions by combinations of gesture and thought to read user intent and produce results. The House of Reason issued a secret arrest order for Boothe. But why was Dark Ops executing it instead of the Justice Directorate? They didn't know.

Braley held up a hand to halt the man before he continued to spout. "Where is he? Tell us that, and you're clear of us."

The man looked relieved. "Axis Mundi. Boothe hasn't slept in days. Whenever he gets like this, he goes there. He gambles, sometimes for days. I was relieved it was my turn to stay behind. He goes on quite a bender when he gets... antsy."

Axis Mundi. Kel searched the name on his datalink, but Sims already had a holo open and pushed it into the center of the room. "It's an orbital vice palace administered by a private corporation. Claims independent status from any terrestrial governing body."

"He keeps a suite," the man added eagerly. "He's got company on call for him up there, if you get my drift. He used to have girlfriends around, but not even the dim ones want to hang around with him since he's gotten so jittery."

Bigg sighed over L-comm. "Okay, say we believe this guy. Seems we have one option. We don't have the support to go in and covertly pull him out of a floating casino, so that's out. What about we nab him in his yacht? You're doing good, sir. How 'bout you try and get us more info about his ride?"

Kel gave the guard the same treatment he'd given the housekeeper and they laid him out on a nearby bed. Sims disabled the protective field and they weren't on the green long before the Talon swooped down to retrieve them. It was an hour before first light. Even if the bird was seen, it might not be thought unusual given the proximity to Xenon Boothe's.

"Checks out," Sims said as they rode into orbit. "*Hespera Sapphire.*" A holo hung in the pax compartment of the Talon. The luxury yacht looked as expensive as it was sexy. "There're only three like it. What are the chances there's more than one docked at Axis Mundi?"

03

Xenon Boothe's yacht was unmistakable. The *Sapphire* was like no other craft. Its violet-blue coating, a color proprietary to the Hespera shipyards, betrayed no wear from repeatedly piercing the atmospheric boundary. The polished surface reflected the pulsing lights of the floating casino in the distance. The ship was too large to dock at the orbital, though the station was itself no minor satellite above Lorrian. The destination for vice held apartments and hotel rooms for thousands, a dozen restaurants, theatres, clubs, and of course, gaming dens.

"Easy to see why he insists on taking care of her himself," Sims said. "She's a gem."

"Something we agree on," Poul replied. "I wouldn't let another man touch her either."

"Well, don't get too wounded when I have to breach her," Bigg chimed in.

Poul winced at the thought, then quickly found the bright side. "If she's damaged, maybe I can get her for half price at the estate sale."

Kel chuckled. "I'm sure she'll be a steal at only a billion credits."

Poul sighed. "Never hurts to dream."

They made a pass in the Talon from a few hundred kilometers, their sensor signature spoofed as a commercial vessel. The docking pens were full of luxury hoppers and small yachts, the *Sapphire* a behemoth in their midst, holding near the facility. Safety regulations mandated craft her size stay fifty kilometers off station in a matching geostationary orbit.

"Time's wasting," Bigg reminded. "No way to know when Boothe might return. We want to have that yacht well locked down before that happens."

Before Kel tranqed the cooperative guard, he'd assured them that their target never stayed on Axis Mundi less than a day, and rarely longer than two. "Guy gets his electrons spun up there, then it's back to his usual paranoia. He'll be back groundside, holed up in his lab or in the mansion for the few hours he stays here anymore. Guy's a wreck."

The picture he painted was of a tortured man. *But tortured by what?* Kel wondered. He was one of the wealthiest men in the galaxy. Kel couldn't sympathize. If he had the kind of money Boothe had, he doubted he'd worry about anything. He remembered his father's opinion when as a child he'd made a similar comment about the rich on Pthalo.

"The very rich are different from you and I, son," his father had tried to explain. "Money does funny things to people. You may not believe me, but I've never seen a rich man happy."

Still, Kel thought he'd like to give it a try someday.

From where the Talon held, it was too far to reach the *Sapphire* by maneuvering jets. The operator delivery skiff reminded him very much of the kind of watercraft Kel fished from on Pthalo. Poul sat in the nose of the faceted, flat-black arrow, ready to pilot their gear across the gulf of space to the luxury yacht as the rest of the team rode individual maneuvering pods. The process began as the grav decking reduced to micro-g levels in the pax area.

They eased the skiff off the ramp, the crew chief hovering over them like a mother hen, fearful they might hurt the bay of his Talon. They pushed in unison to launch Poul and the small ship, little more in size than an oddly shaped sofa compared to the sleek twin tailed stealth craft they launched from.

"Ready to exit?" Bigg asked.

Kel picked up the delivery pod and repeated the same diagnostic he'd done three times already. The charge pack continued to show full. The drive checked green. The conveyance was much the size of a repulsor bike, but oriented to ride vertically.

He placed a foot on one of the pegs and hopped toward the ramp. "Ready."

The rest of the team made similar sounds.

"Free and away," Bigg said as he pushed off to where Poul floated a few meters aft.

"See you boys soon," the crew chief waved at them. "We'll be waiting to scoop you up."

The *Sapphire* was stationary and required no complex matching of speed or orbit. Compared to most of their ship seizures, the cutting out was an uncomplicated relief. Of the potential problems awaiting them, at least the trip over would not be one of them. Once on the hull, though... breaching a ship was tricky.

The intrusion and command programs they had were generally very successful in allowing them entry into any denied vessel. It was also the stealthiest way to enter. When mechanical deterrents denied them entry, flying an assault trunk to the target and cutting through a hatch or the hull like a salvage tech worked, though it was slow.

They didn't have an assault trunk.

They'd tossed around every conceivable contingency as they prepared. What if they had to make an explosive entry onto the ship? Could Sims suppress any communications to warn Boothe off from returning to the yacht before they seized the ship? What if the crew defended themselves from a hostile boarding and responded with deadly force, as was their right?

After going through all the usual considerations, Braley summed it up for them. "We're going to get this guy. Period. No one gets hurt on the team. Understand? No one sacrifices themselves. Win fast. Win early. If we have to injure someone... as long as we get the target, I can justify our actions."

Poul bounced Kel on a side channel so no one else could hear him. "If it comes to terminating a civilian, I appreciate Braley's willingness to fall on his sword for us. I'm just not betting on a mere captain, not even Braley, being able to hinder the justice system from frying us, though."

"At least we'll be on Herbeer together," Kel offered. "Maybe what we've heard about that prison planet is all wrong. Maybe no one comes back because it's such a nice change of pace from Dark Ops."

It always helped to be positive.

Their armor shifted hue to match the black of space as they followed Poul's track toward the yacht, still so far away it couldn't be seen without magnification. In an hour they'd crossed the 200 kilometers and eased to a crawl, aimed at the starboard waist deck. Even in space, movement was the first target indicator. Their stealthed armor and vehicles would not return a sensor signal from the ship, even if actively scanning. It would be unusual that the ship's crew would do so, parked in a port of safety, but still, knowing the incredible capabilities of their detection defeating tech was a comfort.

The outline of the hatch was all but imperceptible on the ultra-sleek hull. Kel imagined the shipwright's pride in the fit of the seams.

Sims monitored the port master control channel. "No comms from the *Sapphire*. I checked the traffic register. The estimated departure logged with the controller is for the day after tomorrow."

Day after tomorrow? Kel thought. *We're going to sit on the yacht for two days waiting to ambush this guy?* A plague of potential complications clouded his thoughts as they continued to close with the yacht.

Sims gave them good news. "I have positive intrusion of shipboard systems. They're locked out of any control function. Unless someone shoots a tight beam from outside the hull, there'll be no transmissions from the yacht and she's not moving a picometer."

So far, Kel had no complaints about Sims's mastery slicing the data stream. Of course, even he could insinuate parasite programs; the packages were AI guided. The program did all the work. Even so, it was nice to have a dedicated slicer on the team again.

"What's the manifest list for crew and passengers?" Braley asked.

"Five crew, no passengers. Lists Boothe as captain and owner. A first officer who is also solo-rated, an engineer, and two spacers as deck hands. Want to bet the last two are his bodyguards?"

So, who's left tending the ship? Kel wondered.

Sims spoofed the shipboard systems and within minutes, the waist deck hatch opened revealing an empty lock large enough for the skiff and all five team members.

Things would happen rapidly now. The lock cycled, and as the inner seals broke, the team exploded onto the deck. Sims remained behind, his back against a wall of equipment lockers, allowing him to face the two portals leading forward and aft. He continued to control ship's systems, holos now hanging in front of him as he controlled the data stream.

Kel and Bigg pushed forward to the command deck while Braley and Poul moved down to engineering. Once they controlled those, the ship was theirs. Bigg keyed the hatch. "Republic agents. Do not resist."

At the sight of them the thin man at the pilot's console turned as ashen as his radiation tanned features would allow.

We often have that effect on people. Kel chained him. The man's surprise kept him silenced as they escorted him away.

Back on the waist deck where Sims continued his ethereal control of the ship's systems, Braley and Poul had the other member of the yacht's crew braced. Both men had gotten over the initial surprise and now protested.

"Whatever you're doing here, it won't work," the flight deck officer asserted.

The portly man in the stained fatigues agreed. "Mister Boothe won't pay a ransom for this ship, if that's your goal."

"As we said, we're Republic agents." Braley showed the men the arrest order, hoping it would sober them. He'd also already explained to the older men that at the first hint of trouble, Kel would tranquilize them and attach autoairways.

"We can execute this warrant with your help, or without it," Braley told the two officers matter-of-factly. "One is easier for us, the other easier for you. You'll like the one that's easier for us better, though."

The two gave each other a look of honest resignation. The kind of look that told Kel a story was coming. The flight deck officer was the one to speak. "Mister Boothe has always been good to me. I respect him, too. But he's not himself."

The pot-bellied engineer who looked every bit his part, shrugged. "He's done gone and gotten the Republic so scalded off at him that they sent you all to arrest him. I'm not going to interfere. Can't say the same about Mazer and Quaid. I think they're both stim heads."

Their lone information source in the mansion had warned them about his fellow guards. The security contractor had been forthcoming about the detail guarding Boothe.

"They're not professionals—at least, not professional-minded. They're thugs. They haven't been on Mister Boothe's detail for long. The last of the old crew, contractors who had police or military experience like me, they already left. Guess I should have followed them. These two, they're muscle. Frazzle heads and juicers. Nothing more. They seem to really identify with Boothe's weirdness."

Frazzlers were paranoids themselves. The stims they took synergized with the performance enhancers that gave them freakish size and strength. Delusional thinking was an irreversible side effect of the drugs.

"I know you guys can handle yourself, but watch out. They're not going to listen to reason."

Kel thanked the man for his assistance before he placed the patch on his neck and eased him onto the bed. He'd been honorable. Plus, Sims and Poul said he'd made a good showing of himself in the fight before realizing he was outclassed. Kel could respect that.

"Two juicers as bodyguards. Stim heads. Who knows how they'll react?" Kel said out loud. Now that they had the ship, the situation would no longer be something to deal with later. It would be next on the list of things to do. Wrangle two juiced frazzlers.

They took shifts. After searching one of the state rooms, they bunked the two officers together and locked them down. Sims was able to sequester the room to any data stream access. The two had been the picture of cooperation. Braley agreed there was no reason for Kel to tranq them. Kel was hunkered down in one of the command chairs on the bridge when the ship's comm alerted.

"*Hespera Sapphire*, Axis control. Runabout with three crew preparing for rendezvous. Please clear with control for exit corridor before leaving. Axis out."

Kel came fully awake. "Heads up. The runabout is on its way with three passengers."

Bigg was next. "Places, boys."

Kel hustled down the companionway to find the rest of the team and the ship's first officer standing outside the docking bay lock. The man agreed to act as the distraction and remain on deck to welcome the returning Boothe and his bodyguards, as would be the norm. The guards wore shields like their compatriot had in the mansion. Shockers would be ineffective against those. Besides, doped as those guards were, shockers might be useless even without the shields. It was amazing how when neuron receptors were blocked by toxic drugs, normal means at less lethal control often proved useless.

It wasn't a complex plan. Two each would dogpile the bodyguards while Bigg took control of Boothe. Kel told

Sims he would take the lead. Getting the suspect face down on the deck was the first task. Kel knew he could blindside anyone and floor them before they could react. He and Sims should be able to pin their thug, immobilize, and chain him in seconds.

His adrenaline throttled him up as he heard the exterior bay doors seal and the hum of the runabout power down. He hugged the curving bulkhead, just out of sight of the lock. Sims was stacked behind him. The rest of the team lay on the other side of the curve, waiting to spring. The lock cycled open.

The first officer played his part perfectly, coming to a loose position of attention as Boothe strode ahead. "Welcome back aboard, Cap—"

Kel sprang at the next body. He slammed his gauntleted fist into the side of the bull neck from behind, then threw the thick beast onto his face. He followed the man to the ground, Sims's body following his to crush the man beneath them.

Gravity reversed as Kel flew upward into the air. The grip he'd had on the man's neck was broken. Impossibly, the juiced thug sprang off the deck, loosing Kel and Sims from his back. Sims was first to land, off balance. The thug turned on him and struck. Sims staggered backward, the blow catching him square in the bucket.

"Republic officers!" Bigg yelled from where he knelt on Boothe's back. "We have a legal arrest order."

Kel landed in a crouch, near enough to aim a punch at the rear of one of the thug's knees. It wasn't enough to hurt the man, but it had the effect of buckling the leg. Sims recovered and tackled the man from the front.

Enough! he said to himself as he pulled a wrench he'd swiped from the engineer from his back. The first body part he saw was the man's knee, bent as he tried to push off to roll Sims from his chest. Kel drew back and delivered an overhead swing onto the man's kneecap. He held nothing back. He felt as much as heard the bone give way.

"Gah!"

Kel had the man's attention. He dropped the wrench and grabbed his enerchains and flung them over the nearest wrist and twisted. The arm folded as Kel encouraged it toward the man's back. "On his stomach. Get him on his stomach!"

"I'm trying!" Sims grunted. "Kark this."

Sims's hands crossed to find either side of the man's neck. Grabbing inside the thug's collar, Sims sunk down onto the man as he pulled his elbows apart. The man thrashed and gurgled for a long moment. The bucking increased. Then stopped.

"All right, Sims. Let's get him rolled over and chained. He's had enough."

Sims heaved a breath without moving, still applying the choke. "I'll make sure he's had enough."

Kel fought laughter as he turned to see how his teammates were doing. *I love a good fight, but for Oba's sake...*

Bigg had a knee in the back of the prone Xenon Boothe. Enerchains clamped the man's forearms and legs. Boothe sputtered and screamed incomprehensibly in shrill wails. Braley and Poul rolled a limp thug onto his side, chains likewise glowing on the man's limbs. Blood ran from the man's skull, pooling on the deck.

Kel tapped Sims. "Come on. He's out. Let's get him chained." They rolled the man over and finished chaining his limbs.

Sims exhaled loudly. "No way I was going to chance him getting up. I might not have been able to put him down again without shooting him. Hey, what was all that about being able to blindside anyone?"

Kel had made the boast. "First time for everything, I suppose," he admitted sheepishly.

"Kel, come look at this guy," Braley said.

Kel trotted and dropped to his knees to examine the thug. He was even larger than the titan he and Sims had tackled. "What happened?" he said as he slapped a vitals card on the man's chest, bending lower to listen for breaths until the card gave a reading.

"What happened?" Poul parroted incredulously. "Our guy was last out of the lock and saw what treatment his buddies were getting. He tossed Braley aside like a toy. I had one of the same spanners you found in the deck locker. I didn't even think about it. I parted that farm animal's hair with everything I had."

Kel wanted to laugh, but concern restrained him. The card on the man's chest confirmed good vital signs, for now. If the man suffered a brain bleed or intracranial swelling, he could die.

"Is there a medcomp on the yacht?" Kel asked the first officer who stood frozen, staring from his same spot on the deck.

"Yeah. There's a medic station. Three forward."

Kel would have been surprised if a trillionaire's personal yacht had been without one. "All right. Help me get this guy to it."

"Hey," Sims said. "Our guy's coming around."

Kel grabbed his med kit and pulled a tranqpatch and put it on the stirring man's neck. "I'll get an airway on him after we get him locked up. Bigg, how's our target?"

Bigg had Boothe rolled on his side. The man had stopped the wailing and now sobbed, "It's all a lie. It's all a lie. They're going to come back."

Kel knelt by the gibbering man. "I'm not going to hurt you," he said in as gentle a tone as he could muster. "I want to see if you're hurt. Are you all right?" He placed a palm on the man's forehead and pried open an eyelid. The pupil filled the iris. "Bigg, he's on something. I think our target's a frazzle head, too."

"He's not himself," the first officer said. "You wouldn't recognize him if you knew him even a month ago. It's the scum he hired to guard him. He was going downhill, but after he hired *them*... You didn't give 'em half of what they deserved," the man said angrily.

"Well, let's get him to the med station, too." Kel sighed. "I've got some work to do."

The thug Poul had put down did not have a brain injury. Kel sealed his wound and they tossed him, chained and tranqed, into a crew berth next to the other goon and sealed the doors with a weld.

Braley stood with Kel in the med bay. "I think we can bring Boothe around now."

Kel pulled the gantry out from the chamber. The still chained Boothe met his eyes. "Feeling better?"

"Am I still alive? Then no, I'm not feeling better."

Braley stepped forward. "Mister Boothe, you understand I have an arrest order for you? I'm to turn you over to agents from the Justice Directorate for return to Liberinthine."

"Figures they sent the monsters after me," the man mumbled. "Maybe it's best. It's all a lie. We're doomed anyway. Someday they're going to come back."

Braley spoke to Kel over L-comm. "Guy's a psych case. He's frelled his brain."

"I know what you're thinking," Boothe blurted, as if he could hear their conversation. "I may be skizzed up, but I'm not crazy. Why do you suppose the House of Reason sent you after me? Because I'm an obnoxious trillionaire? Or because I know too much?"

"What do you know?" Kel asked him.

"You wouldn't believe me." The man closed his eyes as tears ran down his cheeks.

"Try us," Braley said. "What did you mean? What's a lie? Why are we all doomed?"

Now the man laughed. "I suppose it doesn't matter now." Boothe struggled to rise.

Kel helped him to sit on the edge of the table. He put a pouch of water to the man's lips and let him take a long pull.

Boothe smacked his lips and nodded his thanks. "Everything we know is a lie. FTL? We stole it, we didn't discover it. Hypercomm? It's second-rate tech. They trickle out what they want us to have and use the rest to keep themselves in power."

"Who's they?" Kel asked.

Boothe scoffed. "The ones who sent you to kill me."

"I've heard about enough of this nonsense, Kel." Braley's patience was wearing down. "Put this guy in stasis and let's get him in the Talon and get going. I'm going to check on progress."

"Mister Boothe," Kel said, "we're not going to kill you. I'm going to help you stand and we're taking a walk. We're delivering you to justice agents. You will be well cared for and protected. You have my word."

Boothe looked at him in a way that made Kel feel he'd been caught in a lie. "When a man doesn't even exist, what's his word worth?" He broke into tears again.

Kel took him by the arm to escort him. As they walked, the man's sobbing stopped. Unable to restrain his curiosity, Kel asked, "Mister Boothe, how do you know these things?"

Boothe halted and Kel didn't force him on. He wanted to hear this.

"You might as well call me Xenon. You're probably the last person I'm ever going to talk to." He gave a brief sob, gone in the span of a second. "You seem kind. Thanks for that, at least."

Kel couldn't help feeling sorry for the man.

Boothe's shoulders drooped lower. "They brought me into it. They wanted my help. I was too good, too young. I felt flattered. Thought I was smarter than everyone else. Maybe I was. Too smart for my own good, it turns out."

It seemed Booth was explaining all this to himself more than Kel.

"We need to keep moving," Kel said.

They came to the waist deck lock where the rest of the team waited inside.

Boothe saw the stasis chamber in the stealth skiff and tensed.

"So that's it. The long sleep. Tell me the truth." He looked up at Kel. "Will I ever wake up?"

Kel placed the tranq patch on the man's neck. "You will. I promise."

Kel believed what he said. *Why would the House of Reason ice this guy? If they just wanted him dead, there are other ways to do it. We wouldn't be involved. Would we? Not like this.*

Kel eased the man in the chamber, compliant and cooperative with each and every direction as the trillionaire sunk into sleep.

"I know the truth," Boothe said, his voice dreamy and slurred. "They know I know. Now, you know, too." His breathing slowed.

Kel applied the auto-breather and closed the chamber. After activating the program and checking that stasis was stable, he stood. "We can move him."

The first officer waited outside the lock. Bigg extended a hand to him. "Thank you for your assistance. There may be agents waiting for you on landing back on Lorrian. We'll let them know you're one of the good guys."

The captain took the hand. "Thanks. You know," he tilted his head at the chamber where Boothe slept, "he really is a genius. I hope they can help him."

The Talon was waiting for them just off the starboard side of the yacht, ramp open. It was a short glide into the pax bay. Kel helped the crew chief secure the stasis chamber to the deck and checked the readouts before taking his own spot in a jump seat.

"Let's get this package dropped off and get out of buckets for a while," Bigg said.

They'd dock on the cruiser within the hour. The justice agents would be on the flight deck, waiting for their parcel. In two short days, they'd be back on Victrix.

"What'd that frazzler mean about 'the truth' and 'you know too'?" Poul asked. "What'd he tell you?"

"It was just nonsense," Braley grunted.

Kel wasn't so sure. "I couldn't get a straight answer out of him. The only thing he said plainly was something about FTL being stolen tech, and that 'we' didn't discover it. Said 'they' were holding back the best tech for themselves."

Poul made a noise with his lips. "What?" he scoffed. "The stolen alien technology theory? Pfft. Heard it before. Guy was delusional. Seen too many holos."

Bigg joined in. "But he never said who 'they' were, did he? Forget about him, gentlemen. He's not our concern anymore. We did our job. Did it well, too. I'm proud of you all."

Sims frowned. "Remember Five's old team sergeant, Iverson? He left not long after I got on the team. The other guys said he was a big believer in the stolen alien tech conspiracy. Read about it all the time. He apparently had this theory that hypercomm was crummy tech, that the House of Reason had a secret FTL comm system they kept hidden for their own use. Didn't require relays like hypercomm. Said he'd even witnessed instant comms from across the galaxy with no working relays."

Bigg scoffed. "Ivey was a good leej. One of the best. I'd want him with me in a fight anytime. But he got a little flighty near the end. Too much time behind the blaster without a break."

Should I tell them? Kel wondered. He hadn't mentioned Boothe's rant about hypercomm being second-rate tech.

Poul interrupted his thoughts. "That. Was. Exhausting."

"Exhausting's the word for it, Radd," Sims sounded off.

Poul sensed the simpatico forming with his new teammate and continued in the same vein. "Hey Braley, can't we go back to some normal missions? You know, they shoot at us, we KTF them?"

"I'm sure we can find you a home back in the regular Legion, Radd, if Dark Ops is getting to be too much for you," said Bigg.

Kel winced. *That was a low blow.* Even joking about being sent out of Dark Ops was enough to cause an existential crisis. Even for Poul.

"Sorry," Poul said in a little boy's voice. "Just kidding."

"I'm with you," Sims whispered to Poul, even though he was still on the team channel, rendering the effort as comical as it was comforting. "How 'bout some of what Three is famous for? Good old-fashioned dark ops leej stuff."

Poul whispered back, "I knew you were right for Three."

04

**Four months later
Planet Qulingat't**

"Sergeant Kel-boss, the route is clear up to the pass. I will return to the vanguard now." The large Qulingat't warrior, the havildar of the battalion reconnaissance platoon, stood at attention, waiting for Kel's dismissal. He stood beside his repulsor bike, near the lead vehicle of the convoy.

"Yes, K'listan, do so. Maintain a security perimeter and wait for the rest of the battalion. The captain will have new orders for us then," Kel replied in Standard, a nearby, repulsor-powered, miniscule translator bot relaying to the Q language in a string of clicks and hums.

The large insectoid clucked something the voder—voice decoder—around its neck could not translate. Kel knew it was the noise they made that approximated a laugh.

"We will kill many of the apostate mughal's troops soon, yes, Sergeant Kel-boss?"

"That's the plan, K'listan. Bask well."

"Bask well, Kel-boss."

The voice decoders translated the Q's undecipherable language into Standard surprisingly well. Without its assistance, Kel thought he could make out certain phrases, and knew he could recognize many names spoken in the Q's clicking speech. Attempting to speak the Q language was futile. The human mouth was not capable of formulating their clicks, nor could the Q approximate human speech.

But where physiology failed, tech stepped in. The voders rendered a distinct intonation to the sound of each Q's voice, making recognition of individuals easier. When the voder came to a word that did not directly translate to Standard, it gave an approximation that was uttered in a flat-toned mechanical voice, catching the listener's attention. The translator had done so when it chose the word "apostate" for K'listan's description of the renegade Mughal D'idawan.

Some of what the voders produced were transliterations of proper nouns in the Q language, their names being a prime example. Other words were substitutes that had been selected by the xenoanthropologists and linguists as best approximating equivalents from the history and human culture of the Republic.

The team had gotten accustomed to the approximations used by the voders, though Kel had needed to consult a dictionary for many of the terms the translator selected. Just because they were in Standard did not mean he knew all the definitions. Kel felt he was well read and had an interest in history, but some of the references were arcane, especially many of the rank titles the program had settled on.

The Qulingat't, while a single planetary species, were decidedly not a homogeneous culture. Team Three had worked with the Q before, but on the western continent of Tikalasa'at where the societal practices were fairly consistent across all the inhabitants. Here on the eastern continent of Mukalasa'at, or what they called "Big M," the Q clans were divided by many religious and societal differences.

Q as a planet and a race had many stark contrasts. The Q lived primitively, in Kel's opinion, yet were a star-faring race. The mantis-like creatures had advanced tech and used it adroitly, but lived for the most part in mud- and saliva-cemented structures with few comforts or conveniences. The same Q that lived in an earthen mound would operate complex holo-linked machinery, drive a repulsor sled, run a factory that produced jump coils from the rarest materials in the galaxy, and then repair its own domicile by regurgitating chewed sand as a paste onto its walls.

Kel watched the recon platoon sergeant get on her repulsor bike and start the journey back to the lead element of the native troops' battalion, the commando's dark purple carapace streaked with white feather-edged stripes disappearing into the distance. The Q all varied slightly in their coloration and pattern, thanks to the photosynthetic single-cell organisms that lived symbiotically in their exoskeletons. The chlorophyll compounds that provided the organic carbon source for metabolism, growth, and reproduction also provided the wonderful coloration of the exoskeleton. Parents transmitted the organisms to their offspring during reproduction, and they could be shared over the course of long-time close association. The recon platoon all had the same coloring, making them easy to pick out among the other Q.

After their first month on the planet, Sims had confided in him about his discomfort with alien races. "This I-squared stuff gets to me. I mean, indig are indig wherever you go. Even the most backward of the human planets are easy compared to working with races like the Q."

"Indigenous" was the descriptor for human, non-Republic military or police forces they worked with. They called them "indig" for short. I-squared was their slang for alien forces. That was because alien troops usually presented twice the number and complexity of problems carried with training and leading indigenous human forces.

"Well," Kel told him, "you wanted to be on Three and go where the action is, this is what you get. I-squared missions are gonna happen."

If Sims was having any problems adjusting initially, he'd long gotten over them.

Kel pinged his team over L-comm. "Recon platoon gives the all clear up to the pass."

His four teammates were spread throughout the column of vehicles carrying the battalion of Q native troops. The halted column trailed behind him down the thin, winding road and around a series of hills, making it impossible for Kel to see the end of the convoy.

"We're catching up," Bigg answered. "That number twelve sled keeps conking out. We're about a kilometer behind the rest of the convoy. Two platoons of Third Rifles are moving ahead on foot. I have two other sleds held up behind us; the slope is too steep to allow them to go around."

Bigg had stayed toward the rear of the column with Four Rifles during the movement, riding on his own repulsor bike, jetting up and down the column of vehicles and encouraging the Q drivers to maintain a close interval during the movement. They had to take frequent halts to let stragglers catch up to the rest of the column, the troublesome sleds revealing their weaknesses as the operation continued. They were on their third day of movement.

"Shouldn't be more than another few minutes before we're moving again. Power coupling keeps blowing. I think we only have a few more spares before we're going to have to abandon it and cross load onto the other vehicles."

That would be difficult. The eight hundred–strong Q battalion was crammed into and on top of every repulsor sled available. They'd already been forced to abandon one vehicle. If they lost another one, they would have to dismount many of the troops to continue on foot, slowing down their progress greatly.

There were two days from reaching the rally point to begin the combined assault on the stronghold of the renegade Mughal D'idawan.

Kill Team Seven was approaching from the south with the Second Battalion of the Sun-Loyal. They'd been in constant contact with Sergeant Dari and Captain Jaimie over L-comm. They were experiencing the same issues Three was having while moving the First Battalion over such a distance.

It was the largest operation the Q Army had undertaken in the civil war. Three and Seven had been on the planet for months, building on the successes the last iteration of DO kill teams had achieved in forming and training the native infantry battalions. The troops were primarily conscripts, females who had undergone a mating cycle and could now rejoin the warrior caste. The troops would only serve in the army for a year before having to return to carry out another mating cycle. So, it took considerable time to train the recruits, get them semi-competent in their basic tasks, and then utilize them effectively before they departed and the army had to be rebuilt once again.

The exception to this pattern were the Q who composed the reconnaissance platoons for each of the battalions. Kel didn't have a clear understanding of why K'listan and her commandos were different from the rest of the Q soldiery, but they came as close to his definition of "professional" as any group of soldiers the Q had.

K'listan had once tried to explain it to them.

"The Disciplined are rich and even stronger in tradition than the clans of the Chachnam. We have no separation by caste. Our males are many in number. My people threw off rule by the Mughals long ago. We come from the north country. Naca'hamir is ours. We need no other lands."

The predominate group that comprised the Q army were ethnically Chachnam, in distinction to Kel's commando friend and her compatriots. The xenobiologists had decoded the life cycle of the Q in a manner that was digestible by the human kill teams. But most alien life had differences compared to humanity and DO operators were accustomed to working around those differences. The xenoanthropologists had written volumes about the Q species and the planet's native cultures, but almost exclusively regarding those societies located on the western continent of Tikalasa'at.

The populace of the Big M was still being studied. Their societal intricacies were poorly understood. It was confusing to Kel and the team and even after their months here, they still felt unsure about the internal forces that drove behaviors of the Q.

The reproduction cycle and the possession of land were tied closely together with the ethnic majority of the Chachnam. Fertile females mated with males who in turn were killed by the females during the mating ritual. Kel thought that was bad luck for the guys, but more than common for insectoids, sentient or otherwise.

When a female Q successfully mated with a male, her collective gained land from the decapitated male's family. This resulted in frequent changes in territory by a family collective as they absorbed, or ceded, territory. Biologists emphasized that this practice enabled the collective to maintain a strong and diverse gene pool. Anthropologists admitted that the practice was primarily a cultural manifestation and not necessary for the survival of the Q as a species, as the practice did not exist elsewhere on Qulingat't.

The Mutual Prosperity Accord between the Solar Wind Mining Consortium and the most powerful mughal on Big M was aimed at stopping the practice. Resistance to the implementation of the accords had led to them now being on the hunt for the renegade and her forces.

The Disciplined did not participate in the same mating ritual. Males had a more or less equal footing with fertile females. Only a certain number of females were needed to reproduce, and as something about Q biology across the planet made the sex imbalance ten to one female to male, females who did not become fertile had other options in the culture of the Disciplined.

K'listan had explained to Kel and the others that though she was technically a female, she and the other warriors of the reconnaissance platoons were truly more of a sexless class. They could undergo the biologic conversion to fertile female if driven to do so by a declining population, but otherwise would never produce offspring. Serving as lifelong professional warriors in the southern armies of the Chachnam Mughals was a traditional role for the Disciplined.

The battalions had native officers, mature females who'd had many successful matings and offspring, and now served as the leadership of the armies at all levels.

Kel had a hard time thinking of the officer corps as professional. They did little soldiering that he could see. Conscripts were treated as slaves; forced to attend to the officer's needs and carry their gear. The officers participated in no training except that which they chose to do. The class distinction that separated these Q from the conscripts, beyond their fertility status, seemed to be their relationship to the family collective of one of their mughals. Kel assumed the officers would have previously served as troopers before becoming senior enough to become officers, but if so, it appeared to have no effect on their behavior toward their lowest echelon of troops.

During their time with the First Battalion of the Sun-Loyal, the team had made little progress in motivating the officer corps to perform their duties, but had made some advances in training junior non-commissioned officers in the roles of troop leading.

"Sergeant Kel-boss, we wait for rest of convoy?" one of the havildar squad leaders asked him. The Q stood at the tailgate of the sled, his weapon slung on the back of his carapace.

"Yes. Pass the word to all vehicles that we are taking another security halt. Get everyone..."

The whistle of an incoming mortar stopped Kel midsentence.

"Mortars! Everyone out of the vehicles! Incoming!"

An impact and explosion erupted from the plain, two hundred meters short and broadside of the halted column. Kel ran to the back of the next vehicle, ordering the troops to dismount and get out of the vehicles.

"Out of the sleds! Squad leaders, get your troops moving." Switching to L-comm he repeated, "Get them all out of the vehicles. Poul, get your heavy weapons platoon moving and get some counter mortar happening."

"Check," Poul responded, likely already on it.

Another round whistled overhead and this time landed a hundred meters past the line of vehicles onto the hillside beyond them.

"They're bracketing us. Get the vehicles moved and the troops dispersed," Braley called.

The rounds had impacted toward the front of the convoy. Some of the troops were slowly dispersing from the backs of the vehicles, acting groggy and sluggish as each troop dismounted and looked about, orienting to the surroundings. Squad leaders managed to get troops moving away from the line of vehicles, bounding to both sides of the road and finding small depressions to hide in.

Kel had been traveling at the front of the column with the First Rifles. He grabbed the driver of the lead vehicle as the Q attempted to leave the cab, and pushed him back into the control compartment. "Drive! Get this sled out of the impact area. *Go!*"

The troop said something the voder could not translate, but seemed to understand the order. The sled's repulsors fired up and the large vehicle sped forward, bouncing over the uneven dirt road like a boat riding over waves.

The next vehicle in the column followed as a round landed in the open space between the second and third vehicle in the line, a dozen meters between them. Shrapnel ricocheted in all directions. Kel dropped to the ground, spall pinging off his armor. He raised his head to see the driver of the halted third vehicle frozen in place.

"They're on us now. Get moving!" Kel yelled at the driver, hoping to spur him to action. He doubted the Q could hear him.

Behind the stalled vehicle, the next sled moved off to the gentle sloping side of the road attempting to go around when a round struck dead center. Kel ducked again and heard the impact of the explosion, looking up to see both vehicles in pieces and on fire.

"I got them, Poul," Sims said over L-comm. "I saw a trace northeast of us. I'm bouncing you a grid now." He'd moved up the embankment on the opposite side of the road and was looking north. "They must be behind that far cluster of hills. They've got a forward observer somewhere."

Braley's voice came over the L-comm. "Kel, can you find the mortar team's forward observer?"

"Moving," Kel replied. He was already up and running to his repulsor bike. He hopped on and sped off the road and up the embankment, racing to the top of the rise. Cresting the peak, he grabbed his N-22 out of its scabbard on the bike, and leapt off as the vehicle continued to coast forward.

"Poul, how's that mortar coming?" Braley asked.

"Almost there. Keep feeding me grids. Find me targets."

Kel had a good vantage point from the hilltop. The road curved around the hill to his right, the open rolling plain beyond. It was an excellent spot for a strike by high angle weapons; the only place to escape was down the plain and closer to their attackers. He could see the heavy weapon crew to his right, Poul running between his troops, assisting them in getting their mortars ready.

He went prone and got behind the optic of his N-22, leaving the magnification at the low setting as he scanned the horizon near the small outcropping of hills where Sims reported seeing the trace of the mortar fire. With his unobscured left eye, he moved the weapon to place the optic in front of his right eye, now co-aligning the two images. He was now viewing the far ridgeline under his optic. He increased the magnification, looking for movement. He saw nothing.

They're in that defilade behind those hills. They've got to have spotters on this side with a direct line of sight, he thought, straining to find an indicator of movement in the area.

Scanning either side of the hills, Kel looked for motion or a shape to indicate the location of their tormenters, when another round landed onto the road below him. The mortar impacted into the middle of the empty road, where only minutes before several sleds had been clustered, full of troops.

They've got the range. Now they're adjusting to walk their rounds down the column. Kel felt the urgency build to find the forward observer.

The two destroyed sleds continued to burn another fifty meters farther up the road, flames rising up ever higher into the air. Some vehicles had made it around the burning hulks and were moving forward out of the kill zone. Others in the convoy were reversing course slowly, trying to move behind the cover of the hills. Braley stood in the open, attempting to make order from the chaos. Troops lay in the depressions on either side of the road, some crawling farther away from the roadside, some frozen in place where they'd first landed.

"Braley, get the hell out of there," Kel yelled to his team leader. "They've got the range, they're going to start firing for effect any second."

"Don't worry about me," Braley drawled.

Sims broke in. "Poul, I followed that last round on the regression program, sending you a grid now."

Sims had been able to track the path of origin from the last mortar round and now had a location for the enemy mortar team narrowed to within a reasonably small area.

"Someone adjust fire for us," Poul said over L-comm to them all, hoping Kel or Sims could observe.

"I got you," Sims returned.

The distinct "whump" from the mortar team's first launch conjured for Kel the desire for many more of the distinctive sounds. And soon.

"Shot over," Poul said over L-comm.

"Shot out," Sims said. The man had scaled the hill and was now on the hilltop as well, farther to Kel's right.

"Splash over."

"Splash out."

After several seconds no impact was apparent.

"Doubtful," Sims replied, meaning he couldn't see the impact of the round. "Send another and get that baseplate settled." No sooner had he spoke than another round launched toward the hills in the distance.

Kel wanted to direct his attention to the impact zone to try to spot as well, but kept his attention through his optic. Where in the nine hells was the enemy forward observer?

Another round impacted their position, this time a hundred meters short of the road. Below him, injured troops buzzed in pain. Kel continued to search.

"Poul, the OT line is good—impact was short, right on top of the ridge. Add two hundred and send it."

"Short, add two hundred," Poul repeated to his troops. "Shot over."

Kel's attention focused on a dark area on the military ridge, just below the crest of the ridgeline topping the cluster of hills, behind where the enemy mortar team was obscured. He lost awareness of the communication between his teammates trying to walk their mortar rounds onto the target. He ranged the spot through his optic and let his bucket show him the data. 2,374 meters. His attention was drawn to movement. Something in the dark area shifted slightly, reflection from an optical device glinted. Heat waves of mirage lifted unevenly around the shape he now focused on.

Got you, he thought, relieved as he checked the data. The particle beam effect of his blaster would be maximized at this distance. Kel stroked the side of the weapon's receiver, arming the sniper rifle. He closed his eyes momentarily and then opened them again. The sight picture of the reticle on his target shifted slightly. He picked his hips up and slid them to the right to get himself squarely behind the gun, and repeated the evaluation. When he opened his eyes again, this time nothing shifted in his view through the scope.

He looked at the indicator inside the optic to tell him if the gun was slanted left or right in any amount. At this distance, if the gun was canted even a fraction of a degree, the shot would deviate laterally. Even if everything else was correct, the error would cause him to miss the target altogether. Doing it right was in his control alone.

He took in a deep breath and blew it out in an unhurried fashion. When he'd reached an empty chest and was happy with the stability of his reticle on the target, he waited to time the shot between heartbeats and unconsciously pressed the trigger. He continued to concentrate on the picture of his reticle superimposed over the spot where he'd seen the glimmer, aware of the sensation of the click underneath his finger.

Almost instantly he was rewarded with the dark shape under his reticle changing from an amorphous blob into a prostrate shape of a Q, limbs flailing as he watched. A brief feeling of satisfaction warmed him. No matter how incredible the technology in his hands, he was the most important part of the weapon, the part that made it a human system, made him more than a cog switching on a machine.

"Found the observer. He's out of the picture." Kel didn't wait for a response. He knew Sims and Poul were still working.

"Airburst. Fire for effect. Drop it on them, Poul," Sims said, the excitement in his voice apparent.

Kel lifted his head off his rifle to gaze down toward their mortar team's firing position. Poul had three mortar crews organized and was racing between them, checking their adjustments as the Q troops hung a round over each of the large tubes, dropping them one at a time on Poul's signal. Round after round spurted from the tubes. Kel put his head back behind his optic to watch downrange as the rounds exploded several hundred meters above the presumed location of the enemy mortar emplacement. The thermite impregnated explosive rods, fifty of them clustered into each mortar round, rained down. Trails of smoke wafted behind each projectile, filling the air space above with an artificial cloud.

"I've got the view on the drone now," Bigg said to them all. "You can end the fire mission, Poul. Enemy troops on the ground and mortar silenced."

Bigg had been monitoring their eye-in-the-sky from the rear of the column. How the drone had missed the enemy mortar team would be a subject of discussion later. "I'm making a wide sweep to look for runners. Braley, what's our status?"

"Checking now, Bigg. Kel, Sims, sound off."

"Sir, I'm headed down to start organizing aid," Sims responded and trotted down the slope of the hill toward the road.

"I'm on my way down, too," Kel answered. "I'll start getting the companies marshaled and meet you at the casualty collection point, Sims."

He looked for his bike; it had traveled another twenty-five meters from where he'd leapt off it. He placed his N-22 carefully in its scabbard and mounted the bike, turning it to take a course down the ridge of the slope and across the road, then raced to the two burning vehicles. Both had collapsed into flames, burning plasma streaming from the engine compartments. Small arms rounds cooked off, cracking explosions from within the covered beds.

He rode to the next impact crater and halted, dismounting as he saw one of the jemadar staring at the hole in the road. The junior officer looked stunned.

"Jemadar, take my bike and go retrieve the vehicles," Kel said, pointing ahead to indicate the direction the first sleds had taken. "Bring them back. Do you understand?"

After he repeated the order, the junior officer answered affirmatively and headed toward Kel's bike. Kel grabbed his large medkit before the Q rode off, and headed down the slope to the location of the last mortar impact. Troops milled about, neither rendering aid to the wounded nor forming into a security perimeter.

He identified one of the battalion's subadar by the three bands on his arm, standing alone, giving no indication he was directing his troops.

"Subadar," Kel called to him, "get your company organized. Get the jemadar and havildar to find their troops and get them organized. We must be ready to move soon."

The dappled green Q turned to face him.

"Yes. You are correct, Kel-boss. We must move off this plain." The Q started yelling at his troops and his subordinates listened. Kel moved on, hopeful that the company commander could get his unit into some semblance of military order again.

Up ahead, Sims was evaluating the damage to the Q strewn about the mortar impact crater. Several partially intact bodies lay at the outer edge of the blast radius where Sims knelt to evaluate each casualty. Green ichor puddled across the brown grass.

"Any survivors?" Kel asked, stepping over an insectoid leg.

"Not found any yet. Everyone who could, got up and split after the impact. We'll have to check for minor wounded later, but as far as this site, no survivors. I'm guessing at least six dead here."

"I checked the destroyed sleds. The drivers had to be DRT," Kel said, meaning "dead right there."

"Captain, Sims and I are at the CCP. There appear to be no survivors and I'm estimating we have at least eight dead and two sleds destroyed."

"Rog. Let's get our vehicles together and get the battalion loaded and ready to move again. I want to make the high ground of the pass before dark." Braley immediately switched recipients. "Bigg, what's your loc?"

"Pulling up to the end of the column now. I'll move forward and find you."

"Three, everyone, make for my location," Braley finished.

"The mughal knows we're coming," Braley said when they were gathered.

"You think?" Poul offered. "Why didn't we see that ambush coming?"

Bigg spoke. "The Q don't have much of a thermal signature to begin with. If they were deliberate and camouflaged, we could easily miss a small group. The algorithm wouldn't pick up anything to alert us and we wouldn't see anything even live viewing over the drone."

"That's right. The drone's program is good for detecting movement, reflective surfaces, and thermal signatures. I've defeated that algorithm dozens of times on stalks," Kel said, referring to his sniper practice sessions.

Everyone nodded, knowing the drone technology could be a crutch and was not infallible.

"I wish we had a dropship on call for close air support, or that we had more OSPs overhead," Poul said as he turned to Braley. "We knew we were going to be exposed this entire movement, and still we get no support."

Braley put his hand up, but before he could speak, Bigg jumped in.

"Poul, stow it. There are two Talons on the planet and we'll have them for the assault. As for the orbital strike platform, we have one. One. And even if it had been overhead, we couldn't have used it. You know that."

The Orbital Strike Platform was an incredible tool. The OSP satellite orbiting Q was launched by the Navy the same time they delivered Three and Seven to the planet. The package gave them awesome, but limited, ability to destroy isolated targets from orbit. The satellite fired small tungsten rods that could be placed to within a few centimeters of the bounced grid or laser-designated target. The damage the rods did to a target belied their small mass. When accelerated to a fraction of the speed of light, the projectiles wrought massive damage because of their kinetic energy. Kel had seen a single rod make a large crater where a moment before a tank had been.

The OSP projectile rods were extremely effective against those types of targets, something hard and stationary. Against a target like they'd just faced, it would have been unlikely to have been effective. The rod required an exact target grid. Launched at a general area, the rod's impact did cause a significant crater, but had no explosive or fragmentary effect to kill personnel in a large radius. And, without knowing the exact location of the mortar crew, they could have rained a dozen of the rods on the general area by guess and never have eliminated the threat.

The satellite was in a low planetary orbit, and while it could be tasked to remain over an area for an extended period, its ability to do so was limited. The sole OSP they had was going to be tasked to remain available for the assault on the mughal's stronghold in two days. The small satellite carried less than a hundred of the special rods, and those were being saved to hit the armored vehicles and artillery emplacements, and perhaps the compound itself if necessary. When either its fuel or ammunition supply was gone, the OSP became space junk.

"I'm sorry, Bigg. Sorry, sir. I'm just frustrated," Poul said. "I know we couldn't have called the OSP in time or have gotten the Talons from the capital. Sometimes I just miss rolling with more hind-end."

Everyone felt Poul's frustration at a time like this.

"You did a great job with your mortar team, man," Sims chimed in. "I've never seen the Q move that purposefully before."

"Getting shelled is quite the motivator. If you hadn't spotted the trace so early, we would have lost a lot more troops."

"Yeah, Sims, glad you're finally carrying some weight around here," Braley said, clapping him on the back. "Look, everyone, get back to your company subadar, get accountability of personnel and equipment, and let's get moving. We're two vehicles down—"

Bigg interrupted him.

"Three down. We lost number twelve. We cannibalized what parts we could."

"Three down. We're going to need to put some troops on foot and it'll take us the rest of the day to make it to the next RON."

The remain overnight position was on a plateau above the crumbling road they traveled along. It had taken weeks to assemble twenty vehicles needed to transport the battalion for the attack on the stronghold. They had been on a tight schedule from the beginning. Now on the third day of the movement to the western province, it was doubtful they would make it to the rally point on time to stage with the Second battalion and Kill Team Seven.

"All right, everyone, get back to your companies. I'm going to find the nawab and update her. Get me your status as soon as you're able. Let's try to be ready to move out immediately or sooner."

05

They found the First Battalion commander, Nawab Q'stalt, still in the covered flatbed of a convoy sled, surrounded by several of her junior officers. They had not dismounted during the attack.

"Nawab-boss, I'm glad to find you safe," Braley said, restraining his desire to berate the battalion commander for her indolence.

"All is well, Captain Braley?" the short, orange-hued Q asked from her reclining position on a wide pillow.

Returning troops crowded around Braley to peer into the sled's bed. Braley climbed in and took a knee beside the lounging insectoid.

"We came under attack from a mortar crew. We've silenced them with our own. It was excellent work exemplifying the bravery of the First Battalion under your leadership, Nawab-boss. Two vehicles and eight lives were lost. We continue on to the next rally point and should arrive by nightfall."

The nawab seemed pensive as she considered Braley's report.

"So, our movement has been exposed. Was it by battlefield intelligence or by treachery, do you suppose?"

Whether the Mughal D'idawan's forces had interdicted them as a result of the force being observed moving west, or whether they had been compromised much earlier as a result of espionage within their own camp, was a good question.

"Excellent question, Nawab-boss. No survivors from the attacking force have been spotted, so it is unlikely that any report of the effect on our force will make it to the mughal. We are extending our drone sweeps to detect any other interdiction attempts. Our movement will be slower as we have lost three more vehicles."

"Did you not say we had two destroyed in the attack?"

"Yes, Nawab-boss, but another has failed and must be abandoned. That will leave almost a company at a time on foot for the rest of the campaign."

"I question how important we are to the Republic and the Consortium if they refuse to give us the support we need to wage this war on their behalf."

Braley had heard a similar complaint from Poul not five minutes earlier. "We go to war with the army we have, not the army we wish we had." Braley paused to let the translation complete and to gauge the nawab's reaction. The Q's large outer mandibles stayed mated together, concealing the inner mouth parts that formed the softer portions of their speech. No response.

"The mining consortium has pledged that they will support your mughal and her army," he continued. "They have promised more aid in the future. First, you must prove your worth by being capable in the coming campaign. Otherwise, the consortium may not only withdraw their support, they may petition the House of Reason to place their trust elsewhere on Mukalasa'at."

Mandibles clashed, the nawab chittering an objection the voder did not translate.

Braley didn't wait to stroke her ego again. "However, I'm confident that with your determination and leadership, we will have a great victory. Mughal D'shtaran and you, Nawab-boss, will be rewarded greatly when we have defeated D'idawan. New weapons, armored vehicles, artillery, even aircraft have been discussed as part of the reward for success. It would make your clan the most powerful on Mukalasa'at, perhaps on Qulingat't."

One of the trooper attendants loped forward, a plate and a wide cup in each claw, and sank to the nawab's reclining height. Her knees bent to their most acute angle, folding back on themselves so she could lower her abdomen in deference as she offered the dishes. The nawab waved her away.

"I know the game you humans play. We have value only because of what we can offer. My mughal has ordained that the accord will be a good thing for our clan. We are adapting and changing to comply with the decrees of the Consortium. Mughal D'shtaran is strong. Our clan will obey her. The changes the humans wish are not popular. We grow human crops on our land and allow humans to inhabit larger parts of Mukalasa'at because of the promises the Consortium has made." The nawab rolled over, her abdomen touching the floor, the articulations of her limbs bent as she looked up, leaving her in position to spring. A bearing signaling threat.

"My mughal is interested to see how the promises of the humans are kept. I have pledged the life of every Chachnam under my command to see D'idawan defeated and our clan made powerful." She rocked back on her rear legs and stood erect.

Braley relaxed slightly. This was a posture of ease for the Q.

"See that you do your part, Captain."

Braley knew a dismissal when he heard it. With a curt nod, he headed back to his repulsor bike. "All right, Three, the nawab's been briefed. Are we ready to roll?"

"Where was our fearless commander?" Bigg asked.

"Still on the sled, being attended by slaves."

A general silence fell over L-comm. Kel broke it by sounding off first.

"We're ready in the vanguard. I've dismounted some of First Rifles and put them in the lead to set the pace."

Sims seconded the ready to move, followed by Poul and Bigg. Some of Sims's Second Rifles filled in spaces on the lead vehicles, the rest of the displaced riders assuming two loose columns along the road.

"All right, Kel, get us moving. We'll break every hour to rotate troops for dismount. We'll get a rotation schedule by company organized tonight so tomorrow the company on the ground has one chain of command. Right now, it's most important we get moving. Halt us if there's an issue. Let's do it."

This is going to be a slow haul, Kel thought as he gave the order to march.

The Q could move quickly for short distances but were slow to march, their legs more adept at leaping than the gait needed for steady ambulation. The road ahead led across the plain to disappear on the horizon, blending with the brown terrain as it rose to the plateau that would be their resting place for the night. After leaving the short span of hills where they'd been halted, the plain ahead provided no likely cover from which another mortar team could ambush them.

I wonder what else the Mughal D'idawan's army has in store for us?

Ascending the plateau, they marched across a grassland that covered a dozen square kilometers before the road westward sloped down again. At a lower elevation, they'd arrive at their rendezvous with Kill Team Seven and Second Battalion. The staging area for the combined campaign was at the tail of a long dry channel leading to the renegade mughal's stronghold. The dry season meant there was no chance of water washing through the huge wadi. Once assembled, movement in force to the target would be swift.

K'listan met Kel as the column crested the plateau. Her recon platoon was dug into fighting positions, forming a perimeter larger than that needed for the small section of commandos. K'listan had anticipated how much space the battalion would need to form a perimeter. She and her twenty Q had already gotten a good start on security for the battalion by digging positions at several key locations.

"Sergeant Kel-boss, I am glad that you are well. You bring death to the D'idawan's army before the battle even begins. We rejoice but are saddened to not be with the battalion for the victory."

K'listan ambled closer. By now Kel was well accustomed to the Q gait, but the swaying motion of their ambulation always struck him as jerky and clumsy in comparison to their graceful hops. At a full "run" the Q could cover a half a dozen meters in a single launch, and do so in rapid succession to cover a hundred meters in seconds. After that, they had to rest for a prolonged period, making the loping gait their only means of sustained movement for long distances.

"We'll kill plenty together soon, K'listan. Lead the first vehicle into a perimeter and the rest will follow. Make it large, K'listan."

The recon havildar moved to the first sled and got the driver's attention as she walked the path ahead, instructing the driver to follow her.

Kel returned to L-comm. "Guys, I've got a perimeter forming with the vehicles. Make sure your drivers follow into the circle and let's get the companies dug in for the night and get OP/LPs pushed out. Sir," he directed to Braley, "I'll set us up centrally. You'll see my bike."

"Roger, Kel. Poul, when you get your mortar crews placed, we'll see you at the Team RON," Braley said as he rode to halt his bike near Kel's and Sims's.

Poul continued past, following the heavy weapons platoon sled. He directed his mortarmen as they crawled out of the vehicle. Not long after, Kel saw the last of the vehicles make their way into the perimeter. From the end of the column, Bigg rode to the team's position near the center of the large circle.

"Last man, Captain. No stragglers." Bigg removed his helmet and produced a large hydration pouch out of his carryall. It was always refreshing to get a large gulp of water not provided by the nipple in their buckets. Everyone removed their own lids and did the same.

Bigg took a breath and wiped his hand across his forehead. "Let's get the heavy slug-launchers laid in first at nine, twelve, and three, and let's get two heavies positioned outside the perimeter facing up and down the road. Get fighting positions dug at twenty-five-meter intervals all around the perimeter. I want them at least ten meters past the perimeter of the sleds. After that, the troops can dig graves inside the perimeter for sleeping. We'll keep a twenty-five percent watch tonight. Kel, take your recon platoon and scout out your OPs."

The repulsor sleds formed a rough circle, fifty meters between each of the vehicles. The plateau was a huge expanse with no additional terrain features. It would be difficult for a ground force to attack them in this location. High-angle fire from artillery or mortar would be their biggest threat, making it essential that everybody had ground cover.

While the Q were not fast at dismounted movement, they were astoundingly fast excavators. They had no need for shovels or other implements. The tough consistency of their exoskeletons and the way they cupped their terminal graspers allowed them to dig furiously and with great rapidity. While one group dug fighting positions a meter deep, another group processed the tailings by scooping the soil into their mouths, mixing it with their thick saliva, and building berms around the fighting positions another meter in height. The mixture grew hard like duracrete after curing. Working together, within minutes the positions were nearly complete.

Kel followed K'listan to where the Disciplined had already selected locations for observation and listening posts. At the edge of the plateau overlooking the road, they'd dug and concealed fighting positions that were nearly invisible from both approaching directions.

"K'listan, I can see prints in the road where your troops stood to admire their camouflage work on the OPs. Get those swept."

K'listan said something to her troops too fast for the voder to translate and two of the Q took a bundle of long grasses and moved into the road, sweeping as they walked backward to remove the sharp gouges left by the Q hind legs.

"Apologies, Sergeant Kel-boss. It escaped my attention. It will not happen again."

"No need, Havildar K'listan. Just remember to think like your enemy."

"Yes, Kel-boss. It would be a shame to spoil the opportunity to surprise *apostate* troops and kill many of them. It is my favorite kind of joke to play."

K'listan clucked with laughter.

I like to think of surprising the enemy as a kind of lethal practical joke myself, Kel thought. But it was only funny when you were not the recipient.

"Recon platoon will man the east-west OPs watching the road. Let's find a couple of locations for OPs a hundred meters or so outside the perimeter, somewhere in between the heavy gun positions. We'll have the companies in those sectors man them with four-person teams, and they can keep a fifty-percent watch."

Meter-high grass covered the plateau. Prone from within a fighting position there would be little to observe. The teams on OP/LP watch would have to observe standing from their fighting positions to spot anything. They would keep watches from the top of the repulsor sleds as well. Several of the vehicles had medium caliber automatic guns on turrets that Sims had expediently constructed for the campaign. They were still not proper armored vehicles for a mounted patrol, but it was what they had.

Kel returned to the center of the perimeter to find several Q troops digging a large grave for the team to sleep in. Kel didn't feel guilty about the troops laboring in their place. What they did in minutes would have taken the humans hours to accomplish excavating the hard ground. He waved in thanks as they moved off.

Bigg stood with his bucket still off. "Poul's going to stay with the weapons team. The rest of us can split up watch. Captain, you take the first watch; I'll take second. Sims, you want third or last? Seeing as you did such a good job spotting today."

"Hey, I'll take an uninterrupted night's sleep. I'm an early riser anyway. That leaves you with the third watch, Kel." Sims smiled at him.

"That's all right. They always attack on third watch. More killing for me."

06

Kill Team Three had the battalion "stood to" and alert two hours before first light. They were moving before the sun rose.

First Rifles took the dismounted role as they left the plateau, Kel walking with them at the convoy's midpoint. He had turned his bike over to the company subadar for the march. The subadar had shown herself to be more interested in her leadership duties than many of the other company commanders, and merited further trust.

The night had been quiet. Kel made the rounds of the fighting positions during his watch, impressed that he found no sleeping sentries. He'd encountered none of the native officers during his inspection of the perimeter and the camp, which did not surprise him. Even when assigned a watch, the native officer's habit was to sleep and assign a trooper to wake them if needed during their duty period.

The sun rose behind them as they made their way down the slope of the plateau.

"We'll change off in an hour and rotate Second Rifles to the dismount position. I'm figuring we can make the wadi by nightfall if we don't screw around," Braley said to the team.

If we don't get ambushed. If we don't lose any more vehicles. If the Q can keep the pace. Kel knew the others were thinking the same thing. No need to say it out loud.

What few artillery pieces the renegades were known to have, they couldn't operate. None of the crews had accompanied D'idawan in her rebellion. Without crews, the guns were effectively useless. A weapon wasn't dangerous without the knowledge to use it. Unless another mortar team was dug in and camouflaged well, they would meet no serious resistance today.

The biggest issue would be the pace. They were moving at a six-kilometer per hour rate. It was going to be grueling for the Q to maintain that speed. Working them for an hour at a time and giving them three hours recovery in the sleds was their best hope of reaching the rendezvous by the end of the day. It was going to be a twelve-hour movement if everything went by their best estimation. The troops would then only have a brief refit before the assault.

Second Battalion fared better. Braley had spoken with his counterpart on Kill Team Seven, Captain Jaimie, the night before. The Second contained two mechanized companies of light-armored vehicles and infantry, and two motorized companies. Each had a heavy weapon section with mortars. Captain Jaimie reported that unlike Three, they'd lost no vehicles nor encountered resistance. They'd reach the rally point by midday. Their movement from the south was over a smaller distance, but over roads which were much worse. They'd had multiple delays crossing difficult terrain features with the large, spherical-wheeled vehicles. The light-armored trucks handled grades much better than repulsor sleds which lost lift traveling over the combination of rough and steeply angled surfaces. The vehicles were slow but dependable.

The Mughal D'idawan's army had a thousand Chachnam and heavy armor. Tanks. When D'idawan's army had been the Third Battalion of the Grand Army of the Sun-Loyal, it had served as the largest and best outfitted of the three battalions. The First and Second were light infantry, barely motorized, and attacking the heavier Third ready on the defense. The very definition of not good.

What the Third didn't have: a kill team to advise them.

It was vital that the First arrive as soon as possible to combine the two remaining battalions for the attack. Once assembled, the attack would have to proceed quickly before D'idawan's forces moved against the lone Second.

Timing such assemblies was difficult with native troops and resources. Braley and Jaimie decided that the Second would slow their pace so as to not be in the battle space too prematurely without support from the First. If D'idawan launched her armor against either force alone, it would give Dark Ops a real distinction in the annals of military history. The stuff military planners would study to learn what a full blown, New Vega–level disaster looked like. The kind of plan you hoped someone got flayed over.

They reached the halfway point along the route.

"This isn't going well," Sims shared with Kel over an L-comm side channel. "The columns are getting strung out and we have a lot of stragglers falling behind."

He was right. The Q just couldn't keep the pace. They'd learned to expect that after just thirty minutes into a unit's turn on the march, the Q resorted to taking short hops to keep the pace, fatiguing themselves even faster. Those that fell out of the ambling gait and hopped ahead to catch up invariably burned out after a few leaps, then stopped to recover, only to fall farther behind. At the end of every hour dismounted, the exhausted troops had gone as far as they could go before achieving total combat ineffectiveness. If attacked now, those troops would be useless.

Kel thought of options to offer Braley. Slow the pace. Reduce the load. Take longer breaks. It wasn't as if they could shed excess weight to ease their burden while marching. The Q soldiers carried little besides their arms and ammunition. Their armor was integral. It wasn't like they could shed their carapaces. They carried no water or food. What little water they required, they took in once or twice daily. They ate but did not require food more than once a day. Most of their nutrition was supplied by the solar radiation that fed the zooxanthellae of their pigmentation. They basked while they marched, replenishing glucose to their cells, but still needed to remove the toxic buildup of exertion from their muscles like all creatures did. Only rest could supply that.

Kel hailed Braley. "Captain, I'm having doubts we can keep the pace."

"What do you think, Kel? Are the Q going to have anything left when we get there?"

Kel grunted. "I was just with First Rifles as they came off their second rotation. I think we have to go to thirty minute rotations on the march. Even so, they're still going to need every minute of their three hours on the sleds to get ready to do it once more. That and I'm hoping they're going to get a fire in their bellies once the shooting starts. Otherwise at this rate, all we're going to get there with is a bunch of burned out bugs."

"Just talked to Jaimie," Braley replied.

Kel was anticipating the bad news.

"The Second is moving into the base of the wadi. They held back as long as they could. They're going to get in an attack formation and wait until we get there. No sign of movement on the mughal's part yet on drone. Says the stronghold is locked up tight and there's no sign of their armor. Yet. We're both thinking that isn't going to last long. We're out of time. Period."

"Do we have any other options?" Kel asked.

Bigg had been listening and grunted. "Just what we talked about. Overload all the sleds, pile body on body, have them hanging on every square centimeter of nacelle and fuselage, and drive like hell. But when the sleds start breaking down, we're going to arrive with a smaller force."

"Just a second—Jaimie's bouncing me on closed channel," Braley responded.

They waited silently for several minutes. Kel looked over his shoulder from his bike to see Sims behind him on the ground with Second Rifles, marching with his troops.

Braley broke in again. "Okay, the choice is made for us. There's signature of armor firing up repulsors back in the canyons. They're getting ready to move. We have to get whatever part of the unit there that we can, as fast as we can. Guys, get us loaded. Sims, get Second cross-loaded wherever you can, except for the heavy weapons sled. That's got too much mass as it is. Poul, I want you up front with Third Rifles and the weapons section. The mortar section has to make it to the assembly area. Make it happen."

Over the open L-comm channel, Seven's Team Sergeant Dari said, "Hey Three, if you don't get here soon, the party might be all over." He didn't sound concerned. Maybe even jovial.

"Yeah, you wish," Bigg shot back. "Dar, we're moving out double time now. It'll be two hours at our top speed. How long can we hold the OSP on station?"

Too many variables came into play to determine how long they'd have the orbital strike platform overhead in support once they started the attack.

"Two orbits and then I'm bringing her down lower and getting her spun up. If you get here on time," Dari let that hang, "I think we'll have about a forty-five minute employment window at the altitude we discussed. Then let's just say this thing is happening, or else. 'Cause when that armor appears, if we haven't seized the initiative, we're going to have to fight a retreat back into the hills. Get moving, Bigg."

07

The orbital strike platform had an orbital period of about seventy-five minutes. When held stationary along a planned flight path, the OSP could linger over a target area for about an hour. It could be called from another location around the planet for exigent use, but would spend much of its charge to reach the target site, leaving little power left to rain down death. The projectiles it delivered weren't from the gods. Nor was the OSP magic. Despite the reverence those on the ground held for it, the OSP had very real limitations. If either fuel or projectiles were used up, it became useless junk, joining the thousands of other objects orbiting any planet.

    Gliding smoothly on his bike over the rocky path, Kel checked the OSP's telemetry in his HUD. The satellite was in a polar orbit, moving closer to the longitude of the target. When tasked for the attack phase, the satellite would drop altitude significantly, reaching to within five hundred kilometers of the surface, primed to shower down its deadly projectiles.

    OSPs, while useful, were never as good as true air support. A navy cruiser could bombard any target on the ground with impunity, using kinetic or particle-energy weapons. It could remain on station for as long as you needed it. Even a simple dropship like a Talon could use its blasters with devastating effect from anywhere between close atmospheric range to just above ground level and likewise could be counted on to be available over the target area for hours.

The OSP could not.

The assaulters would have two dropships deployed from the capital for the assault—the only two such ships on the planet. Kill Team Seven had reviewed CAS procedures with the Talon crews back in the capital. Dari told Three their confidence level in the Talon's ability to provide genuine close air support was, "somewhere between good enough to help and bad enough to kill us by mistake." Not all pilots were created equal. CAS was complex and required constant practice. The crews had assured Seven they were up to the task. But without the ability to train with the crews live, it was a risk.

Kel remembered Poul's complaint after the mortar ambush. They had no hind end on this mission.

Kel checked the map. If they kept this pace, they would arrive within the hour. They had yet to lose any vehicles, but in Kel's experience it was at times like these, disaster struck. He hoped this time it would be different.

Q hung on every possible handhold around the sleds. Many were held in place by the squadmates on either side, wrapping an appendage around the torso of one Q to link with that of a Q on the opposite side, all rolling together as the speeding sled rocked over the rough road. Q clung to the nacelles, sat atop the driver compartments, and clutched the spars of the canopies over the beds. Their caravan would have made for a comical sight if the situation had not been so dire.

Kel thought about what awaited them. Once at the assembly area with Second Battalion, they'd need to cover a dozen kilometers of open ground before reaching the renegade Mughal D'idawan's stronghold. The battle would take place on the open flood plain below it. The stronghold was a fortress in every sense of the word. At the head of the long wadi the sandy riverbed split to form branches around the cliff where the bastion sat, eons of erosion carving canyons into the plains behind the fortress. During rare rainstorms, the resultant torrents turned the fortress into a peninsula.

From the high ground the castle had an imposing view. Small islands of sedimentary rock pedestals and buttes peppered the desert plain. Features big enough to disrupt the view across the open kilometers of sandy wadi. None big enough to hide more than a few vehicles.

Kel admired the architecture of the fortress. It was unlike other Q constructs he was familiar with. It was definitely designed as a fortification, rivaling what he imagined as the ideal keep of a warlord from the books of his youth. The front courtyard was surrounded by ten-meter high walls, each section several meters thick, parapets standing along their runs. At abutments of faceted wall sections, heavy gun emplacements sat in pill boxes fronting the stronghold, looking down at the wide wadi. A jagged, rocky outcrop rose within the compound and formed its west wall, a small mountain acting as a natural battlement. It descended into the compound and separated the fortress into front and rear courtyards, with a narrow open avenue connecting the two on the east.

Buildings of varying heights were carved from the rocky projection in the compound's center. Kel assumed they were barracks, similar to those back at the battalion garrison. Behind, several smaller buildings did the same to face the larger field at the rear of the escarpment. The rear compound was surrounded by a defensive wall less massive than that to the front.

A road led from the wadi floor rising around the escarpment to the open rear of the complex. Behind, narrow but deep canyons dug into the landscape that led to the mountains beyond. The maze-like crevices offered substantial protection to the fortress; only a single winding road led into the compound from that direction. It would be impossible for any ground assault force to approach the fortress from the plain except by single-file on the narrow trail.

Within the caverns flanking the fortress were caves set into the base of the cliff. Drones and satellites had gathered little intelligence for the operation. They were unable to get a useful estimate of how many tanks the Grand Army's former Third Battalion actually had. The bulk of the mughal's armored forces were somewhere within those natural redoubts, the heavy armor hidden from overhead imaging.

Tanks. Light armor and infantry against tanks, Kel stewed, the prospect weighing him down like a heavy carryall that couldn't be shed. There was an upside to D'idawan relying on the tanks. *Sure, the defector pulled a real coup making off with all the heavy armor. But tanks need maintenance. They need skill to employ.* He doubted the renegade Third had the know-how. They would find out soon.

Kel linked into the feed from Seven's drone, which hung invisibly over the head of the wadi. He knew his teammates, especially Braley, were studying it too. Their unblinking eye bounced a wide view to the operators. The imposing stronghold showed much activity. Troops amassed in the front courtyard. Below, dust rose from the wadi floor where deep shadows from the caverns and caves gave birth to tanks that slowly rolled down the winding road. The squat, gray turtles flowed forward into the base of the wadi, assembling into long files and columns.

The sled in front of him halted. He eased his bike left, only to see that a few vehicles ahead, one sled was at a standstill.

"What's going on up front?" Bigg questioned. "We just stopped back here."

Kel drove up to the halted sled. Climbing up, he leaned into the cab.

"Why are you stopped?" Kel asked the driver.

The Q's voder flatly intoned, "Incomprehensible," several times while the driver chittered, before she spoke slowly enough for the device to translate.

"It has ceased, Sergeant Kel-boss. I know it to be honestly dead for all-time."

"We've got our first dead vehicle," Kel relayed over L-comm. "I'll get the rest moved around and get these guys moving to the assembly area on foot."

"Rog. Make it happen," Braley said, resigned. There was nothing else that could be done.

Kel motioned the trailing vehicles off the road and over the rocky detour. Sims was already at the rear of the dead sled, giving orders to the platoon's havildar as troops sprang out of the bed.

"Get your troops and all equipment and start the march to the assembly area. It should only be another fifteen kilometers," Kel told the Q NCO. "We need you there, so do your best."

"Yes, Sergeant Kel-boss, we will join you in battle soon."

Once Kel saw that approaching vehicles were following the path of the bypassing sleds, he got back on his bike and sped along the narrow dirt road, weaving around sleds, until he found Poul at the front leading the column.

"We should be closing in soon," Poul said. "How many have we lost?"

"Just the one. We're going to make it. Keep this pace."

Kel's comm chimed in his bucket. He was expecting word from K'listan.

"Sergeant Kel-boss, we are with the contact party. I have left a squad at the route into the wadi to guide the main force."

"Good job, K'listan. Stay where you are; I'm coming to you." He broke the connection without waiting for a reply and keyed his L-comm as he veered right and slowed.

"Braley," he said, steering off the road and out of the convoy's way. "We're maybe ten minutes out. Recon is with the contact party and has guides at the turn off to the wadi."

In the distance, the brown plain gave way to the changing hue of light colored sand and shallow spur outcroppings. Erosion created a smooth natural highway that was the wadi. The change in topography signaled impending action. He smiled. They were close now.

It was only a minute before Braley sped by on his own bike, not slowing as he passed. Kel raced to catch up and fell in behind as they wove between sleds.

"Bigg, do you have them on the drone?"

"Sending it now, sir," Bigg replied instantly. A view from the drone appeared in a small window within his HUD. Kel enlarged it slightly, not allowing it to obscure his view as he kept Braley's bike in his left field of vision. A squad of the purple-carapace Disciplined sat on their own bikes at a curve of the road just where red-streaked brown changed to the gradual sandy tones of the wash.

Braley bounced a map projection to everyone, showing their present location and the marker he'd overlaid on the route indicating the location of their recon guides. "Okay, Poul, start slowing them down. I'm going with Kel to meet the contact party. Meet the recon platoon here and wait for us to bring the column forward. I think there's a good way forward from there even if we haven't found the contact party."

A view from the overhead drone panned north. Half-concealed in a small draw about a kilometer away from the turn-off point, Q surrounded a light armored vehicle. Guides from the Second Battalion. A small portion of the weight Kel felt lifted. K'listan and her Disciplined sisters were with them, always easy to distinguish among the Chachnam by their darker color. An icon appeared on the map projection showing their location.

"Excellent," said Braley. "Kel and I'll make contact and then come back to bring everyone up. Get the word passed to the nawab and through the chain of command. It's time."

The repulsor sleds rode better over the wadi floor than the rough road that had been their thoroughfare the last five days. The sleds' seesawing motion settled as they pulled off onto the sandy hardpan. With their escort from the Second Battalion, Kel led the column on a circuitous path around small buttes to finally arrive at the assembly area.

Kel felt relieved to see their sister infantry battalion. The five companies of the Second Battalion of the Sun-

Loyal were lined up in formation, and despite the massive footprint made by the spread of forty armored cars with their heavy blaster cannons, the immensity of the desert wadi engulfed the battalion in its maw. They looked like a fleet of rowboats sitting in an ocean of sand, ready to disappear under the swell of a wave.

His relief dimmed as the inescapable reality hit him again.

We're going up against tanks? With this? Whose idea was this again? Positive thinking and aggressiveness alone could not win the day against the tank battalion. It was going to be a bloody fight.

The team gathered around Braley as Q poured out of the sleds and segregated into their respective groupings.

Braley took his bucket off and laid it on the ground as he took two hands and scratched his scalp vigorously. Kel thought of doing the same. Who knew when the moment would come again? Braley's gaze revealed deadly intent, freezing him from copying.

"Things are going to start moving fast. Let's get linked up with Seven and get it rolling."

"Our drone's on station above us for now until we get the update from Seven," Bigg said through his bucket as he continued to monitor the feed. "I'll put it to better use then. Till then, I have it running counter drone detection."

It was a sound move. It was difficult for the opposing forces to detect their drone but not impossible. By the same rationale, tasking the team's drone to scan the airspace for any enemy eyes-in-the-sky was wise. The Q didn't use drones for much, but D'idawan might very well have learned from the humans in their short time together before her abrupt departure. Just because she hated humans didn't mean she discounted human tactics. Not if she was a military leader.

It remained to be seen.

They found their DO compatriots at the back of one of the armored infantry vehicles, the rear troop doors swung open and a holo-projection of their own drone feed filling the left side of the open portal, a map projection on the right. They rapped each other on the chest with closed fists as was the common greeting when in armor, and spoke on L-comm.

"'Bout time," Dari said to them all. "You guys take the scenic route?"

"I got your scenic route right here," Bigg replied. "Good to see you, too."

Kel noticed that two members of Seven were missing from the gathering. Meadows, Kel's fellow sniper and frequent training partner, and Kim, the heavy weapons man. He knew why. They would be somewhere ahead. Working.

"As I've been updating you," Captain Jaimie said, "and as I know you've followed from our drone feed, their armor is marshaling. I will remain with the command group of the Second as Braley will be doing with the First."

Braley picked things up seamlessly. "The First will fall in behind the armored formations in their thin-skin sleds as we move up the wadi. Dari will run the FDC and the OSP from a Roly."

Roly-polies were their nickname for the light-armored infantry fighting vehicles. The turrets held a particle cannon as well as a medium blaster mounted below the glacis at the front of the vehicle. The advantage of the Roly-polies was they moved fast over any terrain and carried ten infantry in the crew compartment. The disadvantage? They still weren't tanks. Their light armor would not survive anything more than a glancing strike from a tank's heavy particle beam. Their design was similar to many other vehicles but were built on Qulingat't with modifications to meet the unique demands of Q anthropometry.

The same was true for their small arms. The Q infantry carried what was essentially a Stonewell-5. The 7-mm projectile launchers were an almost universal infantry arm because of their dependability. Blaster technology was superior in many ways. The technology was costly for the natives to purchase without Republic subsidies that weren't forthcoming, however, and prohibitively expensive to manufacture. Manufacturing the S-5s locally and modifying the ergonomics to match the needs of the Q was less expensive than purchasing blasters off-world. It was a common pattern in Kel's experience. A world that purchased the rights to the technical data package for an armament and produced the arms themselves, especially one that needed to be modified for a non-human user, saved money in the end.

"I need targeting information in the fire direction center to make this work." Team Sergeant Dari jutted his chin to Kel. "Meadows is out with our recon platoon." He knife-handed at a series of canyons and escarpments west of the wadi. "If you can get eyes on from the east side of the battle space, it'll increase our chances of spotting as many targets as possible."

Jaimie addressed Poul, the subject for the next part of his plan. "If you can end up with your mortar section on one of these eastern slopes," said the captain, "it will put you in good range of the entire field. Kim is already set up on the western slope."

The twelve-centimeter mortars had an effective range of eight kilometers, but were most effective within five.

Fingers flying over a nearby holo, Poul did a few calculations, trying to find the most advantageous spot for his gun crews. They did not have the luxury of time to recon for the perfect site.

Kel and Poul both looked toward Braley for permission.

"Get going, gents."

"I'm ready to get this holo-drama bouncing, brothers," Sims said to them all. "See you in a few." They each took a moment to slap each other on the shoulder before Kel and Poul trotted off to their bikes.

"Find us targets, man," Poul told Kel as he ran off to join his waiting gun crews and mortars, leaving Kel to remount his bike and find the reconnaissance platoon havildar K'listan and her troops.

I'll be out of the melee spotting targets while Sims, Bigg, and Braley are right in the thick of it, Kel thought, feeling guilty. But the success of the attack rested on the team's ability to identify and mark targets for the mortars and the OSP.

If I do this well, maybe those tanks never get a shot off.

Kel sped his bike faster at the thought.

They backtracked to where they'd first entered the bottom of the wadi to start the race along the outward slope and up toward the head of the long, wide depression. The small group on their bikes and fast attack sleds flew, unencumbered by the sluggish transport sleds that held them back when moving as a battalion.

Mercifully, the sun sank lower on the horizon. Kel had an imperfect sense of what natural night vision the Q had. Vision and visual perception were very different. A well trained person with mediocre vision had better perception of things at night than one in the converse position. K'listan and her Disciplined had proved to him that they saw well in darkness. The Chachnam troops, not so much. Regardless, the encroachment of night always made him psychologically stealthier.

The rise of the slope gave way to edges of sharp inlets and deep crevasses as they neared their objective. They had to turn east to skirt a large crevasse before turning west again to follow the plain to their chosen vista. Kel raised a closed fist and slowed; the others followed his lead. He dismounted and motioned for everyone to kill their repulsors.

"K'listan, leave a party of four to guard the vehicles. The rest come with us to form our patrol base."

The large Q clicked in understanding, departing to issue orders. The rest formed up on Kel, instinctively forming into a wedge as they patrolled cautiously toward the edge of the overlook. There were many rocky outcroppings and depressions, locations equally good for the enemy to have posted a forward observer team. It would not do to be ambushed on their way into the site from which they planned to direct the rain of carnage down on the mass of tanks and troops below.

The last rays of light reached them as the sun dropped below the distant cliffs. Kel crouched as he moved forward. He could not see the stronghold yet, which he knew to be farther to his right. As he neared the edge of the cliff, the far side of the open expanse yawned below him. He got down on his stomach and crawled the last ten meters toward the edge, brought his N-22 up, and pushed it in front of him.

He'd been monitoring the sub-channels of his L-comm, and keeping mental track of everyone's progress and activities. He listened to Jaimie communicating with the Talon pilots now in the air to the west, fifty kilometers away and below the horizon. Poul updated Dari in the FDC that they'd made a fire base and were laying in base plates for the mortars.

The plan was to advance the mechanized columns far enough to entice the tank battalion to move farther into the wadi. For the tanks, it would be a necessity. The one bright spot in the whole scenario lay in the incompetence of the Q's procurement officers.

"Man, they really got sold a bill of goods," Bigg had commented when studying the tanks purchased by the Sun-Loyal Army. Everyone agreed. It was baffling why the Q had purchased tanks with particle cannons for main guns. Two options existed for the armored vehicles' main weapon systems: particle cannons and traditional neutron-projectile cannons. Particle cannons were extremely effective, powerful, and had an essentially unlimited range. Any hybrid energy-projectile had a more modest range in comparison, resulting from the ballistic arc caused by the pull of gravity. The Q opted for particle cannons. This was their mistake.

Particle weapons could only engage line of sight. In the current situation, until the enemy tanks had targets in sight, the cannons would be useless. Knowing that, the plan was to entice the tank force into the open. Had the tanks been outfitted with traditional projectile cannons, they could have rained the high-angle weapons on to their lightly protected force from the start.

Particle cannons were a good choice for a weapon system to use as air defense artillery against dropships or from fixed positions of superior elevation like a mountaintop. For use against ground forces, the arcing projectiles of an energy-cannon only made sense as the superior choice. But evidently not to the Q. The salesman probably made the biggest commission of their career when the Q procurement officer signed off on the more expensive item, one with unlimited range albeit useless for all intents and purposes.

We're going to teach them a hard lesson about believing a sales pitch, Kel thought. *At least, I hope. Except for the mortars, we don't have any high-angle weapons to speak of, either. What I wouldn't give for some artillery. Mortars, two Talons, and one OSP against an army! No one will ever believe it.*

Earlier, Kel had heard his friend Meadows from somewhere on the western cliffs feeding target data to Dari in the FDC. Now it was his turn. As he peered through his sniper rifle's optic over the plain, the armored titans sat restrained. Tanks clustered in groups of three, the clusters arranged geometrically to form patterns like a massive hive. The stings and bites to come he felt already.

"FDC, I'm in position. Bouncing targets to you now."

"Roger. Send it," Dari replied.

Kel placed the reticle of his optic over individual tanks. He paused over each one as the microsecond burst of invisible infrared light from his weapon painted the target and registered its position. He continued this process, identifying every target within his field of view. The program at the FDC would do the same as the program in Kel's bucket registered the tanks, assigned them a location on the map, and fed it to the drones. The drones could now follow the targets and track their locations, supplying the fire direction center with instant coordinates.

"Good target registers, Kel. You identified a lot of targets below Meadows's line of sight." Kel heard a break as Dari directed his communication to the team leaders.

"Jaimie, Braley, this is FDC. We have observers set and targets registered with gun crews. Drone feeds active. Talons on standby."

"All units, prepare for advance," Jaimie said over the main channel. On the sub-channel, the two team leaders and team sergeants conversed.

"What do you think?" Jaimie asked. "We only get one shot at it. Is it time to task the OSP?"

"The orbital track is on schedule for a perfect pass in forty-four minutes," Dari noted.

"We still don't know how many tanks are in reserve," Bigg said. "Let's try to draw them out. Advance the Rolies to just outside their line of sight. That'll catch their interest. Meanwhile let's get mortars and gunships on 'em."

"I agree. Draw as many out of those caves as we can," said Braley. "When we've lost the OSP, we'll regret it if there's another company of tanks in reserve."

The channel was silent a moment.

"I say we advance and try to draw out more tanks," Jaimie said.

"Do it," Braley responded.

The main channel broadcasted Jaimie's voice.

"All units, advance."

08

The mechanized battalion moved forward up the gentle slope of the wadi, forming a front two kilometers wide. The wadi took a slight eastward bend that would bring them to within the enemy tank formation's line of sight. The units on the left flank would be exposed first as the columns reached a point four kilometers from the fortress.

Kel continued to watch the oddly impractical tank formations below him. Their symmetrical assembly made no tactical sense. K'listan lay prone at his side. The rest of the platoon was spread out in a perimeter facing outwards, providing security for Kel during his critical task. He'd told K'listan to turn up the volume on her link so that the troops nearest could hear the communication traffic. Very soon noise discipline would not be an issue.

On the wadi floor the front column of tanks suddenly lurched forward.

"It's about to happen," he said to K'listan just as twelve-centimeter mortar rounds whistled above, the crump of their launch reaching their ears a moment later. He held his breath and waited. A string of explosions flashed around the middle of the tank.

"It's on!" Kel cried, the anticipation of the battle finally met.

"Fire for effect," he heard on a sub-channel, knowing Dari was observing the impact area by drone.

The mortar impacts increased, the sharp scream of their approach hidden in the noise of the explosions. He stared at the lead tanks, still exempt from the pounding the middle of the column was taking, willing the next rounds to land there. His mental powers were insufficient. To his disgust he missed the next series of impacts by anticipating where they would land, and guessing wrong. He broadened his view. There. A tank shimmered where the plasma of an explosive shell turned the air into a ten thousand degree furnace. The air around it boiled in his night vision.

No matter how many times he'd seen ones like it, the sight was intoxicating. For the next several minutes the FDC talked to Poul and Kim with their mortar teams, the heavy explosive rounds pelting the tanks with partially pleasing effect; few were the burning hulks he wanted to see. The tanks rolled forward, unchecked. It was time for something else.

From across the wadi Meadows talked to the Talon pilots. "Dropship runs coming up," he said for the benefit of K'listan and the Disciplined around him. The black, angular birds appeared just over the western cliffs. They flew across the wadi, one staggered behind the other, and made a diagonal run over the tank formation below, white blaster bolts erupting from their cannons as they pelted the armor with fire. Just as quickly the Talons disappeared over the horizon.

Kel muted the thermal augmentation to his vision. The explosions and blaster impacts were too intense to view through his optic, now too much residual heat blurred everything.

His vision cleared.

As he'd feared, the tanks were less armored on top than before, but otherwise it appeared that little damage had been done. A few of the tanks in the middle of the pack had been halted, and none outright destroyed. The line of gray beetles in front continued their gliding, steady course forward as the rest followed, some having to alter course around the damaged vehicles before again closing ranks. The mass continued to move slowly past him and down the wadi. Kel ranged the nearest tank. They were three kilometers away.

"OSP on station in ten minutes," Dari said over the L-comm main channel.

Kel watched both the drone feed and the map projection. The Second's left flank now rolled across the last barricade to the line of sight of the opposing armored column ahead. Kel couldn't see the Rolies even under his sniper rifle optic, but looked left into the distance toward the azimuth where they would soon appear.

Now the enemy began their turn at war, quiet until now, like a dormant monster awoken to anger. Within the stronghold, mortar fire launched. Particle cannons erupted from the first line of tanks.

Kel shifted attention back to the drone feed, knowing his naked eye could show him little. Mortar fire was unlikely to have any effect at that range; the Rolies were at the far edge of the enemy mortars' capability. It added to the chaos of the battle, but only demonstrated to Kel their enemy's lack of ability at war. Dust rose as shells impacted well short of the Rolies, the nearest being a kilometer from the vehicles. Splashes devastated swathes of open sand. Completely ineffective.

Poul could have made those shots. But they don't have a Poul.

The particle cannons fared better. A flash of an impact against the Roly-poly on the outermost of the flank heralded contact. The flare of ejected photons faded. From what he could tell on the drone feed, it looked like it hit the vehicle dead-on, the energy dissipated by the glacis since it still rolled forward. None of the other vehicles had been struck.

A faint ray of light, out of place in the melee, flashed for a microsecond across his view. He'd allowed himself to be distracted, anticipating the dread of the confrontation between the tanks and the Rolies. He hadn't been doing his job. He cursed himself as he killed the feed from the drone and settled behind the optic of his N-22. He reduced the magnification to give himself a wider field of view and clicked through a menu of options. He selected the one he wanted as he searched the vertical terrain across the wadi, along the faces and crests of the cliffs beyond.

Got you!

What he'd seen earlier was a brief, bright flash of a beam. The short pulse flared off the front of a Roly-poly but remained long enough to burn a trace on his retina. Mortars and tank fire erupted. There was a forward observer spotting from somewhere on the western cliffs.

Now Kel could find her.

Even in the storm of lights. He knew what to look for. The tell-tale beam used to range and mark targets had not escaped him. It had been a brief exposure, but the beam was not invisible to his augmented sight. He further changed his optic inputs to include all spectrums. Whatever targeting device the forward observer was using had a strong signature. The full-spectrum analyzer was useless for most visual observation, turning everything into a noisy blur, but for detecting a tight beam of energy in an unknown wavelength, it was unbeatable.

Kel watched and once again saw the pencil-thin beam, following it back to its origin. He held his optic in place and scrolled back through his menu, adding a thermal overlay and short-wave infrared augment to his night vision. The cliff's features were visible now, as was the dark area that most likely was a small cave mouth or ledge where the forward observer was hiding. He saw the beam again for a split-second, very faint in the spectrum intensification of his optic, but enough for him to locate the source exactly.

"FDC, request CAS from Talon," Kel broke over comms to Dari. "I have identified an enemy forward observer position."

Dari's response was instant.

"You are cleared to direct. Blackbird, Blackbird, request CAS, take direction from ground controller Rapier-three. Go ahead, Rapier-three."

"Blackbird, this is Rapier-three," Kel said. "Request CAS. Target, forward observer position. Bouncing grid now. Target is a cave on the face of the cliff facing eastward. I will paint with laser, over."

After a moment a reply came back. "Rapier, we are two minutes out. Have any friendly forces turn on burst locators, how copy?"

Dari broke in from the FDC to repeat the request over L-comm. "Meadows, are you following this? Hit your locator."

Meadows and his recon element would be the only friendly troop near the target.

"Roger, good copy. I'm lit," Meadows responded, glee in his voice.

Another minute passed. The tanks below continued to roll as sporadic cannon fire belched from their turrets.

"One minute," a Talon pilot said flatly.

"Talons," Dari said, "when you finish this pass, I'm going to start sending you on runs on the stronghold grounds, so stand by."

Then on a sub-channel, Dari told Poul and Kim to halt their fire missions. They'd been steadily dropping rounds into the courtyard of the stronghold, answering the ineffective rebel fire with their own brand of efficient destruction.

Kel watched through his optic, his reticle held over the dark spot of the cave as he maintained the infrared laser on the spot. The Talons screamed overhead from his rear, their repulsors adding their own distinctive noise to the battlefield. They sped over the wadi and were already pulling away as they unleashed a torrent of fire against the cliff. The rock face exploded, the ridge above collapsing and cascading rubble to the floor below. A waterfall of crushing death. Nothing could have survived that cataclysm.

"Good pass, Talon. Take direction from FDC. Rapier-three out."

Watching the drone feed again, Kel mentally urged the camera to show him farther north when the drone seemingly responded and shifted view. Bigg or someone had picked up what he was seeing. A line of tanks filed down the wash from behind the stronghold, making their way to the wadi floor to join the fight.

"Dari, you seeing this? Get OSP to respond," Bigg said. "The time is now."

"Captain, do you concur release for orbital strike?" Dari asked.

An out of breath Captain Jaimie gasped into the L-comm, "*Do it. Do it now.* They're lighting us up."
Seven's team leader was with the advancing column of Rolies.
Kel checked the other drone feed. Numerous Rolies on the left flank were in flames. Faint thermal images of Q ran in multiple directions, scattering from the backs of Rolies, trying to escape the intense heat of the burning vehicles and failing, only to succumb and fall to the ground. Kel felt the fire on his own skin.
"Talon, break off and clear the area. Orbital strike inbound," Dari directed. "Meadows, Kel, keep painting targets on the ground. One minute to strike."
Back on his optic, Kel highlighted targets again, one at a time. The program would continue to sort and update the targeted tanks, prioritizing the order of engagement based on directives from the FDC. The nearest tanks were only a kilometer north of his position.
"Inbound," was all Kel heard before one of the tanks in the front file disappeared in a blinding flash. He'd been looking directly at the first tank to be struck. A stroke of good luck. It took his bucket a millisecond for the white noise to fade and vision return. The tank exploded into a thousand pieces. Was still exploding. The turret with its particle cannon barrel defied gravity to rise in the air a dozen meters above, giving the appearance it was hovering, not rolling or spinning. It was almost comical. Finally, it took a course more natural, hurtling away, impossible to follow the arc of the large shape along its inevitable path to impact. Another blinding flash, and the tank next to it exploded.
Kel went back to painting targets. With each one he received a confirmation on his screen, "Registered."

Got ya.

Hopefully Meadows could see the new group of tanks heading into the wadi from his vantage. Kel could not.

He'd painted every target several times over. Kel lifted his head off his optic to view the wadi floor. Beside him, the Disciplined troops had left their prone positions from all over the perimeter and stood. Watching. Children captivated by fireworks on a summer night. Sunflowers at full bloom.

Kel shrugged. For now, he'd done what he could. *I guess I can stop to smell the roses, too,* he thought and joined them.

Tanks continued to disintegrate in spectacular fashion. Every three to five seconds another one disappeared as a screaming bolt struck it from above, a faint yellow streak from heaven intersecting the tank to produce a flash of blinding white light on impact. An explosive cacophony rolled and boomed across the cliffs creating a deafening orchestra of echoes, reflecting the destruction from the valley below again and again.

Some of the tanks at the rear of the formation turned to run for the cavernous hideout from which they had come. No sooner had he noticed this than the OSP worked from the back of the formation, starting at the lead of the retreating vehicles. In the FDC Dari must have prioritized the target sequence anew. It was like watching a forge hammer metal. Only instead of forming the basic into the complex, some of the most advanced tech on Q was being violently morphed into slag. Fires blazed, his visor never pausing in its search to find the correct gain for the constant shift of dark to bright.

A new noise entered his bucket. Something not created by the clash of energies in front of him. Something almost melodic. The Q were in ecstasy. As tanks erupted in purple and yellow blossoms from the kinetic strike, the Q hummed in chorus. The pitch started low, then rose with the intensity of the energy released with each strike, direct hits and secondary explosions producing a more rhythmic variation in their chant.

"K'listan, everything all right?" he asked, the havildar standing with her arms stretched to her sides, eyes closed, and mouth open. She quickly resumed a normal posture and turned to face Kel.

"All is well, Sergeant Kel-boss. I never imagined such a thing was possible. The explosions produce light as bright as the sun on a clear day and warm every part of my being. It is beautiful. How is this possible?"

The energy discharge from the strikes was definitely in a wavelength favorable for the Q.

"Rods from gods, K'listan. Rods from gods."

They stayed in this position for many minutes. Kel marveled at the sight just as much as the Q around him appeared to. The wadi was a monument to devastation rivaling the works of any mythical world-ending gods. Fires raged. Dark smoke poured skyward in the windless night. Nothing moved. He continued to listen to the traffic over comms. There was little else for him to do.

"Meadows, Kel, can you identify more targets?" Dari asked.

"Negative, FDC," Kel replied.

"Negative, FDC," he heard Meadows answer. "I know I saw some escape behind the escarpment, but I don't have a grid on them."

"Bigg, can you track with Three's drone?" Dari queried. "If you do that, we'll direct targets off your feed. I'm going to drive ours for a damage assessment of the battlefield then get us a better look into the stronghold compound. Time's running out. Whatever else we can find I want to hammer before we lose the OSP."

"Dari," Braley broke in, "I want that stronghold demolished if there's no other targets for the OSP."

"Roger, Captain. We're working the problem now."

Kel linked into the drone feeds, placing Dari's on the left and Bigg's in a screen on the right. The Team Seven drone moved low over the battlefield at an altitude of five hundred meters. Dari ran a search program allowing the drone to track a grid pattern, sweeping horizontally back and forth, zipping toward the head of the wash. A graveyard. Tank hulks glowed and smoldered, the funeral pyres of the vanquished.

Bigg drove Three's drone two thousand meters over the head of the wadi, the expanded view from above orienting them to the next threat as the fortress crept into view. The drone followed tank tracks leading back into the maze of canyon trails, then slid down a wash leading back into a smaller canyon, the tracks evident in the sand there as well. Tread sign disappeared at right angles into the rocky face of the canyons below. If tanks had escaped the battlefield, or if there were any still in reserve, they sat in caves under the shelves of those canyon walls.

Now both drones hung over the stronghold. Each took a circular orbit, the Three drone from its higher altitude, showing the interior of the compound; Seven's from two hundred meters above the wall of the stronghold, showing the exterior and low angles over the walls.

The castle's battlements were manned. Atop the vertex of the wall's intersections sat the pill boxes, complete with heavy particle guns and crews. Waiting. Mortar-strike craters pocked the interior grounds. Whatever damage had been done to the mortar crews within had been cleared. Only the craters remained. Troops milled about in the open. The earthen multi-story compound was alive with tiny lights bouncing from troops scurrying to prepare. It struck Kel oddly, like a joyous gathering about to occur. Villagers preparing for a festival. A magical summer night, festive lights enticing them to join the party.

Braley's voice broke his reverie. "Bigg, start feeding targets to the FDC. I want the abutments of every one of those wall sections hit. Then hit the interior structures until we run out of rods. Poul, are you up?"

"Yes, sir. Crews are ready."

"FDC is going to feed you targets inside the canyons. Use every bit of HE you have on IMP"—meaning, impact burst on contact—"and send as much frag as you can into those caves. Do we have any of the special AP left?"

Special anti-personnel rounds for the 12-centimeter mortars were nasty. The rounds worked best against large numbers of troops in the open with the fuse set on airburst. They'd used them against the mortar ambush only two days before. Kel knew what Braley wanted.

When set to detonate a meter off the ground, the thermite impregnated explosive rods would travel radially for hundreds of meters. Detonated within the canyons, the rounds would not only horrifically maim any troops within the caves, they'd detonate any munitions and volatile material stored inside.

If they got lucky.

"Yes sir, I have about twenty-five rounds of the special AP left. I assume you want them for near surface airburst to reach into the caves?"

"Right in one, Poul. Get your crews ready for another fire mission."

Kel looked to K'listan. "They're about to start another bombardment. What say we move up the slope toward the head of the wadi to get a better view?"

K'listan ticked happily. "We are of the same hatch to think so much alike."

They set off along the outer slope, chasing the steel rain illuminating the skyline to the northwest. After traveling another kilometer, Kel veered toward the escarpment's edge. This time they rode forward to a clear, flat overlook and were rewarded with a vista overlooking the north end of the wadi and the stronghold, the final destination of the long journey it had been. The finish line.

The OSP dropped its payload at a slower pace than it had against the tanks. Drones painted each new target by laser, bouncing locations one at a time to the satellite. Two moons had risen behind them, their pale light casting long shadows into the wadi below. Each impact flashed, not as bright as what had been created by the tungsten rods smashing into the tanks, but still releasing enough energy from impacts with the earthen walls to cause the light show they associated with the OSP.

Kel bumped up the magnification through his bucket to see the walls fallen and the buildings beyond now taking the brunt of the barrage. The one currently under assault was several stories high and collapsing. With each strike, another portion of the structure gave way and crumpled into rubble. It was the only source of motion in the compound. Troops? Deep in a hole if they were smart. He listened to the sub-channel comm chatter as Bigg, Dari, and Braley discussed the ongoing strikes. He'd not heard Jaimie on the comm for some time.

Mortar rounds whistled overhead and exploded in the canyons beyond, to his disappointment. It would be more satisfying to see the impacts. It was most often the case they saw only the end result of such bombardments, rarely the destruction itself in its simultaneous malevolence and wonder. Tonight had spoiled him forever.

Finally, quiet settled in.

"OSP is off-station and spent. Thank you for a job well done, OSP. Take a well-earned rest," Dari said, anthropomorphizing the satellite. Their friend would now start its fall into the atmosphere before it found its final resting place somewhere on the planet, a small crater marking its grave.

Poul chimed in. "FDC, we are spent as well. Not a round left and two of the three tubes are heat damaged and deadlined. If we need more indirect fire, Kim and Second Battalion will have to provide it."

"Three, sound off and give me your status," Braley ordered on the main channel to just his kill team.

"I'm with First Rifles at the rear of the echelon," Bigg replied. "We're in a perimeter waiting to move forward. I've been on the drone feed. We have no casualties here."

Kel sounded off next. "I'm on the eastern escarpment with recon. No casualties."

"With the mortar section on the lower eastern escarpment," said Poul. "No casualties."

Sims went next. "I'm forward with Seven helping with wounded at the casualty collection point. The left flank got hit pretty hard. Kim, Jaimie, Liu, and I are working. We'll be ready to move soon."

Braley finished the assessment. "I'm with the command group. No casualties. All right, everyone, hold fast where you are. I'm going to confer with Jaimie, and I'll bounce you as soon as possible. Looks like we can consider the threat of heavy armor eliminated. Stay alert."

With his own status report Sims gave a good indication of where everyone in Seven was currently located. Kel wondered how badly Second Battalion had been hit; it looked like the company on the left flank had been devastated. He'd been busy performing his mission—finding targets—and lost track of that part of the action.

Even so, they'd gotten lucky. Had the OSP failed, they would have been in a gunfight against a tank battalion with only a handful of light armored vehicles to throw against them. From what Kel could tell, it had been a full-strength unit. Every piece of armor they had was on the field by the end. He knew that in nights to come, he would lose sleep thinking about how things might have turned out if they hadn't had the orbital platform.

Braley's voice returned in Kill Team Three's buckets. "We're going to hold our positions until dawn. At that time, we're going to make a full assault across the wadi and occupy the stronghold. Kel, do you think you're best off taking recon farther forward on the slope to get closer to the stronghold from up top? Get us eyes on the objective?"

"No question, Braley."
"Do it."
K'listan's attention was on Kel, waiting in anticipation of his next directive.
Kel gave her a nod. "Time to work."

09

Kel led the recon platoon's mounted patrol up the eastern slope, pushing farther northward to what he hoped would be a better position to view the fortress. Security halts slowed their progress as they sent scouts on foot to search small crevasses and rock outcroppings for signs of enemy activity. It would be easy to be overconfident under the cover of darkness and speed into an ambush, especially after such a decisive victory.

"K'listan, we should be almost on line with the stronghold. Let's find a patrol base. We can't go too much farther without getting too deep into the canyon. If those crevasses need to be bombarded, I don't want to be on the receiving end of any rounds that miss the mark."

"Agreed, Kel-boss. We should be able to locate a vantage point from which to view the castle escarpment and the main tank path below."

K'listan gave orders and two of her team headed over to Kel, while the rest formed a perimeter around the vehicles. The havildar had positioned the fast attack sleds with their light machine guns pointed up the slope toward the head of the wadi.

Kel nodded in approval. Any troops that escaped the stronghold and moved down the eastern slope could only come at them from that direction. Down the slope or from over the edge of the escarpment were improbable directions of attack.

The four of them staggered into a loose wedge and moved up the slope toward the crest. There were no rock outcroppings to provide cover, but nothing to hinder observation either. As they neared the edge, Kel liked what he saw. The stronghold lay directly across the valley a kilometer away. The moons hung higher now, casting an even light. The front and rear parts of the compound were visible from here. To their right and looking north, the main arm of the bifurcated wash passed around the bend and out of sight. Deep in the channel, heavy tank tracks cut the sand.

This will do.

"K'listan, take one of the troops with you and have them lead half the platoon and their vehicles back to this point. Leave one FAV with the troops and their bikes to form a blocking position on the slope. I don't want all of our force pinned against the drop-off if we get attacked from the north."

If they were all hit while in the same patrol base, there'd be nowhere for them to go but off the cliff. Not good.

"Yes, Sergeant Kel-boss. That makes sense." She motioned to one of the commandos, clicking and gesturing with long limbs. They sprang down the slope and were gone.

The remaining trooper crept next to Kel and settled into a prone position. A Q's prone form wasn't particularly flat or low. They could collapse onto their rear legs in a sort of a hunched configuration, but couldn't place their thoraxes fully on the ground. Given enough time, they preferred to conceal themselves in a burrow. This one produced a pair of lenses and scanned across the wadi toward the destroyed fortress beyond.

After several minutes of silence, each of them appraising the terrain, the trooper spoke. "Sergeant Kel-boss, is it permitted to speak?"

The Disciplined embodied their clan name. K'listan conversed freely with Kel, but the troopers never spoke unless spoken to. When Kel conducted training, he'd repeatedly had to encourage them to ask questions. Without that prodding, they never would. In contrast, when given opportunity, the Chachnam troopers were a never-ending font of questions. Some reasonable, most unnecessary.

During Kel's early acquaintance with the Disciplined recon platoon, he'd often wondered if his instructions had been understood. When he asked if anyone had questions, the silence made him wonder if their voders had malfunctioned. In his experience with indigenous troops such silence usually meant one of two things. Either they understood him perfectly and had no questions, or that they understood nothing, which didn't matter because they would reject any new information and do things their own way. With the Disciplined, it was always the former.

"Yes, Trooper. What is your name?"

"G'livan, Sergeant Kel-boss."

"Of course, Trooper G'livan. I apologize for not remembering your name. What do you wish to say?"

"No apology is necessary, Sergeant Kel-boss. I understand. It is difficult for us to recognize humans individually. I recognize you by your voice translator, and your shell. It is slightly different in ways I know to look for."

Kel tried to think of what made his leej armor stand out over others. The only thing that immediately came to mind being that he was the only one on the team to carry a vibroblade on his chest.

"Knowing us by sight must be difficult," G'livan concluded. That was the first time one of the troops had been so personal when speaking with him.

"What is it, Trooper?"

"What will happen tomorrow? It appears we have destroyed D'idawan and her forces. We all saw the rain of death that annihilated the tank battalion. Is the battle over?"

"No, Trooper G'livan. The battle is not over. It is unlikely we killed all the rebel troops. We must observe and report to the rest of the battalion if there are any forces left to resist us. There may also be tanks still waiting within the canyons, deep in the caves. We don't know to what extent we damaged the subterranean areas. The battle will not be over until we have eliminated every potential threat."

The trooper seemed to consider this, then brought her lenses to her face, the glasses wide and bulky to match the distance between Q eyes. It was always the little things, the subtle differences in common tech that struck him when working with aliens. The things familiar, yet different. Kel took the silence as having satisfied G'livan, and went back to work. Movement returned within the compound.

He was about to start an observation log when his companion said, "Will we be ordered to kill any remaining Chachnam from the mughal's army?"

"If they continue to fight, then we must."

"Can you not rain fire down from your orbital on any resistance that remains? If the Disciplined had kinetic energy orbital platforms, we would do so."

"No. Our orbital platform is expended. Now it'll be real infantry work. There's always a limit to what technology can do."

"Is it a technology limitation or a logistics limitation, Sergeant Kel-boss?"

Astute question. The Disciplined keep impressing me.

"You are correct. The orbital is a powerful tool. In the wrong hands it could be misused, so the Republic doesn't allow us an endless supply of them. That we even had one is unusual in my experience. It's an indication of how important this mission is to our leaders on Liberinthine."

"That is logical. So, now we fight."

"Yes. But we hope that fighting will not be necessary. The remnants of the Third Battalion should return to service in the Sun-Loyal. Any who surrender must be spared, and we will insist that they receive good treatment."

The Q lowered her lenses. Her species didn't really have facial expressions, but Kel understood well enough what the tilt of her head meant. It was the same for humans.

"I think not, Sergeant Kel-boss. The nawabs most certainly have orders from Mughal D'shtaran to kill all *apostates* of the Third Battalion." The voder used the approximate word again. "Not that it matters. The Chachnam who followed D'idawan are dishonored."

Intrigued, Kel asked, "Are there Disciplined among the renegade mughal's forces?"

G'livan chittered with laughter. "No, Sergeant Kel-boss. That could never happen. I myself served with the Reconnaissance Platoon for the Third Battalion of the Sun-Loyal, before the Nawab D'idawan thought herself a mughal. The Disciplined left when she declared her disloyalty."

More chittering echoed from the voder.

Kel knew that the Disciplined, as well as being professional soldiers, came from a significantly different culture than the Chachnam.

"Dishonored?"

"We sometimes forget. You act like the Disciplined, so much so that we sometimes forget you are *alien*. In your armor, you appear much like us."

Kel was unsure what approximation was substituted by the voder just then with the word *alien*. He wondered what the literal translation would have been. In some cultures, *alien* more closely translated to *heathen* or *barbarian*, or something betraying insult. He sensed nothing of cultural bias against him from the Disciplined.

"The Disciplined are sworn to the mughal who holds the contract with our clan. The Chachnam who follow D'idawan, who protest the changes on Mukalasa'at, are weak of mind as well as dishonorable. If they cannot follow the will of the mughal, they deserve death."

The Mutual Prosperity Accord that Solar Wind had negotiated with D'shtaran and some of the minor Chachnam mughals had created chaos. The reforms the Consortium wanted to implement had been met with resistance, and naturally so. Among mughals, D'shtaran had shown the least reluctance to cooperate. Kel thought this was most likely not because of her egalitarian view of what the company meant by "prosperity," but primarily as a result of bribery by the galactic corporation. Now on the verge of victory and further consolidating the power-hold D'shtaran would have on the continent, the reforms would be able to move forward.

"Trooper G'livan, what do you think about the Mutual Prosperity Accord? Is it changing life for the Disciplined as well as the Chachnam?"

He'd asked K'listan the same question but received a noncommittal response. That had been a few months before, early in their acquaintanceship. Perhaps if he asked her now, she'd answer him more openly.

"The Disciplined are unlike the Chachnam. We believe in the way of the warrior. We live by our own law. It is a law of honor and duty to the clan and adherence to the way. We do not have a culture of weakness like the Chachnam. Really, all Chachnam are weak of mind. They kill their mates only to gain territory as they eventually cede their territory to others who have done the same. It is chaos."

Once more she lowered her lenses to look at Kel.

"You know they are not to be trusted, do you not, Sergeant Kel-boss?"

Just then came the faint hum of repulsors as K'listan rode into view in virtual daylight, the moons now directly overhead. The FAV took a position to their six o'clock and the rest of the vehicles completed a semi-circle on either side. The havildar adjusted a few of the bikes, then satisfied, aimed her own at Kel.

"Trooper G'livan. Thank you for speaking with me," Kel said as K'listan pulled up. "You've taught me much. I hope we can talk again. I'd like to learn more about the Disciplined."

The Q clucked. "You already know all you need to be accepted among the Disciplined."

Kel remained awake. Prone behind his N-22, he made small shifts with his body to relieve pressure and stay comfortable. He alternated viewing through the sniper rifle's optic and his bucket's augmented vision, though not from necessity. The scope on his N-22 provided endless combinations of overlays and magnification, but switching was a strategy. A respite. A gift to himself. He did so on a rotation every five minutes. Little tricks like this were useful for maintaining alertness. If he needed a stim tab, he'd take one later. He could still go on like this for many more hours. The drugs conferred near-instant focus and energy, but caused a big letdown at the end of their effect. If he could stay sharp until they were moving again, he wouldn't need the extra assist.

What he would really appreciate was a cup of kaff. It would be another day or two before he could look forward to that luxury.

K'listan remained awake with him, refusing to rest. They'd put the platoon at a fifty-percent alert, allowing them to take two-hour rotations sleeping in place on the perimeters. They'd need to be rested for the drive across the objective.

"Will you not rest though, Kel-boss? I cannot at such times."

"I'll get all the sleep I need when I'm dead."

K'listan chittered.

Most of the structures within the fortress were now destroyed; little more than shells of the exterior walls remained. But troops moved in and around the compound. Q worked to move bodies and salvage some of the heavy weapons from under the rubble of the collapsed pill boxes and parapets. They made no signs of planning an escape over the plains to the north. They were digging in.

Kel scanned the open assembly area at the rear of the compound. It was the area where they would marshal troops and vehicles for exit onto the lone path out of the fortress to the plains beyond. There were several low structures facing away from him that he could not fully observe. They appeared intact. They could be barracks or maintenance garages. It was hard to tell.

Several light vehicles moved about and Kel recognized the pattern; sleds traveled from the back of the fortress, along the narrow road wrapping around and down to the floor of the wadi, back to the deepest canyons behind the fortress, then up again. It seemed they were gathering arms and munitions from their subterranean stores to mount a defense of the stronghold's remains.

"They are not giving up yet, Sergeant Kel-boss. Tomorrow we fight."

"I think so, Havildar. The Disciplined may yet draw blood."

She chittered. "You know us well."

From the way the havildar and the recon platoon spoke, they only took pride in kills made by personal combat. No matter how many enemies they killed using long-range weapons, it mattered little to them as warriors unless done so in one-on-one combat. Kel knew many legionnaires who felt the same way.

He'd been listening to the sub-channels as Bigg and Dari conversed during his watch. He wasn't the only one who'd been up. It was about three hours until first light. They'd be getting the companies standing-to within the hour. Time to give a situation report.

"Hey, Bigg, you copy?" he said on a channel to him alone.

"Yeah, Kel. Just getting ready to bounce you. What's it looking like?"

"We've had eyes on the stronghold for a few hours now. They're reconsolidating forces, rearming, digging fighting positions. They're definitely forming a defense. I've not seen any armor, but they have several light vehicles shuttling between the fortress up top and the bottom of the canyon. Where're our drones?"

The drone feeds had gone quiet in his bucket some time before.

"Seven's drone is out. It died somewhere over the wadi without warning. Most likely a catastrophic failure. I've brought ours in and spent the last couple of hours getting it refitted for the morning. I should have it up presently."

"We got an OPORD yet?" Kel asked, wanting to know when the operation order for the next phase of the assault would be given by the captain.

"Braley and Jaimie have been with the nawabs all night. Selling them that we've got to go in and finish this on the ground has been difficult. They want us to just magic everything away with more OSP-type support, which isn't going to happen. We've nearly got them convinced that this is the only way. It really only took hold after they conferred with D'shtaran, who essentially told them to finish it quickly or don't come home. Apparently, the mughal hasn't been impressed with the timeliness of this operation."

"Say what? I'm sure if we were privileged to have the benefit of her leadership here on the ground, we could've had this thing wrapped and been back at her palace sipping kaff by now."

"Yeah. Hey, I'll get the drone headed over in a couple of minutes. Let's see what else we can learn about their defense posture."

"Bigg, how bad was it on the ground? I've been listening in. It sounded like the First Mounted got hit pretty bad."

Bigg sighed. "It could've been a lot worse. Jaimie was with the left flank when they came into range of the tank guns. Three Rolies were destroyed and most all the troops aboard were killed. There were secondary explosions that damaged some of the other carriers, but no troops killed. All total there were forty-six KIA, another dozen WIA, and three Rolies totaled. If their tank gunnery or mortar crews had been better, it would've been far worse."

Kel thought about it for a minute. He supposed that was true. He hadn't liked the plan to draw out the Third Battalion in order to destroy them with the OSP, but had understood the necessity of it. He wondered about the troopers sitting in the back of the Rolies on the left flank, rolling slowly into the tanks' direct fire. How had they felt, knowing they were there to draw out the tanks? Had they held out hope that the OSP would save them? How would he have felt in their place?

Even as a young legionnaire, he'd always felt in control. When on the ground, he had nearly endless options to protect himself during a fight. But as a mounted infantryman, you rolled into battle inside a giant tin can that might afford protection—but in truth were just targets for everything and everyone in the battle area.

"Drone headed out. Stand by."

Back behind his N-22, the drone feed popped up again in his bucket. He waited several minutes as it flew over the wadi until it again brought the fortress compound into view. After several orbits over the enemy encampment, the different perspectives supported what Kel had observed from his limited vantage point; the remnants of the Third were preparing for the final defense. Several mortars were in place, aimed down the wadi. New fighting positions were dug around the rear of the compound, reinforced with rubble from the collapsed walls and buildings from the front of the fortress. They correctly anticipated a ground assault from the rear.

The only way into the compound from the wadi floor was by way of the road that rose up and around the rear of the escarpment. The drone shifted perspective to straight down, showing the rear of the compound, and slid along the track of the winding road that led down and around the huge pedestal of the fort.

The survivors had been busy since the tanks rolled out into the fight. Trenches and berms layered the path of the wadi as it curved off the main canyon. The wadi trail narrowed significantly past the curve. It would be difficult to get more than two Rolies on line at a time to assault the positions that now protected the path up to the fortress. If a vehicle became disabled at the bottleneck, it would be difficult to remove it under fire to clear the way for the advance. A chokepoint if there ever was one.

These renegades had some soldiering ability.

Braley joined their conversation. "No armor down there, huh? I bet if they had, they'd be blocking with them. Bigg, is it worth getting a low pass of the drone in those canyons to see if there are any more surprises back there?"

Their team sergeant sighed. "They'll see it for sure. If they get lucky and kill it, we'll be without an eye-in-the-sky to guide fire for the Talons and mortars on the rest of the compound. Kel, I take it you have pretty limited ability to adjust fire for CAS or mortars from where you are, correct?"

"That's right, Bigg. Not the best. Any farther up the wadi and we'll be exposed to their guns and in the impact area of any mortar rounds that don't make the plunge into the canyon. Still, I'd like to move up to get a broader view of the objective, unless you order me not to. I can maybe direct some fire from there. I can definitely give you sniper support on those gun positions. But I don't want to take the recon platoon with me. They'd just give me away."

The L-comm went silent.

"Bigg, what do you think?" Braley asked.

There was another pause before the team sergeant answered. "Kel, you're the man on the ground. If that's your recommendation, I say go."

"All right," Braley agreed. "I'm about to give the order. We're going to make our move up the wadi as soon as we have the Talons on station. We're going to get runs in on their mortar positions before we roll farther. Poul says they want to move up along the eastern slope to get within a few kilometers and set up a fire base there, probably using your last OP from earlier in the night, Kel. He says he can get the best plunging effect from closer. Kim's going to set his guns in from the wadi as we get within range and concentrate on the compound. Poul was able to get two mortars functional and they have plenty of rounds from Second's stores. I think we can get good effect and wipe out any heavy resistance before we reach the head of the wadi."

"Kel," Poul's voice came up over the L-comm. "I'm plunging those rounds as straight down as I can. I can't promise the winds won't drift rounds onto the top of the slope. Don't get too far up the head of the wadi, okay?"

"I appreciate it. Don't worry. I'm not so hungry to snipe kelhorns that I'll take the risks of eating a stray mortar."

"See that you don't," Braley finished.

Under protest from K'listan, Kel left the recon platoon and started a route that would lead him to a better position for observation over the fortress.

He topped off the charge pack for his N-22 with a fresh one from his bike. He'd only fired the weapon once, but best to start his next task with a full charge. He took a moment to remove his helmet and quickly gobbled a calorie-dense energy pack. He couldn't remember when he'd last eaten. After a swig of water, he put his bucket back on.

Checking the systems of his sniper rifle, he enabled the active camouflage of his armor. The mimetic, phased-array camo projected a three-dimensional image of the surroundings onto his armor so that no matter what angle he was viewed from, the observer would have difficulty picking him out from his background. Motion was still perceptible—always the prime target indicator to be concerned with—but it did help to conceal a carefully planned, smoothly executed movement. Though dark, the moons were still up, ready to backlight his figure on top of the rolling plain.

The final firing point he hoped to establish would put him much closer, directly across from the fortress, and overlooking the mouth of the largest of the canyons that was the head of the wadi. It was quite far forward and would be sitting above the entrenched defenders hidden in the caves below; exactly where he had promised he would not go. He'd done a thorough reconstruction of the area, combining his map with information from the drones, and was convinced that it was the only location where he could be effective.

Half-aware of the L-comm traffic muted in his bucket, he focused most of his attention on careful navigation. Speed was the enemy of stealth. After an hour of walking, he reached the last major terrain feature on his route. He skirted a deep crevice that took him out of his way east and down the slope, until he could follow the rise up again, starting the movement into what would be his final firing point. He'd been using every technologic tool at his disposal and most importantly, his years of experience to avoid detection. Most likely, there weren't any observers to see him, but it'd be foolish and potentially deadly to make assumptions.

Monitoring the comms, he knew that the Talons were in a high-altitude traffic pattern to the south, awaiting further instructions. He continued his stalk up the last part of the rise before reaching a narrow plateau, the fortress a scant eight hundred meters beyond the cliff.

Up to this point, the slope had concealed his movement from any eyes in the fortress. He crawled onto the level plateau, following a natural dip in the terrain before he got on his belly and used just his elbows and hips to snake along. He clasped the sling of his rifle where it attached to the forearm of the stock, the rifle resting on his forearm, keeping the barrel elevated off the ground as the stock dragged over the dirt. He lowered his chest to the ground and crawled, maneuvering his rifle in the same manner. He was now only a few feet from the edge. He eased his rifle to the ground and left it as he inched the last meter to peer over the edge. Down in the yawning darkness, the forward fighting positions and trenches blocked the way into the canyon. He was in a perfect position.

Kel scooted back. Reaching his rifle, he pulled a small bundle from the tiny pack at the small of his back. He took a thin blanket from its container, spread it in front of him, then slid his head and rifle underneath the cover. The repulsor rest at the front of the rifle on, he followed the rifle up with his elbows, and settled behind the gun. The drape's active camouflage, combined with that of his armor, rendered him and his weapon all but invisible.

"I'm in position and painting targets," Kel reported, activating the target designator on his weapon, registering gun positions and mortar pits in the compound. He had a slightly elevated vantage point; little in the courtyard was concealed from his sight. Just as he'd planned it.

Communication with the Talons began. Dari was still running the FDC.

"Blackbird, we've targets painted on the objective. Start your run."

"Roger. Have any friendlies in the area hit their locators."

Kel toggled his on, already prepared for what came next.

"Rapier-three, that is *close*," one of the pilots exclaimed.

"Kel, what the..." Bigg interrupted. "If you get killed, I'm going to put you in for the flame of the eternal idiot award."

"Bring it, Blackbird. I'll give you a damage assessment after each run," Kel said with a grin. He remembered Dari's lukewarm assessment of the Talons. *They did all right by me last night. Here's hoping I'm not giving them the chance to prove him right by killing me.*

A minute later, the Talons shrieked overhead, but Kel kept his attention on the compound through the optic of his N-22. He loved a good show. And this time, he was the director. He was soon rewarded with the flashes of explosions from the first pass, temporarily blinded after each blaster impact.

"Blackbirds, this is Rapier-three. Make another run. Same vector. Troops in the open. Wide effect."

Many of the pits and fighting positions had been hit, and Q scuttled out of trenches to run for the rear of the compound and the road beyond it.

"Roger. One minute."

Some of the remaining gun positions fired wildly into the sky in the direction of the Talons' last approach. It was futile. The Talons made another pass, their blaster patterns dispersed to maximize the effect on the Q in the open. The run continued through the rear of the compound before the Talons veered sharply off.

"Good run, Blackbird. I have fighting positions at the base of the canyon floor. If I light up targets, can you make a run from south to north and try to hit those guns at the head of the canyon?" Kel pulled the camo cover off the front of the rifle, and scooted to the cliff's edge. This was no time to worry about revealing his position. He leaned over the edge and painted the trenches and fighting positions at the narrow canyon mouth, waiting to see the "registered" icon lock over each one.

"Can do. Watch yourself, Rapier-three. One minute."

Kel wanted to stay and watch, but decided to follow the pilot's advice. He reversed his low crawl and stayed prone. The repulsors of the atmospheric drives deafened before his bucket shut off sound, and kept his head down. Reflections from blaster explosions lit up the sky.

The Talons screamed away. Audio returned. He cautiously took a glance over the cliff. The Talons must have flown in from only a few hundred meters above the floor of the wadi to achieve such effect.

Q lay strewn about the narrow, sandy wash. Body parts burned. Blast craters led up to the curvature of the road. The Talons had been utilized to their maximum effect at this point. Now there was little else they could do.

"Excellent effect on the ground, Blackbirds. Job well done. Return to FDC control, Rapier-three out."

Dari took over. "Clear the airspace and resume a pattern at altitude, Blackbird."

Jaimie's voice came over all channels. "Column. Advance."

Rolies would be coming up the wadi soon. It would only take them a few minutes to reach the head.

Dari in the FDC again. "First Mortar section, fire mission. Point targets identified by drone in canyons. Adjust fire from FDC."

This was the moment when he might possibly regret locating himself so close to the canyon below. Which targets did the drones paint? Had the FDC failed to register the positions right below him as already destroyed by the Talons? If they were splashing the stuff right below him and the first rounds impacted short or laterally, he could very well be in for a bad time. He gritted his teeth and awaited the first impact.

Boom. The first round landed deep within the canyon to his right, down into a chasm hundreds of meters away. Safe.

I will not be light on my praise for the featherheads when we're done.

"Fire for effect."

Letting the gun bunnies do their work, Kel settled in behind his optic and got comfortable behind the N-22. Scanning the compound, he manually adjusted his optic to a pleasing contrast. The automatic function usually chose a gain setting close to what he preferred, but was never perfect. Kel liked perfection.

He liked what he saw. Q limped and carried one another from the courtyard to the rear of the compound, where he now had a much better view of the buildings still intact. Wounded troops did not present an immediate threat. He moved on. Other troops recovered mortars and crew-served projectile launchers from bombed-out craters.

We can't have that.

Kel's trigger finger swept the receiver, preparing the big gun to perform. The range was a paltry 803 meters. He selected a fine particle beam setting for the task, wanting to minimize the signature of his weapon. For an anti-personnel effect at this distance, the fine beam wouldn't visually betray the him. Had he needed to engage anything behind a barrier he would have to increase the output, which would produce a visible trace from the muzzle to the target. It was going to be easy work for the light-speed, line-of-sight weapon.

He placed the reticle over the chest of a Q who was bent over to pull a mortar tube from an excavated pit. He pressed the trigger, not waiting to see its effect. He knew.

Kel shifted his reticle to the figure standing in the pit. She was just turning to look in his direction, undoubtedly surprised at the sight of her partner's chest exploding, seeking the source of danger. All sentient beings feared the round they never heard. Another gram of pressure on the trigger, and he shifted his eyes again.

Scanning right, Kel saw similar activity from another fighting position and repeated the performance. He decreased the magnification of his optic, searching anew with a wider field of view. The other Q in the courtyard had scattered. It hadn't taken them long to comprehend that they were in his dominion. Their only safety lay in that understanding. Like desert earth sucking up a cloudburst, the scene was barren again. He'd keep this up indefinitely to ensure that no mortar or gun could be brought to bear on the advancing forces.

Friendly mortar fire continued at an even pace, a round impacting back in the canyons every one to two minutes, as opposed to the heavy barrage Poul had been laying down earlier. It was a good strategy to harass and deter any surviving resistance still in the caves. They were nowhere near depleting their stores of mortar rounds.

Bigg's voice came over his bucket. "Having fun, smart-guy? I see on the drone feed you have everything in the front courtyard pinned down. What was all this talk about 'not putting yourself at risk just to KTF some dudes'?"

Kel could hear the quotation marks around the paraphrase of his own words, now used against him.

"Sorry. I meant it when I said it. Hey, I don't see any reason to waste a fire mission on this part of the compound. I think I've got it handled."

"Looks that way. We're moving up now. The first company of Rolies should be coming up to the mouth of the wadi in a minute."

Kel allowed himself to look up from his rifle and left, down at the wadi's wide plain. He really hadn't spent much time looking in that direction until now. The smoldering remains of the tank battalion covered the dusty plain. Second Battalion Rolies wove between wrecked tanks, closing ranks again as they approached the mouth of the canyon. One company took the path inclining to the right of the fortress toward the larger highway, another column breaking left to form up as it moved toward the smaller left path around the fortress.

Behind came the Second Battalion's light armored transports, then their own First Battalion in their patchwork convoy of repulsor sleds.

Wheeled and repulsor vehicles rumbled and hummed down in the canyons. Over the comms, Dari ordered Poul's fire mission to cease, and the last mortar round exploded beyond. His curiosity got the better of him. He brought up the drone feed in a window in his lower left visual field, still watching the compound in his right eye through the optic. He had the magnification set low and had a broad view of the whole area. Any movement, he would snap attention to placing the reticle where it would do the most good. It was the ultimate game. Better than any holo.

Through the drone hovering almost directly above him, he could see the area where he was lying at the edge of the cliff, gratified that he could not find any visual indicator of his presence. It felt a little narcissistic, taking the time to feel pride in such a thing, but as a sniper, he had to check. The drone view filled the rest of the screen. It was centered over the right-hand pass, two Roly-polies entering the narrow canyon side-by-side. They rolled effortlessly over the berms and fighting positions beneath them as another pair of Rolies came in behind them.

Kel checked the compound again. No movement.

"Braley, I think we just got to eat it," Bigg said over L-comm. "Let me fly this thing down the canyon. If there're any defenders back in the caves, we need to know. Meadows has his recon platoon just about worked around to the rear of the fortress from the plain. He can forward observe into the compound from there if we lose the drone."

"I agree," Dari replied.

"No argument here," Jaimie said from one of the lead Rolies inching into the canyon pass. "I'd like some visual of what's ahead instead of just doing a reconnaissance by force."

"No argument," said Braley. "Do it."

"Let me get one last overhead pass and then I'll send it down the hall to the principal's office," Bigg said. The drone gained altitude quickly, then moved into a high circular orbit around the fortress. "I'll take a clockwise around the fort, then drop into the main canyon."

Bigg flew the bird to show the narrower canyon that led around the left side of the stronghold. A single Roly-poly was poised at the mouth of the canyon, its turret gun lowered and aimed into the depths beyond. Rolies spread out behind the lone armored vehicle, awaiting their chance to follow it, the canyon trail wide enough for a single column of the tanks but little more. Mortar strikes cratered the white sand like meteor impacts.

Bigg's drone traced the tracks back until they led under a ledge and disappeared from view. Kel's curiosity at what the cave complexes still held made him wish he was with the Rolies. Smaller trails marked the dirt. There were most certainly fighting positions concealed under the precipices. Whether anyone survived the mortar strikes into those areas, they couldn't tell.

The drone glided over the craggy plain behind the fortress. Somewhere below, Meadows and the Second Battalion recon platoon were hidden, observing the compound. A thin road took a circuitous route between the crevices of the narrow canyons and led to the back of the fortress. The short walls at the rear were the first layer of defense where inside the large open compound, well-entrenched positions filled with troops dotted the bare field. Movement atop three intact buildings within the open compound indicated gun positions on the flat roofs.

The machine swung over the road leading down from the compound to reach the wash and the path back into the canyons. The Talons and mortars had devastated the area. No Q appeared. The drone halted around the bend, meeting the Rolies waiting beyond.

"All right, time for the grunt's-eye view," Bigg said, as the drone did a spot turn, reversing its perspective, and descended straight down. The sun started to rise, golden bands warming the clifftops and the top of the fortress below him. True color returned with daylight. The crumbled earth that had been the bulwarks and buildings now took on a brownish color. *A lot of chewing and regurgitating wasted*, he mused, knowing heavy equipment would've been used to build the thick walls, not masticating skills.

"I've moved to the lead vehicle so I can direct better," informed Jaimie. "Guide us in, Bigg."

The drone eased forward, a few meters off the floor of the canyon. Bigg added a thermal overlay to the image and projected a wide infrared beam to penetrate the shadows of the canyon's crevices. The path branched, the left arm leading up around the wall toward the fortress, the right trailing off into the canyon and whatever remained hidden there.

Aiming right, the drone flitted forward. Before long, the right-hand wall receded to reveal a large opening. The canyon floor sloped down into the rock face, the roof rising a dozen meters. The drone entered and panned around, showing a huge cavern with a flat floor, wide enough to house at least a full company of tanks. They'd been briefed on the physical layout of the armored battalion's base and had seen holoimages. Whether an improved natural chamber or wholly excavated, seeing it live was impressive.

Deeper into the darkness, a sooty tank sat. A few burned corpses littered the ground. Had they been maintenance technicians, working to get the vehicle back in action? Had flames killed them instantly or had they suffocated slowly as the thermite burned away their oxygen? Kel could only guess. The special AP rounds had punctured the tank; superheated chemicals had scorched the exterior edges of the entrance holes. Apparently, the anti-personnel rounds could penetrate armor under the right circumstances. Another reason to hate being inside a tin can.

"That is something to see," Bigg said. "Do you want to advance to that point and dismount some troops to do a search before moving farther?"

"I'll peel off one of the Rolies behind me to go in and search," Jaimie replied. "I want to keep our momentum and move the column forward."

The drone exited the cavernous lodge and continued down the road at the same slow pace, Bigg panning left and right as it went. It wasn't long before a similar opening appeared on the wall. The drone's cone of illumination pushed into the space, and just as Kel thought he saw movement in the depths, the feed went blank.

"Contact. Drone's dead."

"Well, there's our answer," Jaimie said. "We're pushing up to get guns in there."

Heavy blasters spat and cracked over the comms. Kel heard fire coming not just from the near canyon, but from a distance as well. Sims and Bigg. They were taking the First Battalion dismounted behind the Rolies, pushing hard into the left-hand branch of the canyon. It sounded like they'd made contact on that side as well. Right now, everyone was busy except Kel.

He scanned the compound again, seeing nothing.

Always look for work.

He pinged the Disciplined. "K'listan, mount up and bring the platoon up the slope. I'll be waiting. We're going to find a way around to the rear of the fortress and get in the fight."

She responded immediately. "Yes. It is time to bask in the blood of the renegades, lest we perish of shame while others fight in our stead."

10

By the time Kel reached the point of the crevice that had been his earlier landmark, the recon platoon was coming up the slope, K'listan in the lead. One of the FAV gunners rode Kel's bike. The purple Q hopped off and motioned with an extended appendage, inviting Kel to reclaim his ride.

Kel checked in with Dari on his way to link-up again with the commandos. His plan was to hasten to the rear of the compound and assist Meadows. There was no way for him to reverse route all the way back to the wadi and make his way up to the battalion in time.

"Meadows has been marking targets," Dari told him. "I'm going to unleash the two mortar sections on the rear of the compound before the Rolies get too far forward. As soon as we've hit what we can, I'm shuttling First Battalion troops on the Talons to the plains behind the fortress. Bigg is organizing the loads right now. Hopefully you can get there in time to start the ground push into the fortress proper."

Kel gathered K'listan and some of the junior NCOs into a circle and briefed them on the plan.

K'listan addressed her juniors. "We may have an opportunity to lead the ground fight. This is pleasing. Do not falter."

Kel replaced his N-22 into its scabbard on the bike. "If we can find a path to the compound," Kel replied. He took his K-17 carbine, slung it over his head, letting the sling tighten and auto-adjust to hug his chest.

"Let's roll," he said and mounted the bike.

The plain was rife with narrow canyons that formed a maze behind the fortress. Kel had examined the map and drone feeds. Even with that help, a fast route through the labyrinth seemed impossible. Crevices extended like a branching fungus. The only decent option was to travel farther east and then north before finding the road, but once they'd done so, they'd be at the rear gate within minutes.

"I think I've found a passage. We need to move fast, or they'll have to start the assault without us."

"That would be regrettable," K'listan sighed. "We are kin to the Disciplined with Sergeant Meadows-boss. It would not do to allow them all the honor."

Kel set a fast pace. He liked riding a repulsor bike and wished he could remove his bucket to feel the rush of wind against his face. He would appreciate some fresh air if for no other reason than he was getting rank within the armor. The antimicrobial film that circulated inside the equipment helped greatly with comfort when locked inside the suits for days at a time, but after too long, nothing short of stripping out of the armor for a shower helped.

The bikes glided easily over the angled slope as they paralleled the canyon on their left. He kept a screen open with the map view and followed their location marker as he oriented their route direction.

The slope finally reached a level plain, and they approached the rim of the widest canyon. Mortar strikes thundered. If the renegades thought the rain of death was over, they were mistaken. Somewhere below, the Rolies advanced into the resistance awaiting within the caves. He dreaded the type of fight they'd encounter. Cleaning out a well-entrenched enemy in defense was the toughest fight there was. If they spent every mortar round to silence just a fraction of those awaiting in the depths of the caves, it'd be worth it. Munitions could be replaced. Lives could not.

The sun was bright now. The path ahead clear. Kel increased his velocity, briefly looking over his shoulder to see that the platoon was keeping pace. Now it was a race.

They'd been traveling at their best speed for a half hour. After a minor deviation to skirt around a crevice he'd missed, Kel was excited to see the icon on his map closing in on the narrow road ahead. "We're almost there," he yelled to his counterpart riding next to him. "Once we hit the road, let's pause and get a good head count. Then we're going full-tilt to the fortress."

K'listan's voder made the noise of confusion. "Full-tilt? What does this mean?"

"It means we're going to go as fast as we can safely drive." What a time for the translator to miss an idiom.

"Race to the mating place, you mean."

Kel would love to know what the literal translation of *that* was.

"You got it."

They reached the road, and Kel pulled forward far enough in their new direction of travel to make space for the platoon to gather behind him. K'listan pulled next to him and dismounted, walking back along the road, checking each vehicle and rider as they closed the distance and stopped. Some of the pack had fallen back during the race overland, the two FAVs the last to arrive. K'listan came loping back to her bike.

"The count is good, Sergeant Kel-boss. We are ready to race to the mating place."

Kel chuckled. "I thought the warriors of the Disciplined did not mate."

K'listan swiveled her head. "Simply because one is not fertile does not mean one cannot mate."

"I don't think I wanted to know about that. Let's go." He punched the sky as he raised himself on the bike and pointed down the road as the repulsor whine pitched up and he blasted off. Maybe it was an unnecessary gesture, but it felt good.

"End fire mission," Dari halted the mortar teams over L-comm. Things were going to start happening quickly. Time to find the Second Battalion scouts. "Meadows, we're coming up fast behind you from the north. I'm bouncing you my location."

"Right back at you," Meadows responded. "We're dug in about a hundred meters west of the road near the last turn heading to the compound. We should have Talons and troops inbound presently."

"What's the situation in the compound?"

"We hit it as hard as we could. I'm pretty sure we silenced the guns on top of the buildings, and I tried my best to drop plenty of rounds into every pit I could see. Otherwise, we gave it lots of airburst. I'm about as sure as I can be that we covered every square centimeter of the grounds."

Kel heard the grin on Meadows. "My ladies finally got their kill on smoking squirters hopping our way. Most of them were armed. Well, some of them. We're not in a position to take prisoners. Your gals sharpening their claws to get into this?"

"I think you could say that. Are any of the Roly-polies pushing up from below?"

"Yeah. We've got them held on the incline going up to the compound, waiting for us to give them the go ahead. I'm going to bring the Talons in behind my position. We won't move troops forward until we've got the Rolies up. Wait one."

He paused and Kel could hear Bigg on the sub-channel giving the confirmation that he had the Talons loaded.

"Liu, bring up the Rolies," Meadows said to his teammate in the waiting tin can Roly just out of sight. "Stay buttoned up, but get some guys working on that gate. We'll rally First Battalion with you there."

They followed the winding road at full speed. The rear of the fortress came into view, framed by nothing but blue sky. It was going to be a beautiful day, one worthy of holo stills.

Round the last bend waited Meadows and his recon platoon.

"Just in time," Meadows said, waving. "Liu's leading the Rolies into the compound. Let's get the..."

They all looked west to see the Talons coming in low and starting a slow turn towards them.

"That was fast. I've got an LZ marked for them. Want to bet they don't use it?"

Kel nodded. He'd worked with a lot of pilots over the years. When it came to playing pathfinder and selecting landing zones, he found that featherheads played petulant child more often than not. They'd reject the marked LZ in favor of their own last-minute choice, just to prove they were in control of where their birds touched down, and no one else.

After the third time in his life that Kel had marked an LZ and been rebuffed by the pilot, he stopped trying. It had been three times too many. Standing where he wanted the pilots to land, arms held overhead for the pilot to guide on to, bucket strobe on, facing downwind to give the pilots a perfect approach. Only to see them slide a hundred meters in another direction to land at a site no better than the one he had carefully selected.

One time, he'd tried to guide a Talon pilot into a hot LZ. The pilot ignored all his communications and landed right in the line of a hidden blaster emplacement. Blaster bolts scorched the airframe underneath the pilot's compartment as he veered off and gained altitude. The pilot circled around for another attempt, this time following Kel's instructions.

The panic in the pilot's eyes that day had almost made it worth it. Kel wanted to find the guy after that mission ended. He was curious to know what the man had been thinking, but he never got the opportunity. Had he learned a lesson? In Dark Ops, more than anywhere, they held to the dictum, "Believe the guy on the ground." As a whole, pilots didn't seem to listen to anyone but themselves.

He'd given up on trying to assist most pilots. It was wasted effort. He had better things to do.

The Talons arrested their forward motion as they sunk to the ground, one staggered behind the other, the lead craft putting its nose right over the flashing marker Meadows had staked into the sand.

"These guys must be smart enough to be afraid of getting shot up. Nice to see for a change," Kel said.

"Yeah, they've done a bang-up job so far. Let's meet Bigg."

They trotted to the aircraft, the ramps lowering as the crew chiefs hopped off first, directing the disembarking Q forward around the aircraft, pointing to where they saw Kel and Meadows. Bigg broke ahead and jogged to meet them.

"Talons are going back to get another platoon. What've we got?" Bigg asked and rapped them each on the chest. "What's happening in the compound? Pilots told me they saw Rolies coming in."

Meadows took the initiative. "Liu, what's your status?"

After a short pause, the Team Seven assaulter answered, "I've got four Rolies on line. Not seeing any activity. You ready to get your troops in here and start clearing?"

"Yes. Get those gates breached. We're moving," Bigg interjected.

"Roger."

Bigg jabbed his thumb over his shoulder. "I'll get the platoon jemadar briefed and we'll get moving. You guys want to lead the way?"

"Rog," both Kel and Meadows said almost simultaneously, both turning back to their platoons.

The Talons took off, taking a wide path back around the western slope and slipped below sight.

"We're going to lead the way into the compound," Kel told K'listan to her great delight. "Put the FAVs in the center. The rest of us on foot. We'll form up in two traveling wedges and move straight to the gates. They should have them breached by the time we get there. Meadows's platoon will follow. We'll go into a bounding overwatch if we get any resistance."

"Very good, Sergeant Kel-boss." She had no questions. That was all the operation order she needed. The havildar briefed her platoon just as concisely and in a minute, they were ready to move.

"Meadows, we're moving up."

"Good copy, Kel. We're moving, too."

Kel placed himself up front and just to the right of the FAVs. They set a fast pace, Kel trotting, the Q using their hopping gait. He was just feeling the burn as they slowed to a cautious advance. The huge solid metal gates fell outward with a crash. Purple glows of plasmas cutters extinguished, revealing Liu and several Q on the other side.

"Coming out," Liu said over L-comm, redundantly and from habit. "It's a mess over here. They barricaded this side of the gate with berms. They weren't planning on making an escape out the back. It seems the mughal has ordered them to win, or DIP."

Die in place.

"Coming out, coming out," Liu again repeated aloud over speaker as he walked over the huge panel of the gate, now on the ground. Earthen berms had indeed been pushed against the gates from the inside. The top of the berm was covered in Q troops, digging furiously with their scooped appendages to clear the obstacle.

"Leave the FAVs—let's get in the compound," Kel said.

Meadows and his crew approached. "Kel, we'll strong wall from inside as much as we can before we get too deep. I'll take right."

Kel agreed. "Let's do it."

Liu sounded off. "I'm heading back to the Rolies. Once you guys are in, I'll start rolling us forward. I want to get all these buildings cleared before we go to the front of the compound."

Bigg led his platoon up in a trot behind them.

"We'll bring you through in a second, Bigg," Kel told him. "Hold up."

He followed K'listan and several of the Q through the breach, over the berm, and into the compound. It all looked familiar after spending so much time studying the drone feeds.

On his left, the edge of the escarpment and the wide road leading down around the cliff. Below, Jaimie and Dari would be guiding the mechanized unit through operations to secure the canyons.

Ahead, the remains of the fortress's huge walls. Craters honeycombed the surface of the field, the deepest of them having been occupied fighting positions just a short time ago. Farther right, the buildings that had survived the bombardments cut into the tall rocky outcrop at the center of the fortress. They stood largely intact, but the damage of the explosions was evident on their façade.

Liu's voice came over his bucket. "Platoon, advance."

The Q had dug a reasonable path through the barrier and now Liu led the Rolies through one at a time. The four Rolies moved forward on line, crawling at a pace even the Q would have no trouble matching. It wasn't long before they reached the first series of blown-out fighting positions. Mechanized troops from the Second Battalion spilled out from infantry fighting vehicles as squads organized to search the depths of the excavations.

The Q troopers eased to peer over the rims, the muzzles of their rifles pointing ahead of them. Finding nothing to prevent their advance, the Rolies rolled forward another twenty-five meters and the troops repeated the same searches of the defilades, ensuring that no resistance awaited within that had somehow survived the mortar barrages.

Kel and Meadows kept pace from behind as they followed the tin cans farther into the compound with their troops.

"Liu, we've got enough room to bring Bigg's platoon into the compound. I'm bringing him up," Kel said.

"Good. I'm veering right to get two of our big guns on those buildings. That's the next problem we need to solve. And it's going to be you guys and your ground-pounders."

"Don't go all 'tank commander' on us, man. It's just a Roly-poly," Meadows teased Liu.

Kel didn't know Liu well, but remembered he had a background in armor before coming to Dark Ops. His nickname was Roller because of it. It was natural for him to be running the plays from the Rolies.

"Bite me."

"Coming in behind you," Bigg said to them all, having heard the communications between the operators in the compound.

Stepping through the berm and into the compound, Bigg led two havildars, identifiable by the stripes painted on their carapaces. More Q followed. The platoon leader, their jemadar, was not in sight. Most Q officers had been unimpressive; today was no different.

Not an officer in sight yet. I bet they don't show up until the fight is over, Kel thought.

The Rolies halted in the middle of the courtyard, a hundred meters from where they'd breached the gate. Kel made his own assessment as they passed the already cleared foxholes, noting Q remains and twisted weapon fragments. The mortar strikes had done their work.

The two Rolies on their right flank faced the three buildings that were now their concern. Turret guns elevated to the roofs and split the difference in the arc covering the three buildings, the lower coaxial guns aimed at the faces. The two Rolies on the left continued covering the avenue leading around the rock outcropping to the front of the fortress.

"Seems obvious. I'll take my platoon and we'll clear the left building. Meadows, you want the right? Bigg, how about the middle?"

Kel received two affirmative responses and turned his attention to K'listan and her troops. "Get some guns up on those windows," he told her as he led them ahead of the Rolies.

He broke into a trot, dashing for the arched entrance of their chosen structure. The split doors were partially open. Kel stood back as Q moved forward, the lead troopers pointing their weapons at the entry point, the rest pointing weapons higher at the dark windows, as instructed.

"Get on the door. I'm going to toss a stunner."

The trooper on his right halted beside the door, attention focused on the narrow opening. Another trooper stood to his left, weapon raised, ready to shoot anything that appeared through the arch. Kel held out the stunner, then motioned the trooper on his right to push the door open. With a flick, he tossed the stunner into the space; purple fire danced.

"Roll on through, don't stop. Roll through," Kel said, pushing them to maintain momentum. Any defender in the building knew they were coming. It was time to KTF.

Q poured through the entrance. Kel let K'listan follow the first two troopers and waited until about half of the platoon was through before following. He didn't want to step on the havildar's toes—so to speak—wanting to let her lead her own troops through the structure.

The native architecture and construction techniques rendered the building's interior difficult to evaluate. Surfaces sloped oddly and every corner curved. In the end, it always came down to navigating basic shapes and angles with the correct tactics, no matter the structure's layout.

The first floor was entirely open with no walls subdividing it into separate spaces. Within were multiple mound-like kennels common in Q buildings. They could be storage areas or private sleeping quarters, the larger ones perhaps offices. There was little reason to their location as far as he could tell. He didn't need to understand their design philosophy. If it was a space large enough to hide a potential threat, it needed to be cleared methodically, so that no one was turning their back to a danger area.

An inclined walk ran along the far wall, escalating to a portal through the ceiling and up to the next level. The Q didn't build stairs with rises and runs.

"K'listan, get some guns on that ramp but don't send anyone up until we've finished this level."

K'listan moved with three troops to the base of the ramp, head raised above her weapon, gazing up the ramp. The alien understood the principles of fighting within structures well. He knew legionnaires who had greater difficulty with the concepts.

Troops moved of their own accord and cleared in teams of two and three, but awaited instructions by the mounds. K'listan left her subordinates to guard the incline and joined Kel to inspect the many mounds. Some contained food stores. Some held nothing. No rebel Q troops were hiding in them.

"This is a place for preparation. There will be living quarters above," she said, looking to the ramp to indicate their next direction of travel.

"Agreed. This floor is clear. We have the Rolies outside. We don't need to leave anyone back for security. No one is coming in behind us."

Kel hung back as he let K'listan organize her troops to make the ascent to the next floor. As he waited to join their procession in the middle of the pack, he updated his fellow operators.

"We've got nothing on the first floor. No resistance. We're making our way up."

Meadows came next. "Same here."

Liu broke in. "More Rolies are coming up to join us. Jaimie says they've got control of most of the caves and will worry about going farther back into the smaller canyons after we've completely secured the fortress. As soon as I get another platoon up here, I'm going to break off and take them to the front of the fortress and start there. I'll leave the rest of this platoon here outside until you're done."

"Good copy," Kel replied.

Bigg got in next. "Kel, I'm coming to you. Our building is totaled. Enough rounds penetrated the roof to collapse everything inside. Just the exterior walls are standing. Meadows, there's another platoon that just hit the plateau on the Talons. I'm detailing a naik to lead them into your building to join you."

"Copy. I'll have a party meet them on the first floor. We're pushing up."

To Kel it seemed the operation's momentum was being fully achieved, and they were on their way to securing the fortress at last. He knew they could be in for a surprise and many hours of tough work remained, but he allowed himself the minor optimism. Maybe they'd be out of the combat phase of this operation soon.

Always alert for the sound of shooting, he joined the procession up the ramp, the only noise that of skittering exoskeletons tramping the compacted earth. As he crested the ramp, he saw even more earthen mounds. They filled the floor space and were arranged if not in neat rows, at least in patterns. Kel moved farther in to evaluate the rear wall behind him. Another ramp was set into it. Three troops stood at the base of the next ramp, already covering the rising egress. Q troops poured into the large room, searching each mound. Kel shifted over to the base of the next ramp and peered up into the dark space beyond. He brought his rifle up and activated his weapon-mounted white light to penetrate the empty darkness for the troops with him.

He glanced over into the huge room and the progress being made as the Q cleared it. In pairs, commandos peered into each of the mounds. Soon the troops gravitated to the base of the next ramp, ready to push up into the next unknown.

"Coming through. Coming through," came Bigg's gruff voice. The leej led a few dozen Q troopers from the ground floor, spotted Kel, and strode over.

"Looks like a barracks," Bigg opined. "Not much different from ours."

"True," Kel replied. "Meadows, no contact here. Moving to the third floor."

"We're matching pace with you over here, man. Looking good so far."

"K'listan, what do you think, more barracks above?"

"No," her voder answered. "It will be officers' domiciles or command headquarters, I believe. Time to find out." She gestured at the troops beside her, and ascended the ramp behind several commandos.

Following the troops, Kel made his way up the ramp, turning sideways to pass between troops in his way until he reached the top of the incline.

"I was not anticipating this, Sergeant Kel-boss," the havildar said as he came to her side at the front of their group.

The buildings they worked to clear were built into the side of the rocky outcrop at the center of the fortress. A chamber had been carved into the heart of the mountainous rise from the top floor of the building. Where a rear wall had been in the lower two levels, here the space gave way to a large excavation. Opposite them sat a rock face covered with switchback ramps leading to multiple portals cut into the face.

The Disciplined trooper that had talked with him the day before conferred with K'listan.

"Trooper G'livan has no memory of this place," K'listan told Kel. "This construction has been completed recently under D'idawan's command."

Kel considered the rows of portals. "Bigg, move up to me. We have what looks like a tunnel network ahead."

He clicked over to Meadows. "Meadows, we are on our third-level and have run into a huge tunnel complex."

Meadows responded. "Kel, we are on our third level and have met no resistance. It's been all empty mounds and huts. Do you think that's where the rest of them are holed up, in your tunnels?"

"I'm going to take that into consideration."

"Should we join you?"

Kel thought a moment. "We've got a lot of troops in here already. Maybe it's best for you to link up with Liu and see if you can help him push out to the rest of the compound."

"Copy. Holler if you change your mind and need us."

The commandos spread out onto the landing, and K'listan directed teams to cover both directions. Troops headed left to clear the last floor of the building; others went right to put guns on the many open thresholds cut in the rock face.

The many holes reminded him of the houses his father made for the winged lizards native to Pthalo. The colorful creatures preferred nesting in the structures his father crafted rather than the eaves and rain channels around the house. His mother painted them in colors to match the lizards' palette. They congregated in large families, where they cooed and sang at all hours of the day and night as their hatchlings grew. He could imagine Q sitting on nests full of eggs in these honeycombed structures, just like the lizards of his home world. He knew that was not how the Q raised their young, but that's what it looked like to him.

Bigg walked up behind him. "Want to bet that the little mountain in the middle of this fortress is nothing but an anthill full of tunnels?"

Kel shrugged. "One of our Disciplined troopers has been here. Says that this is new excavation."

"I'd better update Braley and Jaimie on this," Bigg said. "Keep working the problem."

He joined K'listan beside the tunnels.

"The floor is clear," her voder chirped. "What next? Do we start in the tunnels?"

"I'm listening in on the command channel now. We'll have orders in a minute."

On the sub-channel, Braley and Jaimie spoke with Bigg and Dari. Kel was forming a mental image picture of what the battle space outside was looking like. The smaller canyon around the fortress held multiple caves concealing a platoon's worth of D'idawan's troops. They were poorly organized and fought individually rather than as a unit. Several dozen were easily killed or captured. Braley and Sims agreed that their area of responsibility held no more immediate threats. Braley was on his way to the top of the fortress with the First and Second Rifles. Sims would stay below with a small force and hold the area.

Jaimie's action in the larger canyon had been more eventful. The destruction of the drone had presaged an organized defense. There'd been strong resistance within the large caves, troops that the AP mortar rounds had not eliminated. The Rolies had been able to clear out most of it, but they'd had to push dismounted troops into some of the deeper spaces. They'd taken a few casualties, but had pushed deep within the canyons. No further armor had been found. Dari remained below to hold the ground they'd secured, while Jaimie made his way up to the fortress with more Rolies.

"Kel and I each have an Inquisitor to launch," Bigg told the team. "If these tunnels lead to anything significant, we're going to have to divide forces to start searching."

Braley's voice sounded mildly strained as he spoke from a full run. "Agreed. I'll make my way to you. Jaimie, you and Liu finish the front of the fortress. Let's lock it down. If that outcrop is nothing but more caverns and tunnels, we need to anticipate that it could communicate all the way to the wadi floor. You guys downstairs reading me on this?"

"Yeah," Sims said. "If you chase anyone down into the wash, we're prepared."

"Good hunting, men," said Dari.

"It's on us now," Bigg told Kel on closed channel. "Let's send Inquisitors out. My curiosity is getting the better of me and I'm feeling impatient to know what we're up against."

This was a good use for the nano-drones. Kel had one in his day-pack, and removed it from the small of this back as Bigg did the same. Kel pulled out a small ball, scrolled through the menu in his bucket, and activated the Inquisitor program, selecting the manual controller. The ball awoke and unfurled in his open palm into a vaguely insectoid shape. He thought it looked like something a Q engineer would design, but this was pure Republic R&D. The drone ran a system check, spread its wings and flapped a beat, then crawled up to his shoulder to await his next command.

Kel brought up a small window and placed it in his central vision. He couldn't divert any attention to follow Bigg's feed, but knew Bigg was probably able to keep an eye on Kel's drone feed as well as his own. He was a real multi-tasker when it came to this tech. Kel had seen him run as many as three of the drones at once on manual, and direct each of them perfectly.

"I'll start on the top row, you start on the bottom, and we'll see what's there to find," Bigg said.

On the bottom row were three tunnel entrances. Kel chose the center one and guided the drone into it using the holo-controller. A chittering chorus broke his concentration, and glancing up, he saw Q peering over their shoulders at the controller projections as the drones flitted off. Kel shrugged, and selected a larger holo-projection to share with the Q troops.

The recon platoon guarded the tunnel entrances, but the Chachnam Q of the line companies were now transfixed by the holos. Kel didn't mind their display of curiosity.

Pretty soon they'll be patrolling those tunnels, Kel thought. *If I were them, I'd want to see what's in there before I went in, too.*

The tunnel stood a full two meters tall. It was unlit and the drone automatically switched to an infrared view, illuminating the tunnel ahead with its own wide beam of invisible light. Kel drove the drone forward and initiated the 3D mapping program to start receiving inputs from the drone. After a dozen meters, the tunnel spiraled down, sloping shallowly as it went. He followed it for several more turns before halting and hitting the return icon. No immediate threats down the first portion of that passage.

He selected the far-left tunnel and started the same process again. This trail led farther left along a gradual curve. Kel could see twenty meters ahead of the drone and increased the velocity to cover more ground quickly. He pictured where the tunnel would lead—around the interior of the outcropping toward the front of the fortress. The drone flitted around until it came to a place where rubble obliterated the tunnel's path. He keyed the mapping program to see what progress it had made reconstructing the subterranean route in relation to the fortress. As he suspected, this tunnel had traveled forward to the front of the fortress. The end of the tunnel sat behind what was one of the analogous buildings they had destroyed at the front. He again activated the return function and let the drone autonomously reverse its course.

That left only one route. He sent the drone into the far-right entrance, starting slowly as he had before. The tunnel traveled straight before sloping to the right in a gentle curve.

"I see you," said Bigg. "Check this out. Look at the map."

Kel panned around to see an adjoining tunnel from above merging into his, with the other Inquisitor hovering in its center. He changed viewers to look at the map projection.

Like Kel's far left-hand passage, Bigg's had terminated in destruction far along its path to the front of the fortress. Bigg's middle tunnel also spiraled downward, but followed a right-hand corkscrew instead of the left-hand one that Kel's followed. Neither of them had investigated past the first few spirals.

Kel had missed it on the first two tunnels, but the map showed cross-branches connecting the tunnels at multiple points along their paths. Bigg's right-hand tunnel had done so from above Kel's, letting Bigg drive his drone up behind Kel's and into his blind spot.

"Let's go this way together," suggested Bigg. "We'll check this out, then go back and follow the spirals in the middle tunnels down. Looks like they go deep. Wouldn't be surprised if they do travel all the way to the level of the wadi."

Bigg's drone took the lead.

Kel set his drone on auto, letting it follow Bigg's. The Q were still mesmerized, chittering in hushed tones. What could be so significant about tunnels, holes, and dirt? Whatever it was, they seemed transfixed.

"Contact front!"

Through the drone feed, Kel saw what had caught Bigg's attention. A gun position on a berm guarding the tunnel. "I think they've spotted the drones."

Automatic fire echoed down the tunnel toward them, the delayed sounds lagging behind the images they watched. But the gunfire had no effect. The drones continued to transmit images. Kel nudged his Inquisitor left to look down the corridor to see a large opening beyond.

They had their answer.

Barricaded beyond, an unknown number of the former Third Battalion of the Sun-Loyal awaited.

It was time for a gunfight.

11

"Braley, we've got something. Drones are giving us feed on a fighting position in one of the tunnels. Looks like there may be a substantial force beyond. Time for us to get busy," Bigg informed their team leader.

"Coming into the building now. It's the one on the left, correct?"

"Yes," Kel said. "It's clear up to the third floor. We're at the top of the last incline." He thought about their options, as he knew Bigg was too. "But we don't have any gas to smoke them out with."

They had some irritant gas back at the compound but not with them. Even then, using it would likely be as a last resort. The legionnaires were the only ones who'd be immune to its effects in their armor.

"Bigg, I think I can get close enough to skip some energy grenades into their laps. Then we'll have to pour it on."

"It's time for the Rifles to earn their pay. Full-on assault. I'm leading," Bigg said.

Kel reluctantly agreed. "All right. Let me work this first fighting position though, then we'll fall in behind you. I've got an idea to clear some of that berm, so don't crowd me. Might get a little messy."

"Sure thing, hero. I'm going to find me a subadar and get her working. Time to see if one of these so-called officers can show responsibility to match their rank. See you in a minute." Bigg headed down the ramp in search of the Q officer, a mother looking for a child shirking chores.

"I'm going ahead to clear that foxhole with some grenades," Kel told K'listan. "Try to blast away some of the berm, too. We're letting First Rifles take the lead on the assault."

Instead of protesting, K'listan's large eyes twitched several times. "It is time the Chachnam showed some courage. Do not worry, we will be there to carry the fight when—I mean, if—they falter."

Clearly she didn't think much of their soldiering ability.

Bigg returned, nudging forward a Q bearing the insignia of three circles painted on her green carapace. "The subadar will be up front with her troops. We're ready, Kel. Waiting for your signal."

"I'm behind you," Braley said, joining them. "I'll push more troops to you as we go."

"I'll follow with the drones," added Bigg. "They're probably going to be skrilled after your grenade.

Kel set off down the right entrance. "If they don't get trashed, make sure you get my best side."

"Just be careful, funny guy."

Kel moved forward, keeping a small window of the drone feed in the left of his HUD. He loaded an energy grenade into the launcher under his K-17, and set it for wide effect. Inching forward, hugging the wall as it curved ahead, he experienced a sensation of apprehension and stopped. Looking at his map and the drone feed, Kel estimated that any farther forward would take him into the line of sight of the fighting position just a dozen yards away.

No time like the present, he said to himself as he launched a grenade off the left wall as far as he could aim it.

As soon as it fired, Kel immediately loaded another and sent it in the same direction. The first grenade skipped off the wall and detonated beyond, just as his next one launched. A wave of overpressure pushed against his armor and shoved him back. In this tight space, explosive grenades created enough overpressure to scramble the brains of anything within twenty meters of the explosion. His armor protected him from the destructive shock waves. Had his un-armored Q troops been with him, they would have been rendered combat ineffective from the pressure waves bursting ear drums and shearing brain cells. Whether or not the grenades had created any effective shrapnel missiles, the overpressure should have badly hurt anyone around the curve.

As Bigg had predicted, the drone feed was gone. Kel stepped decisively forward and slid to his left, into what he thought should be a clear line of sight to the barricade. Behind the berm, the Q had been tossed from their cover and back into the tunnel. With his K-17 set to maximize the coherent light energy effect, Kel aimed it at the top third of the berm. He'd never tried this before, and was unsure what effect the blaster would have on the hardened earth of the berm.

The effect always issued with a buzzing sound.

Clods of hard dirt blasted in a debris shower, pelting his armor with chunks of the berm. He loosed another quick blast, though dust clouds obscured his aim.

"Move in, we're through," Kel bellowed, repeating his order to move and waiting to see Bigg in the lead with Q crowded around him as closely as their carapaces would allow in the corridor.

Kel found himself swept up in their ranks. *Fine*, he thought. *I want to be where the fight is, anyway.* He forced his way up front with Bigg. Kel was gratified to find much of the berm blasted away.

"Worked pretty well," Bigg mumbled to him. "Nice."

Bodies lay on the other side, crunching underfoot as they continued their steady flow forward. Kel returned his K-17 to particle effect and checked the charge. About two-thirds remained.

"Volley fire with me," Bigg invited.

Kel needed no further prompting. He raised his weapon and joined Bigg up front, sending blasts into the space ahead. As they marched forward, they fired on every other footfall. Though their visibility was poor, the precaution seemed justified. It was a trade-off. Un-aimed fire was not only usually ineffective, but also a certain way to hit unintended targets. Still, it might keep any defenders pinned down and unable to get a bead on them. Better than nothing. Armor didn't make you invulnerable.

The dust cleared. Up ahead, the tunnel widened and gave way to a great expanse. He didn't have time for a detailed analysis, but it reminded him of magma chambers he had been in. What most captured his attention were the dozens of Q spread around on the floor below them. And of course, the weapons they discharged in his direction.

"Keep pouring it on! Pour it on!" Bigg repeated his KTF mantra.

Kel had heard it many times. It required no reply. Small things like that never registered at the time, never passed into conscious thought. They were just there. Like the slugs whizzing past him.

Kel moved into the cavern. Muzzle blasts flashed, lighting up the floor. As fast as he could form an instant sight picture, Kel fired, the trigger resetting with a click before shifting to the next lurching shape.

"Get in the fight. Start shooting!" he yelled over his shoulder at the Q behind him.

Bigg yelled the same as Kel faded back and pushed Q into the chamber. "Get going! Start fighting!"

Kel grabbed each Q within reach and pushed them forward. One Q brought her gun up, pointing it at Kel's chest. He brushed the barrel aside and shoved the careless trooper toward an open space on the skirmish line.

Only to those with no sense of time would the delay have been insignificant. The chatter of weapons discharging from their line signaled the end of a solar year in Kel's subjective reality. *Finally.* In what was objectively the span of a few heartbeats, every Q they'd brought had moved into the cavern and was firing uncontrollably in the sympathetic response they called the "mad-minute."

Months of teaching disciplined aimed fire, wasted.

Kel's bucket's audio override muted the deafening hammer of the slug launchers. Q sprayed rounds onto the floor below them, their fire-control set on automatic, hosing down everything in front of them. Some of the wild shooting spun their targets in a wild ballet of green blood. Most of the slugs pocked the cave floor and walls. Kel had stepped back from the frenzy, but now moved to get between two shorter Q in front of him to evaluate the kill zone ahead.

"Cease fire! Cease fire!" both he and Bigg yelled repeatedly.

Silence and smoke.

Q bodies lay piled on each other. The cavern was ringed by a wide escarpment where they stood, overlooking the carnage on the sunken cave floor. A lone Q renegade knelt among the bodies, weaponless and bleeding, in shock, head dropped forward onto its carapace, no longer aware. A shot rang out. The wounded Q slumped forward, dead. The shot came from their line. The company subadar stood with her weapon extended, chittering loudly. It was the frenzied rush of murder.

"There will be no killing unarmed or defenseless troops!" Bigg yelled. He repeated it several times over his bucket's speaker. He switched to L-comm. "Killing the wounded. Great example their commander is setting for them. These troops are on the verge of being out of control. Watch yourself, man."

"Trust me, I am," Kel said, thinking about the trooper who'd just pointed her weapon at him.

"Let's see what we have. Braley, you in yet?"

"Almost," Braley answered.

Kel moved forward, motioning the troopers to lower their weapons.

"You, naik," pointing to a Q with two stripes on his carapace. "Get your fire-team into the cavern and block anything coming from that direction," he said, pointing in the direction he wanted them. To the left a wide tunnel menaced. The junior leader chirped affirmatively and gathered her troops.

"Coming in." Braley joined Kel on the rim. "Talk to me, brother."

"So far, so good," Bigg told the team leader. "Kel and I got the drop on these guys. With some encouragement, the Q got into the fight. You know."

Braley chuckled. "I can imagine."

The legionnaires hopped off the escarpment. Kel gestured for the troops to follow. Time to check the kill zone and ensure their victims were truly dead and not going to reanimate. The dead ones killed you when you assumed.

The Q hesitated.

"Check to make sure they're all dead. Any weapons you find, stack them against that wall," he said, pointing to the spot. "I'll show you." He walked over to the nearest Q body and aimed his carbine at the creature's head as Bigg kicked the thorax. No response. Bigg knelt down to remove the weapon from underneath it, and then passed it up to a gawking troop watching the process, probably for the first time.

Watch and learn, kid. I think you're going to get the chance to get good at this. Kel always found a demonstrative example to be a clearer form of communication than words at times like this. Q troopers hopped off the ledge and skittered about the dead, searching them and removing weapons.

He took a moment to evaluate the scene. Kel had put his fair share of bad guys in the ground. The look of death was something he was accustomed to. He wasn't a ghoul; it didn't entertain or excite him. It was just another part of doing what he did. Accepting what went along with death was part of being a professional. Whatever color the blood was, whatever the innards looked like outside of the body, it always stood out for not being where it was supposed to be. The look. The smell.

The carapace of a blaster-shot Q blanched to a pale white. Quickly. Any other method of death, it took time. On the western continent, reaching the state of pallor was part of their religious dogma. Bodies weren't ready for interment until total blanching had occurred, indicating the spirit had risen. It took days.

Blasters wiped out the zooxanthellae rapidly. Those Kel and Bigg dispatched were going through the process now. The proof they'd nixed more than half of the renegades was unveiled as the dark greens faded into paler shades until... white. An even, unnatural white.

The rest had been gunned down with slugs by their rifle company, albeit wildly and inefficiently. The mix of colors on the floor made a strange palette for a gunfight, the bleached-white bodies sprawled among the dark green corpses, all splattered with light green blood.

"Bigg, block right, we're moving left," Braley announced. "Kel, get your platoon and trail behind us."

Braley took charge of the fire team guarding the tunnel entrance on their left, and brought up the rest of a platoon to join them. He was stepping up to take the lead to clear the next tunnel. Whichever element made contact or had work to do—like dead-checking or controlling prisoners—surrendered the lead to the trailing element, thus maintaining momentum. Braley wasn't snatching the lead from Kel and Bigg. He was doing what any of them would do: finding work and doing it.

It was time to regain combat momentum, to project the mass of a capital ship plowing through enemy space. Unstoppable. It was a good feeling, to be on the hunt. K'listan and her commandos clustered near the cave.

"Nice to see you. Feel like joining in? Come with me and we'll follow the captain," Kel said, gesturing them forward.

K'listan and her Disciplined whirred in unison. There was no translation from their voders. But he knew that sound. The call to war. They were anxious to get into the fight.

KTF, ladies, he thought. *KTF.*

"I don't have an Inquisitor, so unless you have a better idea, we're moving," Braley said over L-comm. "Bigg, maybe we need to get Meadows and anyone else we can to start working these tunnels?"

"No L-comm with the others from down here, sir. Already tried. I'm not leaving you with only Q behind you to watch your six."

To Bigg's side of the chamber smaller tunnels lead in new directions. Too many places to cover. Not enough bodies to do it right. They were going to need more help to clear everything, and they couldn't do it alone.

Bigg continued. "Braley, I'm sending one of the havildars and a small fire-team back to update the rest of the team and to bring more help."

"Rog. We're bleeding momentum. I'm not waiting. If we lose comms with each other, I'll send a runner back in twenty minutes. If we're out of comms for more than twenty minutes, go make that call yourself and bring help. If you make contact with an enemy force and have no comms with us, fight your way out and back to the surface to get help. Either way, we're going to need more troops down here."

Bigg flashed a thumbs up. "Copy. See you in twenty."

Kel was about to move when he heard Bigg ask a perplexed question.

"What gives?"

Many of the Q troopers stood in the middle of the killing floor, looking at the bodies of the slain renegade troops, mesmerized.

It was not entirely unusual behavior. Kel remembered his first combat engagement. He and his fellow youthful legionnaires were stunned by the results of their work, at the destructive force they'd unleashed on other beings. A body that a moment before had been full of life, now mangled and torn, was disturbing. He supposed it was the same for the Q troopers who'd never seen battle.

But a few Q troopers wandered, heads craned up at the tall chamber ceiling. Kel stole a glance upward. He saw nothing except a rocky dome. Odd.

"Let's get 'em going, Kel."

"Moving," Kel agreed.

They were losing the initiative. Anyone farther down this tunnel or the others were well aware that they were coming for them. The deafening explosions and sustained firefight would have echoed throughout the maze of tunnels. If the remaining renegades had not already prepared a good static defense, pressure off them now gave them time to prepare. A classic not-good. Like running out of toilet paper.

They traveled en masse, jammed into the tunnel. Not very tactical, but sometimes there wasn't much else you could do. To fight, first you had to get there. Kel moved with K'listan; another trooper by her side. Behind them, the rest of the commandos skittered along. Ahead, a train of Q bodies moved like drunken partiers, pushing and stumbling to make it to the bar for last call.

Taka-taka-taka.

"Contact front!" Braley yelled. "Another chamber. Big one." More fire erupted, echoing down the tunnel. "This is a big one. There's balconies spread all over this thing. It's raining down on us from every direction."

Kel shoved his way forward. "Coming through, coming through!" he yelled as he wove between halted Q.

K'listan matched his steps, her voder exploding with translated speech, repeating Kel's words for the troops to make way for them to pass.

The tunnel rumbled beneath his boots. Grenades. Braley wouldn't use them indiscriminately. There had to be a massive space ahead, otherwise the overpressure would damage his own troops. Maybe Braley found himself severely outnumbered, desperate, and the launcher was all he could use? Kel pushed harder through the last of the halted Q troopers.

Ahead he could see the tunnel opening into another of the caverns. Braley knelt near the opening, several wounded Q troopers lying on the floor beside him. None of the other Q had moved forward to take their place.

"Coming up behind you."

Braley did not respond. He loaded another grenade into the K-17 launcher and fired it into the chamber. Its trail arced toward the far wall of the dome, exploding in a billowing debris cloud.

Kel knelt beside Braley. Now it made sense. Like a theater, balconies were cut into the face of the domed chamber. In each, two or three Q crouched behind mud revetments, firing down at them. There were more of the positions than he could count.

"Bigg, we've kicked the hornet's nest," he said as he launched a grenade of his own. That's what it was. An angry hive.

"I've been keeping up," Bigg replied. "We're already moving to you."

Thank Oba they were still in L-comm range. K'listan, now beside him, fired into the room. Several more commandos joined the fight, kneeling on top of dead Q to get a better position.

He picked targets as he saw them and fired quickly and methodically. A warning light flashed, indicating his charge pack was almost depleted. One-handed, he found his other charge pack and dropped the spent one, clicking the new one in place. Impacts glanced off his chest. He spotted a muzzle trained on him from one of the low balconies. Shifting right, he spat off several rounds; the Q collapsed behind the short wall.

Kel didn't have time to check himself or his armor for damage. He felt fine so whatever hit him didn't bring much force with it. He would know right away if there were something gravely wrong. Or, he would figure it out later. If he suddenly dropped dead a minute from now from some unperceived wound, what would it matter? There was a fight happening, and he was in it.

"Braley, we'll never get in there if the whole dome is covered with these. It'll be like a reverse slope defense inside."

Even if they could suppress the fire from all the positions on the far wall, they could never engage the positions effectively on their own side of the dome.

"Coming up at your six," Bigg announced. "Braley, Kel, pull everyone back. I'm going to launch a special at them."

A special? Kel thought. That word was used to describe many types of munitions. But the only "special" fired from a K-17 launcher was...

"Fall back. *Now!*" Braley yelled through his bucket's speaker to the Q around him. K'listan and the other Q skittered backward, still firing, with Kel and Braley doing the same on their sides of the tunnel. As they reached a short turn and the mouth of the tunnel was no longer visible, Kel turned around to see a mass of Q troopers frozen in the corridor.

"All troops, fall back!" Braley screamed. "*Do it now!* Back it up!"

"K'listan, get everyone back," Kel told her. "Get them out of the caves. All the way out. I'll follow you."

The commando havildar issued commands too rapid for Kel to understand.

"You guys get back, too. Just in case," Bigg said to Kel and Braley. He'd assumed a prone position and crawled forward on his elbows.

Kel looked to his captain. "Braley, is he launching a TB at them? He'll kill everyone!"

"We'll be fine, just get the Q out of here! You go, too."

Kel trotted down the tunnel after the Q. It didn't take long for him to catch up, and as they made their way back into the chamber, he saw troops retreating yet farther back, into the main tunnel. K'listan waited for him.

"Sergeant Kel-boss, what is happening?"

"Listen, my friend: get everyone out of here. You too. Bigg is going to launch a thermobaric grenade at them."

"I do not understand."

"If you stay behind, you'll die. Move."

The thermobaric grenade was a devastating weapon. It was a miniaturized version of an older conventional weapon still in their inventory, used to destroy fortifications. The nano-particle-sized metallic dust within the grenade was released during the first part of the detonation. The particles saturated whatever space they occupied, only to carry the charge of the second, larger detonation that followed a microsecond later, spreading the destructive force of the explosion evenly throughout an enclosed space. It created an immense pressure wave and consumed any oxygen present.

They used them to destroy bunkers and buildings from a stand-off distance of at least two hundred meters. A round launched into the opening of a small house engulfed it in flame from the inside. The pressure generated was so enormous, it could be felt in your chest through your armor. He'd only ever used them in the open, never from inside an enclosure like they now found themselves in. It would be suicide! What it would do inside this cave complex, Kel didn't know.

Bigg's calm voice conveyed urgency. "They're mounting a counterattack and moving into the tunnel. Here goes."

Kel dropped to the floor of the chamber as he heard Bigg say the last. *This is going to hurt*, he thought, not knowing what to expect.

Dull thunder rumbled down the tunnel, then tapered off.

That's it?

Energy grenades made more of a report.

The tunnel looked untouched. Kel trotted into the entrance. A fine gray mist expelled from the mouth. He doubled his pace and raced forward, ready to see Bigg and Braley injured or dead. The mist turned into thick smoke. He turned on his bucket's white light to cut through the cloud. Rounding the last curve, he found Bigg and Braley standing in the middle of the tunnel, smoke whirling around them.

"You guys all right? What happened?"

"Not sure," Bigg said. "I want to look."

"Me, too," Braley said. "I'm a little surprised to be alive. Maybe we didn't get a high-order detonation. We better go slow. They might be really mad now."

Kel moved in between the two and extinguished his white light and keyed his bucket to add more infrared. At the opening, lanky Q bodies cluttered the floor. The renegades' counterattack hadn't gone far before Bigg fired the TB grenade into the cavern.

They peered into the cavern and saw nothing but smoke.

"We don't need to rush. Let's wait a few," Bigg suggested.

"Okay. Let's give it a minute," Braley agreed.

Kel assumed a prone position. Soon his two teammates did the same. As they watched, the smoke settled into a fine ash, dusting the corpses. Smoke cleared. The far wall of the cavern became visible. Q draped over the parapet walls; others lay writhing and gasping. The sounds of impending demise. They were no threat.

Bigg stood and peered into the cavern, stretched forward to look left, then right around the rim of the tunnel mouth. A shrug. "I think we got them. Let's look."

Tiers of limp Q hung above them like drooping vegetables, ripe and ready to drop. The scene above him was similar to what he saw across the dome, only there were no dying Q. The defenders above were dead as wrapped fish.

"Look!"

Bigg raised his rifle, aiming deeper in the dark space at the base of the dome. Kel stepped on line and brought his own carbine up. Out of the depths of another tunnel was a small procession of Q. Three orange-hued Q covered in soot staggered forward. Behind them, a fourth larger Q walked.

"Who do you think that is?" Braley asked. "They're orange. You don't suppose..."

As the procession moved closer, they could see the Q in the back, painted in whirling patterns of gold, her shine undiminished by the circulating soot.

"Those are the colors of a mughal. It's D'idawan!" Braley blurted. The staggering quartet of Q had not yet seen the legionnaires.

Braley raised his weapon and activated his white light. The Q responded and swiveled in their direction. One raised a weapon. Kel and Bigg fired at the same time. The large insectoid dropped in its tracks. One Q turned to run, and the third started to raise a weapon. Braley joined in as they cut them down. After the last one dropped, Kel jumped into the chamber, charging the red and gold Q now standing alone.

D'idawan stood petrified, in seeming shock. Violence happened in the span of a thunderclap. It was paralyzing for all but the conditioned. Even a mughal. As he reached the red and gold Q, he raised his weapon and pointed it at her head menacingly.

"Do not move. You are in my custody."

Bigg appeared at his side, rifle raised to multiply the peril. The large Q had no weapon, but made noises. There was no voder around her neck, and Kel's bucket struggled to translate in a timely matter.

"Demons. Cursed humans. Demons." The software repeated D'idawan's chorus in his ears.

She screeched, then went limp and tumbled to the ground.

"We have to get her out of here. There's no oxygen." Kel let his carbine drop to his chest and knelt. "Grab a side and we'll carry her."

Braley knelt to grab an upper appendage and draped it around his neck. Kel did the same. They held onto her arms, grabbed the alien's carapace, and stood together, lifting the large Q.

"We've got to hurry. Bigg, lead the way. Double time," Kel said as they began a trot, heading down the tunnel as fast as they could, her lower appendages dragging to slow them. The air cleared. Heading into the final tunnel into the outer building, their L-comm came to life.

"I'm coming in, do you copy?" It was Meadows.

"We're coming out. We have a surprise. Get Jaimie and the rest of the team. Tell 'em we've got D'idawan."

The First and Second Battalions were now formed in the rear courtyard. A dozen Rolies and all the troops were circled in a large perimeter. Q cradled rifles, crouched at the ready. Mughal D'idawan stood in the center of it all. She revived when they brought her into the bright sun, in time to be restrained by several Q officers.

The two orange nawab from the First and Second battalions had appeared on the fortress grounds not long after the legionnaires announced that they were coming out with D'idawan. The Q were now oblivious to the requests of the legionnaires. Braley and Jaimie had tried to organize the army to continue operations to clear the tunnels and caves. That had stopped when the nawabs began issuing orders to their fellow officers. A chant spread among the Q.

The legionnaires gathered between two Rolies, a sea of Q around them.

Liu shivered. "I don't like this vibe I'm getting. The Q are acting strange."

"No kidding," Bigg agreed. "This is the most military-like discipline I've seen them demonstrate. Could be bad."

The orange nawabs strode into the circle, the troops parting for the commanders, the green gate of bodies closing as they passed.

"What's going on?" Kel whispered to K'listan, who stood at his side. "Are we in danger? The troops aren't listening to us. What's happening?"

The Disciplined of both his and Meadows's platoons had formed a layer around the legionnaires. If the Q were getting ready to turn on them, the Disciplined would either act as a barrier between them and the other Q, or lead the attack on them. Kel hoped the commando's intentions were to protect them. He was ready for either. The legionnaires were bunched together. It was a bad strategy. More not-good.

"No. I do not think we are in danger."

Kel noticed she said "we."

"But the Disciplined are ready to fight with you if the Chachnam attempt any treachery."

"K'listan," Braley interjected. He was standing closest to their private conversation and listening in. "What's happening? The nawab won't talk to me. Are they putting D'idawan on trial?"

"I believe so. I cannot say. This is Chachnam tribal law. I have been around them my whole life, but even so, I cannot predict what will happen next. We are ready to fight with you, Captain-boss."

"Maybe we should call the Talons to get ready for a rescue, just in case we have to fight our way out of here?" Jaimie said over L-comm.

"Not a bad idea. I'm on it," Bigg said, shifting to a sub-channel to bounce the capital.

"Tell Kim and Poul to stay where they are and get ready to escape and evade," Braley said. The mortarmen were still distant from the fortress. "Sims and Dari, too. Everyone needs to get ready to E and E."

An escape and evasion would be difficult without the Talons to meet them.

"Hey," Kel whispered. "Something's happening."

Kel recognized the First Battalion commander, Nawab Q'stalt, as she raised her upper appendages and began speaking from the middle of the circle. Her voder was still on, and they heard the translation over the loud squawks and chitters of her speech. She walked around the inner circle, speaking to the circled crowd. In the center, D'idawan stood, a subadar on either side of her, restraining the larger Q.

"The Chachnam gather to bring the law. The Chachnam gather to bring justice. Who thinks themselves so great as to be above the law? Who thinks they do not need to follow the Way? Only you, D'idawan!" the nawab said as she turned from the crowd to point at the red and gold Q with the spear of her upper appendage fully extended.

Nice knife hand, Kel thought.

D'idawan shrieked in what Kel could only assume was protest.

The orange-hued nawab continued. "Where are the humans who led us to victory? Where are the human leaders who see us to victory this day? Captain Jaimie. Captain Braley. Step forward."

The army of bugs turned to the humans.

"I've got a bad feeling about this," Liu said. "I'm slipping out and making my way back into a Roly. I'll start raining fire as soon they make a move on us."

"Be cool, Liu," Jaimie said. "You can get us a Roly, but be cool."

"Let's go," Braley said, as he gestured Jaimie toward the circle. "I don't think we're in danger."

"Let us handle this, men." Jaimie said. "If things go bad, we'll make our own way back."

Hundreds of Q heads tracked the two officers as they made their way into the inner circle. Like a predator watching prey, waiting for the moment to strike. The nawab who had called them forward waited, while Liu slipped unnoticed into a Roly-poly.

Kel's plan was simple: gun down every Q between him and the captains, then fight back to the Roly Liu was prepping. Jaimie's instructions be damned.

The pair stopped before the beckoning nawab who greeted them with a deep bow. "Mughal D'shtaran, commander of the Grand Army of the Sun-Loyal, is pleased and sends her exalted thanks to you for your assistance. She says that you are to take part in the honor of the *Ashkalant.*"

Kel whispered to K'listan, "What does 'Ashkalant' mean?" The voder gave a transliterate response for the last.

"It means we are in no danger. They are going to punish D'idawan for her apostasy."

Kel relaxed. He watched intently as the second nawab rushed to the side of the first. Before Kel could blink, the subadars holding D'idawan released her and leapt away. The two nawabs sprang onto D'idawan, closing the distance in a heartbeat. They set upon her with ferocity, ripping off D'idawan's upper limbs as her screeches echoed.

The audience clicked and chittered as the nawabs continued their grizzly dissection. The large Q attempted to fight back. She recoiled to spring, only for the nawabs to tackle her to the ground, yanking, biting, tearing as they did. Her carapace fractured with loud cracks as the two stood above her, hammering blows onto her thorax and abdomen. The sharp sounds of impacts softened as guts and green ichor flowed.

Kel had lost track of who was who in the bloody assault. The two nawabs, now covered in blood and body parts, looked indistinguishable from each other. D'idawan clicked piteously until one of her executioners bent over her, her mouth gaping wide.

"Oba! They're eating her!" Meadows exclaimed.

The nawab bit down on D'idawan's neck and grabbed her beaked head. Twisting violently back and forth, she decapitated the corpse. She raised the glossy-eyed head above her and shrieked a shrill chant.

"Ka-ka-ka-ka-ka," the Q army repeated.

"Ka-ka-ka-ka-KAAA."

"Okay, I guess not," Meadows continued. "But still—she bit off the head."

The nawab lowered the head and dashed to where Braley and Jaimie stood. Kel tensed again and brought his hands to his carbine, ready to fire. He saw his teammates do the same. The nawab stopped short and extended the head to Braley, gesturing him to hold the head up high, as she had done.

Braley did as he was invited, and raised the head high above his.

The nawab again gave the chant. "Ka-ka-ka-ka-ka."

The Q horde responded. "Ka-ka-ka-ka-KAAA."

Braley lowered the head and gave it back to the nawab, who then proceeded to Jaimie and repeated the same gruesome exercise.

"Ka-ka-ka-ka-ka."

"Ka-ka-ka-ka-KAAA."

The nawab received the head back, held it aloft, walking around the inner circle, displaying it to leave no doubt that the apostate was dead. Finally, she returned to the center where the twitching body of D'idawan lay.

"The justice of the Chachnam has been fulfilled." With that, the nawab tossed the head onto the body and stood aside. She gestured wide at the mess that had been D'idawan.

The crouching Q sprang from the circle in a frenzy and fell upon the still twitching body. The writhing mass of the tribe converged on the spot, crunching, rending, chomping, ripping. Kel couldn't take his eyes away.

"Oh! *Now* they're eating her. How about that?" Meadows said.

"Shut up, Meadows," Kel heard at least three others say with him.

Kel felt a nudge; Disciplined Trooper G'livan was at his side. The rest of the Disciplined still maintained the protective wall around the legionnaires.

"Is it not as I told you, Sergeant Kel-boss? The Chachnam are not to be trusted."

12

"The company is doing whatever it can to help these people. I understand their resistance to change, but it is for the good of their race. We're lifting them up. At some point, they will be equal partners in the company. They'll be shareholders and there'll even be Qulingat't seats on the board. This is just a phase that their culture needs to go through. The rest of the planet is adapting nicely, and I think you'd agree the benefits we've brought have enhanced their way of life, rather than destroying it. It's only Mukalasa'at that is having such difficulty adapting to a modern galactic consciousness. The MPA is necessary for their development. Their leaders see it. We are not trying to acculturate these people. They have a beautiful, distinct culture that will bring a wealth of heterogeneity into the Republic. I'm trying to help preserve the beneficial aspects of their culture while we help to advance them."

Sims and Monica's paths had intersected early during their mission on Big M. The team had been doing small unit operations with the First Rifles, providing security for a joint team from the embassy and the company. The Provincial Development Teams spent a week at a time in the different villages and hamlets, selling the changes proposed in the Mutual Prosperity Accord to the locals. A senior diplomat from the court of Mughal D'shtaran accompanied the teams to make the medicine less bitter as it was dispensed by humans.

Even then, Kel could see the friction developing. Q in the hamlets were resistant to the proposed changes, and it had proven necessary to have armed security whenever human intercessors were present to negotiate with the matriarchs of a family collective. There had been some intimidation and hints of violence against humans, even against the Sun-Loyal Army. Most of the hamlets had followed the edict of their Mughal D'shtaran, especially those in the sector of the First Battalion. Some had not, particularly those in the large region to the north where the Third Battalion was garrisoned. This was before D'idawan had gone full rogue and taken a third of the Sun-Loyal with her.

Sims riveted himself to the bright, attractive young xenoanthropologist from first sight. They'd seen each other on an infrequent basis, getting acquainted whenever Sims was back in the capital. Having an uninterrupted week, there was opportunity for Sims to further pursue the relationship.

Kel smiled at her as he turned over onto his stomach. He didn't like getting into political discussions with silvene tower-types. Especially when all he was doing was trying to relax. He enjoyed stimulating conversation as much as the next guy; with an attractive woman—all the better. But she wasn't a great listener and hadn't responded to Kel's gentle hints that he didn't want to engage her in conversation. The company xenoanthropologist had a never-ending pool of opinions to share, no matter that Kel had prompted her for none of them.

He'd had a rigorous workout that morning, and was looking forward to a day of relaxation by the pool. He'd earned it. They'd all earned it. While he hated downtime in general, after a sustained combat operation like the

D'idawan assault, he was looking forward to doing nothing except getting back in shape and recharging. Returning to Diakasa'at for an extended rest period suited him fine.

Their quarters in the capital were comfortable if not luxurious. A nice change of pace from their mud hut at the First Battalion compound. Kel was glad to have his own bedroom and to not have to resort to plugging his ears every night to escape the sound of everyone snoring. If he got to sleep before the festival of horns began, he could remain asleep. If he hadn't, then it was a struggle to block out the throat noises, no matter how tired he was. When he returned to their hut after two hours on their rotating guard schedule, the small space was an orchestra of power tools sawing at a forest of petrified trees. He needed the break. It would be pleasantly strange to stay in bed the entire night without having to pull a watch.

They'd gotten in the day before, fortunate to have had a Talon available to transport them the 1500 kilometers to the capital on the coast. Kel hadn't felt a pleasantly cool breeze since their last visit to D-Town. The Republic Club was an oasis on the alien world, but it would have been more enjoyable for him if he'd been able to come alone. Sims had invited himself and his girlfriend along, but what could he do? Refuse his teammate? They would've come anyway. There weren't that many other places to go for relaxation around D-Town. That would've made for an awkward time around the pool. No, Kel figured it would be kindest to go as a group and hope for the best. So far, it wasn't going well.

They had three loungers pulled up alongside the length of the pool on the sunny side. Monica lay between the two operators, hers and Sims's lounger backs elevated as they played their get-to-know-you games.

The deck around the pool was serene. The trees surrounding the deck area were topped by wide, fuzzy branches, densely intertwined. A breeze ruffled the branches, the light filtering through to cast unusual patterns on the duracrete.

Kel thought about activating the sunshade to reduce the temperature to an agreeable amount while he took a nap in its shade. It didn't seem like that was going to happen.

The club was a popular spot for the families stationed in the capital. This morning it was populated with a few wives of company employees and embassy types, also lounging in the sunshine. Young mothers entertained their children in the shallow end of the pool. It was not yet lunch, so the pool would not be packed with older kids for another few hours.

Right now, Monica was the primary irritant preventing Kel from drifting off into a pleasant slumber.

"I mean, you're well-traveled here, Kel. Don't you think things are getting better for the average Q?"

Kel inwardly groaned at being forced to participate in the conversation. Sims had been the picture of attentiveness, smiling and nodding at her every proclamation.

"Yeah, Kel. Don't you think the consortium is doing a bang-up job helping the Q? You know, that's in no small part to Monica's cultural expertise and advice," Sims said, raising his shaded specs to look directly at Kel. The message was clear: *Say something nice to my girlfriend.*

It seemed there was no avoiding it.

"Well, I haven't been back to the western lands for a couple of years. That part of the country was still in a civil war last I was there, so I sure hope things are better for them now that the conflict is settled. As far as life for the Q here on Big M, I couldn't say."

Kel looked over to Sims and saw that he hadn't given the right answer. Sims was shooting death rays at him through squinted eyes.

Kel tried to recover. "I mean, I think it's great how much you care about the people here on Q. The Q have an interesting culture. I really enjoy working with them. The Solar Wind Mining Consortium is lucky to have you."

"That's right! Smart *and* beautiful. *I'm* the lucky one," Sims said, a stupid grin plastered on his face. Monica smiled brightly and gave Sims a kiss on his cheek. Sims's grin grew even bigger.

This is torture, Kel thought. *So much for a nap.*

Kel produced his datalink and started scrolling. If he couldn't take a nap, he might as well find a book to read. He was in the mood for something light. He'd been reading a series about a group of adventurous pioneers who were the first to use hyperdrive to explore the galaxy. The books were fantasy, but a great distraction. In the last story, the characters found a clue about an ancient civilization that had guided the creation of all the habitable worlds in the galaxy. When he finished the last installment, his heroes were on the trail to find the home world of the technologically superior aliens. It was a common theme in many of the serials he'd read or watched as a kid. Kel didn't care. Every fantastic race or survival situation thrust upon the characters engaged him still. Maybe there was a new release he should be searching for now?

"I've got a book you should read, Kel. Especially if you're interested in the Q. I can bounce it to you. It's called *A Partial Investigation into the Sexual Dimorphism,*

Ethnography, and Kinship of a Phasmatodean Culture by Harlan Squibb-Davies.

"Squibb-Davies is probably, no, definitely, the greatest xenoanthropologist of the last two centuries. It's simply the best thing ever written about the Q culture. I'm hoping that I can contribute an update after my time here."

Kel tilted his link toward Monica to show her the title already existed on his device. "Thanks. I've read it. *Partial* is the word. Didn't seem like he actually spent any time among the Q. More like he wrote an interpretation of what he *thought* was the significance of what someone else had in turn told him. It's all derivative. So much of it is wrong. I can't imagine the author spent more than a month on the planet."

"Say! Who needs something cold to drink?" Sims stood up. "Where did that waiter go? I swear I just saw that Q server make her way around the pool area. Isn't that how it always is, though? Just when you need one, they're never around, but any other time, they're right there to interrupt you in the middle of your conversation. I swear, some things are truly universal. Honey, would you like something to drink? Kel and I will go fetch something. I know I'm dying of thirst. C'mon, Kel."

"Well, yes, that would be lovely," Monica said, Sims' distraction successful. "Iced kaff for me. You know what? You boys stay and relax. I'll get us all something. I'm going to see if they have any snacks. I'm getting hungry. Be right back." She blew Sims a kiss and walked to the bar. When she was out of earshot, Sims sat on the edge of her empty lounger next to Kel.

"Hey man, don't be a jerk! She's got a cute friend and Monica's been telling her about you. If you play your cards right, we'll go on a double date tonight. I need this, man. So do you."

Sims had been seeing the young academician once or twice a month, whenever they'd taken short breaks to return to the capital for a brief refit or to get supplies. Monica Andrada was the mining consortium's cultural specialist, and a nice person. Kel felt bad that he'd needled her with his comments about the textbook.

"I'm sorry, man. You're right. She's a great girl. It's not her fault that she hasn't been out with the Q as much as we have. What she's doing with the company to implement the negotiation terms means she's only dealing with the senior clan leaders. But she also doesn't seem to accept that there's a different perspective to be had from working with the warrior caste. Look, man, I know she's trying really hard to do what she thinks is right."

"Thanks, Kel. I hear you, but you're not going to convince her of anything, so don't even try. She's been in school her whole life until this year, and Q is her first posting with the company. She's a little idealistic. And opinionated. She'll figure it out. In the meantime, let's try to enjoy ourselves, okay?"

"Sorry. Just feeling irritable, I guess. To tell you the truth, I think I'm a little worried about how things wrapped up after the hit on the fortress. I'm anxious to hear what's going to come out of the meeting today."

Braley and Bigg were at the embassy, briefing the members of the Republic Ex-Planetary Mission on the events of the operation to dethrone the self-proclaimed Mughal D'idawan. They'd invited Kel along, but he begged off. They both understood. Kel had a sour taste in his mouth after his last mission dealing with politicos. It was Bigg who had suggested that he spend the day relaxing at the club. Poul had been out late the night before, and was still sleeping when Kel and Sims left the team house to go retrieve Monica for a day at the pool.

"Well, I don't think there will be anything to criticize. We accomplished the mission. So, here's how I see it." Sims held up his index finger. "Point A. D'shtaran is firmly in charge as the most powerful mughal on Mukalasa'at, and seems to be squarely in the pocket of the mining consortium. That's going to change the constant territorial shifts caused by the Chachnam's mating practices."

He held up a second finger.

"Point Two. Now the company can lease even more land to grow human crops. They're going to have the ability to sustain more human workers and their families, and the company can bring in more labor."

He held up a third finger.

"And finally, C. The mining of the asteroid belt can continue unabated. It seems pretty straightforward to me. The consortium will be even more profitable, the House of Reason will get their taxes, and another planet will be drawn into the sphere of the Republic. What's not to like? All thanks to a few Dark Ops legionnaires."

Kel chuckled. Sims always did the same gag, mixing numbers and letters when he made an oratory of lists. It was always amusing.

"If only it were that simple. Believe me. With pols, it's never that simple."

"Sometimes it is, Kel. Don't make things out to be more complex than they need to be."

Kel sighed. "It's not just the political creeps or the mining consortium buffoons. Didn't you notice how things seemed different after the operation? The Chachnam have not been the best troops, but they got positively weird after we returned to the garrison."

As they began a new cycle of maintenance and refit for the battalion, the Q troops seemed less eager to follow instructions from their human advisors. The Q had always seemed a bit indolent. After all, they were conscripts. Now the troops and junior NCOs had grown disorderly, even disobedient.

But not the recon platoon. The Disciplined were as professional as ever. They were even eager to start training immediately upon their return from the operation. Kel ordered them to take a week to rest after completing maintenance on all weapons and gear. K'listan was confused by the order.

"Why rest, Sergeant Kel-boss? We have much to learn from you and only a short time to do so. We prefer to remain prepared."

"Yes, K'listan. I understand. But the team and I will be taking a week for rest in the capital. I think you should do the same."

K'listan agreed to allow the commandos some time for rest, but said she and the platoon would continue to train daily during at least part of the time while he was gone. They were eager to learn, and were always appreciative of their time spent with the *tak-craw*. Kel picked the word out while listening to the Disciplined. He finally got K'listan to translate after the voder blanked on it too many times. It was slang for "soft-shell." *They use it endearingly*, he decided.

The Chachnam, on the other hand... not so much for endearing talk about the humans. When Kel corrected some troops for having dirty weapons, they ignored his instructions to clean them, and later that day, still had dirty rifles. Many troops had stopped wearing their voders.

Poul had reported no problems with his heavy weapons section. Maybe it was Kel's imagination?

"Yeah. I did notice that they seem a little lazier than usual," Sims said, lounging in the sunlight. "But so what? We've got, like, maybe another couple of months here? The conscripts probably aren't motivated because they'll be discharged soon to go back to a mating cycle. The battalion has gone through the only major combat op it's going to have while we're here. We just keep doing our thing for the rest of our time here, maybe we get to do a few small ops, and we're out of here. I think we can start spending every weekend in the capital, too. We should make the most of our remaining time."

Kel raised his eyebrows. "Sure. It's just that you weren't there to see the creep show that happened when they executed D'idawan. Just about everything that changed seemed to follow what occurred that morning in the fortress."

"What happened? Who got executed? What changed?" Monica said as she walked up behind them. "The waiter is going to bring us some drinks and snacks." She sat next to Sims. "Now, what happened out there that was so weird?"

Monica knew that Kel and Sims were advisers to the Q military, but did not know they were legionnaires, much less Dark Ops. As far as the mining consortium was concerned, they were "planetary technical advisers," and that had sufficed.

Sims shrugged as if to say, *No harm in telling her.*

Kel nodded. As a high-level employee of the mining consortium, she would be getting most of this information eventually. He launched into a brief description of the actions of the Sun-Loyal Army in tracking down and punishing the renegade battalion and its leader. Kel kept out many of the specifics of their involvement, but when it came time to describe the events of the skirmishes in the tunnels, and then the capture and execution of D'idawan, he gave her all the detail he could remember. It was actually nice to have someone to tell the story to. For her part, Monica finally listened.

"But when we got back into garrison with the troops," Kel continued, "it was more than just a unit finding itself again after seeing combat. It was like the basic dynamics between human and Q had changed. We'd led them on a successful operation, but when it was over, instead of the troops being more simpatico with us, they started acting like they held us in contempt. Yeah, that's how I'd put it. It seemed like contempt."

Monica considered this. "We know so little about the Chachnam tribe and their culture. They are quite a bit different than the Q anywhere else on the planet. Many Q cultures have a history of cannibalism and consuming mates or enemies. The Chachnam are the only ones I've heard of that still practice it, though.

"The Chachnam have made it hard for the company. Not being able to grow human crops anywhere else except Big M really forced the company's hand. The problems the Chachnam have caused the consortium in trying to maintain consistent leases for agricultural have been vexing. Thankfully, that's going to come to an end after D'shtaran's victory and the wider implementation of the accords. But you actually witnessed them murder and eat another mature female?" she asked Sims.

"I didn't," Sims said. "I was elsewhere, securing a section of the canyons that we'd cleared out under the fortress. But most of the team was with Kel. He wasn't alone in seeing it."

"There's no mistaking what happened," Kel said. "A ritual killing. But the troops had already started to act strangely back inside the tunnels. They seemed put off by just being underground."

Monica pursed her lips. "The Q are different from many insectoids. Physiologically, being underground is not natural for them. They derive so much of their energy from the solar-glucose generation cycle that it might even be detrimental to them. Hmmm. I'm going to have to reread our xenobiologist's evaluation of the Q. It's pretty dry stuff, but I'm sure I could get you a copy if you're interested."

"That's kind," Kel replied. "It might help me to make sense of what I saw."

"I'd like to interview you about the operation. I'll eventually get the report from the embassy, but it'll be watered down with a lot of editorializing by diplomats who weren't even there. It'd be great to have an oral history of what you witnessed. You know, you guys have probably spent more time with the Q than the whole anthropology section put together. You could make a really important contribution to our knowledge base. I'm jealous."

"Don't be. What's ours is yours, princess," Sims said, putting his arm around her.

I'm going to be sick, Kel thought, trying not to wince as he forced a smile onto his face. He would never let himself be captured on holo talking about an operation, or anything else for that matter. Sims was laying it on thick.

"What about this other tribal group you mentioned, 'the Disciplined'? There's almost nothing in the research about them. I don't think anyone has ever visited their community. Do you think that it would be possible for me to do that?"

Kel shrugged. "I don't know. I've gotten to know them fairly well the last few months. I admire them. They are quite unlike the Chachnam. They seem the most human to me."

Monica frowned at him. "Careful. Trying to judge them by your own cultural standards can lead to some dangerous assumptions." She was back to being the academic.

"I don't disagree with you." Kel couldn't go into his long history of working with different aliens throughout the edge and the rest of the galaxy, but wanted to. She might have many degrees, but he doubted she had much firsthand experience. "But they place a lot of trust in me, and I in them. Believe me, it's a lot easier to work with a group of aliens carrying implements of war if you can trust them. I suppose I could ask K'listan if a visit to her tribe would be possible."

"Oh, you don't know how grateful I'd be. Thank you!"

"Grateful enough to set him up on a date with your roommate, perhaps?" Sims wiggled his eyebrows.

"That's already done!" she said laughing. "Dinner and drinks tonight, and that's an order."

Kel stood. "In that case, I better get an appetite built up." He'd wanted to get in the pool and do some anaerobic work before it got crowded. He'd planned on doing some crossovers and other exercises to maximize his ability to perform in a no-oxygen state, and the pool was as pleasant a place as any. More pleasant than the confines of a vacuum chamber at least.

"Oh, before I forget. Do you two have plans for tomorrow? I'm taking a hop up to the facility in the morning. Have you ever seen a micro-G ore processing plant? It's pretty fascinating. It's the whole reason we're even here. I'm sure that Phillipe would approve of you joining me on the tour. It'd be no trouble."

"What? Miss an opportunity for your company two days in a row? We'd never dream of saying no," Sims said, planting a kiss on her lips.

"Excellent, then I'll make the call."

"Oba, I need a break. I'll leave you two alone." Kel walked over to the pool. He hopped in the shallow end and broke into smooth, silent strokes. The deep end was without occupants. Kel began to hyperventilate as he prepared to dive below the surface and do as many laps as he could from one side of the pool to the other in one breath. He set a goal of ten laps before surfacing or blacking out, whichever came first.

Either way, I won't have to listen to Sims gushing over his girlfriend. Maybe if I'm lucky, I'll drown.

They dropped Monica off back at her quarters and took the short drive back to the team house. The house was little more than a barracks building with multiple bedrooms sharing a central hall that ended in a common room with a small kitchen. At least it was human construction and not a secreted mud hut. They shared the house with Team Seven, who would be in next week for their own refit period. There was also a decent hotel in D-Town, and Kel had stayed there once when he felt like experiencing a little more comfort than the team house could offer.

They walked into the common room to see Braley and Bigg sitting around the dining table. Poul sat on the one couch, looking the worse for wear.

Kel plopped next to him. "Rough night?"

"No. Great night. I'm planning a repeat. I went out with a couple of engineers from the portside ore processing station. Fun guys. We ended up at a party over at one of the administrator's homes overlooking the bay. Pretty swanky. Anyway, long story short, I won three hundred credits playing tiles and drank them out of their best liquor. I got invited to do it again tonight. You?"

"Great day. Sims took his girlfriend to the pool and I went along to chaperone."

Sims pulled out a chair and sat. "Yeah, yeah. What he didn't tell you is we have hot dates tonight with my girl and her friend. Don't wait up. In fact, we need to get ready for our big night." He stood to head for his room.

"Hold up," Bigg said. "Let's have a quick team meeting before everyone heads to the four arms of the galaxy."

"Sorry, Bigg. How did it go today?" Kel responded for them all.

Braley answered. "It went surprisingly well. The ambassador is a pretty savvy character. Not at all like the typical diplomat. He had a lot of interest in the tactical description of the operation. I thought that was unusual. The Republic Intelligence officer is kind of a reptile, but that's not surprising. The rest of the military-political section that we met with were decent enough. They actually listened to our entire brief before interrupting with questions whose primary purpose was to make the speaker look smarter than the last person to have spoken. Classic political one-upmanship at its most irritating."

Bigg chuckled. "That's about the size of it. But we got a lot of compliments, which surprised me. I didn't know pols could give credit to anyone but themselves. The ambassador was pleased with the outcome and sends his compliments to the whole team."

"Tomorrow we have more of the same," Braley continued, "but with the mining consortium people sitting in. It'll be a rehash of today, but for their benefit."

"So, what do you anticipate?" Sims asked. "Are they going to green-light the buildup of D'shtaran's army? They pretty much bribed her to crush the renegades with promises of more weapons and armor to replace what D'idawan made off with. It's not like they can give it back. We destroyed every operable tank they had."

Braley nodded. "Yeah. It's gonna be time to put up or shut up for the company. Or find a new planet. They promised to bankroll a new army for her. She delivered, so now they're going to have to come through."

Everyone waited for Bigg to answer, anxious for his input.

"My take on the ambassador," he said, "is that he views the process favorably. D'shtaran has showed a lot of flexibility and willingness to cooperate with the Republic and the mining consortium. She's proven her loyalty, or at least, that she understands the concept of self-interest. The company and the Republic have bet on D'shtaran, and her ability to keep the other petty mughals in line."

Braley took up. "There's no directive from the House of Reason against sharing tech with Qulingat't. If the consortium wants to arm their own private native army with better tech, it doesn't seem like the Republic will stop them. Anyway, we'll know more tomorrow."

"So, most likely we'll spend the next two months getting the Sun-Loyal up to speed on new equipment for their army?" Kel inquired.

"Looks like it," Braley agreed. "Some of the rebuilding is already taking place. The company had already bankrolled the Q tank depot on the southern coast to work on replacing the Third Battalion tanks. It's not new tech, just a rollout of more of the same model. I talked to Jaimie. Seven is going down with a company of Roly drivers to take delivery of the new tanks. They're going to form the core of the new Third from the Second Battalion. The Rolies and tanks aren't that different to operate, so, it makes sense.

"Anyway, Bigg and I are the only ones who have to work tomorrow. You guys keep getting some refit time. But don't be surprised if at the end of the week we've got to make an appearance at some embassy shindig held in our honor. The ambassador's personal secretary gave me a warning order before the meeting broke up."

Sims sheepishly spoke. "Bigg, do you mind if Kel and I take a hop up to the orbital ore refinery tomorrow? My girlfriend invited us on a VIP tour."

Bigg looked at Braley, who shrugged. "Sure, hotshot, knock yourselves out. How are you planning to travel? Civvie or armored?"

"That's one of the things we wanted to talk to you about," Kel said. "We could go civvie, but..."

"Go armored," said Braley. "We're not worried about exposure. You're here as technical military advisers. Be yourselves, so to speak."

"Not you, Sims," Bigg added. "Don't be yourself. Go as someone who isn't in heat."

13

Early the next morning, they picked Monica up and drove the winding route east from the capital through the pass between the bay area hills. The other side of the pass opened into the low rolling plains and fields that led to the small company spaceport. As Sims drove and made small talk with Monica, Kel rode in the back and watched the scenery around him.

"So, I didn't know I'd be getting the full fashion show today. Is this what you guys dress like all the time?" she asked, referring to their armor. She'd seen them in full kit when they'd first met during their embed with her provincial development team, but not since. Kel and Sims had put their buckets inside their day packs, and had chosen to travel with their sidearms and to leave their carbines at home.

"Yes. You see, it's a work requirement. Plus, I'd never forgive myself if I wasn't ready to protect you from any dragons or black knights that we encounter. Or at least, Savages and zhee."

"You should be more tolerant. The zhee are a fascinating race. I think there's a lot we could learn from their culture. And the Savages are as much a myth as dragons."

Sims glanced back over his shoulder at Kel, begging him not to retaliate and attempt to correct the young lady in her naïve misconceptions. Kel's ears went hot. He looked out at the fields and concentrated on the feel of the wind in his hair to keep his blood from boiling.

"Well, in that case I'd slay any myth to keep you safe, princess," Sims said and made a kissy face.

"That's my hero," she said, returning the expression with pursed lips.

Kel inwardly groaned.

"Did you have fun last night, Kel?" she asked over her shoulder.

"Yes. I did. I hope we can do it again sometime." He meant it. Tatiana was smart, very nice, and a good listener to boot. She'd been shy at first, and they'd both let Monica and Sims do most of the talking over dinner. It turned out that she was a xenobiologist and a fount of information about the Q and their planet. Kel had peppered her with questions, not just to avoid talking about himself, but because he was genuinely interested in what she had to say. Kel had a curiosity about the way things worked in general and the difficulties of growing human foodstuffs here was one of those mysteries. He thought about their conversation as they passed rows of planted crops.

"I'm not an expert in xenoagriculture," Tatiana had told him, "but I've learned a lot since I've been here. As you know, it's a common problem on many habitable worlds. The best human compatible worlds need no genetic modification for crops to thrive. Not as many as we might like, but the galaxy wasn't created for just humans.

"Some unaltered crops will germinate here. The temperature, water, light spectrum, and soil-oxygen content are adequate to allow the seeds to grow, but still not good enough to produce satisfactory yields. The grasses we've grown, like some of the wheat species, do okay without any modification. But the highest yield species always need modification of the soil to get best results.

"We've had to go with gene-mods on some of the other crops, and in most cases, we have to do both gene modifications of the crops as well as soil mods. Now that we'll have long-term leases on the same arable tracts, we can build richer soil and also start regular crop rotations.

"For the flowering vegetables and fruit trees that need pollination to produce, we're getting around that with some pretty innovative tricks. The climate on Big M is actually pretty conducive to abiotic pollination by wind and rain vectors for some of the crops, like the melons. For the ones that require biotic vectors, it's been a little more difficult. I don't mean to sound like we're doing stuff that's never been done before, but it's always a little different for each xenobiome.

"The agri-gene guys are working on a local insect they think can be modified to pollinate the fruit trees. They'll be sterile, so they won't be able to reproduce or pollute the gene pool of the unmodified native insects. The downside is that we'll be breeding them in the lab indefinitely."

"Isn't that expensive?" he'd asked. "I thought the goal was to minimize the cost of feeding humans here."

Tatiana shrugged. "Yes and no. It's all about yields. Insects are still the most economic pollinators, and even if we have to breed them on a continual basis, it'll be cheaper and more efficient than having robots pollinate each flower individually. We'll get better yields and do so cheaper if we can get insects to do it."

"What about proteins?" he asked.

"That's where the biologic pollinators like the insects come in. If we can get the nut trees to produce, plus the legumes that are already working out, we will have a natural protein mix that will feed humans here indefinitely. That plus the vat grown animal protein and we may not have to import any additional foodstuffs.

"We're lucky here. The Q and humans have a lot of DNA in common and can actually digest many of the same carbohydrates. Of course, the simpler the starch, the more likely it is that we share a common food source. We've found isomers of saccharides in plants here that are identical to human dietary starches and sugars. The Q can digest polysaccharides that are way too much like cellulose for us to digest, but they could be broken down by processing into something we could."

Kel remembered his mother plucking red glowing quiver worms off her flowers. "What about pests? I've seen some of the bugs here. They must have some varieties of pest that'll eat your crops, right?"

"It's a good question. The local insects may learn to eat some of the crops, but so far, it's not an issue. As I'm sure you've seen, most varieties of insects are similar to the Q in that they get a lot of their nutrition from photochemical conversion of sun to carbon sources like glucose through the symbiotic bacteria in their carapaces. They just don't seem to be big competitors for other sources of food."

Kel had seen some amazingly colorful insects. He'd always been taught that in nature, bright colors on animals frequently meant venom or poison. It seemed that did not hold true on Q. Above anything else, their coloration was an indication of their ability to use photosynthesis. That the symbiosis produced a coloration the humans deemed beautiful and interesting was a bonus.

Tatiana saw that Kel had followed her explanations. "So, we could grow some native Q crops and just process them to our needs, and we may end up doing exactly that.

But if we can get real human crops to grow with as little modification as possible, it'll be so cost efficient that at some point, it'd be profitable enough that Q could become a food exporter. That'd be a first for the consortium."

As they drove to the spaceport, they passed Q laborers harvesting what looked like tomatoes from bushy waist-high plants. A human in a lab coat stood by a resting repulsor flatbed and waved at them as they sped by.

Maybe it's possible, Kel thought. It inspired hope in him to think of the Q and humans working and living together. It would be unlike any relationship he could think of on any planet he'd yet visited. Coexistence between races hadn't worked out for the Kylar. He tried not to think about Monica's comments regarding the zhee. How anyone could think that the zhee were an interesting culture was beyond him. A zhee with a kankari would split her in two just for breathing the same air. It was hard not to resent Monica's ignorance. He remembered a quote he'd once read that seemed to apply.

> *The galaxy they never knew*
> *Is like that*

He hoped the rest of the day in her company would be less egregious.

"Phillipe, I heard you can't join me today. I'm disappointed," Monica said to the man in the gray business suit. "At least come meet my friends."

The man rose from behind his desk and extended his hand as he walked toward them. "I'm Phillipe Cardoso, head administrator for Solar Wind Mining on Q. I'm very pleased to meet you gentlemen."

A tall, lean man, Phillipe moved like a former athlete. His sun-aged skin and graying hair suggested that life had ended many years before.

"Likewise, Mister Cardoso," Kel said as he took the man's firm grip.

"I'm sorry I can't join you up at the facility today. I'm on my way into the embassy for some meetings. Congratulations on your victory. I've heard the summary, but I'm really looking forward to meeting your people and getting the details."

Kel and Sims gave modest nods.

Phillipe studied them for a moment, a broke into a gleaming smile. "Monica's finally taking me up on my offer, and here I've got other responsibilities. Such a disappointment. I've been trying to get Monica to go up to the ore refinery ever since she got here. We try to get every member of the team up to see the processing plant at least once. I'm only too glad that you men are able to accompany her in my stead. It's an amazing accomplishment—I'm sure by the end of the day that you'll agree. I'm prouder of it than of anything we've ever done."

Monica touched the executive's arm. "I'm sorry, Phillipe, it's not that I haven't wanted to. We've been so busy in the field working on the negotiations and resettlements that I haven't had time. I think this has been the first two days I've taken off since I've been here. If I'm being honest, I also don't like being in micro-gravity. I get space sick easily."

"That's why you're a great member of the team, Monica. You get the job done and think about yourself last. That's a quality you look for in your line of work, isn't it, gentlemen? Maybe you could use a legionnaire like Monica."

Monica threw Sims a confused look.

Kel spoke up. "Putting the mission first is an admirable trait in many kinds of work, sir."

Phillipe seemed to take the hint. "Indeed, it is. Well, I must be going. It was a sincere pleasure meeting you both. Please take care of Monica; she's very important to us. I've arranged for one of our senior engineers to escort you today. You'll be going up with the shift change and will be met by a guide on docking at Sumendi Station. If I can ever be of assistance, don't hesitate to bounce my secretary. You better get fitted into your vac suit if you're going to make it in time, Monica. Thank you for stopping by."

Once in their speeder again, they followed a company security vehicle around the headquarters complex to the flight line. The security man pointed at a small building near the operations tower where they could park. On the short ride over, Monica grilled Sims.

"What did Phillipe mean when he said, 'legionnaire'? You never said you were military, much less that you were in the Legion."

Sims had it covered. "We're not. We just look that way to some people in our armor. We work as technical consultants. It's mainly fixing gizmos and stuff. It's just that we have to do our jobs in dangerous places sometimes. All this is just for protection."

She considered his explanation. "Well, that's what I thought. I'm glad. You know, the company is always hiring. We're going to need more help with the resettlements and farms. I'm sure we could use people with Q expertise. I could put a word in with Phillipe?"

Kel took over. "That's very kind, Monica. We're on contract for another six months to the Republic Embassy. It wouldn't look very good if we reneged on a contract. That wouldn't impress anyone wanting to hire us."

Monica seemed ready to let it go. "Well, just think about it."

The trans-orbital hopper sat on the flight line. It was not as sexy as a Talon, but was slightly larger, built primarily for transporting passengers to the orbital station and back. Monica told them that the crews worked twelve-hour shifts, three to four days at a time, before getting a three- to four-day rest period planetside. It sounded like the workers had a very accommodating schedule. He'd often heard that work outside of the core paid well. Plenty of days off combined with a lot of credits for your work were an attractive incentive, even to core-worlders.

In the executive flight lounge, an attendant stood at a counter awaiting their arrival. Behind her, a luxurious sitting area surrounded by holo projections on the walls beckoned. Kel caught the scent and saw trays topped with snacks and kaff.

"Miss Andrada and company? Please come with me. We have a vac suit ready for you, ma'am. It will only take a minute to fit you. You won't need to wear the helmet except in a few sections of Sumendi Station where the actual processing is done, but it's a good idea to have it with you at all times. Will you gentlemen be needing... I guess not. Am I right that you're wearing combat armor? That's vac rated, isn't it?" the young woman said, with a lilt in her voice.

"Yes, that's correct," Kel said, impressed. "Have you seen combat armor before?"

"I have. I was in the Republic Navy as a Talon crew chief before I came to work for Solar Wind. I've seen it once or twice. Say..."

Kel didn't let her ask her question. "We'd better get Miss Andrada buttoned up, don't you think? Do you have any Three-V to give her? She gets space sick."

"Oh, thank you for reminding me," Monica said. "Do you have something I can take?"

"Of course, ma'am. We don't have Three-V, but I have an auto-injector with Postremadon. That'll do the trick. Come with me, please."

Kel headed straight to the kaff table and grabbed a pouch. Sims joined him. "Twice in one day someone pegs us as legionnaires and it's not even lunch. Monica's going to have a fit if she finds out."

The lift up was smooth, but Monica wasn't doing well. Usually chatty, she now sat quiet and rigid between the legionnaires on cushioned seats near the front of the aircraft. Behind them, workers and engineers in vac suits were packed into tight rows of narrow seats. Sims snored lightly, having fallen asleep as soon as he'd belted in. He did the same every time they got on an aircraft.

Kel felt sympathy for her. Her manner sometimes irritated him, but he didn't like seeing her in distress. He knew how difficult it was to do something that caused you apprehension.

"How come you guys don't seem to be nervous? He's sleeping and you're eating. How can you eat while we're accelerating?"

Kel chuckled. "I'm hungry." He'd gotten up early to work out and hadn't had time to get a decent breakfast before they had to leave. On the way out of their quarters, he'd grabbed the ration pouch he now sucked on. It was the best he could do.

Monica now sat with her eyes closed and started to breathe rapidly.

"Monica," Kel said. "You're doing fine, really. Hey." She opened her eyes to meet his. "Anyone can do something if they have no fear. Be proud of yourself. Knowing that you're going to be scared, but doing it anyway, takes real courage.

"I'll show you a trick. Breathe with me. Slowly in through your nose, deep into your belly, then slowly again out through your mouth. Put your tongue on the roof of your mouth when you breathe in, like this," he showed her his open mouth. "That's it. Keep doing it like that.

"We're going to stop accelerating soon and it will feel better. They have the gravity decking on, so you won't feel like you're in freefall. It gets easier. Trust me."

She followed his directions and did so for several minutes with her eyes closed. Kel watched her as she performed the routine.

"Good. Now try this. As you take in a deep breath, I want you to tense every muscle in your body and hold the contractions at the top of the breath. Make really tight fists, like this. Now as you slowly exhale, let your body relax. Feel everything go limp. Then do it again."

She nodded and repeated his instructions. She did this for a few repetitions with her eyes closed, then opened them and smiled. "Thanks. That helped. You sound like my dad. He used to tell me things like that. Thanks. I'm going to be all right."

Sims was awake and had been listening to his coaching sessions with Monica. "Yeah, it's just like dancing. Kel's terrified of it, but he does it anyway, even if he shouldn't. That's what I call courage."

Kel immediately regretted telling Sims that he hated dancing. They'd done some last night at the club, but only a few slow numbers. Tatiana had quickly realized that she had to lead, and he'd trodden on her feet only a couple times. How had Sims remembered that small foible he'd shared with him? That'd been months ago.

Stretching, Sims let his arm rest behind Monica and closed his eyes once more. "I see all. I know all. I remember all. Even in my sleep, you can't escape my sight. I'll always be there to embarrass you. Don't forget that, tough guy."

The ship settled against the docking ring and in a minute they all unbuckled and stood. Kel and Sims gathered their daypacks and watched as the miners made their way through the open hatch and out to the docking gantry. They fell into place at the end of the line, and were the last ones off the ship.

Standing at the foot of the ramp was a man in a vacuum suit.

"I'm Beck Alford, senior mine engineer. Are you Miss Andrada?"

They made introductions all around, the engineer noting the legionnaires' dress and sidearms.

"Expecting trouble today, gentlemen?"

"You never know," Sims answered. "But seriously, we needed vac suits anyway, it just seemed to make more sense to wear our armor for the tour."

Monica interceded. "Our guests work for the embassy as technical advisers to the Q military. They just assisted in the last phase of the negotiations to secure the company its new farmlands."

The man raised his eyebrows. "Wow, that's great. I'm going to get to bring my family in a few months if everything goes according to plan. Thank you. Well, are you ready to take the tour of Sumendi? We're pretty proud of her. Have you ever been on a major orbital station before?"

Kel answered for both of them. "Oh, you know, about as much as the next guy." Being vaguely evasive was a way of life for an operator. Kel knew he shouldn't take so much pleasure in frustrating people's attempts at making small talk, though.

"Ah. I see. Well, why don't we start on the observation deck and I can give you an overview of the operation. Follow me."

They left the docking area and followed Mr. Alford through large, well-lit corridors, workers coming and going all around them.

"We've only been fully operational for a year," the man said as they walked. "Everything has occurred in stages, and we're about ready to move on to the next phase of development. We started with an asteroid that we towed into geosynchronous orbit and began hollowing out as the original worksite two years ago. The station really took shape as we added the graphene constructed habitats and went from there."

Kel had seen the massive orbital grow on the holo feed during their approach. Although every bit as large as

Orion Station, rather than being a hub for commerce and transportation, it was solely dedicated to the processing of ores gathered from the asteroid belt. The original asteroid that they'd used as a base was gigantic, easily a kilometer in length. It was covered with evidence of construction protruding from all points along the oblong rock.

"It's enormous," Monica gushed. "A bright spot in the sky over Diakasa'at day or night. It's almost a moon."

"Yes, ma'am. It certainly is. Even at twenty-six thousand kilometers above the equator, it makes an imposing feature in the sky. As I was saying, the first phase of construction was establishing the framework of Sumendi and getting the solar arrays and fusion plant constructed to power everything."

The men and women they passed were immersed in their duties. Everyone seemed cheerful, and none gave the party a second glance.

Whatever they're doing, Kel thought, *it must be interesting.*

Mr. Alford kept talking. "The first asteroids were brought from the belt by haulers one at a time. Virtually all of the first materials we processed were used to expand the station into what you now see. To get the station built we initially did more manufacturing than we do now. While we still make some finished products, we mainly process and purify the ores into constituent elements for use by other manufacturers."

"What about the processing station at the north end of the bay?" Kel asked. He'd seen the massive dropships making controlled splashdowns off the coast. Tugboats guided the huge floating ships into the north bay before lifting off again to repeat the process.

Alford smiled. "Space manufacturing lets us do a lot of things better and more economically than we could under gravity, but some things are still best done planetside. Let me show you the whole scheme."

They made their way to the observation deck. They passed through a wide air lock that had the inner and outer doors open, and into an expansive ceilinged room. A dining facility sat at their left, with tables and lounging areas spread around the multilevel sunken floor. A holo projection dominated the space above the center of the room, showing a schematic of the mining operation. The wall opposite them was basically a large transparent viewing panel ten meters across. A few miners on break sat in front of the window, sipping pouches and admiring the view. The bright albedo of Q shone below them. Outside in the distance, a field of multicolor flashing lights floated on line with the horizon of the station.

"Of course, the holo is not to scale, but it serves to show the relationships of all the moving parts of our operation." Alford pointed up at the holo above their heads.

"As you know, the asteroid belt is the next orbit out from Q. Whereas we used to have haulers driven by human crews manually select and ferry the rocks to us here for processing one at a time, we could never keep up with our capacity to process by doing so now. The field teams select asteroids by size and composition, and attach ion thrusters to ones that are suitable and can be timed for a transfer orbit.

"Those crews work the longest rotations. They're out in the belt for thirty days before they come back in for a break groundside. Those crews make sure we have a constant supply of rocks heading to the parking lot to await processing," he said, pointing through the viewing window to the distant forest of small blinking lights.

"They move at a low delta-v, and it's taken us about a year to where we now have a pretty much constant chain of rocks moving from the belt into the holding pen."

"Why so slowly? Why not rocket them here as fast as possible?" Monica asked.

"Economics. It would be too expensive to run a fleet of haulers back and forth shuttling rocks to us. We could move them faster, but it would be more expensive, and dangerous. Rocks speeding this way could cause a lot of damage if there was a bot error. It takes a lot of energy to slow something down which is that large and moving that fast. The ion thrusters don't create huge velocities, but are cheap and reusable. They use material from the rocks they're driving for fuel. They accelerate the rocks, then slow them down as they approach. At a low velocity, the tugs have no problem intercepting the rocks on their way in, and the crews just have to nudge them into place. They take a little bit of corralling by the tug crews on a regular basis to keep them penned, but they aren't in the pens all that long before we process them anyway."

Kel looked up at the holo to see the representation of the station in orbit around Q, with the orbits of Q and the asteroid belt highlighted around the helios. Small icons showed the position of the field teams in the belt, and a dotted arcing line showing the path of the asteroids to the station's holding pen outside. Kel assumed every blinking light along the path was another asteroid on its journey from its home to the ore processing station.

Mr. Alford broke their reverie after allowing them a few moments to marvel at the holo. "Come on, I'll show you where the processing takes place."

They followed him back through the lock and deeper into the station.

"We're going to go into a micro-G area of the station which is also under vacuum. We'll need to put our helmets on when we get there. Miss Andrada, I understand you haven't had much time in a vac suit. I'll help you activate your grav-boots if you're not familiar with them. You'll get the hang of walking in them in no time. It's pretty natural."

"Thanks. I'm kind of nervous about it. I've never done it before."

"I think you'll have plenty of help from your guests. I bet they know their way around micro-G enviros, huh?"

Sims grinned. "We will absolutely be close by to help. I won't let you out of my grasp, Monica."

She smiled back at him weakly. Her nervousness showed.

They approached a lock station where several workers stood, putting on helmets and running systems checks on their vac suits. Sims helped Monica put her helmet on and ran a check on her suit diagnostics as Kel retrieved his bucket from his day pack. Large signs surrounding the lock said:

DANGER
Entering Vacuum and micro-G work environment.
Take all precautions

Other signs said:

BUDDY CHECK ALWAYS
COMPLACENCY KILLS

A small caricature showed a worker in a vac suit with oxygen escaping a tear in the suit, hands at the neck in the universal sign of asphyxiation. Kel nodded approvingly at the warning signs. Safety could never be taken for granted. The ways they did things in the Legion were a result of procedures and methods that were continually re-evaluated. An injury or death in combat was often unavoidable. The same outcome in training was unacceptable. He appreciated the formal display demanding attention to safety. Complacency truly did kill.

A green panel lit up and the outer door of the lock opened. Alford led the way and Sims held Monica's hand as they all crowded into the chamber. The lock cycled and they made their way through the inner lock out onto the floor of one of the processing bays.

"This is where it starts," Alford said as he turned to face them. "The tugs deliver the rocks there," he pointed to a gigantic bay open to space. There was an asteroid about fifty meters across being manipulated by robot arms into the bay, the lights of the departing tug disappearing into the darkness. A human worker monitored a holo in front of her as she walked along with it, guiding the huge boulder through the bay toward a chamber to their left.

"The ores are separated by several processes, culling the different constituents during the run. Come on and we can go to an observation deck and I'll show you."

They followed him up some stairs to a catwalk above that ran the length of the huge bay. Looking down into the bay were rows of large chambers, most of them containing rocks about the size of the one heading in now.

"This bay handles rocks about seventy-five meters or less in diameter. We have a few larger chambers for bigger or irregularly shaped ones. The really big ones, we first have to bust them up outside with blaster cutters. We lose some material that way, but not so much to be a concern. It's worthwhile to transport the larger ones because the cost is essentially the same as to move the smaller ones here from the belt."

He pointed at one of the chambers as the doors closed. "The solar panels power everything else on the station but these. The fusion plant powers our electrostatic levitation furnaces. The ores are superheated and allowed to diffuse in the chambers under micro-G. As they cool, a lot of the magnetic elements are easily separated and removed by their relative attractive forces. As things continue to cool, we apply a gradually increasing gravity field, and things fall out of the gravity suspension by their different weights, and are removed. The gas vapors liberated during the process are saved, and the oxygen is used to feed the atmosphere of the station."

"What constituent elements are you refining from the ores?" Kel asked.

"One of the reasons we're here is because of the richness of the ores from the asteroid belt. Gold is pretty easy. It almost always exists in its elemental form and takes just about no processing. The nickel, iron, and copper are all in high concentrations and are also pretty easily separated out.

"The really rare metals are why we're here, though. The belt is rich in promethium and most of the lanthanide metals. As far as we know, we have ores with the highest concentration of promethium of any mining operation. It's an essential element for charge packs, so it's probably the most profitable of what we're processing here."

Kel understood. Charge packs were an important part of everyone's daily life, none more so than a legionnaire. Kel fingered the pistol at his side as he considered this.

"Not much else to see here. Let's go back down and I'll take you to one of the sections where we still do some manufacturing."

He led them to another area of the massive micro-G work bay to show them a foundry. They stood on another catwalk looking down at an open furnace.

"By a similar process to what you just saw, we produce iron alloys. As you know, the amount of heat energy required to alloy several elements together is a lot lower in orbit because of how well the constituents diffuse in the low gravity. We produce very pure impervisteel up here. The cost would be crippling to manufacture it planetside and then lift it into space to a shipyard."

They could actually see the processes as they occurred. Robotic bucket loaders dumped materials into a huge crucible as it was heated cherry red by the plasma jets surrounding it. Another hemisphere joined the crucible to seal it from above and it began rotating as the plasma jets heated the sphere evenly. A technician on the floor watched a holo showing an indicator of the gravity force in the chamber as it reduced and the process continued.

After several minutes, the indicator showed a rise in gravity. Soon the crucible divided and the molten material poured into a casting ingot and was rolled away by bots. They moved farther along the catwalk to an adjacent bay overlooking a rolling mill. The ingot was removed from its mold and then was worked back and forth through the mill as it was reduced in thickness with each pass until it was moved by the bots out of sight.

Alford looked at them quizzically. "I don't want to tell you more than you want to know. If I get too technical or boring, please stop me."

Sims spoke up. "No, sir. I know we'd all really appreciate you continuing. It's truly fascinating."

Alford smiled back at Sims's sincere curiosity. "Very well. Tempering is pretty economical. We just expose the product to the vacuum of space to lock in the grain structure, which is very difficult to do uniformly in an atmosphere. We can also manufacture much larger sections than you ever could dirtside. We can forge pieces to specified dimensions, so the shipyards buy the plate from us ready to install."

Kel had a question. "So, you said you don't do a lot of manufacturing up here anymore. Why is that?"

"We process so many materials into immediately usable form, it's already hard to keep up with the demand to supply purified raw material to other manufacturers. We don't want to compete with our customers for the same materials. We may expand to produce other things as the facility grows. Isolinear crystal cable will probably be our next venture. There are others. I don't know if you noticed on the big holo, but there are icons up there for three transports lined up to take on raw materials for destination elsewhere in the core."

"What do you process at the plant on the bay?" Sims asked. The large complex sat on the north side of the bay in the capital. Between it and the huge floating ore carriers that regularly floated off the coast, it was a center of attention.

"Ah, glad you asked. Remember I told you about the rare earth metals we get? They need to be processed dirtside. It takes a combination of electrolysis and chemical means to separate out those elements from each other, and that requires a lot of water. It wouldn't be economical to do up here. So, those big floating dropships you see in the harbor from time to time? We load those with the rare earths and send them down to Q.

"Come on. They're loading one now. I can show you."

They followed a path around the inner walk of the foundry to another bay open to space where one of the huge carriers sat. The hull had a wide v-shape like a watercraft.

"The rare earth carriers hold a massive amount of product. Very heavy. No ship could produce the repulsor power it would take to land such a mass at a spaceport, and even if it could, the load would simply collapse the ship under its combined weight. The only place they can land is in the water, and as I'm sure you've seen, it's kind of a controlled crash."

Buckets ran along gantries that filled hoppers at the top of the long ship with the powdery gray mixture of the rare earth metals.

"It takes about a month to get enough rare planetary product to ship down for processing. Even then, that is not a lot of material mass. Most of the mass is other processed products that can be used planetside. The Q are customers too, and the need to mine materials on Q has decreased dramatically since we can supply them with refined ores cheaper and cleaner than what they can make on the surface.

"The skirt you see around the rim," he said, pointing to the contracted tube circling the ship, "is inflated with inert gasses recovered from the refining processes. The skirt is inflated during reentry and buffets the ride down and also helps to float the ship. During lift, they collapse it to reduce resistance. Pretty slick, huh?"

Kel and the others nodded in agreement. Monica had said little. Kel thought it might be a result of anxiety at being in the constrictive vac suit. Instead, she was wide-eyed and clearly engaged with what they were seeing, her discomfort apparently subdued.

"I've talked to the pilots," Alford continued. "They tell me the landings aren't as bad as they appear. The huge water plumes are impressive, but apparently aren't a good indicator of how rough the landing is." Kel had seen one of the landings and it was striking to see something so large in an atmosphere, much less to see it landing on the water.

"There's not another shift change for several hours. Why don't you take a meal and enjoy the view until then?" He led them back out of the processing area and to the observation deck again. "This is where I must leave you. It was a pleasure."

They all thanked him. It had been worth the trip. It was indeed as impressive as Mr. Cardoso had led them to believe.

Kel had a question. "Mr. Alford, has there been any attempt to train the Q for work on Sumendi Station?"

"Funny you should ask," Alford's eyebrows shot up. "Yes. We did try. They don't have many capable space engineers or personnel who can work in micro-G, even though they are classed as one of the spacefaring races. They manufacture their own vac suits and maintain quite a few orbitals. We did hire Q engineers on a trial basis. We had to let them go."

"Why is that?" Monica asked.

"None of them would work a full shift. We kept finding them basking on the surface of the asteroid. One of them went into a kind of psychosis and removed her vac suit. Seems she was enjoying the solar radiation so much, she forgot she was in space."

Monica slept on the drop back to the spaceport and again on the ride back into the capital. It had been a long day and even Kel felt tired. Sims spoke in the same tones he would use on a recon. "Hey buddy, I'm going to drop you off at the team house. I'll take Monica home. Probably just stay over there tonight."

They both rode in the front seat as Monica slept in the back. "She's got to work tomorrow so I'll be back early."

"Sure," Kel assured him. "No prob. Hey, she did a good job today. For her first time in a vac suit, she did well."

"I can remember feeling kinda claustrophobic the first time I got into armor."

"Yeah, I heard they almost bounced you out of leej basic and sent you to the Republic Army."

"That's a lie!" Sims said, breaking out of his whisper.

"Claustrophobic, huh?" Kel gibed. "Who'da thunk it?"

"Hey, I said 'kinda.' Once. The first time. I'm obviously not claustrophobic."

"All right, all right. I'll find a weakness to exploit yet."

"Don't bet on it, mister dance shoes."

Kel thought about the events of the day while he lay in bed. He was glad he had the opportunity to see the ore processing station. It was easy to take for granted the everyday miracles that went on around him, and the skill and education it required of the people who made such amazing things a reality. It always fascinated him when he considered the diversity of occupations in the civilian galaxy.

He was a master at what he did, but he didn't have any kind of education or skills outside of his training in the Legion. What could he do that was of use to the galaxy at large? Could there even be a life for him outside the Legion?

14

The ambassador's obligatory party was slated to happen the night before Team Three's return to the First Battalion garrison. They all secretly hoped their return would predate the event, but the timing ensured they could not use that as an excuse. Apparently, the success of the meeting at the embassy with the head of the Solar Wind Mining Consortium, Mr. Cardoso, had resulted in a change of venue from the Republic Club to the director's estate overlooking the bay.

"Too bad it wasn't next week," Kel said to his squad mates as they gathered in the common room before starting the drive toward the estate. "Then Dari and Team Seven would be there in our stead to bask in all the glory."

"Free food. Free drinks. Female companionship in abundance." Poul affected an accent from a holo-drama about a family of hereditary monarchs. "I rather think they should throw a soiree in our honor every time we're in town, what. It would bring joy to the peasants, seeing their betters in public."

Poul brushed lint off his dress tunic, a very dark shade of purple. "Besides, aren't you looking forward to seeing your new girl before we go back out?"

"I'd hardly call Tatiana 'my girl.' We've only gone out twice, and it was in the company of Sims and his girlfriend. She's just a nice date. Very smart. I've learned a lot about the Q listening to her."

The four of them had made a trip to the beach the evening before to swim and watch the sun set. The water was very alkaline and had an unpleasant odor, but was entertaining because it took no effort to remain afloat in the hyper-mineral solution.

"Kel's just worried there'll be music, which may lead to dancing," Sims teased.

Kel chose to ignore him but vowed to double his efforts to find his teammate's weakness.

"Also, Kel, nice variety in your wardrobe there. Own any color besides black?" Sims flayed him from another front.

Kel knew his civilian dress tunic was unappealing, as it was the same color as his Legion dress silks. He selected the clothing for its comfort rather than flair.

"Just smile and make polite conversation. It'll be over before you know it," Bigg told them. "Poul's got the right idea. Eat, drink, and be merry, for tomorrow it's back to a mud hut. And don't do anything stupid."

Braley came out of his room and joined the conversation without missing a beat. "We won't have to worry about Sims. He'll be glued to his girlfriend. The rest of you, try to not cause any incident that would make us persona non grata with the embassy. Dark Ops may get you a new identity, but I'd prefer to keep my own, thank you very much."

There was a story about a Dark Ops leej who had caused a minor incident at an embassy event. When liquor flowed, as it often did at social gatherings, inhibitions lowered. This particular operator had experienced a tense working relationship with one of the diplomats, and their mutual dislike came to a head. When the diplomat called the leej a "slack-jawed Savage," the operator, who'd patiently suffered through many of the diplomat's poor decisions, was at a moment of weakness.

And anyway, it was unlikely that the operator would have actually *dropped* the man out that second-story window. Dangling the kelhorn by his ankles made the point well enough. The diplomat overreacted—it was never in any real danger. Who wants to deal with that kind of paperwork?

As the story went, the operator was due to leave at the end of the week anyway. Had the insult been given during the middle of the man's mission, he might have shown more restraint. As the incident occurred at the end of the mission, his subconscious, guided by the alcohol, had given the green light to his volition to scare the life out of the pompous ass of a diplomat.

Kel's theory about being an operator was to be invisible whenever possible. He could never imagine doing such a thing, but then again, he didn't drink. Not much to speak of, anyway. Scuttlebutt had it the operator was still in Dark Ops, but did have to use a cover name when working other planetary security missions. Apparently, Colonel Hartenstein, the DO commander, had some sympathy for the man.

Who hasn't wanted to dangle a politician out a window at some point or other? Kel reasoned.

But Bigg's point was well taken. Team Three had a spotless record in DO. Best to keep it that way.

Phillipe Cardoso stood with his back to the open veranda, the bay behind him reflecting moonlight across the gentle waves. "I'd just like to say a few words of welcome and thanks to our many guests in attendance. First off, my thanks to Ambassador Grealy for allowing Solar Wind and me to host this event. The ambassador and his staff had the event planned, but kindly allowed us to move the venue as a way of showing gratitude for the excellent work done by the embassy and the diplomatic staff. Thank you so much for all you do."

Phillipe started the applause and the gathered crowd joined in.

"The events of the last few months that have propelled the mission of Solar Wind here on Qulingat't to the heights of success we are now enjoying, is due to the tireless work and professionalism of the Ex-Planetary Diplomatic Mission as well as our own dedicated employees. The working relationship that has been fostered between us under the guidance of Ambassador Grealy is unparalleled in my experience, and again I say thank you."

More applause followed as Phillipe gestured for the ambassador to take the dais with him and to say a few words of his own.

Sims spoke quietly through the side of his mouth, "Pretty posh place, don't you think?"

"Yeah," Kel agreed. "Not sure who lives more lavishly, diplomats or company executives."

On the slope of a hill overlooking the bay, the stately mansion looked like it came straight out of a core resort holo, albeit one built by Q mandibles. Multiple terraces were excavated into the hillside, buttressed by thick walls and columns, leaving the mansion open to the bay. The living spaces were dug into the slope, joined by staircases composed of transparent steel, an off-world design touch, no doubt manufactured by the foundry in orbit above them.

From the podium, the ambassador made pleasantries, returning compliments to Phillipe, while Kel and Sims mumbled to each other.

"I'm ready to eat," Kel said, making small talk to avoid having to listen to the head diplomat's remarks.

"It's about that time," Sims whispered. "I'm starving."

The two stood between Monica and Tatiana, each with a drink in hand. Kel's held water as the other three had some type of imported beverage that Sims assured him was rare and therefore expensive.

"You're missing out. As usual. This is the good stuff, man," Sims said as he sipped the pale green liquid. "Poul is already on his third glass."

Kel stole a glance at Poul, farther back in the crowd, surrounded by several women dressed in high fashion, much as were the two ladies on either side of them. Poul caught his glance, and closed his eyes as though falling asleep. Kel nodded ever so slightly; this whole event was a bore.

"I would be remiss," Phillipe continued, "without extending my admiration and respect for the men who put themselves at such risk to ensure the victory of our partner on Mukalasa'at, the Mughal D'shtaran. They faced unbelievable danger. It is due to their bravery and expertise that we are moving forward as rapidly as we now are."

Tatiana's hand slipped into his. Kel returned her smile, feeling flushed as she admired him. Monica smiled brightly up at her date. Sims's face looked anything but amorous.

He knew what Sims was thinking. *He isn't going to blow our cover just to...*

"I'm of course speaking about the brave men of the Legion who..."

Tatiana pulled her hand away. The smile disappeared from Monica's face.

"What in the name of Oba is he saying?" Sims whisper was more of a growl.

"Captain Yost, please make your way forward and say a few words," the director said, leading the audience in applause once again.

Poul joined Kel and leaned over to whisper, "The guy's trying to score points by outing us to his underlings. The big important man has the Legion doing his bidding. You know he was instructed to keep our presence here confidential. What a jerk."

Without a glance at the legionnaires, Monica took Tatiana's hand and pushed through the crowd.

"Let them go, man," Kel whispered when Sims moved to follow them. "We'll find them later."

Braley made his way from the crowd up to the dais, looking stern. He took Phillipe's hand and shook it with a few small pumps; the director winced. Kel had seen their team leader do one finger pull-ups to prove a point. It was an item of contention as to who was strongest on the team—everyone had one attribute that they thought was superior to the rest of the team—but no one questioned Braley's grip strength as being the best. He could have crushed the older man's hand effortlessly.

"Thank you, Mister Cardoso. I'll just say that we serve at the pleasure of the House of Reason. Thank you." Speech over, Braley stepped down and cut his way through the crowd, Bigg following close behind.

"Let's go," Poul told them.

Sims didn't move with them as he strained to see where Monica and her roommate had vanished into the crowd.

"Come on, man. We'll find them later," Kel assured his friend. "It'll be all right. We gotta link up with Bigg and Braley first."

Sims shrugged and moved to follow as the mining consortium director continued to speak. People holding drinks parted out of their way, some smiling in appreciation, both men and women patting them on the shoulders as they passed.

They found Braley and Bigg standing alone on a darkened veranda, Phillipe's speech droned on in the large room behind them. "The Q are being brought into a new era of prosperity thanks to our efforts..."

Braley took a long pull on his drink.

"I know, men. I'm mad too. But no harm done. We aren't here on a covert mission. Yes, any aspect of our identity is supposed to be shielded from official use. Period. Mister Cardoso simply ignored his brief from the embassy. There's nothing to be done about it. My recommendation is we stay and not make a scene. What do you think, Bigg?"

"I agree, boss. Just play cool, keep being friendly, don't retaliate against any of the company people, especially Cardoso, and just do what you'd always do to deflect any inquiries. Smile and nod. Personally, I'm going to try to bankrupt the company by eating and drinking all I can. Everyone good?"

Poul nodded. "Yeah. I'm good. I'm going back to my harem to see if I can capitalize on my newfound fame. I also have a feeling that the tiles are going to be dropping in my favor later tonight. I plan to pad my retirement account off these company types some more. Getting to play with a real-life legionnaire might draw some easy players."

Kel nodded. "Yeah. I'm good. I think I'm stag the rest of the night, though."

"You and me both," Sims sighed.

Session over, they went back into the hall and eyed the train headed for the buffet. Kel stayed with Sims, who kept scanning the crowd for Monica.

"It's not like she wasn't going to have to learn who you were sooner or later if you were going to get serious, man. The civilian technician cover is pretty light stuff. I've had to do it all under deep official cover before. That gets tricky when you meet people you care about," Kel told him, drawing on recent experience.

"I know. It's just that Monica has been good about not probing too much into my experience and background, but you've heard her. She has that general distaste for the military. Typical academic. I was really starting to like her. Ah, who am I kidding? Where would it go, anyway? C'mon, let's get some grub."

Kel noticed Tatiana standing by herself near the entrance, looking in Kel's direction. "Hey, I'll catch up. Let me talk to Tatiana and I'll get a read on the situation."

He made his way over to where Tatiana stood. Alone. She twitched an anxious smile as he walked over.

"Hi, Kel."

"Hi. Are you okay? Are you leaving?"

"Yeah. We're going to go. Monica is kind of upset."

"Sorry. I wish I knew what to say, it's just..."

"No. It's okay. Look, I knew you were some kind of military guy, or had been in the past, or something. Who else would be a military adviser working for the Republic? We're not stupid. We thought you might be Republic Intelligence, or something. I understand that some things related to the embassy are sensitive. I just... I just didn't know you were a legionnaire."

"Is that so bad?"

"No. It's only that, I don't know, I've never really known any legionnaires before. I've just always heard that they were fanatics."

Backtracking, she hastily said, "Sorry. I know you aren't a fanatic, it's just, well, Monica is upset. She really liked Sims and, I guess she's freaked out right now."

"Well, Sims is hurt. I can tell. He really likes Monica. We're leaving tomorrow to go back out into the field. Maybe tell her, I don't know, tell her it isn't Sims's choice to share with people who he is and what he does."

Tatiana frowned. "That doesn't *change* who he is or what he does."

"No. It doesn't. But what is it that you think we do that's so egregious?" Kel was starting to feel less like making a case for his friend, and was more curious to know how Tatiana saw him.

"You kill people."

Kel was stupefied. "There are people in the galaxy who need killing. You are safe from Savages and zhee and all the forces that want to see everyone in their silvene towers dead, safe because of people like me and Sims."

Tatiana looked at the floor. "I have to go. Take care of yourself, Kel."

Then she was gone.

Kel wanted to feel mad. He wanted to care. Instead, he just felt pity for the two women. Both highly educated. Privileged. Naïve.

I've done nothing wrong and there's nothing for me to feel guilty about.

Kel walked over to the buffet line where Sims waited.

So, why do I feel bad?

They ate standing around in small groups, attempting to feed themselves gracefully while holding their plates in one hand. Kel was failing. Trying to manage the mechanics of eating while standing was annoying. He'd just filled his plate for a third time when he spotted an opening at one of the high-top tables, and quickly made his way to a clear spot where he could set his plate down and actually eat with both hands.

Several other attendees arrived with him to do the same, and they all smiled to each other politely and exchanged brief greetings as they crowded to place their plates around the table. He recognized the embassy's regional security officer and her husband. He'd met her a few months ago when they arrived on Q, but since he had avoided the embassy, had not seen her since. He thought her name was Reynolds.

"Hi, Mister Turner. Allow me to present my husband, Dillon. He works in the economic development office."

"Kel. Nice to meet you," he said between bites. The RSO had not reintroduced herself, so Kel was still not certain of her name.

"And this is our friend, Chetan. He's a manager for Solar Wind. Dillon and he have been working together on the rollout of the new partner programs between the company and the Q."

Kel tried to make polite conversation with the RSO's husband—what was his name, again? He didn't want to alienate anyone by seeming unfriendly.

"So, how is the development going?" he asked. A general enough question.

The man—was it David?—took a drink before saying, "It's going really well, I think. Chet here has been a great help. I thought we were on an ambitious timetable, but now it looks like we will be proceeding without delays, thanks to you guys."

"Glad to hear it," Kel replied. "What, ah, what sort of programs are you rolling out?"

The other man took over. "We are working to integrate the economies of the locals with the human expatriate community to help tie us together. We're working to convince as many of the local farmers as we can to try to grow human crops. What we'll be paying for produce will be far above what the Q farmers would receive for the crops they currently grow for local consumption."

David—no, Dillon—took over again. "The company is having great success selling materials to local manufacturers. The orbital facility produces better refined materials than they produce themselves. It's already obvious to the Q manufacturing sector how beneficial the new material source above them is. As we branch out into things that can be produced in micro gravity, like isolinear cable, the first market will likely be right below us, here on Q."

"That's the kind of talk I like to hear." A hand clasped Kel's shoulder. Phillipe had walked up behind him to join their conversation. "Mister Turner, I tell you, you have no idea how much the Q are going to benefit now that the way has been paved to start trading in earnest. And with a team of the Republic's finest like these great people, there'll be no stopping us."

Kel swallowed his bite of food as he forced himself to remain relaxed. He despised someone touching him from his blind spot. "I certainly hope so, Mister Cardoso." It was the only polite thing Kel could think of to say as he fought his hypervigilance. Throat punching the person who startled him would violate Bigg's dictum to stay cool.

"Please. Phillipe, *Phillipe*. No need to be so formal. How did you enjoy your visit to Sumendi Station? I haven't had the chance to follow up with you. Wasn't it everything I said it would be?"

"Yes, I was truly impressed. Thanks again for the opportunity."

"You're most welcome, and I assure you the pleasure is ours. Tell me, any thoughts to share after seeing our operation?"

Kel looked at the Q servers moving about the party goers. "The technology involved is simply brilliant. Phenomenal would be the word for it."

"Exactly. It just overwhelms, doesn't it?"

"Yes. But—" Kel paused. He wasn't sure how best to communicate his next thought.

"Please. Continue. I didn't get where I am by being afraid of criticism. Be honest with me."

"All right. You may have a negotiated settlement with D'shtaran for now, but I think your real challenge is going to be maintaining it."

Phillipe's eyebrows raised. "Please. Tell me more."

"I've worked with many cultures, human and alien. I've seen insurgencies, and I've implemented counterinsurgencies. I've gotten to know a lot about the Q on two major regions of this planet over the last several years. Mukalasa'at is quite different from the rest of Q. I don't pretend to be an expert. You have many of those. I simply have doubts about the Chachnam's ability to integrate into the company's plans for Big M."

There. He'd said it.

"What do you mean? I would argue that things are going smoothly, especially since the mughal's consolidation of power. She has her own best interest, and the interests of her people, at heart. I would expect that of any rational being, human or alien. We've found her to be a skillful negotiator. We've gotten where we are by achieving a reasonable agreement."

"I don't disagree. However, alien minds are alien. Even humans as a species are not homogeneous. On Big M, the Q are as tribal a culture as any I've ever seen. We've had a lot of challenges working with them. What I'm saying is that just because we've destroyed the most obvious opposition to the changes you want in the Chachnam's traditional practices, don't count on it staying that way."

"And why is that?" Phillipe asked, his face flushing pink. His claim to be fearless of criticism was ringing hollow for Kel.

"Why do you suppose D'idawan went rogue and declared herself a mughal?"

"Why does anyone make a power play?"

The rest of the table leaned in, as if to watch a trexxo match.

"Possibly for power. Or perhaps, partly for power. She didn't have such a cult of personality that she could persuade an entire battalion of troops to desert just because she asked them to. No, there was enough sentiment against the Mutual Prosperity Accord that it took little in the way of convincing to get the battalion to desert with her."

Kel pushed out a breath, then plunged forward. "It wasn't a simple power play. I think she was driven to do so by her breeding caste. Call it whatever you want: culture, religion, custom, or habit... asking the Chachnam to change their way of life so that a few at the top could benefit by company handouts would not be popular with the masses. We may think of the Q as insects, but there's little about them I've found to remind me of a hive collective. The Chachnam are a tribe. And tribal leaders aren't monarchs or queen bees. They're leaders because the tribe allows themselves to be led by them. And when the tribe decides the leader isn't doing the will of the tribe... then they're no longer leader.

"D'idawan declared herself mughal because her tribe was opposed to the changes encouraged by the MPA, and so was she. D'shtaran may be more powerful and have a longer history leading the tribe, but to think that she holds a hegemony over the breeding caste would be foolish. And if they become dissatisfied with the changes, they'll push someone else to declare themselves mughal and revolt again. The seeds of their discontent are being planted as we speak."

Phillipe gave a condescending smile. Kel knew one when he saw it. "You're an expert in discontent and how to exploit it, I see. Work the problem with me from the other direction. If you were trying to release the pressure valve on that plasma conduit and prevent that discontent from boiling over into another rebellion, what would you recommend?"

Condescending or not, Kel appreciated the astute question. "Okay. You've started with the farms. What you're trying to do is an excellent idea, and I hope it comes to fruition. But by itself it's not going to win over the breeding caste. Only a small portion of them farm."

Phillipe nodded, clearly interested now.

Kel went on. "The breeding caste's power is derived primarily from the land they bring to the collective by successfully attracting mates. When that's gone, what power do they have? A few cycles alternating between breeding and army service is their path to senior position, either in the army, or in their family collective. How will they secure a better future for themselves when that path is taken from them?"

Phillipe seemed less patronizing as he asked the next, stroking his chin. "So, we need to be working harder to win over the breeding caste rather than concentrating on the mughal?"

Kel nodded affirmatively. "D'shtaran is a realist. She knows the Republic and the humans aren't going to go away. She knows she isn't strong enough to win a war against us. She made a bargain with you to make herself more powerful, with you betting that she could keep her people in line. So far, she has. Now you must pay your debt to her and honor the agreement. So, you upgrade her army. When her own army decides to overthrow her, like D'idawan attempted, they become an even more difficult bunch of renegades to bring to heel. Will the Republic fight that battle for you again?"

Phillipe's poise faltered. "I heard you and I understand your point. I'll ask again, how do we win over the breeding caste, in your opinion?"

"Bear with me, sir. You've developed the technology adroitly. Impressively. But your development of the psychological terrain of the Q didn't keep pace with your tech development. If the mughals, the senior females, and the breeding caste don't see their own people being integrated into the highest levels of prosperity on their own world, how will they ever feel invested in the company being on their planet? A few extra credits for their crops aren't going to be enough to maintain the new status quo. A few more tanks to keep D'shtaran slightly more powerful than the other mughals or upstarts also won't do it."

Phillipe seemed about to ask the question for a third time when Kel answered.

"There were no Q working on Sumendi Station. The jewel of your operation on Q, and there are no Q working there." Kel paused for that to sink in. "You can pay off the mughals. You can even make them stockholders and put a few of them on your board. They don't have the power to control their people indefinitely. If the breeding caste don't get a taste of the good life, or at least have a path to a better one, there will be rebellion. In my humble opinion."

Phillipe grunted. "Not entirely original observations, my friend."

Kel's conviction was about to show in full color. "I've never had an original idea in my life. If it isn't historically documented or proven science, I don't know it. You're right. Nothing happening here is a unique occurrence. It's happened before. Therefore, it will again."

Phillipe burst out laughing. "A reductionist! It's rare to meet a man with that philosophical bent in this day and age."

Kel shrugged. "I'm in good company. Men much smarter than me have found wisdom by not ignoring the truth of history."

The older man smiled indulgently. "I'm not saying that you're wrong, especially about having Q working on Sumendi. We've tried. Perhaps we'll revisit the problem. But Q spacers removing their vac suits in a fit of orgasmic pleasure to bask in cosmic rays is not conducive to safety or social justice!"

Kel conceded the point. "Agreed. But that was a single incident, wasn't it? What if that was just an aberration? What if that individual were psychotic? Psychometric inventories probably don't exist to screen the Q. Develop one. Train space engineers. Invest in their education. In the meantime, get Q up there in labor jobs. If they need extra breaks to bask, then compromise. Get some kind of visible presence of Q up there. Get them working in the rare earth plant on the bay. Do something, but do it quick. That's my recommendation. Or there's going to be a whole generation of Chachnam breeding caste on this continent who are going to be without social status or power. Their only option will be to return to what they know, and that will mean rebellion."

Smiling, Phillipe spoke as much to the other diners as to Kel. "Well, Mister Turner, I'll take that into consideration." Then, leaning close to Kel, he whispered, "We own D'shtaran's army. The company's army. We own her. If she starts suffering delusions of grandeur, then at a word from me, the House of Reason will have the Legion right back here to bring her to heel. I can't spit without hitting another petty mughal to take her place. Your job is to get our army working so that if there are any more D'idawans out there, they can take care of it without you. The new armaments have been on Sumendi awaiting your victory. You'll have them soon. Train them and put yourself out of a job is what I recommend."

He placed his hand on Kel's shoulder, the urbane company director once again. "What an evening! Thank you for your bravery, and thank you for your thought-provoking comments. If you all will excuse me?" He made his way to another table to generate his well-practiced routine as the chief executive.

Kel said goodnight to his dinner companions and turned to find his teammates. At the table next to his stood a small group that included Ambassador Grealy. He met Kel's eyes but said nothing, nodding to Kel before turning back to his party.

The ambassador was listening in the whole time! I was so intent on showing how smart I am to that stuffed shirt I lost awareness and completely missed who was listening in. The frelling ambassador, at that! So much for playing it low key around the pols.

Phillipe had shown Kel his true colors. Not that he'd had any doubts. Kel had worn out his welcome. He only hoped the rest of his team had done a better job of playing it cool than he had. How much damage could one dark operator do?

15

"It's a pointless task," Poul said as they sat in their team hut days later. "Their army's only a few months away from a mating cycle. They're all gonna leave, and the battalions will be filled with new troopers. A good number of them will be first-timers. We'll have to train the whole army all over again. Why bother?"

"Orders are orders," Bigg said. "We'll still start by training their trainers on the new blaster tech. It'll be up to them to sustain the capability once we're off to new adventures. We'll have done our job." Bigg pushed documents around on a holo projection, organizing their training schedule. The problem was that they'd made little progress in teaching their junior officers to be proficient trainers themselves. Few were motivated for the task.

Sims chuckled. "Maybe the shiny new things will motivate them. Even a Q's got to appreciate how sexy a K-17 blaster is compared to their slug throwers."

Kel sighed. "Instead of giving them more powerful and better tech weapons, they need to train them how to stay proficient with the arms they have. If they can alter the entire structure of Chachnam society for the company's benefit, why can't they get them to organize their army better?"

"Yeah. Giving them shiny new toys, that's a manager's type of solution. Or a politician's," Poul said. "Let's say we get the battalion trained to a minimum proficiency on the blasters in the next two months. The army has a complete turnover in troops the month after that. If the officers are too lazy to train the new troops up to standard, who cares if they have blasters or if they have sharpened sticks?"

Braley had been looking at his datapad. He set it down.

"I know. But, instead of complaining about it, let's do the job. We've motivated worse troops than these. We just led these troops to a victory that would rival anything in their history. Two battalions of dismounted and lightly armored troops took on a heavy armored battalion in the defense and wiped the planet with them. That's T-Rex kind of stuff!"

Kel had to admit it, Braley was right. When seen from that perspective, it was an impressive accomplishment.

"We need to build them up, and using their victory is a righteous way to do that. We influence change one mind at a time. We aren't going to win over the nawab. But all these subadars and jemadars we're putting our effort into, someday will rise to the rank of nizam and eventually nawab. They're going to remember that we took the time to train them correctly. Even some of these havildars, naiks, and troopers will eventually rise to be officers after enough mating cycles to become senior caste-members.

"If we continue to lead by example, show the officers and troops that we care about their welfare, encourage them to be professional and proficient with their arms, maybe the next team that has to work with the Sun-Loyal won't think that we accomplished nothing in our six months here."

Everyone considered that.

"Sorry, sir," Poul said. "Of course, you're right. I didn't mean to lead the team in a complaint session. I was voicing my observations about the Q in an unconstructive way. What we say here stays in the team room. It won't affect how we do our job."

Poul grinned widely. He knew how to disarm tensions by always being the first to admit fault and apologize, even if he'd done nothing wrong. If Kel or Sims ever said or did something stupid in front of Braley or Bigg, it was Poul who stepped up to take the blame or apologize on their behalf.

Braley smiled back at them all. "I know it won't, Poul. Admittedly, I've felt a little pessimistic myself. A week off after a killer combat op may have done us more harm than good. That jackassery at the party the other night didn't help. I know hanging out in garrison won't be an exciting conclusion to our time here. I just hate to see us end the next couple of months on a low note. You guys have all done an incredible job. If I haven't said so, I couldn't be prouder of you. I just want us to finish strong."

Poul was the first to get up and shake Braley's hand. "You know it, sir."

Kel and Sims each followed and did the same. Everything was back to normal. Now they could get back to organizing the training plan.

Bigg took over again from his seat behind the multiple holo-projections. "We will sprinkle in as much team training time as we can for ourselves as well. Not to worry. We don't have to resign ourselves solely to the drudgery of training the Q in marksmanship. Again. There'll be some kind of ops for us to pull off. It's bound to happen."

Bigg was right, too. Something critical that required them to use their skills was still likely to happen. And if not, they would go back to Victrix trained up as a team and ready for the next mission.

Bigg closed every holo but one, a schedule. "Anyway, ladies, the blasters are due to arrive in three days. We'll spend the next week reviewing basic marksmanship with the battalion, identifying weapons needing level one service by the armorers, doing maintenance, getting their S-5s turned in for storage. Then begin training on the K-17s. It's going to be a big change transitioning them to blasters. I think it'll be a change for the better."

Kel laughed. "True. With the exception of the recon platoon, the majority of the Q can't shoot to save their lives. Maybe blasters will be easier for them."

Poul took the opening for a major backslide. "We've almost mastered pointing them in the right direction. What could possibly go wrong by giving them deadlier tech?"

They spent the first day of the training cycle with the junior officers reviewing the principles of marksmanship and then on the range zeroing weapons. One of the problems they'd encountered with the Q was their inability to get low enough on the ground to assume a true prone position. With their hind legs tucked, they could lower their abdominal segment, but couldn't touch their thoraxes to the ground without flexing their forearms underneath them. In such a position, they couldn't extend their upper limbs to properly stabilize their rifles.

The weapons the Q used were an almost identical copy of the Stonewell-5 carbine. The 7-millimeter slug throwers were ridiculously reliable and effective, and Kel had no qualms about carrying one himself whenever necessary. The guns were produced on Q and had undergone modifications to accommodate the ergonomics of the Q anthropometry. The Q had no problem manipulating the weapons. The difficulty lay in their ability to stabilize the weapon effectively to aim it accurately.

Zeroing weapons was a nightmare. The process of adjusting the sights to the point of desired impact was dependent on the shooter's ability to shoot consistently. If the shooter was unstable and wobbly while firing, one shot could be twelve centimeters above the aiming point, the next could be the same amount below the aiming point, the next could miss the target altogether. How did one know what adjustments to make to the weapon's sights?

The solution was to let the Q do what they did naturally. Dig holes. Within minutes, they could scoop out meter-deep foxholes that allowed them to squat on their hind legs and rest elbows and the weapon's magazine on the ground in front of them.

Transitioning to the blasters, while not providing any improvement to their accuracy, would at least improve their hit probability. It was possible to use the weapons on a wide dispersion, as opposed to a point dispersion, where the energy beam projected in a wider arc. It used more energy, drained charge packs faster, and delivered a less powerful blast at successively farther ranges, but required less accurate aiming control to hit a target in that mode. An upright Q could aim a blaster well enough to hit a Q-sized target out a hundred meters or so, and do significant damage. Each charge pack could deliver about twenty blasts on that setting. It was a reasonable tradeoff for them, improving hit probability while losing some shot capacity.

On their first day of training the battalion's commander was as usual nowhere in sight.

Braley wasn't surprised.

"Officers of the First Battalion of the Sun-Loyal," he addressed the unit, "we are proud to once again be among you. My human brood-mates and I are humbled to be with such great warriors. Your courage and leadership in bringing D'idawan to justice has brought great honor to you all."

Kel couldn't tell, but he thought the dozen or so assembled Q seemed attentive. Their heads swiveled in Braley's direction, their large multifaceted eyes staring unblinkingly at him.

"Our task is to assist you in preparing for the arrival of your new armaments. You have won a great victory for your mughal and in proving your worth, the terms of the Mutual Prosperity Accord are being completed.

"Let us work together with you to share our knowledge and provide our assistance so that the Sun-Loyal can continue to be an even mightier army than they are already."

The Q hummed, clacking their graspers all around in agreement.

Leave it to Braley, Kel marveled. *Instead of a bunch of malcontents, they're acting almost like soldiers.* Sims took center stage to begin laying out the morning's lesson; officers pulled out their datapads as if to take notes. Kel was impressed.

Braley was right. If we're motivated, they'll be motivated. Maybe this won't be so bad after all.

The next day, the full battalion joined them on the rifle range. The company's junior officers ran the day's activities while the human team stood back. Things progressed smoothly as they rotated squad after squad of troops to the range.

Sims joined Kel behind the firing line. "Not too shabby, eh? Maybe Braley's right and we're going to rub off on the juniors."

The officers seemed keen, perhaps because new weapons were coming.

"Seems so," Kel allowed. The troopers, he had a harder time assessing. It was still difficult for him to read the Chachnam Q, though he thought he could interpret nonverbal cues from the Disciplined a little. "I've seen a few things that make me think the troops aren't in synch with the plan."

From what he could tell, discipline seemed to be breaking down, much as he'd sensed before they'd left for their break in the capital. Preparing for the range, several troopers seemed reluctant to participate. More than slacking or shirking, some of the troops required physical encouragement to fall in and draw weapons from the armory.

"Yeah, well, every army has its screwups." Sims seemed to dismiss the most stunning incident of the day so far.

It was on the range that the outright disobedience occurred. A trooper refused to pick up her S-5. A havildar approached. Kel couldn't make out anything useful from their voders. Suddenly, the much larger noncommissioned officer struck the smaller Q to the ground.

Discipline among alien forces was frequently harsh. The humans never dispensed discipline to the native troops themselves. If infractions occurred, they allowed the Q to punish their own. Kel had no desire to punish a troop no matter what race they were. In this case, the havildar barked orders and two Q troopers raced over, pulled the disobedient Q to her feet, and carried her back to the compound. Kel wondered what would happen to insubordinate and unfit troops. He hoped they didn't get eaten.

Kel was kneeling behind one of the trenches, observing one of the Q troopers as she fired, while conversing with the platoon's jemadar.

"Sergeant Kel-boss, does it appear that the shooter is raising her head off the weapon after every shot? It looks as though she is having to reacquire a new body position each time." The young officer raised her mag-glass to her face to view the target downrange. "Her accuracy is not acceptable. How do I tell her to improve? Telling her not to lift her head does not seem a reasonable piece of advice to change that behavior."

It was an astute observation. Kel enjoyed helping a sincere person. "It is a good example of failing to follow through. I would tell her to concentrate on seeing the sight as it lifts from the target when she fires. If she can train herself to be aware of that, she will naturally keep her face down on the weapon where it belongs. Proper follow-through cures many ills that cause sick shooting."

Kel hoped that his analogy translated well.

The jemadar clucked. "*Follow-through.*" The voder repeated in the flat intonation indicating there was not a perfect translation of the concept. "Yes. That sounds reasonable. I will try that."

He walked off the line to where Poul and Sims stood under an enormous heavy foliaged tree, the same that grew sparsely around the garrison compound. Its purple leaves sat still on the windless day.

"Man, it's hot, even in armor. Like the seven hells." Sims removed his bucket. "Itchy neck be damned; it's better to stay buttoned up."

Kel removed his as well to join his two teammates in the shade. The heat was oppressive out of armor. It was early summer on Big M, but already the nights were getting uncomfortable in the team house. Last night Kel had climbed onto the roof to sleep in the light breeze until his turn came for watch.

"Hey. What's that?" Kel pointed at something moving within a hollow area at the base of the tree. It had to be some creature. Kel was always fascinated by animals. Wherever he went, he delighted in finding local fauna. Besides the Q, all he'd seen on this planet was the occasional insect.

Getting down on one knee, Kel peered into the darkness of the small hollow. Multiple eyes reflected back at him.

Poul knelt with him. "Whatcha got there, Kel? See something?"

"Don't know."

He looked for one of the Disciplined. Trooper G'livan with her squad awaited her turn to join the training on the firing line. Kel got up and moved to the group.

"Trooper G'livan, greetings."

"Greetings, Sergeant Kel-boss. How do you bask this day?"

"Very well. May I ask for your help? We see some type of animal in that tree over there, and I'm curious about it."

G'livan looked toward the tree. "It could only be a 'waste-consumer.'"

"Waste-consumer?" Kel said

"Yes. That is not their real name. We call them that because of what they do. The correct name is *chak'chak*. It means 'eat-eat' in the northern tribal voice. It's a child's name for the things. They do not bask as we do, but consume garbage and waste products. Very useful animals. Many keep them as pets for entertainment and companionship. Would you like me to try to coax it out? It may come into the shade of its tree if I can find something to feed it."

When Kel told his teammates about the critter, Poul perked up. Sims frowned.

"Is that like a kuatamundi, I wonder? We had them where I grew up. Cute furry things, but they were always digging in your trash."

G'livan strode over, and Kel pointed to where he'd seen the small creature hiding. "I saw it in there."

Ducking down to the hollow, G'livan set something on the ground, then skirted to the side and waited. In a moment, spiny legs appeared out of the recess, followed by a body. A small ovoid critter sprouting ten thin, spindly legs. Several segmented eye stalks protruded from its back, looking in all directions. The creature skittered over to the small piece of food and crouched. A proboscis extended from its carapace and sucked at the offering.

"Disgusting!" Poul said.

"They are quite harmless. I had one as a pet when younger. Would you like to hold it?"

"Yes!" Kel said. He removed his gauntlets and knelt beside G'livan. The commando took out what looked like a sweet potato.

"Offer it this. It will eat from your hand. Then you can pick it up."

Kel did exactly as instructed. He held his hand on the ground, a bit of potato cupped in his palm. The creature turned all eyes to the offered food and skittered closer, climbing into his hand to suck on the vegetable. Small fine hairs formed a whirl on its black carapace. Kel lifted the creature. It inspected him with all three of its eyes as it ate.

He stroked it several times with a single finger. The creature buzzed in his palm.

"I think you've got a friend," Poul said. "Hey Sims, what do you think? Sims?"

They looked around for their friend. He was gone. They examined the creature for another minute before Kel lowered it to the ground. It hopped off his palm and returned to its hollow in the tree.

"They are quite harmless. They live in these trees. You can find them at night searching for food. They are good to have around a dwelling. They keep the area clean."

Kel looked up. "Thank you, G'livan. That was very educational."

"You are welcome, Sergeants-boss. I must return to training now."

Kel stood. A realization came to him. "Sims is an entomophobe!" he blurted out in excitement.

"What? What's that?" Poul asked.

"He doesn't like insects. It makes perfect sense now. Ever notice he won't remove his bucket when he's close to any Q? He just did this thing I've seen him do before. If he's got his bucket off and any Q approaches, he's the first to put his lid back on. Oh man, you know what? At the party the other night, when we were eating, I saw him flinch when a Q server walked up behind him to clear plates. I thought it was just a bit of hypervigilance. No way! He's creeped out by things that look like bugs! This is fantastic!"

Poul looked at him queerly. "Um, okay. Why is this fantastic?"

Kel cackled. "Because I am going to *destroy* him with this!"

Poul put his bucket back on, shaking his head. "C'mon. Let's get back at it."

Kel followed, taking a long draw from a hydration pouch before hearing his L-comm erupt from within his bucket. He quickly secured his lid.

"Say again, Braley," Kel said as soon as his helmet was connected.

"Three, we've just been alerted that there's a situation. One of the provincial development teams is in trouble in our sector. They're scrambling a Talon, but it's going to take them at least a half hour to get there. We're closest. Embassy wants to know if we can respond. I've already told 'em we're on our way. Doubtful the Talon crew could make a recovery on their own anyway. I've told them to send the Talon here and get us. Kel, let's take K'listan and a squad from Recon. I'm going to retrieve the subadar from Second Rifles to go with us, too. I want one of the senior Chachnam to be available on site to try to defuse things."

"What's the situation?" Bigg asked.

"One of the joint teams is barricaded. Apparently, the whole village is trying to kill them."

16

The Talon landed in the garrison courtyard. The squad from the recon platoon crouched on the deck, preferring it to the jump seats along both sides of the compartment. The Disciplined held their weapons in front of them, much the same way the humans did: at the ready.

"Heads up, everyone," Braley said. "The embassy tells me the provincial development team is composed of five humans, a representative from D'shtaran, and two company security guards." He waited for everyone's voder to catch up.

"They put a distress call out to the embassy an hour ago. They were attacked during one of their public forums and one of their guards is wounded. We don't know if the agitators are armed or not."

The provincial development teams traveled all over Big M to bring the word of the Mutual Prosperity Accord to the Q. The teams were composed of specialists from the company and the embassy, as well as Chachnam elders who were there to issue D'shtaran's edicts.

The teams usually traveled with company guards and frequently had extra security provided by D'shtaran's army. With combat operations taking priority, Kel bet that the Q had not returned to detailing security parties for the provincial teams. Who was with them for protection right now, they did not know.

Kel had experience with civil unrest. "Doesn't really matter if the crowd's armed or not. That team's in great danger. A mob is a deadly weapon all its own. We watched Q tear one of their own limb from limb without weapons."

Braley agreed. "Let's just get over the village and get a read from the air. The embassy comm center is getting me a link to the PDT now.

"Everyone. We are not going in to harm civilians. Our goal is to rescue the development team. Just be ready to fight through an angry mob. Subadar, will you be able to calm any elders in the hamlet?"

The subadar's voder replied over her staccato clicks. "I will endeavor to calm them. We must also consider that the mughal's representative is on the scene. If an elder of the mughal's court was not able to calm the situation, I may not have better success. I am concerned about the welfare of your human brood-mates, but I must attend the mughal's representative. It is a crime to molest a messenger from the mughal."

Braley spoke to someone from the development team. The speaker was not doing well. The male voice quavered, panicked.

"Please get here soon. I don't think we can hold out much longer. Our one guard who can still fight is running low on his charge pack. They really hurt our other guard. We're trying to stop the bleeding."

"What part of the hamlet are you in? Can you turn on a locator?"

"Yes. Okay. We can do that. Please hurry. They're starting to dig through the walls. Some of them are up on the roof. Hurry!"

Their pilot's voice came over the comm in the crew compartment. "Five minutes."

Braley talked to the voice again. "I'm Captain Yost. I'm on my way with a team to help. We'll be over your position in five minutes. Do you have any weapons?"

"Just the one the guard has. The other guard, Jun, they ripped his arm off and took his weapon. They ripped it off him. It was horrible..."

"I understand. What's your name?"

"I'm sorry. This is Matthew Ballard. I'm the team lead from the company."

"Mister Ballard, I'm going to put you on with one of my team. Kel, you listening? Take over. I'm going up to the crew compartment to get a visual. I'll send a link back to you guys."

Braley moved forward and up the small ladder that led to the crew deck.

"Mister Ballard, my name's Kel. We're almost there. Hang on. What's your situation? How many people are with you?"

"There's five of us on the team. We've been working this sector for the last month. We've never had any problems until..."

"Mister Ballard, who else is with you?"

"Um, Jerry is okay. He's one of our guards. Jun, he's the one they attacked. The other Matthew is helping him. Then there's Jason, Terril, and Simone. They're working to build a barrier at the door."

Kel was relieved to not hear Monica and Tatiana's names. "Okay, five of you on the team and the two security guards. Seven humans. Is there anyone from the mughal's court with you?"

"D'alak is dead. The crowd grabbed her and tore her apart. I've never seen Q move so fast. If you don't get here, they're going to do the same to us."

A holo projection came to life at the head of the compartment. One of the forward cameras on the Talon broadcast the view over the hamlet as they descended in a tight circular orbit. The hamlet sprawled on a rise overlooking a floodplain of fields and farms. On the plateau, the tallest buildings fronted a rock bluff. A central plaza radiated smaller buildings to fill the rest of the plateau.

The magnification increased to focus on one portion of the village. It was obvious where the human team was barricaded. A mass of shifting Q surrounded a two-story structure abutting the cliff.

"Subadar," Kel said, catching her attention, "the humans in the hamlet tell me that a Chachnam elder named D'alak was with the team. She was killed by the crowd."

"D'alak is a diplomat of the mughal's court. If she has been murdered, tell Subadar Braley that he may kill everyone in the hamlet."

Had he heard that right?

"Braley," Kel said on L-comm. "The subadar is telling me that if the diplomat from D'shtaran's court is dead, we have her permission to kill the entire village. It's apparently a capital crime to harm a member of the mughal's court."

"Yeah. That won't be happening." Braley switched to the open channel in the passenger deck. "We're going to make a low pass over the hamlet and try to scatter that crowd. Pilot says he can hover over the roof and put us out there. Kel, Poul. Get on the tailgate and be ready to suppress any fire. Get all threats off that roof. I'm heading back."

Braley wanted his two snipers on the job.

Kel clicked to the development team's channel. "Mister Ballard, you should be hearing us overhead now.

Tell your guard not to shoot. We have Q troops with us. Do not shoot at us."

There was no response.

The ship banked as their forward momentum slowed. Bright sunlight spilled in through the lowering ramp, and Kel glimpsed treetops and buildings, some covered with Q waving their limbs and hoisting scythes. Their attitude leveled and the craft did a spot turn as it continued to descend. Kel pushed himself toward the ramp where Poul and Sims already stood, K-17s in hands.

Kel brought his rifle up and peered through the optic. Q used their raptorial forearms to hammer at the flat roof, some whacking away with tools. A Q holding a scythe turned toward the Talon's open ramp; Kel shot him in the chest. The other Q kept attacking the roof. Without a word exchanged, Kel's two teammates opened up, drilling each Q with a bolt until there was no movement on the roof, only bleaching insectoid bodies.

The crew chief knelt at the corner of the ramp, guiding the pilot. The edge of the ramp eased back to the roof, the Talon's split tail practically kissing the cliff. The crew chief's thumbs up was all he needed. Braley beside him, Kel sped off the ramp and landed in a run, checking bodies as he went. There was no question the Q were dead. All were bleached a pale white, growing fragile in the sun.

The last of the Q troopers cleared the tailgate. "We're clear, Blackbird. Take off and stay on station above us," Braley said as the Talon levitated up and away, bending the laws of gravitation.

Q troopers spread out to face the crowds below, who still hammered at the building face as they'd been doing on the roof.

"Let's try to get these people backed up," Bigg said. "Everyone, drop a stunner over the edge. Maybe we won't have to kill any of them." Anticipating its use, Kel had placed a stunner from his daypack onto his chest during the flight over. "Kel, pass me one," Sims said. Kel handed him the one in his hand, then grabbed one off the pouch on Sims's back for himself.

"Toss 'em," Bigg said as he swiped and released it over the edge. The rest followed closely. The purple-silver arcs danced, light bouncing and reflecting up and off the cliff, the building face, and onto the crowds in front.

Looking down at the crowds, Kel's visor dimmed at the blistering energy release. The Q who'd been hammering at the walls fell in waves, squinting and squirming in the dust. Apparently, the stunners didn't produce light in a spectrum the Q found pleasing. To have the devices attract rather than repel Q would've been suboptimal.

"MOVE BACK. MOVE BACK," Braley's translated voice projected from his bucket's external speaker. "CLEAR THE AREA. OTHERWISE WE WILL FIRE ON YOU. MOVE BACK."

Q collapsed from gunfire like cut wheat. The Q subadar was shooting into the crowd below.

"Knock that off!" Poul shouted as he pushed the barrel of the subadar's weapon down, more rounds discharging as he did so, bullets riddling the roof at their feet. The crowd dispersed, those in front turning and pushing into their motionless brethren, those behind confused and resistant, not yet understanding what had happened to spur the retreat.

"Subadar," Braley said as he confronted the Q officer. "No. Do not do that again. We will not tolerate that behavior."

The Q chittered something unintelligible, then the voder translated, "They are breaking the law. They are immature males. It is only right. They will be punished."

"Yeah, but not like that and not here. Don't do that again. Poul, stay with the subadar."

"Yes, sir," Poul said as he took a step toward the Q officer.

Kel tried to raise Ballard again. "Mister Ballard, we're on the roof. The villagers are pushed back. We're coming in to get you. Do you hear me?"

"Oh, thank goodness. Yes, I can hear you. They broke through the wall in the front room. We're in a rear room with some containers pushed against the door."

"Okay. Stay where you are. Hear that, guys?" Kel asked them all.

"Working on it," Bigg said. "You told them to stay put, right, Kel? They're on the first floor? Confirm that for me. I'm going to find a place to lay out this roof charge."

"Rog. Mister Ballard, we're going to be using an explosive charge to make a hole in the roof. It's important to stay where you are on the first floor—"

"Hurry, there's some of them in the building and they're trying to get in!"

"Speed it up, Bigg," Braley said.

Bigg did not reply. He was in deep concentration scanning the roof when he raised his hand to point to a spot on the roof. "Move those bodies."

Several Disciplined commandos sprang to drag the bodies off the spot Bigg indicated. One tossed a body over the roof. Bigg spread a thin strip of black material in a rough circle over the chosen spot, produced an initiator from the breacher bag on his waist, and set it on the charge.

"Stack up. Braley, I'll make the count. Stand by for short count."

"Ready. Ready. Now."

The charge ignited with a dull report and a large hole the circumference of the black outline appeared. No explosion. No dust. The mass converter charge simply transformed the roof material into electrons.

"Go."

Braley turned on his weapon light and peered through the hole before disappearing into its mouth. Kel let his knees and hips flex to take the impact, springing out of his landing to make room for Sims and K'listan.

He brought his weapon up and activated his white light. No villagers here. Braley had ended up on the left side of the space, Kel on the right, closest to the ramp down.

"This way." Kel led. Their priority was to get to the first floor and the hostages. They could search the building for other threats later.

The team at his back, Kel headed down. He knew he was not alone. He crouched as he penetrated the line of the ceiling, trying to cheat the angle to see into the floor below as he flowed.

Three Q hammered away at a wall, one ramming himself against the door.

"Hey! Get back!" Kel hollered.

They didn't quit. Kel shot the Q at the door in the back. The other two rushed him, striking as they advanced. He shot each of them as bolts at his side joined in to do the same. Braley.

Sims and K'listan sped to the door, K'listan dragging the bleaching body out of their way.

"You all right in there? We're here to rescue you. It's safe now. We're coming in." Sims stood in front of the partially breached door. Kel moved closer. People on the other side worked to remove their hasty barricade.

Moments later, a frantic group spilled out. A woman saw K'listan and shrieked.

K'listan's voder spoke. "I am here to rescue you."

"Where's your injured man?" Kel said to the next person.

"He's in here," yelled a voice from in the room.

A man knelt at the injured man's side, pressing a bloody cloth against the wound. It was the man's shirt, balled into an expedient dressing. His left arm had been removed at the shoulder. The man was a pale gray and breathed shallowly. Unconscious.

"Is this Jun?" Kel asked.

"Yes. He's not doing well. He's lost a lot of blood."

"I'm going to help. What happened?" Kel asked the question but tuned the man out. He wanted the man occupied and not in his way. Kel got out his own med kit and examined the man, feeling the man's other limbs. He saw no blood on his gauntlets.

"Is he hurt anywhere else?" Kel asked.

The man blurted out, "No. Isn't having his arm torn off by those freaks enough?"

Kel continued working. Beneath the dark, sticky cloth, blood poured from the wound. Likely the axillary artery had retracted during the traumatic amputation, and was too deep for him to reach. It couldn't be compressed externally. He pulled out a nanogel hemostatic pack. He prepared the injector and probed into the wound with the tip as he deployed the medicine. The man stirred and groaned.

"You're hurting him!"

"I'm saving his life." Kel squeezed a nanocolloid dressing over the wound. It sealed the amputation site and formed into a hardened gel in seconds.

"Stay with your friend, please. We're going to be moving him soon." He clicked his teeth to open L-comm. "Bigg, I've got the wounded man down here. He's lost a lot of blood and is in hypovolemic shock. We need to get him to the capital ASAP."

"Rog," Bigg acknowledged. "Braley, the crowd is gathering again. Best we can do is..." Gunfire chattered from the direction of the roof. "Hey! Knock that off."

Bigg continued hurriedly. "The subadar has ordered the commandos to fire on the crowd. Sket. What a karkin' mess. *Cease fire!*"

"I'm coming up," Braley said. "Sims, get everyone upstairs. Kel, we'll be right back to help move the casualty."

"Roger." Kel pulled a small cube from his pack and unfolded it. "Hey, what's your name?"

"Matthew. Titus."

"Matthew Titus, I'm Kel. You're going to help me. This is an insta-litter. I'm going to spread it out and then you're going to help me log-roll Jun onto it. I'll wrap him in it, and it's going to harden into a cocoon and make it easier for us to move him. It'll also protect him and warm him up. We've gotta get him out of here. You understand?"

"Okay. Tell me what to do."

"Good man, Matthew."

Kel heard the deep rumble of Talon repulsors. Sims helped him carry the litter up the incline. The team had gotten everyone on the roof for evacuation, leaving only them and the patient.

"Ready." Poul lowered a length of mono-line through the hole in the roof, and Kel snapped it in place.

"Okay. Lift." Kel and Sims steadied the litter from both sides as it disappeared through the hole.

Sims clapped him on the shoulder. "You next, man. Go tend your patient."

From a short run, Kel jumped and grabbed the edge of the hole, the hands of his teammates hauling him the rest of the way onto the roof. The Talon was performing the same maneuver that got them onto the roof, backing up as it descended, the tail gate already lowered. More Q bodies covered the ground beneath, and an angry, buzzing mob formed in the plaza.

Braley slid over beside Kel. "We'll get you and your patient on first. How is he?"

Kel checked the man again. "Bad. I wish I'd thought to tell the Talon crew to load some transfusers. I grabbed some synth-blood before we left. I can get him some as soon as we're on board. I probably should have been training the flight crews for a med response while we've been on planet, huh?"

"Can't do it all, man."

"Hey, Braley," Bigg said as he walked up. "The subadar says she's not leaving with us. Says she is staying here with the commandos."

"What?" Braley walked to where the subadar stood as she directed the commandos. It looked like they were about to open fire again.

"Subadar. I hear you are staying. Why do you wish to remain behind?"

The subadar held her communicator in her hand. "I have been ordered by the mughal to remain. The mughal is sending members of her court for an immediate investigation and trial. The Disciplined will remain behind with me. I wish you good travels, subadar."

Kel frowned and hurried over to where K'listan stood with her squad, her hard carapace gleaming in the bright sunlight, the angry mob buzzing in the plaza.

"K'listan, what's happening?"

"We are ordered to stay behind to punish the village."

"Punish? What does that mean?"

"I believe the mughal will order retaliation against the villagers."

He knew what that meant. And there was nothing he could do to stop it. "Be careful, my friend."

"Thank you." K'listan turned back to her troops as the subadar began issuing more orders.

Kel moved back to the litter, and motioned Sims to help him from the other side. "What'd K'listan say?" Sims asked him as they lifted together. The blast of the Talon caused them to sway as they walked forward to the beckoning crew chief.

"Sounds like the mughal has ordered them to massacre the village."

17

Kel prepped the team's one bag of synth-blood for the wounded man. Braley knelt to watch as Kel worked. The osseous injector would use its nano-bots to tunnel a path into the man's sternum while Kel pulled the tab to warm the synth-blood. The blue light pulsed on the injector pad, and Kel rested the warm bag on it. The bag slowly deflated. Within minutes, Kel was gratified to see the numbers on the vitals card improve. Maybe the man would make it.

"We're going straight to the spaceport," Braley said. "The company med facility at the field is waiting for him. They have a larger facility on Sumendi Station and will lift him there once he's stabilized. Think he'll pull through?"

"I do. I'll bounce them and give their medtechs an update. What happened on the roof while we were inside?"

Braley grunted and shook his head in disgust. "Yeah. That. The subadar ordered the commandos to fire on the civilians when they started to mob again. They killed a few dozen before the crowd backed off."

"Sket. K'listan gave me the impression that they'd be ordered to 'punish' the whole village. Doesn't that sound like a massacre in the making?"

"It does to me, too. I hope not. I'm going to report to the ambassador as soon as we touch down."

Kel continued to monitor his patient as he listened to the conversations in the cabin. Bigg and Braley interrogated Mr. Ballard about the events of the morning.

"It started pretty routinely," Ballard told them as he sat in the soft jump seat, a pouch of water in his hand. "We've stayed in this hamlet before and never had a problem. We were in the plaza. D'alak was addressing a small crowd of elder females. I was next to her, trying to follow as much of the conversation as I could.

"I started the address, talking about the end of the hostilities and the next phase of development with the farms. I'd just turned the floor over to D'alak when another group moved on to the plaza and crowded around the elders.

"There was some kind of disagreement between the elders and the new group. There's so much the voders don't translate. They were young males. Immature, non-breeding males, the kind with the bright red splotches. I asked D'alak what the commotion was, and she told me it was a matter of '*Chachnam-kakataaa.*' I didn't understand what she meant, and I told her. It seemed important.

"She didn't get to elaborate, because the mob pushed through the elders and started clicking at D'alak. There were some pretty rapid exchanges between them. The kind the voders miss. I caught only a small part of what was being said. By this time, it was clear that there was some friction, and Jun and Jerry stepped to put themselves between us and them. The rest of the team were behind the platform. Simone and her crew were getting prepared to show a holo on the crop rotations, I remember that," he said as he looked in the direction of the woman sitting next to him.

She nodded vaguely, clearly traumatized.

The man took a deep breath. The pouch in his hands shook.

"I just remember things happening quickly from there. Some of the youths reached forward to grab D'alak off the riser. Jun stepped forward and put his arm on one of them and the next minute... his arm was just... gone.

"Jerry stepped forward and shot several of the mob. D'alak was pulled down into the crowd and they just... they just tore her apart."

Kel thought about the dismemberment he had personally witnessed by the Q. The repulsive sounds of rending that accompanied the act. The ones he could feel in his bones.

"I laid down as much fire as I could," the security guard said. "It slowed them down when they realized they couldn't overwhelm us. Seeing their friends blasted had some effect. Initially. It gave us enough time to recover Jun and run down the plaza strip to reach the house we quartered in. Luckily, being cut into the cliff, it gave us protection from the rear. If they had been able hit the house from all sides, we wouldn't be here."

Ballard nodded at the guard. "Jerry here saved us, for sure. We got the call out to the company and eventually to the embassy staff. It took forever to get someone to understand what was happening to us. It wasn't long after that when the mob reorganized and came at us in the house. I tried talking to them, but they wouldn't engage me. At first, they threw rocks. Once Jerry and I retreated inside, they attacked the walls. Another few minutes, they would've had us."

Calmer now, Jerry added more details. "I shot more of them as they came down the street. It only backed them up for a minute each time. After a while, it seemed like it infuriated the crowd rather than deterred them. They were determined. I knew we just had to barricade and wait for help. I was never so glad in my life to hear a Talon in-bound. Thank you."

Kel checked on Jun. He checked the vitals monitor on his forehead then took off his bucket and gauntlets. He leaned over and placed his ear over the man's mouth to listen to his breathing as the man's chest rose and fell. There was a lot of information you could get from the monitors, but there was every bit an important part of the picture that was enhanced by the tactile examination of a casualty. Kel placed his palm against the man's cheek. His skin was warm, his color improving.

Jun responded to Kel's touch and groaned, his head lolling. Kel searched his kit for a dose of Noci-block. The man was regaining consciousness and his pain was returning. He was always amazed at what the human body could withstand.

Kel looked down at the security guard. Having an arm ripped from your shoulder would be an unimaginable experience. One that certainly would be expected to take even the best warrior out of the fight. As sobering as their story had been, it still puzzled Kel.

"Mister Ballard," Kel said from where he knelt. "Do you understand why they attacked your group?"

"No. Not really. I mean, there has always been some resistance, especially at the beginning, but the mughal's diplomats explained that the accord was the will of the mughal. Things have gone smoothly in most villages, including this one."

"You said you couldn't understand most of what was being said. Could you understand any of it?"

The man furrowed his brows.

"It didn't make much sense. Voders fritz in situation like this. Words in Q and concepts that are very culturally specific, the voder just transliterates, throws out ten-chit words without any context to them."

"Yes sir, I've experienced the same myself. Did they say anything you could recognize? Anything that might give us a clue as to why they attacked your group?"

One of the women leaned forward. "Colorless. They kept saying, 'colorless.'"

The Talon returned them to the garrison the same night as the rescue, and the wounded guard was lifted to Sumendi Station for further treatment. Kel had not seen their medical facilities, but was told by the medtechs that they had a full robotic surgical suite. If they had been able to recover the man's arm, it could have been reattached microsurgically and repaired with nanotech. As it was, the best they could do was save the man's life, and prepare him to be fitted with a cybernetic. It was too high of an amputation for regen.

Kel could think of worse fates. An arm that was stronger than a flesh and blood one, felt no pain, and could be replaced again and again as needed? Not so bad. Lots of leejes had prosthetics. They still wore the armor and served. It took more than that to keep a legionnaire from his KTF... provided they didn't become too much machine. Because the reality was that you could shut down a bot much easier than flesh and blood.

Sitting around the team hut after another day on the range everyone was stripped out of their armor except Kel. He was getting ready to take a turn on watch. He had the first shift of the night, after which he'd get an uninterrupted six hours of sleep before starting the next day's routine. Six hours was something to be excited about. As good as clear skies on Camerone Day.

Someone knocked on the entrance. A Q head peeked into the room. It was K'listan. Braley and Bigg looked up from their datapads. Sims was snoring on his bunk, his forearm draped over his face. Poul poked him awake. The leader of the commando section stepped into the threshold, recognizing Kel in his armor.

"May I speak to you, Sergeant Kel-boss?"

Kel moved to the door. "Please, my friend, come in and sit with us."

The rest of the team got up and slapped on their buckets. Whatever was going to be said, they wanted to hear it too. Another commando appeared behind her. G'livan.

"Trooper G'livan. Please come in and be welcome," Kel said, gesturing for her to sit as well.

"Thank you, Sergeant Kel-boss. We have just returned to the garrison and sought you out for communication."

Braley stepped forward. The undressed humans looked odd wearing only their buckets, even to Kel. He thought he saw the two Q retreat slightly as Braley moved closer to them. Could the Q be xenophobic to their human form?

"We are glad to see both of you. We have all been concerned for your welfare," Braley said slowly and without contractions, trying to make his communications clear. "Is all well?"

K'listan rocked her upper body in the display of agreement. "Yes, Captain-boss. All is well, thank you for your concern."

Bigg brought chairs into a circle, leaving an open area for the two Q to squat. "Come, sit with us. What happened in the village after we left?"

Everyone took a seat while the two Q squatted on their abdomens to rest, their rifles beside them on the dirt floor of the hut. Sims remained on his bunk. Kel thought he knew why.

"It was an eventful two days. The arbiter from the mughal's palace court arrived with a company of the mughal's personal guards. We were ordered to gather all the village, even those from the farms and not present the day of the mob attack.

"We awaited the arrival of the arbiter the next day. Then, the palace guards executed all the immature males in the village. Many of the females of breeding age were killed as well. Then we were dismissed and only now have returned. What we covered quickly in your aircraft took over a day to drive in a repulsor sled."

Everyone was silent. There were huge gaps in her shortened version of events.

"K'listan," Kel said, "why did they kill so many of the young villagers?"

The havildar canted her head. "It is *Chachnam-kakataaa*. It is their way."

That word again.

K'listan tried to explain. "Their way is *Chachnam-kakataaa*. Their law is *Chachnam-kakataaa*. Their belief is *Chachnam-kakataaa*. The youths disobeyed Mughal D'shtaran, who is *Chachnam-kakataaa*. The disobedient killed an elder. How is this not clear?"

"Well. That clears it up," Poul coughed.

"I think we understand why the villagers had to be punished for their crime against the mughal's representative," Braley said. "What we don't understand is why she was attacked in the first place."

K'listan and G'livan spoke to each other rapidly and in tones too low for their buckets to catch. After a few exchanges, K'listan seemed ready to answer.

"It is *religion*," their buckets translated, the inability to directly translate *religion* reinforced in the reconstructed voice. "There is belief that the humans have brought *damnation* to the Chachnam, and the elders are complicit. This was the teaching of D'idawan."

Kel tried to process this when G'livan spoke for the first time. "D'idawan was not alone in her beliefs. The Chachnam have ancient beliefs. Different from the Disciplined. We are not Chachnam, but we have been among them our whole lives."

"And we're grateful for your knowledge of them," Braley said. "Some things we understand. The Mutual Prosperity Accord forces the Chachnam to change their mating and land dowry rituals. The Chachnam have resisted that."

Both Q rocked back and forth.

"True," K'listan said. "But it is more than that. There is talk that the humans are stealing the souls of the Chachnam. Removing their essence. Word of this has spread through all the villages. Stories of the assault on D'idawan's fortress has spread throughout Mukalasa'at."

G'livan took over. "The bask is important to our race, you understand?"

Everyone nodded. The Q biology allowed them to receive nutrition through photosynthesis. The sun literally fed them.

"For the Chachnam, it is part of *Chachnam-kakataaa*."

Of course. A function so vital to their being would likely have religious associations in their culture. Kel had already assumed something like that must be true.

"D'idawan was preaching for a return to the old ways. She not only wanted to halt the new way of life for the Chachnam, she wanted to return to an earlier time in Chachnam history. When the Chachnam were in danger from the great catastrophe, they lived underground. It is known to them all."

"What great catastrophe?" Kel asked.

"It is part of Chachnam lore," K'listan said. "Some of it is true and there is science to explain it. The Disciplined believe the Chachnam ancient history describes the occurrence of a solar flare or other phenomenon that rained over this continent."

This took Kel aback. It shouldn't have. The Q were an advanced race, but sometimes he allowed himself to forget that because of the manner in which they lived. They were not primitives.

"For some part of their history, they lived in caves and caverns and their *prophet* saved them in this way. The Chachnam were led to a period of great prosperity afterwards. The tales of their ancestors' survival of the great catastrophe by retreat underground is an important part of their culture."

Kel understood. "So, the caves that the Third Battalion renegades were making in the fortress were more than just fortifications against attack, it was part of D'idawan's religious fundamentalism?"

The two Q were silent after this. They spoke to each other rapidly and quietly before G'livan answered. "We think we understand your words. D'idawan tried to return to a practice from earlier times from Chachnam beliefs. Yes."

Kel saw a connection. "The Sun-Loyal troops we took with us to search the tunnels in the fortress, they seemed disturbed or awed at the large caverns where we fought D'idawan. Was this because of the great catastrophe myth?"

K'listan spoke again. "It is no myth. Our historians and scientists have documented that an extinction level event occurred on Mukalasa'at several thousand years ago. The Chachnam rose to greatness after this event. They were saved by one of their kind, an elevated one who led them to live in great caves. That part is Chachnam myth. It is not the belief or history of the Disciplined."

G'livan answered next. "The Chachnam troops were certainly awed to see the re-creation of the caverns from their ancient tales," G'livan added. "The Chachnam live above ground and bask their entire lives. It would be a departure from modern life for them to consider housing themselves underground."

"Unless," Braley said, "there was a great disaster looming. Like the changes brought by the accords?"

K'listan clucked. "Perhaps."

"Didn't this occur to you at the time?" Kel asked.

K'listan rocked on her hind legs again. "My sister and I have been talking about these things since we witnessed them," K'listan said. "I know the Chachnam well, but some of their thinking is *alien* to me."

"And to me," G'livan admitted. "I told you, Sergeant Kel-boss, they are weak of mind. Superstitious. Do you understand?"

"I do. It translates well." He remembered G'livan telling him the Chachnam could not be trusted. "What does 'colorless' mean to you? One of the humans we rescued from the mob said she heard the attackers saying 'colorless.'"

"Yes. During the examination by the arbiter, the youths mentioned that the humans stole the souls from the dead. What the simple-minded adolescents were saying was that the blasters somehow stole the life force from the Chachnam in a particularly evil way. You have noticed how bleached the bodies of our race are when struck by the energy-based weapons? Much faster than the normal process of our bodily decay."

Everyone chorused agreement. It was a distinctive feature of Q death by blaster bolt.

"These fools believe that during the time of death, the life force takes time to leave the physical body before reaching the new plane of existence. It is during this time of blanching that the journey occurs, and the soul tested and judged. You humans are somehow interfering with that and causing death to the spirit by blanching the color out of us all at once."

Sims jumped off his bunk. "Hey, wait a minute! The Q already had blaster tech. You have blasters on your tanks and on the Rolies. You use blasters and lasers for industrial processes. Why are these kids so upset about blasters now?"

The two Q clucked.

"Superstition is by its nature irrational, is it not?" G'livan said.

"So, let me get this straight." Sims held up a finger. "A. D'idawan wasn't just opposed to the changes of the accord, she was some kind of religious zealot trying to lead the Chachnam back into their dark ages? Great."

A second finger extended.

"Two. We didn't quash the rebellion by killing D'idawan and destroying the Third Battalion. There's some kind of wacky insurgency in the villages based on D'idawan's screwed up ideas. Awesome."

Three fingers.

"C. The wackos are incensed because when we kill them with a blaster, not only are they dead, they can't find their way to Q heaven? Fantastic. Braley!" Sims said as he turned to face the commander. "I want to go back to killing zhee. It was much simpler. I like my religious zealots easy to understand."

Everyone remained silent as Sims marched back to his bunk and started pulling on his armor. The two Q rose to leave.

"I am sorry that I did not have these epiphanies sooner, Captain Braley-boss, Sergeant Kel-boss. It was only after witnessing the interrogations that this information came to my realization," K'listan said and bowed slightly.

Braley gave a slight bow in return. "Thank you, Havildar K'listan, Trooper G'livan. You are brave warriors as well as our friends. You have helped us greatly."

Kel moved to follow the Q through the threshold and out into the night air.

"I will see you and the platoon in the morning. We are starting the transition to blasters tomorrow. I will start with the recon platoon while the rest of the team has a day to train the officers. Do you think this will be a problem, if there's a belief that the blasters are evil tech?"

The two Q clucked.

"As long as we get our new blasters, we do not care what the silly Chachnam believe."

Kel watched them go before retrieving his K-17 for watch. Sims brushed past Kel's shoulder.

"Where are you going, man?"

"You might as well sleep, Kel. I can't even think about it now."

"What?"

"What do you mean, 'what'? This whole crazy continent is full of whacked out bugs who want to pull us limb from limb because a mining company needs to get richer. I can't wait to get off this planet. It's not too late in the evening. I'm going to bounce Monica and try to get her read on these new revelations. Maybe the xenoanthropologists will know something useful." He walked away, mumbling, "If she'll talk to me."

18

Sleep did arrive, but not before he'd mulled over what their Disciplined friends said. What weighed on his mind was the idea that there could be an ideological resistance so powerful that it could motivate them to harm their own elders, as well as the humans they collaborated with. After he ran through his morning routine and dressed, he woke Sims.

"Hey, did you get to talk to Monica last night?"

Sims scratched himself and rose to sit on the edge of the bunk. "Yeah," he said noncommittally.

"Well? What did she say?"

He shrugged. "She's mad. At first she didn't want to talk to me and closed the link. I forced my next bounce through so she had to. I told her the truth. I just wanted to get her expert opinion about what we learned from K'listan last night."

"Did she listen?"

"Yeah. Eventually. She let me tell her the story of the attack on the provincial development team, and all the weird stuff with the caverns and the blasters and the catastrophe and, you know, all that stuff." He rubbed his eyes as he stood and then stretched his arms overhead.

"And?"

"She said it was new to her. Like she told us, the Chachnam and Big M as a whole haven't been well studied. She heard about the rescue, of course. Said she thought it might have been me on the rescue mission, and was going to bounce me to see if I was okay, blah, blah, blah." He trailed off as he grabbed the sonic shaver out of his toiletry kit. "She was interested in everything I had to say. Except about seeing her when we got back to D-Town, that is."

Kel felt bad for his teammate. "Sorry, man. Give her time. She'll come around."

"Ah, I'm over it. Let's get the day rolling, what do you say?" He yawned again. "I'm looking forward to teaching some giant bugs how to use blasters today. How about you?"

"That's why I signed up in the first place."

Kel spent his day with the recon platoon, getting the new blasters and their optical sights collimated for each shooter. It was not necessary to discharge energy in a destructive power output to zero the weapons. The N-16s allowed for a mode that placed discrete burns into the targets that were virtually the same size as the 7mm holes from their Stonewells. It saved much destruction to the backstops of the rifle range as opposed to using the blasters at any other power setting. The optical sighting systems were easier for the Q to use than those on their S-5s, and the process of zeroing the weapons went quicker than Kel had expected.

They finished the day by taking an excursion on their bikes to an open area several kilometers from the garrison. Kel had planned for the training and prepared the short canyon for the Q's marksmanship practice, much as he did for their own team training. He set up impervisteel plate scraps on small rock ledges and marked some of the larger boulders with geometric shapes.

"The N-16 will range the target and select the energy mode based on the distance to the target, unless you override the selection manually. Most of these targets are around two hundred meters away. I prefer that you try the focused light energy mode to avoid destroying the targets with the particle beam setting. Let's try. First shooters to the line."

Two troopers came forward and assumed their "squatting prone" position.

"On the left. Identify the boulder with the triangle. On the right. Identify the far-right square steel plate in the array. I want a five-shot group on your target. Shooters ready? Fire."

Both shooters commenced firing. The targets were each about thirty by thirty centimeters. The sandstone surface of the boulder where Kel had engraved a triangle was scorched after the second shot, his triangle mark soon obscured. The steel plate fared a little better, but was melted by the final shot.

"That was on the coherent light energy beam setting at twenty-five percent power discharge," Kel told the semicircle of Q standing behind the firing line. Then, to the two shooters, "Check your charge packs."

"Ninety-eight percent remaining, Sergeant Kel-boss," the first trooper reported.

"The same, Sergeant Kel-boss."

Kel faced the group. "The readout will tell you the number of shots remaining as an estimate based on current power mode, but it is just that. An estimate. By learning how your N-16 uses power with different outputs and at different ranges, you'll develop the ability to make a good guesstimate of how many shots you have based on the percentage of charge cell remaining. It takes some experience, but will be a more accurate guide."

As usual, the Disciplined raised no questions.

"Next shooters to the line."

They finished the training day after every member of the platoon had gotten to shoot, and ambled downrange to inspect their targets. All the impervisteel scrap plates and rock faces had been rendered unrecognizable. Kel was glad he'd found as many plates as he had. Any fewer and he would have had to identify random areas on the cliff face for the marksmen to aim at. If it would have been unsatisfying for anyone, it would have been him. He didn't like to shoot at indistinct targets for his own training, and didn't want to conduct what he considered lazy training for his recon platoon.

They rode back to the garrison and before dismissing the platoon, Kel pulled K'listan aside and gave her instructions for the next day's training.

"Havildar, tomorrow we begin training the rifle companies. Once again, we will be assisting the officers and havildars of the First Battalion as they train their troopers. I prefer that the recon platoon be on the range with us for the rest of the week to assist."

"Yes, Sergeant Kel-boss. We have not assisted in training the rifle company troopers before."

"Yes. I am not so much anticipating trouble training the troopers as I am... wanting my most reliable troops on the range in case of trouble."

K'listan tilted her head. "You are expecting trouble."

Kel shrugged. "Let's just say I believe in being prepared. After our discussion last night, I think it would be wise. Captain Braley was going to speak to the nawab and the junior officers today about such a possibility."

The large purple Q rocked back and forth. "The troopers of the rifle companies are from a lower caste than the officers. Many are the same clan as the farmers who attacked Diplomat D'alak and the provincial development team. I think that is a wise precaution."

"Tell the rest of the Disciplined not to be overly concerned, just alert to the possibility."

"It will be done, Sergeant Kel-boss."

They'd gotten through the lecture portion of the following morning, introducing the troops to their new weapons via holo, reviewing the features of the N-16, the modes, and the fire control mechanism. The operating controls were little different than their S-5s, or virtually any shoulder fired weapon, and Kel was amazed that by the end of the introductory presentation, there were few questions.

Late that morning, the troops were lined up by company outside the armory to be issued their new blasters, one squad at a time. Kel and the team milled about, trying to stay out of the way of the Q cadre supervising the operation. K'listan and the rest of the recon platoon likewise crouched under a large nearby tree, putting Kel's guidance into action.

Though the Q did not have facial expressions per se, the troops seemed excited. As each squad exited the battalion armory, the troopers cradled their brand new weapons with blatant admiration.

"Check it out. Everyone looks like they just got the best birthday present of their lives," Poul said laughing.

"I've seen Legion companies less organized. I'd say the level of motivation is pretty high today," Bigg said.

Kel nodded. "Agreed. It's going smoothly."

Maybe there's nothing to worry about, he hoped.

The battalion marched to the range in company order, with the recon platoon bringing up the rear, followed by Kel and the team. The humans could not march to the Q's slow, staggering lope. Their uneven gait made maintaining a sixty-paces-per-minute march difficult. The Q did not sing to keep cadence, but whirred with their smaller mouth parts while their mandibles clicked in unison every other step.

A flat repulsor sled sped by them and the marching formation, headed to the range down the dead-end road.

"Well, I'll go catch up with the nawab so I can praise her troops to her," Braley said as he broke into a trot.

It was all part of the job. Kel was glad it wasn't his.

They rarely saw the plump orange and jeweled nawab. Today she made an appearance, no doubt because of the shiny new presents. The arming of the Sun-Loyal troops with weapons equivalent to those used by the Republic forces was an auspicious event, even for the seemingly detached commander.

"She's probably out here to bear witness for the mughal that the mining consortium paid off on their promise," Kel said to Bigg.

"No doubt."

Soon the battalion stood in full formation, the recon platoon in the rear with Kel and the team.

The nawab addressed the gathered command.

"Today we start the process of strengthening the defense of the Chachnam and our mughal's rule over this land. You are trusted with this great honor because you have proven worthy. The mughal and I demand that your service is unquestioning and fearless. Do not fail." With her petty threats finished, she walked off the field, returned to her sled, and sped away.

"Heading back to the sunning station next to her mansion with slaves to fan her, I assume," Sims said over L-comm.

"Well, she never has been one for long speeches. I kind of admire that in a leader," Poul said.

"Sergeants-boss," K'listan said, stalking over.

"What is it, K'listan?" Kel asked.

"Sergeants-boss, one of my troopers has heard a rumor. Last night, a trooper was encouraging others in her platoon to rebel against the havildars and officers. Trooper K'granda told me she overheard two troopers speaking about it this morning while awaiting the issue of the new weapons."

Bigg spoke. "What did she hear, exactly?"

"She said the troopers spoke of a malcontent who encouraged them to refuse to use the new weapons. That the blasters are evil and bring harm to the Chachnam."

"Sounds like the indoctrination the provincial development team met with," Sims said.

"Braley, you hearing this?" Bigg asked.

"Yeah. On my way. Do we know what company?"

"K'listan?" Bigg asked.

"It occurred during the early part of the issue. I believe the First Rifles were still receiving weapons at this time."

A Q voice rose above all others and filled the air. There was no voder following the noises with translation.

What the kark now? Kel thought.

"Over here, guys," Braley said over L-comm. "There's a trooper out of formation causing the commotion. Her voder and rifle are on the ground and she's lecturing the company. Get over here and bring the recon platoon. The havildar's about to shut it down in a big way."

They double-timed to Braley. The First Rifles stood in rank and file, a lone Q in front facing the columns of troops, a mix of percussion and whistles issuing from her beak like a symphony of reeds and hammers. Frenzied like a zhee revving up for the death by a thousand cuts ritual. The havildar with her three painted stripes returned the challenge, both forelimbs raised to strike.

"Get back in formation immediately. Pick up that rifle and your voder. I'm not telling you again. Who is your squad leader? Naik! Attend your trooper."

As Kel neared, his bucket translated the protestations of the frenzied trooper who strode up and down the front rank.

"It is *blasphemy*. It is an abomination, to arm us with the same weapons that stole the souls of our sisters in the Third Battalion. It is a sign of the coming of the end times for the Chachnam. The Mughal D'shtaran is a false mughal to allow such *blasphemy* to occur—"

"Seize this trooper immediately!" the havildar repeated. No one from the formation moved.

Kel looked to K'listan. "Better get out there with some troops and apprehend that trooper before this gets out of hand."

K'listan barked orders, leading the vault toward the agitator. A swarm of purple carapaces sprang with her.

They raced around the motionless ranks to reach the front of the formation where the crazed trooper continued her call to rebellion.

"Rise up against the *apostates*! Rise up! Use your arms against the humans! It is only just to kill their souls with the same magic that takes the souls of our sisters. Rise up!"

A trooper from the front rank leaped forward and tackled the agitator, just as the havildar reached the trooper to do the same. K'listan and her troops arrived a second behind. A mass of green and purple limbs flailed around the hissing, shrieking soldier.

Bigg must have sensed the team wanting to get into the fray. "Stay out of it, men. Watch the rest of the troops."

Kel wasn't going to get in the mix. He was just ready for it. There were better things he could do if this was going to escalate. "Let K'listan and the Q handle this. Keep your heads on a swivel and let's make sure this was just one lone fanatic."

The team fanned out into a small perimeter facing outward. Kel loaded an energy grenade into his launcher. If a significant number of Q made a move against the team, there'd be little they could do, exposed in the open as they were.

Kel was positioned so he could still see the commotion at the front of the Q formation.

"They're carrying the fanatic away," he told his team. "Someone must've clocked her pretty good. Her head's dangling. K'listan is leading the custody party off range."

A subadar approached their perimeter. Kel recognized her as the company commander of the Second Rifles.

"Captain Braley, are you and your team well?"

Braley stepped forward to meet the subadar. "Yes, Subadar T'klat. All is well. What happened?"

The subadar approximated a shrug. "It seems the situation is now in control. My sister, Subadar T'chan, is busy reestablishing order amongst the First Rifles. Perhaps we continue training and allow my company to begin our work? Will you assist us? There is much to be done."

Braley stepped off with the subadar from the Second Rifles as Kel turned back to where the First Rifles still stood in formation. Their subadar, T'chan, now stood in front of them, their havildar and the trooper who had tackled the agitator standing behind her. The subadar addressed her troops.

"Who knew that Trooper C'shkar was a deviant? Who knew?"

None of the troopers moved.

"Why did no trooper follow the orders of her havildar, save Trooper C'grank? Why did no trooper restrain the deviant C'shkar when ordered? Answer me!"

Again, no trooper in the formation moved or spoke.

"Very well. Company! Attention!"

The troops responded to her command and now stood at attention.

"Lay down your arms. Lay them at your feet. Do it now!"

Kel and the rest of the team were mesmerized as the company commander disarmed her troops.

"Havildar C'kaln, Trooper C'grank. You will march the company back to garrison where they will be confined to quarters under guard. A detail will be assigned to recover the weapons of the disgraced. Move out!"

The havildar and the trooper, now the only ones armed in the company, marched the troops back to the garrison. Kel and the others moved out of the way as the company was directed by its havildar along the dirt road to march behind the line of the other companies of the battalion, still in formation. Troops broke discipline to turn and watch as the disarmed company marched away, the lone armed trooper in the trail position, her weapon held at the ready as she marched.

"What did we just witness? This wasn't a little thing, boys," Poul asked.

"Nope," Sims said. "Did you catch the subadar call the whole company disgraced?"

"Know what I think?" Kel said. "The battalion staff must be aware some of the troops are in the D'idawan cult frame of mind. If so, I don't like that they've been keeping that to themselves. They must suspect that's the case. Why else would Subadar T'chan have disarmed the whole company, unless she suspected that there were more sympathizers among them?"

"Boom." Braley knife handed Kel. "I'm going to go on record here and say I think that's a good possibility."

"We've seen some pretty harsh punishment for infractions of discipline from the Q," Bigg said. "I'm not sure what's going to go down, but we have to be prepared. Let's assume that we're about to experience a breakdown in discipline in the battalion. The same battalion we've just armed with N-16s. No one goes anywhere unaccompanied. Buddy system. That means you too, Braley."

"Okay, Bigg," the team leader responded without hesitation.

"In the meantime, let's get back to the task at hand and try to get this unit acting like soldiers again."

They finished the day's training without incident and spent the rest of the night in the team house, keeping two-man watches throughout the night. Early the next morning Braley received a message from the nawab's adjutant. "Change of plan, gents. There's going to be a battalion formation this morning. By order of the nawab, there will be no training today," he read to them all.

"Any clue what's going to happen?" Poul asked.

"Oh, I think we know what's going to happen," Sims interjected. "These guys punish disloyalty by ritual execution. That crazy trooper is going to be made an example of. I'm just not sure what's going to happen to the rest of her company who did nothing to stop her."

"I saw the recon platoon guarding the First Rifles' barracks last night," Kel said. "I haven't had the chance to talk to K'listan, but I have a feeling her platoon will be the executioners as well as the jailers. Remember when they made her stay behind to handle the village? The Disciplined seem to be the vanguard for every action where the battalion needs professional soldiery. I get the sense this is their hereditary role for the Chachnam."

"Well, let's not be late then," Braley said, pulling on his armor.

The battalion was once again formed by company order, this time on the parade field facing the battalion headquarters building. The parade field was carpeted in fine purple clover and in the center stood one lone tree, its wide canopy shading the otherwise bare field. A woven cable dangled from one of the thickest branches. At its end was a noose.

Nawab Q'stalt exited the headquarters building on the far side of the rectangular parade field, hopping slowly to the elevated platform in front of the battalion formation. Her orange-hued staff trailed behind her as she ambled up the dais ramp, her subordinates moving to the front of the stage to stand on either side of their commander.

"What are we getting ready to see?" Sims asked over L-comm.

"Whatever it is," Poul said, nodding to a nearby tree, "it isn't going to be good. That cable hanging under the tree isn't for decoration. I've never seen it there before."

"Adjutant," the nawab said, "call the battalion to attention."

The battalion's nizam strode forward and addressed the battalion and brought them to the position of attention. The battalion responded and assumed an upright rigid posture. The field was silent.

"Trooper C'grank, First Rifles, present yourself before the battalion."

On Kel's right stood the First Rifles. K'listan and the recon platoon surrounded the company, armed with their N-16s. No one else in the battalion carried arms besides the havildars, the officers, and the recon platoon.

A dark-green Q stepped out of the formation and sped to the podium in the center of the field. She halted in front of the platform and snapped to attention. The battalion commander stalked down, a staff officer trailing behind. Kel increased his bucket magnification to get a better view. He did not think that the trooper, the only one in the company to act against the dissident C'shkar, was in danger. He was correct.

The nawab took the small instrument offered by her adjutant and painted three gold stripes on C'grank's shoulders, said a few words, and dismissed her. The newly promoted havildar did an about face and vaulted away, posting herself to the rear with the recon platoon guarding the First Rifles.

"Bravery and courage are expected in the service of the mughal and will be rewarded," the nawab addressed the battalion. "Cowardice and treachery will be punished. Present the prisoner."

Kel's attention had been focused on the display at the center of the field, and had missed the procession forming behind the gathered battalion. Tall K'listan and three of her Disciplined sisters surrounded a smaller, dark green Q. C'shkar. They tramped over to the enormous tree and the hangman's noose underneath.

"I guess hanging is more humane than tearing off your limbs before biting your head off," Poul said.

Kel somehow doubted what they were about to witness was a simple hanging.

K'listan and her prisoner detail stopped beneath the tree to position the prisoner underneath the cable. They produced coils of rope and worked loops around the limbs of the prisoner.

"Proclaiming heresy against the mughal is a high crime," the nawab continued. "Inciting other Chachnam to take up arms against the mughal is treachery of the highest order. The punishment is death."

K'listan held the end of the rope fastened to C'shkar's lower limbs while the two Disciplined troopers beside C'shkar held the lines attached to her upper limbs. The noose hung around her neck.

K'listan and the two other executioners walked backward, removing slack from the ropes until the prisoner lifted off the ground, spreading her limbs in the form of a cross. The prisoner wrenched and fought as she strangled. The executioners heaved and strained, stretching the prisoner tighter and tighter until her suspended body was pulled taut. As if on cue, each executioner sprang backward forcefully, and with a sickening pop and splatter, the three were suddenly released from tension. C'shkar's body fell, her separated limbs twitching on the ground, the head suspended in the noose.

"They really have this thing about pulling off limbs and heads, don't they?" Sims muttered.

"Disgraced members of the First Rifles," said the nawab, "with shameful cowardice, you failed to follow orders from your superiors to subdue the zealot in your midst. Investigation has revealed the zealot had proselytized to her company the night before her attempt to incite rebellion, and not one trooper obeyed her oath of loyalty to the mughal to report the blasphemy. With the exception of Havildar C'grank, not one of you acted. For that, each of you is found guilty by your mughal of conspiracy and is labelled disgraced. You are stripped of all rights in the Chachnam breeding caste and are discharged to return to your clan, never to rise in station. Escort the disgraced to the gates for banishment."

The battalion remained at attention as the recon platoon marched the disgraced company past the formation in the direction of the main gates, and out of sight.

"All companies are released to their subadars for renewal of loyalty oaths. Upon successful completion of the same, the battalion will resume training tomorrow. Nizam, dismiss the companies to their subadars."

The companies dismissed from the field one at a time and marched to their quarters. Not until they were gone did Kel's team turn inward.

"I think Bigg and I need to request a meeting with Nawab Q'stalt and get some clarification," Braley said. "You guys head back to the team house and we'll be there as soon as possible. When we've got more info, I'll contact Jaimie and Dari and the rest of Seven to let them know what we're experiencing. I would expect we'd have heard something from them if anything like this was developing with the Second Battalion.

"Then I've got to report to the embassy team. They need to be apprised of the situation. We've heard a lot of anti-human stuff. If there's further resistance against the accords, and it's following a pattern of radicalism of the D'idawan sort, it may mean more violence against our people on Big M."

They all nodded. Sims snapped his head up, like a canix hearing a whistle. He stood looking down the parade field lane. Kel looked, but saw nothing.

"What is it, Sims?" he asked.

"Not sure. Thought I heard something."

They stayed silent. Focusing. Straining. Kel increased his bucket volume to max.

"I hear it. It's faint. Sounds like that shrieking the Q make," Poul said. "Say, you don't think..."

"Okay," Bigg said. "You three, stay together and check it out. The boss and I are off to the head shed to see the nawab. Meet you back at the team house. Stay alert. Bounce us and check in with whatever you find."

"Rog," the three said almost simultaneously.

They formed a wedge and moved out at a fast march. Kel's thighs ached to break into a run and find the source of the noise. He knew what they would find. Sounds like an impervisteel rod breaking echoed off the three-story barracks lining the main drag. The closer they got to the front gate, the louder the shrieks became.

"You've got to be kidding me!" It was worse than he'd imagined. Kel broke into a run, his teammates tearing down the lane behind him.

Leading out of the compound were a series of panels erected as a channel, forcing the pedestrians traveling through it into a single file. Disciplined commandos herded the disgraced First Rifles into this funnel. K'listan and several of her troops waited at the other end. Two of the recon troopers grabbed the next Q in line, who wrenched herself away. The purple Disciplined Q again grabbed the smaller Chachnam female by her arms and pulled them out to her side. K'listan stepped forward with a monomolecular edged blade and hacked off each of the Q's wrists, dropping them on a pile of twitching limbs.

As if nothing extraordinary occurred, the First Rifle Subadar T'chan stood in supervision, bordered by her two havildars, C'kaln, and the newly promoted C'grank.

"*Stop. Stop this right now!*" Kel yelled as he halted, shocked at the grizzly sight. "K'listan, stand down!"

First Rifle Subadar T'chan hissed, "You have no right to give orders here, human. This is a lawful order given by the mughal. The disgraced cannot be left with a hand to raise against her. It is the law."

Kel ignored her. "K'listan, stop!"

The two Q from the recon platoon shoved the amputated Q out of the gate and grabbed the next victim who struggled to pull away.

K'listan gripped the blade.

"Sergeant Kel-boss, I must do as I am ordered. Do nothing to taint my honor.

Please. Return to your domicile. I will come later and explain."

Kel's teammates took him by the shoulders. "Hey, man, back off. Let's tell Bigg and Braley. There's nothing we can do."

Kel allowed himself to be pulled away. They took several steps back and watched in horror as the next Q's wrists were chopped off, her shrieking cries piercing the air, no longer a strain to hear. Kel had forgotten to lower the volume on his external audio and did so now.

"Let's get to the team house. Come on," Poul said. "Bigg, we found out what the noise was. You're not going to believe it."

They trudged back toward their hut.

Sims mumbled, "I've never wanted off a planet so badly in my life."

19

"Believe the guy on the ground."

That's what Legion Dark Ops Commander, Colonel Hartenstein, once said.

"You can record all the holos you want for evidence, compile it in a proper report, gift wrap it with a bow, but if those faceless people in dress uniforms and silk robes sitting a half a galaxy away decide it never happened, it never happened. No matter what you see with your own two eyes, no matter what you can prove, facts are irrelevant to someone who doesn't want to hear bad news. The most you can do is do your job right. Forget nothin'. The rest is up to the galaxy to accept, or not."

Informing an embassy team about a hairy situation was never easy. In Kel's experience, most diplomats and pols were skeptical of any information from an outside source. As Braley and Bigg spoke to layers of diplomatic functionaries, repeating their observations regarding recent events over and over up the bureaucratic chain, there was finally a call that included among others, the ambassador, the Republic Intelligence station chief, and the head of Solar Wind Mining Consortium, Phillipe Cardoso.

Team Seven was included on the holo conference as well. Jaimie and Dari were reporting similar occurrences within the Second Battalion's ranks. Q proselytizing against the "blasphemous" blasters. A stand-down from training declared. The leadership confident harsh punishment would restore discipline. Evidently a dangerous ideology was taking hold among the Sun-Loyal.

"It just sounds like poor management to me," said Mr. Cardoso. "And it sounds like D'shtaran is dealing with it according to their laws and customs. Captain, I appreciate your concern, but what you're suggesting sounds a little reactionary. Halt the upgrades of their army? Renege on our agreement and desert our support of the mughal? All because you find their discipline methods extreme? I thought legionnaires were immune to cruelty. Isn't that your way of life? Yet you condemn the Q culture as cruel. Isn't it possible that your perspective is tainted by your own human-centric upbringing? Besides, the only way to influence their culture for the better is by doing what we're doing now—continuing to build bonds instead of severing them."

Lips pursed, Braley listened until he was sure Phillipe had finished. "I wouldn't make the recommendation to renege, Mister Cardoso. We're reporting evidence that some form of ideological, perhaps religious, fanaticism has appeared. The implications are important to us on the ground. We may be seeing the rise of an insurgency against the corporate and Republic's mission on the continent, and most importantly, a very real threat of violence against humans here."

Cardoso scoffed, "That's quite a leap, Captain. One lone fanatic out of an entire battalion of native troops hardly seems like proof of a radical conversion by the masses. I think the fault in your perspective is that you are too close to the problem. You fail to appreciate the scope of our progress on Big M. The terms of the accord are proceeding well and the benefits to the Chachnam are being realized by them as we speak—"

"Of course," the intelligence chief interrupted, "that couldn't be said about the hamlet where your people were attacked, could it?"

Cardoso waved his point away. "Another isolated incident, Mister Cummings. Our development team is already back and cementing the relationship again—"

This time the ambassador interrupted. "Clearly, gentlemen, we can admit that there is the potential for disturbance. Whether at this time it's a small potential that can be contained or one that may be growing, it cannot be ignored."

Ambassador Grealy was measured in his speech and used a gentle tone, one Kel thought reflected a lifetime of practice. It was how Braley spoke. It made him think about how he was perceived when dealing with others.

Giving Braley a steady look, he said, "I'm interested in hearing Captain Yost and his team's recommendations. Captain?"

"Thank you, Mister Ambassador," Braley said, matching the measured tone of the senior diplomat. "I have concerns about the process of upgrading the armaments of the Sun-Loyal. It's having effects not anticipated. I'll go ahead and call it a religious objection for lack of a more precise term, but there is a very real belief on the part of some Q that death by these armaments impedes their resurrection to an afterlife. Captain Jaimie, can you share with the group what you've experienced?"

"Yes," Jaimie said. "We haven't had the unrest to the degree that you've seen, but our attempt to issue the N-16s yesterday was disastrous. The troops refused. Peacefully, but they refused. Most of the battalion petitioned the nawab to reconsider the issue. There was no incitement to violence against the officers or us by any element, but in my opinion, there is a widespread belief among the lower breeding caste that the weapons violate a core religious belief."

The ambassador frowned. "Captain Jaimie, what's the response been by the leadership to this petition?"

"For now, the battalion commander has calmed the troops and made a plea for understanding while she receives guidance from the mughal. She meets with D'shtaran tomorrow, as I'm sure the nawab of the First Battalion is as well," Jaimie said, nodding toward Braley over the holo.

"Yes, that's correct. We received the same assurance from Q'stalt that she'll be meeting with the mughal. I wish our nawab had the same measured response yours did, Jaimie. Maybe meeting with D'shtaran will provide her with the guidance to be less dictatorial and brutal. When Q'stalt perceives disloyalty, her response is institutionalized violence to enforce discipline."

"Sounds like a very tense situation, Captain Yost," the ambassador said.

Cardoso again interjected. "Yes, I'm sure it was, but allow me to remind us all, especially our Legion friends, that the Q have their own cultural norms. Let's not permit our species-centric concepts of morality to prejudice our perspective."

Braley remained silent.

The ambassador seemed to take no notice of Phillipe's comment. "Captain Yost, you were right to bring these developments to my attention. I want you to continue to keep me informed of any concerns or insights as they occur. Contact me directly. That is my directive," he said with a nod to his chargé d'affaires, who sat taking notes.

"Gentlemen, do you think that you can continue with your missions at this time?"

Jaimie nodded. "I do, Mister Ambassador. We're having good success getting the Third Battalion rebuilt using part of the Second. The tanks are being delivered on schedule. If we can get an accommodation from D'shtaran and the battalion commanders on the transition to the N-16s, perhaps we can nip this in the bud. I'm thinking that we suggest a reissue of the Stonewells to try to obviate the conflict in their beliefs. Letting the troops continue to use their projectile launchers again should be the pressure release valve. Let them keep the blasters the company provided locked up in the armory. That way the company has kept their end of the bargain to D'shtaran, and they can figure out over time if there is a way to acceptably integrate their use by the troops."

Braley grunted. "That's a good idea. I'm going to make a similar recommendation to our nawab if it appears there's an issue, but so far, we had only the one company balk at the blasters. The other companies had no issues with the transition. We may not need to use the same tactic, but I'm going to bring that to her attention as an option."

The ambassador smiled. "Excellent suggestion. I think you should implement the plan as discussed. Mister Cardoso and I have more to go over, so I'll let you gentlemen get back to your teams. I'd like to make this a daily event until we have some indication that this crisis has been averted. Neal," he said to his chargé, "budget an hour."

The ambassador continued speaking to others in the room as someone placed a datapad in his hand.

Kel was impressed. The ambassador had shown himself to be an adaptable leader and rather than exclude the legionnaires from the discussions, had made them the center of the collaboration. The link broke and it left Team Seven on the holo with the Team Three operators.

"That went better than I expected," Braley said.

Bigg leaned forward. "We need to keep in closer communication, Dari. Let's link up on L-comm daily to keep tabs on our respective situation."

The Kill Team Seven Team sergeant nodded. "How about twice a day, say 0900 and 2100 for a routine sitrep, then as needed for anything significant?"

Bigg made a finger gun and pointed at Dari. "We'll do it. We're keeping a fifty-percent watch here. I don't have any indication that there's an immediate threat to us, but hearing a zealot call for our deaths because of blasphemy does tend to raise the threat level."

Dari chuckled, "Yeah, I bet. Until tomorrow," and broke the link.

"All right, it took all day, but we've got guidance now. Let's set a watch and the boss and I will hammer out a plan for tomorrow," Bigg said as he opened screens on his datapad and pushed projections into space around him.

Braley sat across from Bigg doing the same. "I'll send a message to the nawab's adjutant and get a meet with us first thing in the morning. I have a feeling training may be shut down another day. I am going to make a suggestion, though."

Everyone looked toward the team leader.

"This goes without saying, but keep your kit ready to bounce out of here at my say so. If we have to activate the E and E plan, well, just know that we will."

The Escape and Evade plan was an important part of every mission planning. Theirs was a fluid one, as they had worked from many locations around the continent, not just out of the First Battalion garrison. If the security situation became untenable and they had to flee, they'd worked out multiple options for independently fighting their way to safety and then finding travel back to the capital. But it would be a virtually impossible fight if they were surrounded by the battalion of Q and had to escape without Talon air support.

"I say we sneak out in the dead of night tonight, boss," Sims said. "They'd never expect it."

Everyone chuckled.

"Sims, I hope we don't look back and wish we had."

The next few days passed uneventfully. Training resumed and there were no further issues. During their daily holo conference with the embassy staff there were reports of unrest from the villages. Proselytizing against the accords and the blasphemous human weapons spread, but no violence against any of the development teams. Kel assumed they would've heard immediately if another rescue mission was needed.

Ambassador Grealy had led the discussion the day before.

"Mister Cardoso and I have a meeting with the mughal tomorrow. We are flying to her palace for the meet. Our Solar Wind executive is certain that this is an attempt to extort more tech from the company. My sense is that

Cardoso thinks he can get things back on track by leveraging the mughal's cooperation with more bribes.

"I am keeping an open mind, but I'm not so sure his assessment is correct based on reports from the development teams and our xenosociologists. I'm not convinced this is a top-down orchestrated ploy by the mughal, but rather a genuine groundswell against the accords. The analysis is that this quasi-religious fear of 'death by blaster' is just a convenient element. A way to propel change in their society. Regardless, I'll have more to share with you gentlemen after the next meeting."

The ambassador was continuing to impress Kel. He shared information, as well as his own analysis, with the legionnaires—as though he considered them another arm of his diplomatic mission.

If only the meeting with the nawab had been so productive. That conversation brought no assurances of compromise or ameliorated treatment of "disloyal" troops.

Braley told the team how it went.

"The mughal is pleased that the transition to the improved weaponry is occurring on schedule for the First Battalion of the Sun-Loyal. I can make no statement concerning my sister and the Second Battalion," Nawab Q'stalt clucked from her reclined position. "However, it is my understanding that an accommodation may be made for them. The clans that make up the Second Battalion are not the same as those that fill our ranks."

"Nawab-boss," Braley asked, "what about the First Rifles? Was that company from a clan that had connections to the renegade Third Battalion and D'idawan? Do you know why they showed, er, disloyalty?"

He wasn't sure how to best ask the question. He hadn't had the best rapport with the commander, and the dismissal of the First Rifles hadn't improved the relationship.

"It is not relevant to which clan the disgraced belong. There is only loyalty and disloyalty."

That had been her last word on the matter to her human advisors before dismissing them.

The next day found them reviewing patrol movement techniques with Third Rifles, having the jemadar and havildars conduct platoon-sized movements in one of the large training landscapes outside the garrison. How to negotiate terrain and provide security while moving a large dismounted element was complex, and needed continual refinement. It required the correct actions of the troops through their individual movement techniques, as well as the integration of those into all larger echelons of organization.

What some took as a walk through the woods with rifles was anything but.

Braley was advising the company subadar, with Kel and the rest of the team spread out advising the other junior leaders. It had been an uphill battle teaching some of the company commanders how to lead with a tactical mindset. They'd seen a spectrum of extremes in the company officers' leadership styles. One subadar insisted on always moving with the traveling element during a bounding overwatch, which was impractical. When two assaulting elements were separated by a great distance, the leader insisted that the trailing element move to her overwatch and "pick her up" on their way to the next overwatch position. It was an example of an officer who did not trust her junior leaders to perform their jobs without her supervision.

The other extreme was one where a company subadar remained with a small headquarters element and watched the advancing elements from a distance. During simulated contact with an enemy, the subadar was never in a position to influence the fight, and relegated all small unit leadership to her subordinates, expecting everything to just work itself out. With time, they had been able to instill a better problem-solving paradigm for the company leaders and now, the team found that very little guidance by them was needed to direct tactical movements. They were about to start another bounding overwatch across the next valley—and introduce a problem that included an opposing force—when Bigg gained their attention over L-comm.

"Team Three. Stop what you're doing and listen in. Dari, go ahead, I've got the whole team up on L-comm. Start over and tell them what you told me."

Dari's voice came over their buckets. "We've got trouble here. The battalion is in full revolt. We recommended that the battalion keep their S-5s if the N-16s were going to present a religious problem for the troops. The nawab agreed, and we began the reissue yesterday.

"That seems to have destroyed the calm more than improve it. The new narrative is that this is proof that we *knew* that the blasters caused 'soul-death,' or else we wouldn't have offered to return to the slug launchers. We're damned if we do and damned if we don't. The troops weren't fomenting violence against us or the officers before, but they sure as hell are now."

"Get out of there," Bigg demanded. "Initiate your E and E. If the troops have gone that irrational, just get out of there. Where's Jaimie?"

"Jaimie's with the nawab, trying to calm things down. Liu's with him. The rest of us are in the team house, getting assembled. I've got a link open with the air detachment; we've got a Talon speeding here now. You guys be careful and we'll keep you updated when we get to the capital. You should consider your own security situation. Dari out."

"Braley, you get all that?" Bigg asked.

"Yes, I did. What's everyone's impression? I'm not having any difficulties out here. Bigg, sound off."

"Ditto, sir. All smooth. Troops have their voders on. Everyone's following instructions. Seems to be just another day of training."

Kel, Poul, and Sims had the same to report. They were within visual distance of one another as they accompanied the individual squads through the long movement across the valley.

"We've had good rapport with the naiks and troopers all day," Kel spoke for the three of them. "No hint of anything negative I'm picking up, not that I'm an expert in reading the Q. We're good."

"Okay," Braley said. "Then we finish what we're doing. Bigg, why don't you and Poul peel out and stay on top of the situation with Seven? The rest of us will link up back at the team house later. Bounce us with any update."

"Rog," Bigg said.

"Man, this is getting weirder and weirder," Sims said to him.

"Well, just because Second Battalion is getting bizarre, doesn't mean our guys are going to."

"Agreed, Kel. But word spreads. Any malcontents placated today, when they hear that their whole sister battalion is in revolt, what then? You know it only takes that hard-core three percent of a group to start a riot. The other twenty-five percent that are on the fence, they won't go full-fledged rabid until the three percent do, then they join in. Everyone else suddenly has a choice—join or get trampled."

Kel agreed. Whether the percentages held true for non-human psychologies, it was still a valid observation.

"How many hard-core fanatics are hiding out in our battalion? Is it three percent? Is it less? More? Second Battalion had enough to push them over the edge into full revolt. That alone could spark it into flames here. What are we waiting for? When I told Braley we should get while the getting's good, I wasn't kidding."

Kel, Sims, and Braley descended the plateau overlooking the garrison, walking in trail behind the Third Rifles. The platoons were organized in a traveling formation, and were marching at a decent pace—for the Q—back to the garrison. Kel felt generally pleased with the efforts of the squad and platoon leaders in conducting the movements as a company.

There was nothing glorious or flashy about patrolling. It was infantry work at its most basic. Closing on an enemy, shooting, moving, and communicating as a team, and doing so with an element of violence of action was as old as warfare itself. The First Battalion of the Sun-Loyal were a light infantry unit, and as far as Kel was concerned, they had shown strong development. Kel felt pride in that. No matter that the Q were alien, no matter that they were part of a system that he could not comprehend or sympathize with, he felt a kinship with their yearning to be good soldiers.

"Team Three, you picking me up?" Bigg's voice filled their helmets.

"Yeah, Bigg, we're with you. What is it?" Braley answered.

"There was a ground fight at Seven's garrison, and now I can't get them on L-comm."

They raced to the team house. Kel had let his level of aerobic conditioning drop the past two weeks, and he felt it as he and his two teammates finished the last kilometer to their quarters, running at their full pace. The sun was setting, darkness rapidly covering the garrison grounds.

In the hut, Bigg sat with his bucket off, monitoring several open screens as he spoke to someone on the link. Poul stood looking over at the screens. He waved them over when they entered the room.

"We don't know much," Poul told them, speaking low. "The team made their way out of the garrison when a running gunfight started. We were listening in on the team guiding the Talon crew on approach to the landing zone. Then we lost them. Bigg's talking to the other Talon crew right now. They launched and are trying to get eyes on. They can't raise the first Talon crew either."

Kel felt a lump in his throat. If they couldn't raise Seven or the Talon crew, it meant something terrible happened. Bigg had the volume of the comms with the Talon crew turned up and one screen enlarged so they could all see the forward view from the Talon's down-looking camera.

Several Rolies and a tank sat on the plain outside the garrison. The Talon fell into a high-altitude orbit, the scene of the disaster told its own story. The magnification increased. A destroyed Talon sat on the ground a kilometer from the garrison. It was only identifiable by its twin tail booms. Scorches of blaster strikes marked the ground in all directions.

"They could be on foot. I can remotely activate their locators for you," Bigg said to the pilot. "Stand by."

Bigg opened another window and swiped through command codes. He could turn on all of Seven's beacons. It was an emergency protocol to identify a downed operator.

"I'm not getting a link confirmation. I'm trying again," Bigg said out loud, speaking to both the pilots and the rest of the team.

Kel pointed at the holo as the view from another angle became clear. Q troops advanced on the wreckage from the edge of the picture. There was no mistaking the bodies. Tossed about. Limp. Armor singed.

"They hit them as they were loading." Anger tinged Poul's voice, his face drained of color. He shook his head in disbelief as he stared at the holo. "They got them at the perfect time, while the Talon was on the ground. The Rolies and the tank got 'em. Blasted them right while they were loading. Look at it. There would've been nothing they could've done."

Kel gripped his shoulder. Last year Poul spent six months with Kill Team Seven, when the other members of Three were deployed on individual missions. Poul knew Seven as well as he knew his own team.

"Threat!" Sims yelled.

They all snapped around to the team house door. Kel raised his weapon only to see K'listan coming through the threshold, her appendages sprawled wide in front of her.

"Peace. Peace, Sergeants-boss. Peace," she implored, freezing under their muzzles.

"It's all right, guys." Kel stepped in front of her, forcing the others to lower their weapons. The team hadn't had contact with the recon platoon since the day of the execution. K'listan had promised to seek the team out later, but it hadn't happened. That raised questions about their relationship with the Disciplined.

"I apologize for not appearing sooner, Sergeant Kel-boss, but I was ordered elsewhere. I have come to share important news with my human friends."

Sims and Poul still faced K'listan, their weapons lowered, but both hands on their rifles. They did not have the same level of trust that Kel did.

"What news, K'listan?"

"The Disciplined are leaving the Sun-Loyal. We ask that you leave with us. We fear for your safety."

20

"Leaving the Sun-Loyal? Tell us what's happening."

K'listan took a cautious step into the foyer at Kel's beckoning. Braley moved to hear the conversation, putting his bucket on as he did so.

"Captain-boss, Sergeant-boss, there is a mutiny occurring in the Second Battalion now as we speak. The Chachnam have openly revolted against the officers of the battalion and have advocated an attack upon the humans."

Sims pointed at the holo in front of Bigg, the charred remains of the smoking Talon as Q picked over the site, pulling out the burned and broken bodies of their leej brothers.

"Yes, K'listan. We know."

The large Q froze, still as a statue, staring at the holo. Kel felt himself flush and his bile rise as Q hefted the Team Seven and Talon crew corpses and ripped them apart.

"Sergeants-boss, this is not the doing of the Disciplined," K'listan chittered. "I am in communication with my sisters in the Second Battalion. They flee with Sergeant Meadows-boss as we speak—"

"How do you know Meadows is with them?" Bigg asked, a sharp edge to his tone.

"I have just spoken with Havildar K'chak. Would you like to speak to Sergeant Meadows-boss?" K'listan produced her Q datalink to show Kel.

"Yes! Where are they? We haven't been able to locate any of Team Seven. Is Meadows okay? Do you know why he can't communicate with us?"

"Apparently when the retreat of the humans started, the reconnaissance platoon and Sergeant Meadows-boss were elsewhere. I do not know why he cannot speak with you; I only know he is alive. Allow me to raise my sister and we will know more."

K'listan spoke into her link. Kel could follow some of the exchange. In a minute, he heard Meadows's voice from the device and K'listan passed the datalink to Kel.

"Meadows, it's Turner, where are you?"

"Kel! Glad to hear your voice. We're moving fast, man, trying to get as much distance from the garrison as we can. I was with the recon platoon at their camp when we got hit by about a company of Q. They came right up our six and just opened up on us. I lost several of my commandos. We smoked the little sewer rats good. We're well off the X now, but it's been hard. We have our bikes and are staying off the roads."

Wind whistled in the background.

"What's wrong with your L-comm?" Kel asked. Bigg had mouthed the question to him twice so far.

"My bucket was off. I was taking a quick break when we got hit. I'd just talked to Dari when they got hit at the team house. I wanted to head back in to try to relieve them, get them some fire support to give them space to get out of there, but Jaimie and Dari told me to stay out and E and E on my own. They were confident they had it under control. It'd been getting a little weird the last couple of days, so it wasn't a big surprise. I took my bucket off for a good scratch just as I was going to give K'chak the sitrep. Rookie mistake, huh? It was hairy, man. Anything not on my body got left. My armor got hammered pretty bad, but I'm fine. Tell you what, they were more motivated going after us than they were the Third Battalion, know what I mean? I wish they'd have been half that aggressive in the fortress battle. We hurt them badly, though. Broke contact to get to the bikes and escaped. Anyway, I was going to wait until we made it to a defendable spot to raise someone on the Q link. Have you talked to Dari and the rest of the team?"

Kel looked around the room for help. Bigg nodded and mouthed, "Tell him."

The squeeze in his chest reminded him of drowning.

"Meadows, they didn't make it."

Dead air.

"Say again. I'm not sure I understood your last."

"They're gone. The Second rode heavies out and hammered them. Waited till the Talon was on the ground. The other air crew's in the air right now. We don't have any way of confirming, but it looks like everyone is down. I want you to find a defendable rally point and we'll send the Blackbird in for you."

Dead air again.

Kel understood. Meadows had just survived an ambush by his own troops. He and the recon platoon were fleeing for their lives. The news that he was the only survivor of his team was a blow. A full scale blast to the bucket.

"Meadows, the rest of the team is dead. Continue to escape and evade. Use the Q link to keep us informed of your location. We're going to get the Talon driver on your band and extract you from a safe LZ. Do you copy?"

Bigg was working furiously on his datapad, communicating with the Talon crew and isolating the Q network to pass the communication channel Meadows was using on to the Talon.

The response from the air crew came back. "Roger. Starting a search pattern from the north garrison. If there is a platoon on repulsor bikes, we'll find 'em. Tell your man we're coming. Get him to find a suitable LZ, and we'll work on locating any approaching threats and suppress them from above. We're coming to get him."

"Meadows," Kel said, "the Talon is coming for you. They're executing a search and Bigg is connecting you to them directly. Keep moving. They'll be able to give you eyes on any pursuing threats. How copy?"

"Good copy, Kel. Thanks, Team Three. Out for now."

Kel handed the Q link to Bigg and turned back to K'listan. "Meadows made it sound like the Second Battalion was attacking the recon platoon, not just him?"

K'listan's whole body shook. "Yes. That is why we must leave now, before the same happens here. My clan leader has dissolved the bond between the Disciplined and the Sun-Loyal Army. We are called home. You must come with us or you may be killed as well. Forces gather as we speak. D'shtaran has lost control of the Sun-Loyal, and no amount of discipline enforced by us will give Nawab Q'stalt an obedient battalion. You must come, I plead with you."

Braley looked at each of the team, still standing in the small foyer with the purple Q havildar. "We've overstayed our welcome. Quasar, quasar, quasar," he said, giving the code for the team to escape and evade on receipt of the order.

Bigg continued to work as everyone but Kel moved to retrieve daypacks. In his bucket Braley was busy communicating with the embassy operations center.

"What's our best way out of here?" Kel asked K'listan. "Have you informed the nawab that the Disciplined are leaving?"

"No. I think it unwise. I do not think you should, either. She will have to see to her own survival. As do we. We have bikes and FAVs waiting at our camp. We should move there now. The platoon is assembling."

Bigg slapped on his bucket. He spoke to them all over L-comm, excluding their guest from the conversation. "I've got the Talon following Meadows's track. They should be retrieving him soon. Braley," he said as the team leader swung his daypack onto his back, "I think we have a better exfil plan leaving with the recon platoon than on our own. What say you?"

Braley moved to where the rest of the team now stood. "I want to hear it, guys, tell me what you think. On our own or with the Disciplined?"

Poul was the first. "Yes. We'll be a stronger force with them. If we get in a fight before we get out of here, they're our best chance."

Sims seconded. "He's right. We can break off later if we have to, but let's get out of the garrison first. Together."

Kel had wondered if Sims's personal revulsion of the Q would cloud his evaluation of the Disciplined. It had not. "I think so too, boss. I trust K'listan and I trust the Disciplined."

Braley nodded. "Then let's let her know. The Talon is going to be busy and it's our only air asset. We're going to be on our own for the near future. Let's try to get out of here quietly."

Kel spoke over his external speaker. "Thank you, Havildar. We're ready to move. Let's make our way to your camp." Kel grabbed his daypack and his N-22 sniper rifle off his bunk. He folded the stock and made sure the maglock on the rear of the pack held the rifle securely before hoisting the combination onto his own back. He checked his gear quickly. He had a full rack of grenades and charge packs on his chest. A credit chit in his pocket, a full pouch of water, and a K-17 in hand.

I'm a killer monk, he mused. *Wandering the galaxy with my few possessions.* E and E was about minimalism. Anything else he'd need, these tools would secure for him.

Except, Oba forgive me, I ain't turning the other cheek.

"I have G'livan outside with a squad." K'listan turned to leave as the muted shrieks of blaster fire filled the air outside.

Sims sighed. "Mama always taught me to get in the escape pod before the ship burns up."

Kel pulled the door open and pinned the face of it with his body as he stayed behind cover, enhancing the night vision of his bucket as he peered through the narrow opening out into the night. Poul did the same from his side as they met in the center of the threshold.

"Moving," Poul said as Kel followed him through the doorway. Commandos squatted, firing steadily at one of the barracks, the blaster bolts leaving an illuminated trail from muzzle to impact.

Kel flung himself into a prone position between two of the crouched Q. "Where's the contact, Naik? Sound off."

"Across the field, two hundred meters, the Second Rifles barracks. Dismounted infantry squad with N-16s and S-5s, firing from the second story," the fire team leader answered as she had been trained, identifying the source of fire by direction, distance, and description.

Kel switched his view to that of the carbine optic, increased the magnification as well as the night vision augment, and scanned. The small squad from the recon platoon had done a good job reacting to contact from the fanatic troops, no longer firing or visible. Particle beam scorches and deep pocks scarred the earthen barracks.

A minute passed.

"Havildar, I saw a laser mark the back of Trooper G'takt as we waited outside," a trooper said, filling the silence. "Then I saw another. Then there was some gunfire. Evidently the renegades are not opposed to the new blasters and tried to ambush us with them. They must have left them on optical collimation mode. Their incompetence gave them away and allowed us to react. When they saw their technical error resulted in no effect, those with S-5s opened up."

"They will not make that mistake again," K'listan said. "Was anyone successful squeezing the color out of them?"

"I hit at least one of the cowards square on," another trooper said with pride. "She'll be pale by now."

"We need to move," Bigg said. "K'listan, let's do it. You form a fire team with your troops; we'll make a second. Let's skirt around the garrison." Bigg pointed left. "Make a bound to the next building and get on overwatch. When you're set, we'll bound to you. Move out."

"Moving," the large havildar clicked. Kel and the rest of the team stayed prone, everyone covering a different portion of the garrison. Their infrared illuminators lit up the buildings, probing the depth of the shadows like invisible suns.

"They tried to shoot up the Disciplined with blasters? I thought the N-16s were soul-suckers, or whatever?" Sims said.

"As long as it's not your own tribe, I guess it's okay," Kel answered. "I'm pretty certain the Chachnam don't have much regard for the Disciplined, especially since they've been the enforcers of the law around here."

"Yeah, pulling off heads and amputating hands kinda causes some resentment, I suppose. Even if you are under lawful orders," Poul said.

Bigg brought things to the maneuvers. "K'listan's set. Let's move."

Off in the distance, their Disciplined friends crouched, their blasters covering a wide spread. Kel rose to a knee as a set of armor on either side rose with him. As one, they dashed towards the waiting Disciplined. He felt the presence of his team around him as they charged. Kel ran holding his carbine by the forearm, stock draped over the front of his biceps so he could pump his arms as he ran the fifty meters in seconds. He picked a spot and dropped between two troopers. A blaster bolt zinged over his head to impact the building behind him as he turned and dropped into prone.

Everyone facing the garrison had seen the path of the blaster bolt from the top of the two-story supply house. Figures moved on the flat roof. Darkness was replaced with orange light as Kel joined to hammer the roof with blaster fire. A missile arced a purple trail from beside him. The flash of the explosion revealed the shooters as their lanky bodies traveled with the leading edge of the energy cloud to throw them off the roof, sparks flying from their burning bodies as they fell.

"Good effect, Sims," Kel said.

"Want me to drop some on all these buildings to keep them down while we beat feet?" Sims asked as he closed the launcher on another grenade.

"Negative," Braley responded. "We've only had a few renegades shooting at us. I find it hard to believe the whole battalion is in revolt. There may be just a handful of malcontents who got into the arms room. Let's not kill anyone we don't have to."

Kel agreed. They'd just spent the day with Third Rifles, and there'd been no hint of animosity. Some of them might even be working to restrain the fanatics among the Sun-Loyal.

"K'listan, start your next bound," Bigg told the havildar.

The Disciplined vaulted away to the next position as Three kept heads up and eyes out. After their devastating barrage on the last malcontents, Kel doubted anyone thinking about trying the same had the steel in their bellies to risk the ballistic retaliation that would follow.

"Bigg, what about the repulsor stables?" Poul asked. "We don't want anyone giving chase. Should a couple of us peel off and destroy all the vehicles before we rally with you at the recon camp?"

"Almost forgot," Bigg replied. "Wait one. Okay. Done. I loaded a worm into all the vehicles when we prepped for the operation on D'idawan's rebels. It's activated. They'll never get a single sled running again."

Kel laughed out loud. "That's awesome."

"Yeah," Bigg said. "Those derelict sleds are held together with plasma sealant and prayers. I probably didn't have to do anything to get them to conk out. But I like a little insurance."

"You were just going to keep that to yourself, Bigg?" Braley asked.

"Slipped my mind, boss. Sorry. We're set. Let's move."

Three more bounds took them to the garrison's outer edge. They passed into the thicket that covered the rear slope of the garrison plateau, formed into two tight wedges, and set a hard pace. Soon they entered the last of the forested hills before crossing the single road leading from main garrison to the smaller recon platoon camp. They halted before the tree line, and waited for K'listan and a trooper to make contact in the camp and reenter their own friendly lines. It was bitter to think of the garrison as enemy territory now. A place of refuge that represented months of their sweat and strain. Lost.

Braley and Bigg were talking on a sub-channel, just loud enough for the rest of the team to listen in as they discussed the next phase of their escape.

"If the battalion's vehicles are disabled, once we get clear of the garrison area, we should be able to hightail it and create some distance. Unless they've set up roadblocks, which I doubt," Braley said.

"I'll get the Blackbird on the blower," Bigg said. "We were in the middle of a firefight when they called for a sitrep last. They got the idea we were busy. Hope by now they got Meadows. Soon as we have some breathing room, we should be able to bring them in for extraction."

"Okay. Make it happen, Bigg."

A slender figure approached from the darkness and joined their perimeter. The Q crouched beside Bigg and spoke quietly through her voder.

"Havildar K'listan says we may approach. All is clear. The bikes are prepared."

They stood, Kel taking a slow turn before continuing forward, clearing behind them and then following the group out of the woods. A pair of Q crouched by the road in opposite directions. Across the open field, a full squad of Q were fanned out, guarding the entrance and the road leading into the fenceless camp.

No light issued from the camp or its small buildings. Two fast attack vehicles and a gathering of repulsor bikes were rallied in waiting. His thermal overlay indicated the vehicles were running, their repulsor nacelles gleaming orange.

The Q ahead of them broke into their fastest gait, the long spring. The humans raced to match step. Kel brought his weapon up, the infrared illuminator on his carbine lighting up the road. They could see the half a klick toward the bend in the road that led to the garrison.

K'listan stood by a small repulsor sled. She was speaking to the trooper mounted on the rear of the FAV, arming the automatic projectile launcher on its central mount.

"What route do you suggest, Havildar?" Braley said, flicking open a holomap into three screens: one showing their current location in fine scale, the next showing the camp and the garrison, the last a large scale of the entire battalion territory.

"I recommend we travel overland southwest. When assured we are not being followed, we can make our way north and follow one of the great routes to the high plains. We can move well off-road on the bikes and it will be difficult for any pursuers in large vehicles to follow. Will you travel with us to Naca'hamir? You are welcome to remain with us there."

"Thank you, K'listan," Braley replied, sounding touched by K'listan's offer. "But we must travel to Diakasa'at. We have a Talon waiting to retrieve us. We'll regretfully part company then. I don't think you'll have to worry about vehicle pursuit from the First Battalion," he said with a chuckle. "We've disabled all their vehicles."

K'listan rocked in approval. "I am pleased to hear that you have done so. Yes, I thought you might be returning to your people in Diakasa'at. If something changes, know that you do not need to be isolated. We can provide you sanctuary."

"Thank you, K'listan," Kel said. "You have been a good friend to us." Kel knew he wasn't alone in feeling humbled at the Disciplined's offer.

K'listan bowed deeply. "Equally felt. Now, we must depart."

"Hey," Bigg said over his external speaker. "The Talon made pick up on Meadows. They're on route. I'm lighting my beacon."

"I wish we could get you all the way home, K'listan," Kel offered. It already felt like they were abandoning her and the Disciplined. "Will you rendezvous with the Second Battalion commandos if they're headed back to Naca'hamir?"

"I will be in contact with them soon. We may have a common route once we make our turn north." K'listan mounted her repulsor bike.

"Kel, Sims, take the lead with K'listan," Bigg told them. "I'll bring up the rear with one of the FAVs. If we get hit from the direction of the garrison, that'll be our best weapons platform with which to break contact. Ready to move?"

Their loose convoy headed out, heading west on the improved road. Bigg and one of the FAVs posted at the road as he indicated, facing the direction of the garrison. Their escape route would turn north, then briefly east again, finishing the large loop that led back to the main entrance of the garrison. He'd spent many hours on foot and on repulsor bike around the garrison and its adjacent landscapes. He could picture the terrain and where it was best to depart the road for an overland route across territory that would discourage pursuit.

Kel slowed to make sure that their group wouldn't get too spread out. He despised when a lead vehicle raced off, leaving the trailers to play catch up. Speed could kill. You'd be better off trying to swim in vacuum. It was just as absurd. They only made it past the first bend when L-comm crackled with a deep *chug-chug-chug*. It had to be the auto-cannon on the FAV.

"Keep moving!" Bigg shouted over the rattle of gunfire. "We've got company coming up our six. About a platoon-sized element moving on us from the garrison. I spotted them early, about three hundred meters up the road. They weren't expecting us. Too bad for them."

"Stay on task, guys," Poul instructed. "I'm closest. Bigg, coming up behind you."

Energy grenades whistled—those could only be coming from Bigg and Poul. As much as Kel wanted to get in the fight, he forced himself to concentrate on finding the path for their escape. He slowed to a pace not much faster than a walk, and altered his topographic display to a ground view. He knew there were not many deep ravines or obstacles that would force them to have to backtrack on the bikes, but he didn't want to take the chance. The bikes would ford most any depression that was not too steep or deep, and would maintain a rideable roll and pitch from about a meter's height. But having to halt the entire platoon and turn around to find a better path would expose them to pursuers. One wrong turn could be their last.

"Braley," Bigg returned to his L-comm, "Poul and I are going to be following at a stagger to deter any pursuers.

They're on foot, so they won't keep up for long, if at all. We just gave them a pretty good lashing and scattered them. Keep the platoon moving. We'll be right behind you."

"K'listan," Kel hollered above the repulsor hum. "There was pursuit headed to the recon camp. Bigg, Poul, and an FAV intercepted them. We're to continue the route."

"It seems they still seek revenge on the Disciplined. Disloyal curs. They do not quickly learn. I would gladly have met them and punished all the Chachnam so they could not raise a hand against anyone again."

I don't doubt she would relish chopping off more of their limbs, Kel thought. He'd witnessed how she performed the ritual punishments with detachment. Executions, beheadings, amputations—it made Kel uneasy, to say the least. For a time, he feared the mughal might direct the commandos against the team, as they had been used against the Chachnam troopers. Learning the Disciplined's clan leader nullified the contract that kept the commandos in service to the Sun-Loyal Army reinforced what he thought he knew about his friends from the north. Tradition or no, the mughals crossed a line with the Disciplined that was felt all the way in Naca'hamir.

Kel's mind drifted as he wondered what the boiler plate of their contract with the mughal looked like.

Section seven, subparagraph c: *The Disciplined (the party of the second part) may be directed on behalf of the party of the first part to perform behavior modification of conscripts (party of the third part) by methods to include but not limited to lashings, hangings, limb removal, purging by fire, and strangulation. Except on Tuesdays. And months with an 'S.'*

Section nine, subparagraph d: *Failure by the party of the first part to prevent fanatical religious and/or politically motivated rebellions by the party of the third part that results in attempted harm (e.g. revenge killings) against the party of the second part, renders any contractual obligation by the party of the second part to fulfill the terms of the contract null and void. Penalties to be levied against the party of the first part as described in appendix D.*

They skimmed across hilly fields and thin forests of wide canopied trees. Braley had been communicating with the Talon crew as Bigg provided their rear defense. Braley tagged several suitable sites for a landing zone. The Talon reported that it would be overhead within fifteen minutes.

"Bigg, what's your take? Any sign of pursuit?" Braley asked the team sergeant.

"Negative. We're closing on the tail of the formation. Let's keep heading for one of your proposed LZs, and when Blackbird's overhead, have them do a sweep. Wish we had some drones left; I'd do it myself."

"Rog."

Red icons appeared on Kel's map view over three separate clearings along a string of shallow valleys. Braley's suggested landing zones.

"I'll start steering us to the first valley," Kel said, picturing the route to reach it.

They passed a small hamlet to their south, a faint glow above bounced off the low cloud cover rolling in. Kel listened for the pop of gunfire, expecting an ambush to be sprung on them from the village.

None came.

Kel guided them around a slope and into another forested area. He rode into a surprising area of planned growth; gnarled but uniformly planted trees, spaced evenly every ten meters. *Fruit trees? A grove planted by the hamlet?* He was still curious about the Q, even when some of them were trying to kill him. He halted them when he was far enough into the stand to provide cover for the entire group.

"Braley, we're about there. Another eight hundred meters and we'll be into the first clearing."

He knew Braley heard him, but got no response as the team leader spoke on a sub-channel to the Talon circling somewhere above.

"Rapier-six, we have no dismounted activity on the ground in your vicinity," the pilot reported. "The village to your south is quiet. We locate no vehicle traffic for three kilometers. I agree with your selection of LZ. Are you prepared to mark and exfil, how copy?"

"Roger, Blackbird. Five mikes out to authenticate our marker." Braley broke back onto their common channel. "Sims, Poul, mark the LZ. You got five minutes and I want the bird identifying our beacon and them down on the deck. As soon as the bird touches down, we're out of here. Kel, get K'listan prepped to secure our exfil."

Two bikes sped into the clearing, his teammates racing to find the best landing area free from trees or anything that could damage the aircraft. Even with augmented vision, the pilots would appreciate a ground party evaluating the landing area at night. The team would appreciate a ride out in an uninjured bird.

A slip of a moon broke through the patchy clouds and the tops of the trees. The long shadows draped over the glade where two armored men stood.

Back from scouting, the havildar waited as Kel shouldered his pack and slung his rifle into place.

"The Talon saw no activity for kilometers around us. It should be clear for you to start your turn north to pick up a major route," Kel told her. He wasn't sure what else to say. Their association was coming to a close. "We're all very grateful to you, K'listan. Is there anything we can do for you or the Disciplined?"

The havildar clucked. "It is we who are grateful to you," she said, hefting her N-16. "We traveled an honorable road together. You taught us much. You and your sisters are great warriors. I had wanted to show you Naca'hamir and the home of our clan. I hope you may yet visit the Disciplined. Until then, bask well, Sergeant Kel-boss."

"Friends call each other by their given names, K'listan. Mine is Kelkavan."

K'listan's neck elongated. "Kel'ka'van? How did you acquire a name from the *totem* of the Disciplined?" She clucked several times over her voder. "We knew there was much about you that made us bonded. Bask well, Kel'ka'van."

"Bask well, K'listan."

"Thirty seconds," said the Talon pilot in his bucket. Kel had heard the authentication of their transponders and the landing zone beacon in the background while he spoke with his friend for what was likely the last time.

"Let's move," urged Bigg, arriving with Braley to where Kel stood with their friend.

As if warriors from an era long since past, the two legionnaires bowed their thanks.

"You can always bounce us. If we can help, we will," Braley said.

Moonlight glinting off her carapace, the tall Q bowed in return.

The Talon approached from the west and put its nose into the slight east wind. The ramp was already lowered, faint blue light spilled onto the clearing. They sprinted for the Talon as Sims and Poul approached from the nose. The pilot's helmet was illuminated by another faint glow of blue in the flight dome.

They didn't stop running until they reached the ramp, Bigg pushing everyone up in front of him.

Bigg's external speaker blasted to the crew chief before climbing the ramp himself. "Five operators. Last man."

At the head of the ramp, Meadows clapped them each on the shoulder. The Talon lifted slowly until, ramp raised, they accelerated upward and banked away. Everyone swayed and swung themselves into jump seats. Braley spoke to the pilot before switching channels to talk to the embassy. They'd been on the ground less than ninety seconds. Kel wondered how long the other Talon had been on the ground before they got hit. Had the guys been feeling as relieved as Kel was right now? Had the bird even started lifting before getting fried to a crisp?

Poul sat next to Meadows with his bucket removed to match the state of his friend from Kill Team Seven.

Good. Kel could have increased the audio gain of his own bucket's input to hear their conversation, but let them have their privacy. He knew how he'd felt when he'd lost a teammate last year. He couldn't imagine how Meadows must be feeling after losing his entire team.

"We're going to set down at the embassy. The ambassador and his senior staff are meeting us in the que-diff," Braley said, enunciating the acronym for the quantum-dampened intelligence facility. Time actually passed minutely slower in the isolated office, surrounded by a field of energy that made intrusion by any known means of espionage impossible.

"Apparently, we're not the only ones on Mukalasa'at being shot at."

21

"Gentlemen. Remain calm," Ambassador Grealy implored. "The facts are unfolding, and rather than trying to lay blame, we must now direct our attention to protecting all humans on the continent."

Kel and the team sat in the QDIF with the ambassador and the other department heads from the embassy and the Solar Wind Mining Consortium, including its chief officer, Phillipe Cardoso.

"My instructions to you were to act like realists, not idealists!" Phillipe fumed, ignoring the ambassador completely. "If you had supported the mughal's wishes and simply punished, or executed, any fanatics as she directed, none of this would be happening. Instead, you ran out at the first sign of danger. We're in this situation because you can't follow orders, Captain."

Kel was too tired to react with anger to the man's idiotic accusations. Meadows, however, leaped to his feet. "Buddy, I didn't see you with us when the shooting started. What gives you the sand to think that you can criticize—"

Bigg placed a hand on Meadows's forearm. He was too gigantic to physically restrain.

"Mister Cardoso," Braley interjected, "that is a rather bizarre interpretation of the facts, which we have gone over extensively. The disintegration of order within the Sun-Loyal Army is not a failure of military discipline; it is occurring as a result of the many factors we have discussed. Repeatedly."

At the head of the table, the ambassador raised his palms to silence the room again. "Phillipe. I prefer to move forward with Solar Wind's participation and help. If that's not going to be possible, the Republic Diplomatic Mission will do so without you. Please, calm yourself, my friend."

Kel had a brief fantasy of being asked to remove the corporate shill from the QDIF, and the pleasure he would feel putting a choke hold on the man, dragging his limp body from the room.

The older executive took in a deep breath and blew it out forcefully. "My apologies, Ambassador. I'm only concerned given the immensity of our presence here, and of course, for the safety of all our people." He looked at Meadows. "Sorry for the loss of your fellow soldiers. It was a poor choice of words on my part."

If looks could kill, Meadows would have rendered Mr. Cardoso into a pile of ash. "Legionnaires," he coldly said.

Cardoso shifted uncomfortably in his seat. "Of course."

"Robert," the ambassador spoke to the Republic Intelligence Chief of Station, Mr. Cummings. "How many incidents have occurred and where?"

The thin man swiveled his chair and swiped a holo-projection from his datapad into the space above the table. "I'm continuing to get reports from our liaisons in the local constabulary and militia forces, and are of course exploiting sources of local news and other intelligence. In the last twenty-six hours we have seen a sudden explosion of incidents that could be characterized as fanatical or quasi-religious in nature across most major cities and settlements on the continent, save the northernmost provinces. We are characterizing the insurgent activity at this time as being endemic to the areas under Chachnam tribal majority rule."

The map projection was overlaid with blue irregular splotches of varying sizes and shades, corresponding to population centers across the continent. Where they now were, the coastal capital of Diakasa'at was the largest and darkest of the highlighted areas. Cummings gestured and small red dots appeared, many coalesced into large irregular shapes that equaled the area of the blue shading underneath them. Kel was relieved to see that only a few small red dots marked the capital.

"Some incidents we characterize as minor and non-violent. Virtually every rural development team has reported some type of protest, mainly groups of younger females banded together to disrupt agricultural and trade activities. Unfortunately, many incidents have been of a more serious nature."

He again swiped and another holo appeared, showing a full-blown riot, complete with burning buildings and limp human corpses. Whirling dark green Q cheered and chanted as they danced around the carnage.

"This came from a local source who was on the scene this morning when the events you are now viewing occurred. This is the village of P'shar'at. The human victims you see we believe are the remains of the Panggabean family."

One of the mining company executives leaned forward. "We have a dozen or so civilian experts contracted that are establishing farms and trading outposts throughout many of the most suitable agricultural communities. The Panggabeans are a family of exo-agricultural specialists who have successfully implemented similar programs on other worlds. Most of the other contractors are the same. They were one of the first to start a cooperative farm working with the local Q farmers. They're a husband and wife team, with three children..." the man trailed off as he choked up.

"I met them when I first arrived," the ambassador said. "I toured their farm and their homestead. This is... unbelievable."

The intelligence man continued. "This has been one of the worst incidents that we know of so far, but I'm sorry to say that it is not the only one. We recovered this bounce from a Republic geologic survey specialist a few hours ago. He was calling for help as this occurred." He again swiped and another holo opened above them.

A terrified man ran, swarmed by a horde of scythe-wielding Q. The man's link was secured to his chest and the holo view showed his face from the low angle as he fled. "Come and get us!" he panted. "Please—help. Get us out of here!" He continued to plead and pray unintelligibly as he was pursued. The first scythe cut caused the man to stumble. He pushed himself up just as several more Q set upon him. The view went black as the man fell on his chest. He did not rise again.

"That's Tompkins-Waite! I know him," a man sitting across the table from Kel gasped. Kel recognized him as one of the economic development specialists he'd met at the embassy party.

Ignoring the gasps and murmurs in the room, Cummings continued his brief. "We just received a report from one of the embassy wives that their Q house staff tried to poison their food. She became suspicious when her children complained the food tasted bad. The mother examined the plate to see what looked like sand mixed in the mashed potatoes. She thinks it was ground glass or a similar substance. She called the constabulary and they responded along with an RSO liaison. When they confronted the servant, the Q servant became violent and had to be subdued. The matter is being investigated.

"And I wish that were all but there are more incidents. I'm bouncing our preliminary report to everyone in the room."

"Why aren't the local police deploying to restore order and protect our citizens?" someone shouted. "Why aren't our Marines out protecting people?"

Julie, the regional security officer for the embassy, said, "The embassy has a single detachment of ten Marines for physical security of the embassy grounds and the ambassador's residence. I have a dozen contracted Q from the Disciplined clan whom we use as well. But we do not have a force to respond to such contingencies."

"We are insisting that the local security forces and militia respond to these events," Mr. Cummings said, "and I have personnel in the field trying to push the responsible parties into action. The response so far has been lukewarm at best."

"What about the company security forces, Phillipe?" the ambassador asked.

One of Cardoso's fellow executives answered for him, "Our security personnel guard the company offices and the surrounding spacefield. The mobile security teams that accompany the provincial development teams work in two-person groups. For some of the teams, there is only a single security officer."

The ambassador looked to Braley. "Captain, can you do anything to assist?"

Braley nodded. "Yes, sir. We can immediately assist in evacuating all human personnel from their outposts and get them back to the capital, but there are only six of us. We'll also need air support. We have only the one Talon left in the air detachment, and we're going to have to co-opt the assistance of all available resources from the company fleet to recover everyone."

"Hold on a minute," Phillipe said. "I understand your concern, but I cannot order civilian contractors to abandon their homesteads, nor do I think that abandoning the missions of the development teams is warranted. Mister Cummings just said so himself—the teams are not experiencing any violence directed at them. I appreciate and respect the expertise of my people on the ground, and when they tell me they have things in control, I believe them. Abandoning their posts is not to going to reinforce the perception among the Q that the company is here to stay."

The ambassador frowned. "Phillipe, the development teams are joint teams, comprised of company employees as well as members of the embassy planetary team. They go where I say they go. It is time to pull everyone in for their own safety."

"With all due respect, Thomas," Phillipe slowly said, "you don't have authority over the company."

The ambassador scoffed. "Yes, Phillipe, I do. I have authority over all Republic citizens on the continent and the plenipotentiary powers from the House of Reason to back up my decisions."

Cardoso clenched his arm rests, his knuckles white.

"I am ordering the recovery of all human personnel on the continent to the capital," the ambassador continued. "This applies to all humans on Mukalasa'at. We'll worry about any citizenship issues later if we happen to have any residents from unincorporated edge worlds here.

"Captain Yost, I am placing you in charge of the operation to recover our people. You have absolute authority under my name to use any assets available on the planet to do so." He looked to his aide, who was furiously typing the ambassador's orders on a holo screen as the words were spoken.

Braley nodded in receipt.

"The QDIF will serve as your operations center, Captain. Please make it so."

Braley stood as the RSO and the intelligence chief joined him. As was his nature, he already had a plan of action formulated and orders to give. "Get the communication officer here. We need to send out a blanket recall order. Julie, please draft the message and we'll review it. We need to have it ready in the next few minutes. I'm sure you have a good handle on it, but it needs to say that because of the deteriorating security situation, and the murders of several Republic citizens, all humans are being recalled to the capital. Anyone who can make their way out of a population center by their own conveyance should do so now."

"Yes, uh… Captain," the RSO said, unsure how to address him.

"Braley is fine. Next, we need to identify anyone who cannot make their own egress and anyone who is in imminent danger. Those groups we prioritize for recovery by air as soon as possible.

"Anyone who cannot start their egress we advise to barricade in the safest location. They can await recovery by our teams. Let's get that written up and then we'll bounce it to all links. We'll also have the ambassador read the statement on holo and bounce that, so any stubborn holdouts will understand that this is coming from the highest human legal authority on the planet."

Braley studiously ignored Cardoso who had cornered the ambassador and, with his finger flying in the man's face, continued to make his protests known.

"I'm going to be stuck here," the captain told Bigg. "You take command of the team and get everyone working on the logistics. Someone's going to have to get over to the spaceport and start organizing company air assets for the recovery. Why don't you fly over with the Talon crew and get them to take charge of the air coordination? Pilots like to talk to other pilots."

"Right," Bigg nodded. "We'll move the whole team to the spacefield and stage there. We'll end up sending out any recovery mission we can with one or two of us as the muscle. If we have any situation with heavy ground resistance, we'll reorganize to beef up as needed."

Braley grunted. "Good. I'm hoping to have missions to assign by the time you guys have landed at the spacefield."

So they had a plan. Kel and the team gathered up their datapads. Bigg rapped them each on the chest. "Well, you heard the boss. No rest for the wicked."

The next three days they slept on their feet. Sortie after sortie launched from the company spacefield to destinations around Big M. Their first runs were to the hamlets where the security situation was most rapidly deteriorating. None had proven as desperate as their rescue of the besieged development team a few weeks prior, but Kel did have to drop a stunner from a company lifter as they hovered over a large crowd. He'd subsequently fired a few blasts on low power into several buildings in the main square. It had the desired effect. The crowd scattered long enough to land the transporter and load civilians for their return to the capital. The angry Q mob were just a passel of rural farmers armed with tools, and Kel hadn't needed to take a single life to accomplish the rescue.

Poul wasn't so lucky. He'd had to wade through a swarm of Q to reach a family homestead, and after struggling with too many of them, had finally resorted to blasting a path through the crowd. When the first bleached carapace hit the ground, the crowd scattered. Unfortunately, the demon weapon's mark also served as the proof the insurgents needed to cement their belief in the evil human campaign to extinguish Q souls.

Sims, Poul, and Meadows teamed up for one of the early rescues. A development team in the province just north of the former Second Battalion made egress from their village in a repulsor sled and were driving north, trying to follow an overland route but making little progress.

Their panicked description of an enormous armored military vehicle rolling into the village as they made their way out of town brought instant response.

"The whole way in, I was kind of skeptical that there was a Roly pursuing them. I mean, I doubt one of those eggheads would know the difference between a Roly-poly and a capital battle cruiser," Meadows explained later.

"So, we locate the repulsor sled," Poul picked up the story. "These guys are stuck in a ditch. We tell them to stay put and to not go wandering off. We have the location by their links, and we race there at nap of the earth altitude. The pilot is below treetop level; we ease in as the crew chief drops the ramp. The pilot slides around this ridge to put his nose uphill into this wash, and as the tail swings around, we're looking out the ramp right at a Roly driving up the valley straight toward us."

"We flew in so low, we never had eyes on it," Sims added. "It was just, follow this turn—and boom! There's a blaster turret pointed right at us. We must've surprised him as much as he surprised us."

"What happened?" Kel sipped a ration pack, trying to stay awake without taking another stim tab.

"What do you think? Everyone started yelling at the pilot to get the kark out of there. We went from a low hover a few feet off the deck to FTL in about a microsecond. I had to grab Poul by his drag strap. He almost went right off the tail and out the back, we took off so fast."

"That's no lie!" Poul agreed. "I thought I was going out myself. There's nothing to grab onto when you're standing in the middle of the ramp!"

Kel nodded knowingly. "Don't keep me hanging, finish it."

"Nothing much left to tell," Meadows said. "Pilot got some altitude, turned a racetrack, and came up behind the Roly. They took two runs at it and smoked it with particle cannons. They didn't stand a chance—once we saw them, that is."

Bigg chimed in. "So, the locals sicced a Roly on them? The only Rolies on Big M are from the Second. That's telling me our former Second Battalion is still in the business of hunting humans."

Meadows nodded. "I thought the same, Bigg. I'm promising you all, they still have a serious beatdown coming to them. Smoking one Roly-poly ain't enough.

I'm going to see that whole battalion fry before I leave this planet."

The rest of the recovery sorties were less dramatic. Most of the other missions involved a peaceful escort out of the area by members of the team. In several of the villages, Kel witnessed the Q travel with the humans to the aircraft, carrying their bags and gear for them as they departed. The human evacuees were cooperative, but puzzled by the forced exit from their peaceful part of the world. When they saw the holos that the rest of them had seen, they'd understand. Kel was certain.

After three days, they tallied two hundred and twelve humans successfully recovered. There had been sites where the human occupants couldn't be contacted. For now, the personnel were listed as missing. Kel felt certain any human who was out of contact was likely the victim of Q homicide. They'd start a new phase and search for those unaccounted for, but a sinking feeling told Kel that it was already too late.

Kel checked his chronometer. It had been three days—seventy-eight hours—that they had been recovering humans to the capital. No one had slept more than twenty or thirty minutes at a time since their own escape from the First Battalion garrison.

He looked around the flight hangar for his teammates. Sims and Meadows lay on their back on the duracrete underneath the wing of a lifter, their buckets off, their heads resting on their daypacks. The hangar looked like as good a place as any to get some shut-eye. Kel made his way over to his friends and removed his bucket. Both of his fellow legionnaires snored loudly, as he intended to. He dropped his pack and lay back, finding the familiar depression between a spare grenade and a ration pack at the bottom of his pack, and passed out.

"Guys, we have to go. Braley wants us in the QDIF."

Kel stirred. He checked the chrono panel on his forearm. He'd been asleep for almost three hours.

Bigg stood over him. "We have to go. The Talon is waiting outside. There's been a development."

"Development?" Sims scratched his head. "What is it?"

"War."

"My people have spoken. I have spoken. The Chachnam are no longer the tool of the human conquerors. As mughal of the Chachnam and the highest representative of the Great Giver of Sun and Life, I demand that the soft-skins pay for their blasphemies against us. The Army of the Sun-Loyal declares war on all humans."

They sat in the QDIF watching the message play again.

Braley closed the holo. "So. That's it. D'shtaran has switched sides. She's no longer a reformer who wants to bring change to her people. Now she's claiming leadership of the insurgency, and making the case that it's the humans who are to blame. A few days ago, she was ordering the execution and mutilation of her own troops. Great."

"'Soft-skins,' huh?" Poul said.

The ambassador sat at his usual place at the head of the table, dark circles under his eyes. He looked as tired as Kel felt. "We've been in communication with D'shtaran for the last three days. Both Mister Cardoso and I have exhausted our attempts to convince the mughal of any other way forward besides complete dissolution of our diplomatic relationship and the commercial cooperation between our peoples."

Braley looked each of his men in the eyes. "War means that we can expect an escalation of the insurgent attacks against humans on Big M. We have to act accordingly."

"I believe it is much worse than that, Captain." Mr. Cummings swiped his datapad and another holo appeared. A satellite view of the continent came into focus. It was not a map projection. Moving weather patterns proved it a live feed. The images shifted and magnified in scale. As the scope narrowed, Kel recognized the area near the former Second Battalion's camp. Meadows leaned forward to better view his former operational area. It was shocking.

"We've been observing activity in the garrisons of the First and Second Battalion over the last three days. They are massing troops and vehicles, assembling into a movement formation. The tank battalion is leading the movement and is beginning a route toward Highway One leading north."

North to the capital.

The room erupted.

Kel remained silent as Braley whispered to Bigg, "I thought we deadlined all of First's vehicles?"

Bigg shrugged. "They got around the worm, or they scavenged more sleds. Either way, they're on the move."

A knot formed in Kel's stomach. The stim tabs and the kaff were taking their toll on him. He inhaled a ration pack on the short Talon ride to the embassy. It was time to ignore the physical and focus his mind.

"Please, let's have some quiet while we analyze the problem," the ambassador urged.

Phillipe sat stone faced and still, a smug look frozen on his countenance. Kel hated few people he'd ever met. Cardoso was one of those few people.

Mr. Cummings continued. "I would appreciate a military appraisement of the intelligence, but my initial assessment is that until proven otherwise, the Army of the Sun-Loyal is marching toward the capital to attack the bastion of human presence on the continent."

The room again broke out in whispered fears.

"Captain Yost, do you concur, based on the information we currently have?" the ambassador asked, loudly enough to regain everyone's attention.

"Sir," Braley said. "I don't think that there's another reasonable conclusion."

The ambassador nodded. "I need options, gentlemen."

Everyone in the room broke into their separate groups to converse hurriedly. Braley and Bigg remained seated and turned to each other while Kel and the others gathered round.

"All right, guys, let's hear it," Braley encouraged.

The rest of the room was an orchestra of voices.

"Buckets," the captain ordered, and the operators donned their lids. "Okay, that's better."

Bigg started. "We can't fight them. We have no ability. No OSP. No Navy for an orbital bombardment, and no way to get them here in time. It'll take that force of Q three days to get here once they hit Highway One. We've got to evacuate everyone off the continent west to Tikalasa'at or get them off planet to the refining orbital."

"Even a single OSP couldn't hit all those targets. Some would still get through," Poul said. "Meadows, what was the count on tanks when you left?"

Meadows sighed. "They'd completed delivery on probably three companies' worth of tanks. They don't have full crews to operate them all, but they drive just like a Roly. I didn't count them on the satellite feed, but it looked close enough to a full battalion to me."

"I agree. Anyone else?" Braley asked. Kel and the rest of the team remained silent. "Okay, let's get our lids off. I'm going to make the recommendation that we get everyone out of D-Town and now."

They removed their buckets. The room was already silent, all eyes on the legionnaires. Hope warred with fear. Did the legionnaires have a plan? Kel found his seat and set his bucket on the table in front of him. Without being prompted, Braley spoke.

"Mister Ambassador, in consultation with my team, I believe the correct course of action is to evacuate all humans out of Diakasa'at to Tikalasa'at until the Navy can come for a retrieval. The company may prefer to move their people to their orbital for safety, or they can join the evacuation to Big T. There is simply no way to militarily engage the armored forces to stop their advance on the capital."

The ambassador rose as he continued to address his experts. "Robert, do you see any alternative?"

The intelligence officer steepled his fingers. "Mister Ambassador, I'm not an expert in military affairs. If our most senior military representative tells us that there is not a force solution to deter an armored assault on the capital, I'm inclined to believe him. Yes, I think that evacuation is our only option."

Phillipe sprang to his feet. "Unacceptable. Unacceptable. This is madness! We have an incredible investment here. A half a trillion credits. I don't expect any of you diplomats to truly understand the magnitude of what you are suggesting. We haven't exhausted all our options. I've negotiated with D'shtaran for longer than any of you. This is a ploy to extort more concessions out of Solar Wind. I have plenipotentiary powers as well, Thomas." He shot the ambassador a haughty look. "I can leverage our position on behalf of the consortium to calm this down. I haven't even begun to offer D'shtaran all the jewels in our trophy case. We can—"

The ambassador raised a palm again. "You may certainly try, Phillipe. But in the meantime, we have an army descending on the capital. We cannot pin the hopes of a peaceful resolution on your ability to appeal to her profligacy with more bribes."

The room broke into mass discussion again. Kel's head started to throb. He pushed away from the table and stood. He left his bucket on the table and moved to the back of the room. Kel was a peripatetic thinker. He would often pace in a small track in his room, back and forth, as he worked through a problem. His teammates used to joke about it as he did so. "The genius is making tracks. The wheels are turning. Look out." That had been Tem who used to gibe him about his habit. He missed his brother fiercely.

He was exhausted, but something ate at Kel's subconscious. He tried to focus, but the individual pieces would not come together for him. He knew there was a solution, he just didn't have clear view of it right now. He started to match his breathing with his pace. One deep slow breath in through his nose as he took three steps, then he turned, and took three steps in the opposite direction as he slowly exhaled through his mouth. Soon, the voices around him were silent. He closed his eyes as he stopped in place and took another deep breath. As he exhaled, his mind snapped into focus and a thought occurred to him. The thought of all thoughts. He opened his eyes. His flash of inspiration seemed to brighten the entire room.

"Kel," Braley said, noticing Kel's expression. "What is it?"

Kel turned toward the group. The whole team had been staring at him.

"I have an idea. But I don't think you're going to like it."

22

"No. Absolutely not. I will not authorize such a reckless, insane venture! What you're suggesting is madness," Phillipe spurted out, his tan flushed red.

"Kel, do you think you can do this?" Braley whispered to him.

Kel now sat between Braley and Bigg. His teammates stood behind him. In theory the calculations were the same. He whispered back. "Yes, sir. I do. It's never been done before, far as I know, but there is no reason why it wouldn't work."

"What you're suggesting—" Phillipe didn't get to finish his thought.

"Mister Turner," the ambassador said from the head of the table, "we would all like to hear your full recommendation. Is this just an off the cuff idea, or is this actually a workable plan? You think you can drop a kinetic weapon from orbit onto the approaching army? You can—how did you put it—'rain an asteroid on them'?"

Kel nodded. "Yes, sir. An iron-nickel asteroid that we turn into a meteor. With a large enough mass of the correct composition, the kinetic energy of an impact or the resulting air burst, spread over several kilometers, would almost certainly wipe out the advancing army."

"And the Legion has a plan for such an employment?" the ambassador said incredulously. "Can you explain to us how you intend to execute this plan?"

"It involves some math, but I'll do my best to describe the concept of the operation."

The ambassador swiped a hand over his brow. "I was a pretty decent engineer once upon a time, Mister Turner, before I was swayed into a life of public service. You all have our undivided attention. Proceed."

Kel felt everyone's eyes on him. Both Braley and Bigg gave him the nod.

"In orbit with the ore processing facility is an entire holding area of asteroids, culled from the belt for rendering into constituent elements. They're in a very high orbit, but the rocks still have to be tended to prevent them from falling into the gravity of the planet.

"We can use them to make own kinetic energy weapon—a poor man's Orbital Strike Platform. The OSP unleashes destructive force by the KE it creates hyper-accelerating rods onto a target. The mass of the rods is relatively tiny, but the velocity is so incredible that its KE becomes massive.

"We can't duplicate the velocity of those projectiles, but we can use an object of immense mass and let gravity accelerate it to its terminal velocity and onto a target. We have to aim it, of course. The destructive force will be much larger than a single OSP projectile, but will not be as significant as, say, an asteroid of equal size traveling at a cosmic velocity and colliding with a planetary body.

"Okay," the ambassador said. "I can see that. Continue."

"I have two methods in mind to deploy the asteroids. One is essentially a duplication of an orbital freefall release from an altitude of about a hundred kilometers. We can maneuver a large rock, and they have some big ones, calculate a release point, and let gravity do the rest."

The ambassador opened his mouth, indicating to Kel he had a question. "How big of a rock are we talking about?"

"I've personally seen asteroids come from the holding pen that are seventy-five meters in diameter. I'm told they have some much larger that they use lasers to cut to size for processing. A seventy-five meter asteroid of the iron composition I'm going to select is probably in the neighborhood of..."

He typed on his forearm datapad. The math was simple; it was just an estimate of the surface area, by assuming the mass was a cube, and a guess about the density. He remembered a chart he saw on the wall of the processing station that he'd read while on the tour. He'd taken a picture of it just for kicks. Now he pulled it up, found the density estimate he was looking for. Iron ore weighed about 2500 kilograms per cubic meter. The raw asteroid was not pure iron ore, but he was only interested in a simple case scenario for his estimate.

"It would weigh about a million metric tons."

A million anything was a big number. The room was silent. Concentrating on his math, Kel was oblivious to the shock registering on people's faces.

"The kinetic energy in Joules, if we had a perfect retention of mass, would be about... nine times ten to the thirteenth Joules, so not quite a petajoule. We'll lose some mass due to thermal ablation on entry, as well as velocity, so we probably won't get anywhere near that..."

"Mister Turner."

Kel looked up. Intelligence Chief Cummings was speaking to him. "How much energy is that? What would that compare to?"

"What Mister Turner is saying," the ambassador took up for Kel, "is that it would have the energy of a decent-sized nuclear device."

Kel nodded. He had a chart of energy yields of the multiple nuclear weapons in their inventory pulled up, the standoff distances for use in different environments, radiation yield estimates, and the like.

"Yes, sir, I was getting to that. It would be pretty similar to one of our tactical Mark Sevens. They're designed for the destruction of large, hardened installations covering a four to five square kilometer spread. Of course, that's a thermonuclear device. The meteor won't have anywhere near that destructive power or latent radioactive effect, and like I said, we'll definitely lose some mass on atmospheric entry."

"And that's by simply releasing it over the target from orbit?" the ambassador asked again. The rest of the room listened intensely.

"It'll be a little more complex than just dropping it, but we can calculate a release point from an altitude of a hundred kilometers that'll get us a pretty precise impact."

"What do you mean by 'precise'?"

Kel considered. "Well, there are factors I can't estimate, the degree of material loss through thermal ablation being one of the big ones. The asteroid will be of such a size that I think we will end up with a large core no matter how much we lose. How that loss will affect the trajectory, that's what I can't estimate. But I feel we have a safety margin that'll be in the arena of kilometers, and not hundreds of kilometers. Certainly not thousands of kilometers."

"Hundreds of kilometers?" the ambassador repeated. "So, what you're saying is that if there is a miss, so to speak, it is not going to be the difference between the southern and the northern part of the continent, but by a margin that you could cover traveling an hour in a speeder?"

"Yes, sir. I think that would be an excellent way of assigning a relative comparison."

One of the ministers leaned forward onto his elbows as he clasped his hands in front of his face. "But this is just theoretical? You've never actually done this? Mister Ambassador, why are we wasting our time on a cockamamie idea?"

"Actually sir, I've done this sixty-six times." Kel let that hang in the air a moment. "Only, I'm not dropping asteroids on a planet. I drop myself and my team onto a planet under the force of gravity alone. From one hundred kilometers in space, I can land us within a meter of my calculated landing spot." Kel knew he was bragging. He flushed as he said the last, but he was not going to let himself be cowed by a man who had offered no useful suggestions for stopping a tank battalion from murdering every human in the capital.

The ambassador held up a palm to his subordinate. "Mister Turner, you said you had a second method in mind?"

Kel shook his head. "I apologize, sir. In the second case I was truly thinking theoretically. As I examine it now, it seems unworkable in the immediate term. I could accelerate a much smaller asteroid at a low angle into the atmosphere on a trajectory that would give us more of an airburst effect over a very large ellipse. I would need more time than we have to run simulations and come up with a workable solution. Once I actually crunched the numbers to confirm how much energy we could impart to a target area by my first method, I didn't see the benefit of pursuing the other method further. At least, not at this time."

The ambassador grinned. "Well, that sounds like good engineering to me, Mister Turner."

"Kel," said Braley smiling at him. "What's the employment going to look like? We can't fit an asteroid in the back of a Talon."

Kel grinned. "We don't have to. The asteroid tenders maneuver these giant rocks twenty-six hours a day. With a little assistance, we use one of the mining tugs as our platform for the release. My plan is to have several of them working for us, ready to fire for effect."

Phillipe stood, fists clenched. "You're forgetting one thing. I do not approve of this plan, nor will I. This is insane. Besides which, you're suggesting the Legion use property of the Solar Wind Mining Consortium to perpetrate this act of idiocy. But Sumendi Station, the tugs—why, the very rocks themselves—are ours. I do not give you permission, and as I *am* the company as far as anyone here is concerned, it's not going to happen."

Ambassador Grealy frowned. "Phillipe. Please, sit and let's discuss this. I know these developments have been a great blow to your strategy on Mukalasa'at, but wouldn't you want to support a viable plan to save your own company from destruction, not to mention the life and human investment on the continent?"

The man narrowed his eyes. "Thomas, I've already said this is an over-reaction on everyone's part. I have not yet even begun to offer D'shtaran the incentives for cooperation that I have at my disposal. We also have a significant investment in the Sun-Loyal Army. We just paid for the refit of their entire armored battalion, and upgraded the entire army's weapons. Now we're talking about destroying it all? Not to mention the negative perceptions these actions will engender in the minds of our partners here on Mukalasa'at? No. No. I cannot approve this action for those and a hundred reasons more."

The man sat. "Further, I will instruct my personnel to resist any effort by the Republic to co-opt our materials for making war with the Q. Thomas, how can you allow yourself to be swayed by the ranting of these military half-wits?"

The ambassador frowned. "That will be enough, Mister Cardoso. You've been invited to participate in this critical incident brief and are welcome to stay as long as you are productive and civil. Apologize to our military staff, sir."

Phillipe avoided looking at the legionnaires. "I know what I said." The man's voice trailed off as he attended his datapad.

The ambassador's look of disdain for Cardoso was apology enough for Kel.

Kel returned to his own datapad, oblivious to the conversations around him. He continued to work the problem as best he could so that he'd be ready with an operation order when given approval to implement his plan.

"All right. We're going to adjourn. I would remind everyone, both diplomat and civilian alike, that these proceedings are not to be discussed outside this facility. My advisors and I would like the room to confer. Be available for recall immediately. I do not plan on taking long to make a decision. Mister Cummings, Captain Braley and your team, RSO, and all division ministers, please remain. Thank you."

The ambassador remained seated as more than half the room departed. Phillipe stooped to say something to the ambassador, who nodded curtly in return, then left as well. When the room had emptied and the entrance closed, the green light over the door activated, indicating that the disruption field was back in place.

The ambassador led the discussion. "Well, these events are shocking. I think the inescapable conclusion is that there is an existential threat to the human populace on Big M. Any dissent?"

There were no sounds of disagreement.

"I am averse to abandoning the embassy and the Republic diplomatic mission. However, I feel that we must place the safety and security of all personnel ahead of our pride. I am ordering the evacuation of every human from Mukalasa'at at this time. Unless we have a revised estimate," he looked at Cummings, "then we must plan to have completed our evacuation in less than three days' time. Does everyone feel that is a reasonable assessment?"

Cummings spoke up. "I'll have a better estimate on the disposition of the enemy force and their rate of approach soon. I'd appreciate some experienced analysis from our Legion friends."

Braley nodded at Bigg, who spoke up. "Certainly, Mister Cummings. I will attach myself to your section for as long as is helpful."

"Excellent," said the ambassador. "Regardless, I'm issuing the mandatory evacuation order immediately. That we have the human population concentrated here will improve the logistics of moving everyone off the continent. RSO, do you have a recommendation?"

"Yes, sir," the RSO said. "Captain Yost and I've already discussed logistics. The plan to utilize the company assets to move people immediately is a good one. We will also charter as many sub-orbital capable commercial craft as possible from Tikalasa'at to start the evacuation. We'll need a release of funds from the Republic to begin the process."

"Done. Continue, please."

"I've asked Captain Yost to assist me in the coordination of the airlift."

"Worse comes to worst," Braley put in, "we can get an ore carrier down into the harbor and load evacuees onto it. The deck alone would probably hold several hundred people. We could use it as a floating refugee camp and guide it out to deep water off the coast. The mughal has no navy or significant air forces. It would be a temporary solution."

The ambassador looked relieved. "Very good. We're not going to prioritize or segregate evacuation based on Republic or company affiliation. Our first priority is to get families off Big M and to safety as soon as possible. The diplomatic mission here has been very much a joint venture from the start. Regardless of how Mister Cardoso chooses to view the company's financial situation and his sovereignty here, I have the legal authority that supersedes any other consideration when it comes to the safety of our citizens.

"Now, what to do about the approaching threat? I am of the mind to encourage a peaceful resolution if at all possible, but we will not curtail any effort to protect life while those attempts continue. We will continue diplomatic efforts to negotiate with D'shtaran, and I will encourage Mister Cardoso to continue his efforts as well.

"I will be conferring with the House of Reason and the Planetary Security Council by hypercomm presently. Relay delay means guidance may not be forthcoming in time. I will continue to exercise my plenipotentiary powers and responsibilities."

Then the ambassador turned to Kel.

"Mister Turner. I want your operational plan ready to implement. I'm giving you authority on behalf of the House of Reason to exercise all methods at your disposal to engage and destroy the enemy that now presents an existential threat to the life of every Republic citizen here. However, do not execute the plan until I have given you my express order to do so. Do you understand?"

"Yes, sir. I understand. I will need orders bounced to me stating the same." Kel didn't wait for his team leader's input to declare the necessity of lawful orders being issued. He was only concerned with the task at hand, but also knew that later, if things were scrutinized, it would be important that the situation as it was currently perceived was locked into the record of events.

"Done. Where will you be staging then?"

"Sir, the only obvious place would be Sumendi Station."

"Very well. Let's recall the group and get ready for the evacuation."

"No. Solar Wind refuses to cooperate. Sumendi Station is sovereign property of the consortium and is not subject to any declaration of control or influence by the diplomatic mission on Q. Thomas, you may be able to legally order the evacuation of any Republic citizen on the planet, but you cannot order the cooperation of any Solar Wind personnel or take control of its property. There's no planetary government on Qulingat't, and Sumendi is in geostationary orbit over Big M. Our agreement for operation is with the government of Mughal D'shtaran, not the Republic. I will order my personnel to close the station and refuse cooperation. It's as simple as that."

The ambassador remained silent for a moment. "I'm sorry to hear you say that, Phillipe. Your position on this matter is disappointing and places the lives of Republic citizens at risk. You leave me little choice." He looked out at the faces gathered in the QDIF.

"The Mughal D'shtaran has exhibited war-like aggression against the diplomatic mission and the representative of the Republic and the House of Reason. As an agent in their service, I am declaring an emergency, and am exercising the powers delegated to me by our Republic. The property of the Solar Wind Mining Consortium including Sumendi Station is hereby declared resources necessary for military operations, and corporate rights are suspended until the House of Reason determines that the crisis has been resolved."

Phillipe jumped to his feet. "You can't do that! It's not legal!"

The ambassador wryly tilted his head. "I can assure you it is. No matter. The consortium has many attorneys in its employ, as does the House of Reason. This will be settled another time. However right now, your failure to recognize the state of emergency and cooperate with the exercise of these powers places you in the position of committing treason during time of war. That is a matter that can only be adjudicated on the floor of the Senate, not by the courts. I assure you, that will be settled much sooner than any civil dispute between the company and the government on Liberinthine. Please, my friend, choose your next words carefully."

Phillipe smiled coldly. "Very well. I again protest in the strongest possible terms. These actions are not in the best interests of the consortium nor the Republic. In anticipation of this, I've already issued orders to my staff on Sumendi to close operations and seal the station until further notice. My conscience demands no less."

The ambassador sighed. "Very well, Phillipe. You've left us little choice."

The entrance to the QDIF opened and two Republic Marine guards entered. The RSO was already on her feet and moving to where Phillipe stood. "Escort Mister Cardoso off embassy grounds and return him to his offices at Solar Wind Spacefield. Hold him there until you are instructed to place him on a ship for evacuation off the continent."

"Phillipe," the ambassador said as the guards took him out of the QDIF. "I prefer not to have you in enerchains. Your protest is duly noted. If you move to act against the Republic further, there will be consequences."

The executive said nothing, and allowed himself to be escorted out of the room.

"I will be appealing to Mister Cardoso's second-in-command to countermand his orders against cooperation," said the ambassador once the room was secure. "Failing that, do you gentleman have the ability to carry out the plan as you've outlined?"

"Yes, Ambassador," Braley replied. He turned to Kel. "Bigg and I are going to be here coordinating the evac of the capital. You take the rest of the team and get upstairs. A forced entry into the station should be a last resort, but do what you gotta do."

Kel gulped. *Micro-G entry on an orbital. Plan and execute the asteroid drop. Me. In charge.*

"No problem." He did his best to remain stone-faced. Inside, his bowels cramped.

The ambassador stood to leave. "I admire your cool detachment, gentlemen. Good luck to you and good luck to us all. The evacuation is ordered. I am going to issue a statement from my office immediately. Meeting adjourned."

Kel stood as he was surrounded by the rest of his team.

Sims was the first to speak. "Kel, I mean," he shook his head. "Wow. Are we really going to launch meteors onto the Sun-Loyal? Where on earth did you come up with that plan? Do you have an H8 problem we don't know about?"

Meadows grunted. "I only wish I'd thought of it. I'm ready to make them pay. Let's do this."

Poul grinned. "We've got this, brother. KTF."

Kel looked at Braley and Bigg. "I wish you guys were going to be up there with us."

Braley put his hand on Kel's shoulder. "I have complete confidence in you, Kel. KTF."

Bigg spoke last. "I'm glad Braley and I will be down here. You blow this and drop a rock on the capital, you're all going to wish you were dead with us."

23

"Hey, remember me?"

A young woman in a flight suit spoke. Kel had his day pack and breacher kit laid out on the duracrete underneath the wing of the Talon. They were making a brief stop to top off reaction mass for the thrusters before launching to the station. He was flaking out his gear and running a mental checklist when the visitor appeared.

"Um, sure. We met at the, uh, the executive flight lounge the day I went up for a tour of Sumendi Station. I'm sorry, I don't remember your name..."

Just then, their Talon crew chief stuck his head out the back of the open compartment.

"Hey Rox, what you up to?"

"Hey, Drummond. Off again?"

The man answered, "Yeah, you know how it is," and disappeared back into the cargo compartment.

"Rox. Is that short for Roxanne?" Kel asked.

"Yup. Hey, we heard what you guys are doing."

Kel frowned. The team stopped checking gear to listen.

"Um. What did you hear we're doing?"

"You're going to go drop a rock on the Q before they can get here and slaughter us."

Sims laughed out loud. "Q-Dif my left foot."

"Listen," she said. "Cardoso issued a blanket order that the company is not to cooperate with any Republic officials, especially the military. The next guy in line issued a bounce that said that we're to follow the evacuation order, but not to do anything that would harm the company."

"Okay," Kel said noncommittally.

"Look. Everyone heard the ambassador's brief. There's a Q army rolling north to blast us off the planet. We've all heard what you're going to do about it. I was a Talon crew chief. I'm rated by the company in all flight ops. I've worked orbital processors before and can drive a tug. If you get up there and can't get the help you need, who's going to drive a tug for you? One of your Talon crew might figure it out, but I don't think you've got time for that. I'm telling you I'm ready to go upstairs, right now. There it is. Plus, I know most of the people up there. You're going to need a liaison to smooth things over." She stood with her hands on her hips, waiting.

Kel blew out a breath. He gauged the team. Sims shrugged. Poul nodded. Meadows turned back to his gear.

"Get your stuff. We're lifting within the half hour."

On the flight deck Kel caught the eye of the flight engineer as he finished the ascent up the narrow ladder. Sumendi Station, bright as a white rock in the sun on a cloudless day sat ahead.

"All right. Let's raise the station. If I can get us access by talking some reason into them, we won't have to do a forced entry."

The flight engineer nodded as he opened a holo link. "Sumendi Station, this is Blackbird One, do you receive me? Over."

No reply.

"I'll try again."

The man repeated the same transmission, with no response.

"I've got a laser link directed right at their receiver. There's no way they're not hearing us... Do we know for sure they don't have heavy weapons?"

"They don't have military armaments," Kel replied, "but they have plenty of commercial-type blasters and other tools. I doubt they could use them at a distance like this. It's all industrial tech for cutting and ablating stuff at close distances."

"Yeah, well, if turns out they do, it's going to be the worst day of their life."

The flight engineer repeated the message several more times.

"They're ignoring us, hoping we'll go away. What do you want to do?"

"I don't think we've got any choice," said Kel. "We're going to make a denied facility entry. Let's plan to breach on the dark side. I'm sure we can get visual access on a set of pressure locks there."

"Hey, let me try." Rox appeared at the top of the ladder. "I can bounce the ops chief. He'll answer for me. He's been trying to buy me drinks for months."

Kel scooted aside and made room for her to climb onto the crowded flight deck.

"Here goes." She opened her link and a small holo sprang up. Beck Alford, the senior mining engineer Kel had met on his tour, greeted them.

"Uh, hi Roxanne, this isn't a good time to talk. Nice to see you, but—"

"Beck, listen. I'm outside the station in a Navy Talon with a load of legionnaires who are going to blow their way into the station if you don't open up."

"You're what?"

"Beck, you know that Cardoso is an idiot. That order he gave isn't valid. You heard the statement Chien made not long after."

"Yes, but Mister Chien said that we're not to do anything that harmed the company."

"Beck, you realize that there's an army headed to D-Town to kill everybody, right? You understand that not cooperating with the Republic and letting a bunch of people get killed when you could've helped—not to mention, make these legionnaires blow a hole in the station—is the very definition of 'bad for the company,' right?"

"Yes, Roxanne, but what are they talking about? Mister Chien bounced me and said that they want to use the station to drop asteroids on the Q. He said that we can't participate in that kind of thing, that it would be bad for our image."

"Mister Alford, do you remember me?" Kel stepped into the viewing field.

The man's eyes widened. "Uh, yes. Yes sir, I do."

"Sir, I understand the position you are in. I truly do. It's a tough place to be in, trying to assess the facts. How they change. Making the right decision."

The man nodded. "Yes, it is."

"Here's the thing. There's an army of fanatical Q headed for the capital. They're on their way to murder every living human soul still there that they can. I've seen the Q when properly motivated to violence. They murdered four of my friends. I've seen what they do to each other. They decapitate and pull the limbs off their own people.

I can't imagine what they're going to do to defenseless women and children.

"We are working on evacuating every person out of there as we speak. But if we aren't successful and the Q army is able to get there, well, we don't want that, do we? Right now, we're the only ones in the galaxy who can stop them.

"So, what I'm telling you is, you have the opportunity to do the right thing. Right here, right now. Open that station and let us in. Otherwise, I'm going to come in. If that happens, you will not find me in an appreciative mood. I am authorized to use deadly force to achieve the completion of my mission. There is nothing I want to do less in my life than kill or harm a civilian. But sir, if you force me to do so, I absolutely will."

The man gulped. "Yes, sir. I remember you. And your friend. I believe you. All right. I'm giving the order to unseal the station. Flight control will direct you to the main hangar. I have a wife on the ground. She's terrified right now. I don't want anything to happen to her, believe me."

"Thank you, Mister Alford. Oh, and Mister Alford, make sure that you communicate to your people that we are the good guys coming to help. If we end up receiving a hostile reception, you're not going to like that either."

The man shook his head. "Yes sir. I believe you."

The link closed.

Kel chuckled as he looked at Roxanne. "Thanks for the help. That was well done. It's going to save us a lot of trouble."

The woman rolled her eyes. "Pfft. What a jerk. Wife on the ground? That dude must've asked me out for drinks a dozen times. Now I wish you were going in with blasters blazing."

They stood on the hangar deck with their buckets on. The hangar had repressurized, but everyone including the flight crew and their new friend was buttoned up in a vac suit. From the operations center window above the hangar a smiling man waved furiously to get their attention.

"We'll meet you on the other side of the lock," a voice projected from the wall of the hangar.

Kel waved back in acknowledgement. He kept his hands free with his carbine against his chest. "Let's go."

"Doesn't seem like these guys are going to give us any trouble," Sims said.

"No. They're not," Rox added. "I know most of these folks. They're miners and engineers and technical people. A lot of veterans among them. When they hear from you what the situation is, you're going to be drowning in help."

Not long after, the team stood in the observation lounge. Instead of facing resistance, they'd been welcomed with smiles and salutes. It was standing room only. The viewing window was behind Kel and a holo projection floated over his head.

"So that's the situation. I don't know that we're going to be ordered to execute our plan, but if we are, we need to be ready to carry it out as fast as possible. I'm asking for your help. We can do this without you, but I don't want to do that. Our best chance of success depends on me relying on the best people to help me move these asteroids, and that's all of you.

"I can't order anyone to help, nor would I want to. I just ask that if you don't want to help us, please don't get in our way."

One of the miners in a vac suit stepped forward. "Hey, leej. I'm one of the shift leaders for the asteroid tenders. We do all the exterior work with the rocks, so I guess we're who you need. Pretty sure I can speak for everybody on my crew. There ain't nothing you can do to stop us from helping you. What do you say, guys?"

A cheer went up around the room. "Hoo-ah, hoo-ah" and "ahh-roo" thrown in by the dozens.

Rox winked at Kel as if to say, *I told you so.*

Kel took a deep breath. *Suddenly got smoky in here.* There was mist in his eyes.

"Well, all right then. We appreciate it. I think..."

"Sir, sorry to interrupt," another miner said. He was one of the younger men in the audience. "I'm one of the safety engineers here on the facility. We've looked at how to avoid the very thing you're trying to accomplish. Do you have an AI programmed to run this kind of maneuver? I mean, I know you're with the, uh, military and everything, but I've never heard of such a thing."

"What's your name, sir?" Kel asked.

"Dane, sir. Engineer Dane Sharpe."

"Mister Sharpe, I'll tell you how you could help me. I need you and any of your engineers to review my calcs. The sooner I can confirm them, the sooner we can stage into low orbit."

Kel pointed with his chin towards the tug tender shift leader. "Sir, what's your name?"

"Carl Hutchens."

"Mister Hutchens, how many tenders do you have?"

He scratched his head in thought. "Well, it's not a simple question of how many. We got six tugs capable of pushing all but the largest asteroids. One o' them's deadlined. But two others can handle the really big rocks. So, I have seven available. We only run two tenders per shift, 'cause it takes a crew of two per tender. For the big guys, we use a three-man crew. We don't have enough people to run all seven tenders at once. It's your basic manpower issue. Most we can field at once is four and the one big boy."

"I can pilot a rock pusher, and I can do it solo," Rox said.

"Sure, Rox, but you still need another body for safety."

"We're not doing any complex maneuvers, Hutch. We'll just need to move them through open space from the holding pen to the point they've calculated over the planet, isn't that it?" she asked Kel.

He nodded.

"Well, the simplest things always turn out to be not so simple when you're dealing with moving asteroids around space," Hutchens said.

Kel grinned. The man spoke with the gravitas of experience. "Point taken. We won't have a lot of time to respond if the situation deteriorates on the ground. My plan is to have as many tenders and rocks marshaled into position as close to a low orbit as is feasible, ready to release on command. The armored column is moving fast. If the ambassador doesn't come to a decision soon, that means the tanks will be even closer to the capital. Going low-orbit will reduce the margin of error to avoid a catastrophe with a miss."

Hutchens shook his head. "Believe me, we want to help. But there's a coupla' issues. How close do you need us to get to the planet to drop these rocks?"

Kel sighed. "Until I can check my calculations with the engineers, I need to get as close as I can to use a release point that I can reliably determine."

"How close is that?"

"One hundred kilometers."

The man scoffed. "No can do. The tugs aren't capable of that kind of repulsor thrust. That's practically atmospheric. We'd drop just like the rocks from that altitude. I could probably get you as close as a few hundred kilometers. Most of the power usage of the tugs is in managing momentum, not providing lift. The gravitational force will still be beyond the flight rating. If we can release from freefall, I think we can do it. If you expect a stationary release, forget it. Like I said, we'll drop like the rocks."

Kel had been afraid of that. It's not what he was hoping to hear.

"The other problem for us is how long we can stay out, boss. We can stretch a shift to twelve hours. While it's fatiguing to work more than eight, that's not the issue. The tugs just don't have enough juice for much longer than that.

"You see, to get from where we are now at our geostationary altitude of twenty-six thousand kilometers and some change, to where you're probably going to want to stage us, say, a couple of thousand kilometers, it'll take several hours. Then, trying to maintain the position you want, well, it's gonna drain a lot from the cells, quick. We're not gonna to be able to stay on station with you for long before we have to head back for new cells. Three hours out, maybe a few hours on station, then three hours back. That's if we push things to the absolute safety limit."

"What about if we ferry cells to you?" one of the Talon crew offered. "We can act as a tender for the tugs to keep you on station. Fuel cells, life support cells, rations, crew swaps, whatever you need. Can the tugs do clean exterior exchanges or lock-outs, or do you have to decompress and go extra-vehicular?"

"Hmmm. It'd easier for a tender to do the cell exchanges for us so we could stay buttoned up. The charge cell ports are all accessed on the exterior. We do have an exchange lock for small items, so you could get us stuff through them, but I hope we aren't out there long enough to need more survival stores than what we can cram in there to begin with," Hutchens told them. "But yeah, that would work."

Kel waited as the man thought out loud.

"Once we're there, then what? Even if we can get to a staging area within a couple of thousand kilometers above the surface, and we're able to stay in a position without assuming a fast orbit, we can't get you as low as you want to go and hold there. Sorry. We can't do it."

The Talon pilot stepped forward. "We can grapple you. Piggyback you and take you down. We have enough power to take you there, and if we can assume a freefall orbit, once we release the load, I can easily get us both back up to a high orbit to take another tug down for the next attempt."

The flight engineer nodded. "We grapple and sling load extreme packages in atmosphere. I'll do the math, but I'm certain it'll be even easier in orbit."

There were nods all around the room.

Kel felt encouraged. "I'm thinking that if we can get organized and get on station in the next eight hours that at most, we're going to have no more than twenty-six to much less than fifty-two hours to do it, or scrub it. In fact, once I check these calcs with the engineers, I'm going to encourage the command authority to let us do this as soon as possible, if at all. I want the greatest safety margin we can get. The closer the tanks get to the capital, they get closer to other smaller population centers, too."

Everyone nodded in understanding.

What an amazing group of people, Kel thought.

"Folks, if there's anything else that anyone can contribute, this is the critical time to say something." Kel looked around the room. He saw eager faces but no one spoke. "All right, Mister Sharpe, I'm going with you. Gents," he turned to his teammates. "Do you want to go with Roxanne and the Talon crew and start organizing with the tug drivers?"

Everyone nodded.

"Mister Sharpe, lead the way to your engineers."

Kel asked for some privacy. A small office overlooking the hangar is where he collected his thoughts, alone. On the other side of the pressure lock, the crew loaded the Talon with charge cells and other supplies for the tugs. Rox was now in a hard vac suit with an EVA pack attached. She insisted on staying in the Talon to guide the team in any replenishment for the tugs. She hadn't made it an option. He saw no reason to disagree. Outside, somewhere in the holding pen, tug pilots were selecting rocks to carry to their initial rally point. Kel's only guidance to them was, "Make them big."

He knew he should be nervous. He wasn't. He was ready. He opened the holo. In the QDIF were the ambassador, the intelligence chief, Braley, Bigg, and a few others. When he was sure they were receiving, Kel started.

"Gentlemen, we are ready to move to our rally point above the continent to wait on station for an order to execute. I've had nothing but fantastic cooperation from the crew here on Sumendi, and I'd like it recognized that their contribution has been nothing short of phenomenal."

The ambassador smiled. "I'm very glad to hear that, Mister Turner. Please pass on all our thanks. Were you able to get any additional insight as to your ballistic assumptions?"

"Yes, sir. We've had a meeting of the minds and the consensus among the engineers is that we have the best calculations we can hope to have, knowing that this is something that's not been done before."

"Is there a confidence level that they felt comfortable sharing with you?" the former engineer asked.

"Yes, sir. Some engineers expressed a ninety-percent confidence level in the predictive accuracy of the calculations."

The ambassador's eyebrows shot up. "Did they tell you how they arrived at that conclusion?"

"Yes, sir. It was based on the composition of the asteroids. Since the rocks are so dense, they are unlikely to suffer a devastating disintegration on atmospheric entry."

"I assume there were dissenters?"

Oh, boy. Were there. He hesitated to tell.

"One of the older men felt ablation was too big a variable, that we might shower smaller projectiles all over the continent."

Braley remained stoic. Bigg's eyes shot open like exploding grenades. The ambassador's paternal smile encouraged him to share the worst. "Anything else?"

"One of the geologic engineers reminded us about the hydrocarbon vents in the far east. He feels there's a tiny risk of igniting them and possibly burning the atmosphere away."

Braley's mouth fell open. True surprise. He'd never seen that before from his team leader.

"But everyone else dismissed the possibility."

The ambassador's closed his eyes, his shoulders expanded with the deep breath. He blew it out. Kel knew the look. It reminded him of Colonel Hartenstein. Firm like duracrete. "Based on what you've learned so far, what is your recommendation, knowing all the risks?"

"Do we have an update on the progress of the Sun-Loyal Army? Do we have an estimate of their time on target? What's the progress on the evacuation? Will everyone make it out before that time?"

Mister Cummings started to answer.

"No. Don't answer that, Robert." The ambassador pointed a finger at Kel. "Mister Turner, I want you to answer my question. None of the other factors can influence what you're about to tell me. Knowing all the risks, knowing the potential outcomes associated with those risks, based on what you've learned so far, do you advise me that this plan to stop the Sun-Loyal Army is feasible?"

He took his own deep breath. "Yes, sir. I do."

"Very well. Robert, proceed."

"Our current projection shows that if they maintain their current rate of travel, that the lead elements with the tanks will be within range of the capital in thirty-six hours. As far as evacuation, we are approximately fifty-percent evacuated out of Diakasa'at, but at the very best speed, the turn around to get the rest of the personnel evacuated by then will still leave twenty five percent of the population behind."

Braley and Bigg looked as grim as the others in the room.

"Mister Turner. I am authorizing you to execute the operation with haste. We're all depending on you up there. Good luck."

Kel stood on the edge of the Talon's tail gate, just as he would as jumpmaster. He'd considered riding on the exterior of the tug hull to overlook the release, but dismissed it as unnecessary. As it was, the Talon had the tug intimately tethered by its grapples, making its fuselage just a few meters underneath him. The enormous asteroid filled much of his view of the planet below, anyway.

They decided to drop one of the smaller asteroids first. This one was still all of seventy meters in diameter. Its round shape appealed to Kel, like a massive seamball some intergalactic pitcher could hurl with consummate accuracy. They had one of the mega-rocks on station with the rest of the tugs about two thousand kilometers in a higher orbit above them. The engineers estimated that the big asteroid weighed probably two million metric tons. Kel couldn't bring himself to use that one for their first attempt. What if it caused an extinction level event? No. He couldn't have that on his conscience.

His wrist holo showed the orange arc of the optimal track; the green their current. The two curves grew closer every second. He'd already given the five-minute time warning, just as he would for a jump. He watched their altitude as he communicated with the pilots, descending to the 300-kilometer mark. The counter flashed they'd rotate into the release point at an altitude of 301.7 kilometers. The result of the exact calculation. The program wouldn't let him subtract the three meters to compensate for the altitude of the tug below him, but knew it wouldn't matter.

"Thirty seconds. Stand by." Kel watched the chronometer count down. "Go."

The tug's arms released and the shimmering binding field dissipated. The rock started to fall away.

"Missile away," Kel said to Bigg, monitoring from the QDIF, his face a negligible window in his bucket amidst the heavens.

"Good copy, Kel. Missile away."

As the rock fell, he imagined the renegade Q somewhere below. They'd be too tiny to see, even under magnification. But he knew how they looked. Pictured them as if he were on the ground with them.

They hung on the sides of the sleds and sat on top of the tanks and Rolies. They hit a bump. A green Q fell off, crushed under hard wheels to the amusement of her sisters. Spindly arms pumped overhead, brandishing the blasters they cursed. An orange Q whipped the lead driver to go faster.

"Kel," Sims said. "Whatever happens, I'm proud to be here with you."

Kel had been lost to his thoughts. His teammates were with him on the ramp. Sims put his hand on Kel's shoulder. "I've never seen anyone work harder in my life."

Poul stood on his other side. "Me too. You always lead the way, Kel. I've never been prouder, brother." Poul put his hand on Kel's other shoulder.

Meadows voice burned righteous rage. "Thank you for this, Kel. This is for Seven."

The huge rock grew smaller. The bright tail of a meteor appeared. The fire of their hope ignited. The air roiled behind the fiery trail. The meteor was lost to sight as they continued their eastward fall around the planet.

"There's nothing worth seeing here anymore," Kel said. "What we really need is the impact telemetry. We need to adjust fire off this splash. Let's pick up the satellite feed on holo."

The Talon crew anticipated their need. The satellite feed projected as a large holo on the back of the bulkhead behind the flight deck. Inset was a smaller picture bounced to them from the ground. Someone at the embassy had a view captured of the southern sky.

The tail was visible on the ground, but not very dramatic. Not like holos he'd seen of comets and other objects entering the atmosphere. He supposed it was because the angle wasn't shallow and the velocity of his meteor wasn't of the cosmic variety.

He checked his chronometer and compared it to the countdown in the corner of the holo. They were synchronized. A little less than three minutes remained until impact. Kel's heart pounded in his ears. He was ready to give the command to bring the next tug into low orbit to begin the process again. He wasn't sure how he was going to calculate a new release point if he couldn't plot an accurate impact for this shot. He hoped that the satellite would locate the splash and he'd get the information rapidly. Otherwise he wouldn't be able to start the computation of a corrected release point. He started to pull up his calculator.

"It's happening," Poul said to him, reverently. Like at worship.

The satellite tracked south. The detail fine enough to distinguish a column of twos. The line of tanks rolled north on the pale highway. A spring flood gushing down a dry riverbed. Kel counted ten ranks deep to the edge of the view screen, where more would be trailing out of their current view.

Flash.

Orange. Yellow. Then white. The image blanked. The aspect ratio changed. The expanding maelstrom outpaced the camera's attempt to pan wider. Wider. Finally, a rim of normal terrain was recognizable. In its center, chaos. A rapidly expanding pressure wave continued expanding. It swept over as yet untouched grasslands, followed by a wall of expanding gasses and dust. Then the fire followed.

Will it ever stop? he wondered.

The view was now so high, almost the same they'd had looking down on the planet from the tailgate. The death cloud stopped expanding and mushroomed in place. It was tiny. From way up here.

What would it look like when the last of the debris fell, and the air cleared? Would there be anything left of the green creatures he'd just pictured as the caricature of evil they'd become to him? What of the woven figure, the beautiful statuette the one trooper made and gave to Kel. He'd left it in their hut, forgotten as they fled.

Someone grabbed him by the shoulders.

"We did it! *You* did it! Oba's beard, you did it!" He was rocked by slaps against his armor and the hugs from his brothers.

"Hey, hold up," Kel told his compatriots. He spoke into his L-comm. "Say again all, I missed your transmission."

"Damage assessment indicates good effect," Bigg said, joy evident in his voice. "End fire mission, say again, end fire mission. Really nice work, Kel. Congratulations."

"Job well done, Kel, and to the whole team," Braley said. "Finish up and come home."

"Yes, sir. Thank you, Captain Yost," Kel said. He was rarely so formal with Braley, but somehow, it felt appropriate. He took a deep breath, grateful and relieved.

"Now hear this, all asteroid tug pilots, mission complete. Return to Sumendi Station and stand down. We've had a successful strike on our target. The crisis is over. Thank you to everyone. Your service will not be forgotten by me or the Republic. Job well done, team. Blackbird command, out."

The tail ramp closed and he slumped into a jump seat. He attached a harness to his armor and leaned back into the mesh cushion. Tears sprang to his eyes as the stress from the last—what was it? Days, weeks, months?—swelled and burst. He turned off his L-comm. Just for a moment. To himself.

Quiet.

The Talon moved at a pace to match the slowest tug. It would take a few hours for them to reach Sumendi. Before he knew it, he was snoring inside his bucket.

24

It was time to go home. They'd packed their gear and palletized it at the spaceport. Later that night, the Talon would give them a lift to the Navy frigate entering orbit above them. Soon enough they'd be back on Victrix. The home they always returned to. The one they never remained in. A waystation in an endless loop between fights.

There was a week to do the necessaries. Meetings. Reports. The cool bay breeze was refreshing. The changing season brought light rain in the evenings and chilly nights. A thin fog hung over the bay and low areas each morning as the team trained their bodies again, and the brisk mornings put Kel in the mood to push himself hard.

Most of the evacuated personnel had returned to D-Town. The provincial development teams were starting to venture out to their work sites, and Kel and Sims had accompanied one such team the day before. When they arrived on the airfield, they recognized two familiar faces. Monica and Tatiana.

There was hesitation as they came close, loading into the large company lifter. Sims popped his bucket and smiled at her cautiously. The awkwardness dissipated when Monica broke into tears and rushed to give her ex-boyfriend a hug, unconcerned the armor between them was as hard as her feelings about the Legion.

"I was worried about you. We were some of the first personnel evacuated and there was so little information coming out. I tried to find out if you were okay, but there just wasn't any news. Then, to find out that you guys saved everybody..."

"It's okay," Sims said. "Everyone's safe now. That's all that matters."

Her eyes welled up. "I'm sorry for how I acted. It was just... well. It doesn't matter. I'm sorry that I wasted so much time being mad at you."

"I'm the one who's sorry. Not much I could do differently, though. It's my life. But, I'm still sorry."

Sims pulled her into a hug, a tricky feat in armor. This gentleness was something Kel hadn't seen in Sims before. He felt awkward overhearing their private conversation, but he was not alone in disturbing their moment together as everyone moved onto the lifter.

"We're leaving tomorrow. I'm glad we got to see each other and that we can spend my last day together. I wanted us to part on friendly terms. I'm glad I have the chance to do just that. You better get loaded. I'll see you on the ground."

He hugged her again, then watched as she climbed up the ladder into the ship. Tatiana waited for her. She waved to Kel and smiled.

Sims put his helmet back on as he watched her go. Kel walked closer. "That was nice, man. I'm glad you two got a chance to catch up. Today'll be easy. You guys will get to spend some time together. I'm sure of it. The fanatics have settled down. The big fireball was a message from above they were following a false doctrine. Even D'shtaran is trying to suck up to the company again."

"Yeah," Sims said, almost regretfully. "S'pose every fight ends sometime. Guess that means we did our job. But if it had to end now, I'm glad for the chance to make things right with Monica before we get back to it on some other cesspool. Makes me feel, I don't know, kind of hopeful, I guess. It'll be nice to leave without regrets."

Kel had never heard such sensitivity from him before. It was a whole new side to him. Maybe romance brought these things out in an operator? "Brother, I'm proud of you. You're behaving very maturely for a knuckle-dragging leej," he said, trying to lighten the mood.

"And you dance like a twelve-year-old boy trapped in the body of a twelve-year-old girl," Sims shot over his shoulder and headed into the lifter.

They sat in the QDIF with the ambassador and Mister Cummings. The department ministers rounded out the group. Noticeably absent were any representatives from the company. Braley led the after-action report. He kept it as brief as possible, planning to spend most of the hour answering questions and making their recommendations known.

The ambassador's attention was intense. Kel had become impressed with the man's abilities and manner. He'd seen him manage a tremendous crisis and do so with great aplomb and competence. *Maybe I'll have to ameliorate some of my negative attitudes toward Republic diplomats*, he thought.

"Gentlemen, I appreciate your observations on all these matters. If you had to choose, though, what would be your top recommendation militarily for the next avenue of development with the Q?"

"Well, sir," Braley began, "we feel the use of a proxy army by the Solar Wind Mining Consortium was a failure. Someone at a higher level will have to determine if the Republic's participation by Dark Ops attenuated or precipitated the outcome that led to the necessary destruction of the Sun-Loyal Army. In any case, it seems that it would be ill-advised to recommend the rearming of a Q army by the consortium again."

The ambassador chuckled. "That's the understatement of the century, gentlemen." There were polite laughs around the table, including from the legionnaires.

"If I may ask, sir, what's the disposition of the company currently?"

Mister Cummings answered. "Cardoso made his way back from involuntary refuge on Tikalasa'at and is now on Sumendi Station. He's still the nominal head of Solar Wind's operations on the planet, but the ambassador made him persona non grata."

"I'm awaiting guidance from the House of Reason on several points," the ambassador continued, "and leave next week to give testimony before the Planetary Security Council. For right now, the mining operation overhead and at the ground facilities will continue without interference by the Republic. For how much longer, I cannot say. We are allowing the joint-agricultural projects to resume, but as far as the so-called accords, we'll have to see what response we get from the field. The embassy will do nothing to promulgate culturally unacceptable policies.

"And Phillipe Cardoso, he's subject to his board of directors. I can't imagine they'd leave him in place."

Kel wasn't aware of any technology that enabled one to read the future, but if he could take a guess, Cardoso's days in power were numbered.

At a nod from Braley, Kel told the group, "Our team would like to recommend more Republic resources be devoted to developing relations with the inhabitants of Naca'hamir. The Disciplined are by far the most important resource on Mukalasa'at. Our successes on this planet would not have been possible without their aid."

"Yes. The praise in your team's report for the Disciplined stands out." The ambassador looked to one of his cultural ministers.

"It's true, sir. They're an untapped resource," the man said. "But we know so little about them. It's an unfortunate tendency to view any species as homogeneous or monolithic. The Chachnam majority have simply dominated our studies and efforts on Big M. We do need to devote more resources to engage with the peoples of Naca'hamir."

"Then I'd like to see a plan of action as soon as possible, Joachim. The relationship with D'shtaran is most certainly beyond repair. She was not the lone mughal on the continent, simply the strongest. Now that her army is dust, it's likely that there will be a power vacuum. We don't want to see another civil war between petty mughals. We have an opportunity to help guide the direction of the Q, and if we have better options than another mughal, that may be the way toward fostering a better relationship between the Q and the Republic."

Kel was pleased. If he and the team accomplished nothing else during their time on Big M, advancing the position of the Disciplined would make Qulingat't a better place. He was sorry he'd never get to visit K'listan in her homeland. Perhaps their kill team's relationship with her had kindled a lasting friendship between her people and the Republic.

The ambassador stood. "Gentlemen, I cannot express my admiration for you all highly enough. What you've done has been above and beyond the call of duty. My evaluation of your service here will reflect that, I can assure you. It has been an honor." He moved to shake hands with each one of them. When he reached Kel, the ambassador spoke to him. "Mister Turner, remain behind with me for a moment, please. May we have the room?"

Everyone else departed. Kel looked toward Bigg who gestured with his finger out the door, indicating that he would be waiting outside for him. When the ambassador's aide closed the panel behind him, the ambassador was already seated, pointing to the chair across from him.

Kel wasn't sure what to expect. The ambassador smiled in a fatherly way. He doubted he was about to be chewed out, but the possibility was never far from his mind.

"Mister Turner, I didn't want you to depart before I had a chance to speak with you one-on-one."

Kel's chest tightened. "Yes, sir?"

"Son, for a man in a covert unit whose name is supposed to be unknown, by circumstance you have come to the attention of many influential people. Twice."

He wondered what the older diplomat referred to. Did he mean the incident on Meridian last year? How would he know about Kel's participation in those events?

The ambassador laughed. "I can see by the look on your face that you're concerned. I apologize. My purpose was not to cause you anxiety. I'm sure that your operational identity is secure. My meaning is simply that for a young man, you've now been involved in two critical incidents of a planetary scale, both of which were largely resolved because of your direct actions. As this incident becomes known on Liberinthine, your participation will not go unnoticed."

Then, as if an afterthought, Ambassador Grealy added, "It could be that a young man with such ability and good luck could do better than choosing to remain in the Legion. I wish you good fortune, Kel Turner."

With that, the ambassador left to join his retinue, leaving Kel to mull over the implications of what he'd just been told.

"What'd you do?" Bigg asked. Kel found him alone in the hallway.

Kel laughed. "Nothing like that. Let's get out of here, Bigg."

As they walked, Kel knew he would find a time to tell Bigg what the ambassador had said to him. He wouldn't dream of not telling Bigg everything.

From his private office on Sumendi Station, Phillipe Cardoso looked down on Qulingat't and at the continent of Big M. The brown and red sands mixed into maroon near the coast. The outline of the bay just above the equator marked where the rare earth processing plant stood. Over his desk hovered the holo projection of a red and gold Q gesticulating wildly.

"I am the Chachnam mughal and the leader of the Sun-Loyal!" her jewel encrusted voder chirped. "You are nothing more than interlopers. I alone have the power to grant you what you wish on Mukalasa'at. If you refuse to agree to my terms, when my army is again raised, I will order the eviction of your house from my continent."

Phillipe was weary of this negotiation. He'd already made up his mind. The time for placating was over. "Listen to me, D'shtaran. You are only mughal because I say you are, little bug."

Before she could respond, Phillipe severed the link. He opened the screen on his datapad, entered the necessary codes, and swiped the activation key. A new holo appeared as it magnified the terrain below to show the palace grounds. He pushed the floating button. Almost instantly, the palace erupted in an explosion and collapsed onto itself. A second strike would not be necessary.

"The Legion isn't the only one with toys."

Kel sat in his room, patiently listening. The plasteen walls of their living quarters were similar in construction to most all the buildings on the secretive DO compound. The material was ridiculously strong. It resisted the conductive flow of heat as efficiently as a natural rock barrier ten times its thickness. The stuff provided incredible sound dampening, so much so that he could watch a holo at full volume and not disturb a sleeping comrade above, below, or on either side of him.

That's not to say the plasteen eliminated his awareness of the muted noises and vibrations around him. There was always some emanation that let him know that the space adjacent to his was occupied by a neighboring human presence. He sat on the floor and started meditating. He followed the same steps to calm his mind that he always took when lying hidden in ambush, in wait as an enemy approached the kill zone.

It was the preparation of his mind that was important now, readying it to receive any stimulus without distraction. He tuned his awareness to perceive the frequency of hum that was unique to the vibrations created when the sonic shower next door was activated. As soon as he sensed it, he leapt up and exited into the common hall.

He gave the door next to his one knock before swiping the sliding mechanism. They rarely locked the doors in their living quarters, and frequently went in and out of each other's apartments casually without waiting to be invited in.

Kel yelled at the closed fresher door as he entered.

"Hey man, I think you grabbed one of my sets of silks by accident. You know, when we were dumping stuff out of our grav containers in the team room? My fault. I was in too much of a hurry. Mind if I check?"

He heard the muffled voice through the fresher door.

"Yeah, man. Go ahead. I haven't unpacked everything yet."

Kel moved quickly to perform his task. He was careful, and cautious. He would get one chance to do this correctly. Being nervous and bungling the job would lead to mission failure. He would never permit himself to misstep by performing inexpertly or haphazardly. He moved through the apartment and spied his objective.

"Found them," he yelled as he left. "Sorry. I was throwing stuff around trying to get out of there too quickly. See you in the morning."

"No prob. G'night," Sims yelled through the closed door.

Kel returned to his own apartment and shut the door, passing his hand over the inner access pad and securing the lock. He was not going to be disturbed or the victim of intrusion. Not now. He began sorting his personal clothing out of his grav container and small kit bag, readying what needed to be laundered into a pile. There was time, and this would occupy him. He left the holo player off, enjoying the silence within his domicile. It had been many months since he'd had real quiet to be with his thoughts and alone.

The anticipation was tearing at him. He felt nervous, a hollow pit forming just below his diaphragm. He was twitchy; his muscles tensed as he tried to stretch and breathe in an effort to release the building suspense. There was a possibility that it could still be hours before the moment came.

After pacing about his living room for a while, he dimmed the lights and forced himself to lie on his bed. He practiced his meditative breathing, releasing his mind until he developed a feeling of lightness. Time was irrelevant to him as he reached a state where his body felt as though it were floating, surrendering his nervous energy to the universe. In exchange for a suspension of his conscious thought, he received the ability to extend his senses into the fabric of space and time itself.

The noise brought him back from the edge of transcendence.

A muted scream rose and fell, then rose again in a series of crescendos. Sounds that could only be caused by a grown man running naked around the confined space of the apartment next door, screaming like a little girl.

He reveled in the moment of sweet revenge.

His link erupted, a communication forced through the unit by special command, guaranteeing the attention of the recipient in emergency situations. A distressed face filled the projection.

"KEL—COME AND GET THIS THING OUT OF MY ROOM. COME AND GET IT. NOW. NOW. NOW!"

Sims uttered an unintelligible string of syllables as he disappeared out of the edge of the holo emitter's field. He gurgled and sputtered and shadows danced on the wall as Sims darted around his room.

Kel trotted out the door to find Sims standing naked as predicted, long hair dripping. Desperate, Sims pointed into his room.

"NOW!" he shrieked.

Kel shrugged as nonchalantly as he could muster, while trying to restrain his laughter. He bit his lip as he shouldered past Sims into the apartment and walked through the living area to the bedroom. There the bed covers had been thrown back, and the fist-sized chak'chak sat right where Kel had placed him in the middle of the mattress, its ten legs folded above. Serene. Unperturbed despite Sims's pitiable dance of psychotic agitation around the apartment.

Kel opened the lid on the small cube and put it on the bed. He reached into his pocket for a piece of fruit, dropped it in the carton, and waited. The creature's three eye stalks turned toward the food, then it scurried into the box, and Kel closed it. He walked out of his teammate's apartment carrying the container in front of him as a talisman to ward off any attack by his entomophobic friend.

Sims remained motionless as Kel passed. He paused for a moment, as if to invite Sims the opportunity for discourse. When no words came from the large man's mouth, Kel continued to the door of his apartment. As he was about to enter, the faint voice stopped him short.

"Truce, man. Truce, okay?"

Kel turned slowly, the box held in both hands in front of him. He nodded approvingly at his friend.

"Sure. Truce."

Sims shivered from head to toe, like a wobanki shaking water off its fur. "And you're not going to say anything about this to anyone, agreed?"

Now Kel laughed out loud. "That. Is never. Going. To happen."

He turned and closed his door before Sims could plead his case. Revenge truly was sweet. He'd take the little guy to the local zoo where it would have a good home. He thought about keeping it as a pet, but knew that wouldn't work. Tomorrow, he could be sent on a new mission and gone for months. If that happened, who would pet it, and feed it, and tell it that it was a good little chak'chak?

Not Sims.

EPILOGUE

"We'll call it the Qulingat't Reform Act."

Senator Lucius VanderLoot, Chair of the Planetary Security Council, reclined in his private office. It had been a lengthy morning of closed session testimony regarding the recent events. Their ambassador had been succinct and deliberate in his report to the council. Though there had been many opportunities for the diplomat to self-aggrandize, he had not done so. Unlike many others Lucius had elevated to the position of ambassador in the past. Grealy was neither incompetent nor ambitious. He was also obedient. Lucius had chosen well.

He spoke to his chief of staff, Accius VanderBlanc, as he formulated the substance of the bill he would propose in council after tomorrow's testimony. Representatives from the Solar Wind Mining Consortium would be on hand for grilling by his committee. He'd already made his views on the matter known to his colleagues. By the time the corporation had been made to look culpable for the debacle, it would be a simple matter to pass the bill out of committee and move it on to a full senate vote.

Any member of the council who failed to follow his lead and took the side of the company, he would destroy. If not tomorrow, then soon. Once on the floor of the full senate, he would have the majority votes needed to pass the new act. Of that, he had no doubt.

"The unchecked activities of the mining consortium have led to the wholesale slaughter of a significant number of beings, not to mention the deaths of many Republic citizens, and has imposed an immoral intrusion into an indigenous culture. Their ill-advised course of action—"

"Excuse me, Senator. May I ask a question?"

Accius knew that it was tempting the wrath of the dragon to interrupt the senator when he was composing. When he had dared to do so in the past, he'd frequently been rewarded with a glimpse into the mind of a master politician, a path he hoped to someday emulate. Other times, he had been handed his head in chastisement. By the way he saw the Senator return his gaze, he knew that he had been correct to brave the question.

"Of course, Accius. What can I clarify for your inquisitive mind?" The senator was in a truly good mood. Accius only knew him to be so when the senator sensed a decisive victory on the horizon.

"Well, could it not be made to appear that we were responsible for much of the chaos? After all, it was the House of Reason who approved the transfer of military technology to the natives. The Republic also approved the petition for development of local resources by the company, and we authorized the joint agricultural ventures on the planet which led to the accords—"

The older man stopped his young aide right there. "What am I always telling you, Accius? Causation isn't relative. The *narrative* is. We must control the narrative. There are times to separate out specific issues, and there are times to bundle them. The average citizen has not the interest in too many details.

"Giving approval for development of human agriculture on another world is a positive for us. It's an issue that most any human would see as a good for the galaxy."

The young man nodded. He knew to remain silent and listen to the answers to his query before formulating new ones.

"Allowing the company to transfer technology to the peoples of the planet was approved because, in our view, who are we to judge another spacefaring race as being unworthy of sharing the fruits of our great society? It betters the galaxy as a whole."

Accius squinted to show the older man that he was thinking carefully about what he was being told. He found it useful with the senator to practice his acting skills.

"What is truly most important is not that we explain our positions on those decisions defensively, but rather that we go on the attack and bring to light the betrayal of the Republic's trust by the Consortium and their reckless implementation of speciesist policies."

Accusing the company of acting in a manner that treated the inhabitants differently based on their species was always a good tactic, Accius had observed.

"With the Reform Act, I will propose a number of regulatory oversights to prevent such a thing from happening in the future. The House of Reason will have to establish watchful care over operations by the Consortium on Q, and aegis over its inhabitants to guarantee the fair treatment of its natives from a predatory corporation. The House of Reason will be seen as blameless in this crisis or, at the very least, be perceived as taking rapid, empathetic action to correct any injustices."

Accius understood. The creation of another bureaucracy to provide the regulatory oversight of the new law would provide a great opportunity for the senator and his colleagues on the council. It would create a wellspring of positions that could be filled with those seeking political favors in exchange for that most valuable commodity: gratitude. The Consortium would no doubt work tirelessly to lobby against many of the proposals and attempt to reform any parts of the law it found too restrictive or egregious. There too lay the opportunity for gratitude. Only there, gratitude would come in an even more tangible form. Credits.

Accius imagined the future of the senator's legislation. It might even be grand enough to warrant the establishment of an entirely new agency to administer its regulations. There would need to be offices on Liberinthine, as well as on Qulingat't. Inspectors would have to be assigned to every aspect of the company's operations, whether that be related to mining, agriculture, or trade. The sheer number of jobs it would entail was staggering.

Young Accius was beginning to understand.

"Accius. Before I forget. Some other items came to my attention during this morning's proceedings. First, the use of the asteroid to halt the advancing army. We must seal all knowledge of this event. It must be classified. All participants and witnesses must be forced to sign the Secrets Act. We will deny any knowledge that this occurred and have our people develop an alternative series of events to explain the army's destruction. A civil war between factions would suffice. There must be disinformation regarding this episode. We do not want some radical faction to get the idea that it can start using asteroids to bombard the Republic."

"Yes, Senator." Accius knew which agency to employ.

"Second, a name came to my attention, a name I have heard before. Did you notice?"

This was a test. "Yes, Senator. The legionnaire who orchestrated the victory became notable for his participation in the events on Meridian last year."

"Precisely." Lucius had done very well by the expansion in trade with the edge world and his early investment in the commodities market.

"This man bears watching. He has been at the center of two enormous crises in less than a year. He has shown a willingness to resolve them without the input of the House of Reason or the Senate. That makes him a loose cannon. A competent one, but a loose cannon nonetheless. Such a man is dangerous. Dangerous, that is, unless he is secure in his allegiance to us. How else can such a man be trusted? I know his type. He is an idealist. Worse, he believes in military glory, the worst kind of idealist."

"What would you have me do, sir?"

The venerable man remained reclined. "For now, nothing. This is a question I will have to ponder. Leave me, I have much to meditate on."

THE END

ABOUT THE AUTHORS

DOC SPEARS is a veteran of the United States Army.

JASON ANSPACH & NICK COLE are the co-creators of Galaxy's edge. You can find out more about them and Galaxy's Edge by visiting www.GalaxysEdge.us or by joining the Galaxy's Edge Fan Club on Facebook.

HONOR ROLL

We would like to give our most sincere thanks and recognition to those who supported the creation of *Galaxy's Edge: Rebellion* by supporting us at GalacticOutlaws.com.

Artis Aboltins
Guido Abreu
Chancellor Adams
Garion Adkins
Elias Aguilar
Bill Allen
Tony Alvarez
Galen Anderson
Jarad Anderson
Robert Anspach
Jonathan Auerbach
Fritz Ausman
Sean Averill
Nicholas Avila
Matthew Bagwell
Marvin Bailey
Joseph Bailey
Kevin Bangert
John Barber
Logan Barker
Brian Barrows
Robert Battles
Eric Batzdorfer
John Baudoin
Antonio Becerra
Mike Beeker
Randall Beem
Matt Beers
John Bell
Daniel Bendele
Edward Benson
David Bernatski
Justin Bielefeld
Trevor Blasius
WJ Blood
Rodney Bonner
Thomas Seth Bouchard
William Boucher
Brandon Bowles
Alex Bowling

Jordan Brann
Ernest Brant
Geoff Brisco
Raymond Brooks
James Brown
Jeremy Bruzdzinski
Marion Buehring
Matthew Buzek
Daniel Cadwell
Charles Calvey
Van Cammack
Chris Campbell
Zachary Cantwell
Brian Cave
Shawn Cavitt
Kris (Joryl) Chambers
David Chor
Tyrone Chow
Jonathan Clews
Beau Clifton
Alex Collins-Gauweiler
Jerry Conard
Michael Conn
James Connolly
James Conyers
Jonathan Copley
Robert Cosler
Ryan Coulston
Andrew Craig
Adam Craig
Phil Culpepper
Ben Curcio
Thomas Cutler

Tommy Cutler
David Danz
Alister Davidson
Peter Davies
Walter Davila
Ivy Davis
Nathan Davis
Ron Deage
Tod Delaricheliere
Ryan Denniston
Anerio Deorma
Douglas Deuel
Isaac Diamond
Christopher DiNote
Matthew Dippel
Ellis Dobbins
Gerald Donovan
Ray Duck
Cami Dutton
Virgil Dwyer
William Ely
Stephane Escrig
Steven Feily
Meagan Ference
Adolfo Fernandez
Ashley Finnigan
Kath Flohrs
Jeremiah Flores
Steve Forrester
Skyla Forster
Timothy Foster
Bryant Fox
Mark Franceschini

Elizabeth Gafford	Kyle Hetzer
David Gaither	Korrey Heyder
Christopher Gallo	Aaron Holden
Richard Gallo	Clint Holmes
Kyle Gannon	Charles Hood
Michael Gardner	Joshua Hopkins
Nick Gerlach	Tyson Hopkins
John Giorgis	Ian House
Johnny Glazebrooks	Ken Houseal
Justin Godfrey	Nathan Housley
Luis Gomez	Jeff Howard
Justin Gottwaltz	Nicholas Howser
Gordon Green	Kristie Hudson
Shawn Greene	Mike Hull
Erica Grenada	Donald Humpal
Preston Groogan	Bradley Huntoon
Brandon Handy	Wendy Jacobson
Erik Hansen	Paul Jarman
Greg Hanson	James Jeffers
Ian Harper	Tedman Jess
Jason Harris	Eric Jett
Jordan Harris	James Johnson
Revan Harris	Randolph Johnson
Matthew Hartmann	Scott Johnson
Adam Hartswick	Tyler Jones
Ronald Haulman	Paul Jones
Joshua Hayes	John Josendale
Adam Hazen	Wyatt Justice
Richard Heard	Ron Karroll
Colin Heavens	Cody Keaton
Jason Henderson	Noah Kelly
Jason Henderson	Jacob Kelly
Jonathan Herbst	Caleb Kenner

Daniel Kimm	Lucas Martin
Zachary Kinsman	Pawel Martin
Rhet Klaahsen	Trevor Martin
Jesse Klein	Phillip Martinez
William Knapp	Joshua Martinez
Marc Knapp	Tao Mason
Travis Knight	Ashley Mateo
Ethan Koska	Mark Maurice
Evan Kowalski	Simon Mayeski
Byl Kravetz	Kyle McCarley
Brian Lambert	Quinn McCusker
Clay Lambert	Alan McDonald
Jeremy Lambert	Caleb McDonald
Andrew Langler	Hans McIlveen
Dave Lawrence	Rachel McIntosh
Alexander Le	Jason McMarrow
Paul Lizer	Joshua McMaster
Richard Long	Colin McPherson
Oliver Longchamps	Christopher Menkhaus
Joseph Lopez	Jim Mern
Kyle Lorenzi	Robert Mertz
Charles Lower	Pete Micale
Steven Ludtke	Mike Mieszcak
Brooke Lyons	Ted Milker
John M	Jacob Montagne
Richard Maier	Mitchell Moore
Ryan Mallet	Matteo Morelli
Chris Malone	William Morris
Brian Mansur	Alex Morstadt
Robert Marchi	Nicholas Mukanos
Jacob Margheim	Vinesh Narayan
Deven Marincovich	Bennett Nickels
Cory Marko	Trevor Nielsen

Andrew Niesent	Brian Robinson
Sean Noble	Daniel Robitaille
Otto Noda	Paul Roder
Brett Noll-Emmick	Chris Rollini
Greg Nugent	Thomas Roman
Christina Nymeyer	Joyce Roth
Timothy O'Connor	Andrew Ruiz
Grant Odom	David Sanford
Colin O'neill	Chris Sapero
Ryan O'neill	Jaysn Schaener
Tyler Ornelas	Landon Schaule
James Owens	Shayne Schettler
David Parker	Andrew Schmidt
Eric Pastorek	Brian Schmidt
Zac Petersen	Kurt Schneider
Corey Pfleiger	William Schweisthal
Dupres Pina	Anthony Scimeca
Pete Plum	Preston Scott
Paul Polanski	Aaron Seaman
Matthew Pommerening	Phillip Seek
Nathan Poplawski	Christopher Shaw
Jeremiah Popp	Charles Sheehan
Chancey Porter	Wendell Shelton
Brian Potts	Brett Shilton
Chris Pourteau	Vernetta Shipley
Chris Prats	Glenn Shotton
Joshua Purvis	Joshua Sipin
Max Quezada	Christopher Slater
T.J. Recio	Scott Sloan
Jacob Reynolds	Daniel Smith
Eric Ritenour	Michael Smith
Walt Robillard	Sharroll Smith
Joshua Robinson	Michael Smith

Tyler Smith
Alexander Snyder
John Spears
Thomas Spencer
Peter Spitzer
Dustin Sprick
Graham Stanton
Paul Starck
Ethan Step
Seaver Sterling
Maggie Stewart-Grant
John Stockley
Rob Strachan
William Strickler
Shayla Striffler
Kevin Summers
Ernest Sumner
Carol Szpara
Travis TadeWaldt
Daniel Tanner
Lawrence Tate
Tim Taylor
Robert Taylor
Justin Taylor
Daniel Thomas
Steven Thompson
Chris Thompson
William Joseph Thorpe
Beverly Tierney
Kayla Todd
Matthew Townsend
Jameson Trauger
Cole Trueblood

Scott Tucker
Eric Turnbull
Brandon Turton
Dylan Tuxhorn
Jalen Underwood
Paul Van Dop
Paden VanBuskirk
Patrick Varrassi
Daniel Vatamaniuck
Jose Vazquez
Josiah Velazquez
Anthony Wagnon
Humberto Waldheim
Christopher Walker
David Wall
Justin Wang
Andrew Ward
Scot Washam
John Watson
Ben Wheeler
Jack Williams
Scott Winters
Samuel Wolfe
Jason Wright
John Wurtz
Ethan Yerigan
Phillip Zaragoza
Brandt Zeeh
Nathan Zoss

CPSIA information can be obtained
at www.ICGtesting.com
Printed in the USA
BVHW060958260122
627130BV00018B/1859